White Rabbit

Gregory C. Randall

ROUGH
EDGES
PRESS

Rough Edges Press
An Imprint of Wolfpack Publishing
5130 S. Fort Apache Rd. 215-380
Las Vegas, NV 89148

roughedgespress.com

Paperback ISBN 978-1-68549-093-5
eBook ISBN 978-1-68549-092-8
LCCN 2022938392

White Rabbit

"I could tell you my adventures—beginning from this morning," said Alice a little timidly; "but it's no use going back to yesterday, because I was a different person then."

— Lewis Carroll, *Alice's Adventures in Wonderland*

Chapter 1
The Lies We Tell Ourselves

Bobbie Davis: Then
Chicago, Illinois
August 29, 1968

I have never felt more alive. We were thousands marching in protest on Michigan Avenue—against the war, the politics, the dying, and the killing. Ahead, blocking the street, stood hundreds of blue-helmeted Chicago police. Then, without warning, with their batons held high, they surged forward and slammed into our crowd of nonviolent demonstrators. Wild screams and thuds of batons filled the August night; above, a haze of tear gas drifted over the madness. Now, this was no longer a protest; it was the start of the revolution—and I was there.

The batons hit hard, I coughed through the tear gas, I tasted my blood, I heard the cries of those marching with me. We were punched, cudgeled, dragged, trundled up, and tossed into paddy wagons. All was chaos and confusion. I stood my ground and spit more blood. A cop, with an old man's face shadowed by the rim of his helmet, confronted me—there was no way out. He righteously raised his arm and viciously smashed his stick against my head. Stunned, I dropped to my knees and waited for the fatal blow. From behind me, a man's fist slammed into the cop's face, knocking him and his blue helmet across the pavement. Then I was lifted and carried away from the bedlam. Around us police continued to swing nightsticks like they were scything corn; I watched people fall. Then, groggy and beaten, I was bodily thrown into the back seat of a cab. I blacked out.

I woke the next morning in a bed with white sheets and to the aroma of coffee. Debbie Toomey, tall, pale, angular, with green eyes and short red hair, stood over me. Next to Debbie was Abe Klausnick; he was a big handsome man, blond beard, and thick head of hair. His brown eyes were quiet and clear, yet beyond them I always saw an intensity that sometimes was scary. He was wearing an Army fatigue jacket; it was his trademark.

"You look better," she said. "We were worried."

"Did you get the number of that truck?" I answered. The smile hurt.

"From the size of the cop that hit you, he could have been a truck," Abe said. "I took care of him; he's waking up in the hospital. He wanted to smack you again, big mistake. You look better—good color."

"Am I at the house?"

"Yes, you're safe here," Abe said. "I made coffee; there's a cup on the nightstand. I have things to do." Abe left the room. Debbie smirked; she looked tired.

"We carried you until we found a cab on State Street—cost us forty bucks," she said. "The son of a bitch wanted nothing to do with us. He asked if you were dead. Me, I hope you live. I need my money back—you are becoming an expensive comrade and coconspirator."

I pushed myself up on the pillow. "What happened?"

"A cop clocked you on the side of the head with a billy club—it was across from the Hilton. There's a one-inch gash and some swelling, maybe a slight concussion. There's a bandage around your head, and somehow during all that you cut your arm. Not sure when."

I felt the gauze. "Thanks. What about the others?"

"Jimmy and Barbara came in early this morning; it was still dark. They crashed on the couches downstairs," Debbie said. "The riot went on for three more hours. The word got out that it was being broadcast live on TV. Shit, we couldn't have scripted it better. The national TV this morning is calling it a police riot—a fucking police riot. The convention is over—we made history, girl. Big-time history—they will be talking about this for years."

"Yeah, now what? Fingers will be pointed, more lies told, the war will go on; and more men will die. This is all bull-shit." I stopped and took a deep breath. "How's Abe doing?"

"He says everything will all be ready in a couple of days; we are on schedule. It's a go for Monday. No one will be there; it's Labor Day."

Late that afternoon, I managed to stand and walk through the house. The stairs to the basement went through a door in the kitchen. The door was just inside from where the mudroom and outside porch were attached to the back of the house. Steep, outside wooden stairs led from the porch down to the alley behind the house. I tapped on the basement door.

"Can I come down?" I asked, sticking my head around the door and looking into the void.

"You aren't smoking, are you?" Abe yelled.

"No."

"Sure, come down."

Abe sat on a stool at a large worktable made from a sheet of plywood that straddled two sawhorses. A single light hung over the work surface. Tools, wires, and alarm clocks were to his right. A stack of shoeboxes sat to his left. The metallic and resinous odor of something burning hung in the air.

"What's that smell?" I asked.

"Solder. I'm attaching the wires to the clock. Wouldn't want a bad or loose connection, would we?"

There were three alarm clocks side by side, windup types. They didn't have their bells. Wires were attached to each clock, and the clocks were secured to individual wooden boards about the size of a shoebox bottom. Taped to each board was a large battery. On the board was a void where the dynamite was to be placed and held in place by more tape.

"Watch," Abe said.

He checked the wires that ran from the clock on the board to two small switches also mounted on the board. The alarm clock had the face of Mickey Mouse on it.

"Mickey Mouse?" I asked.

"A revolutionary has to have a sense of humor—or they are lost. I think Lenin or Lenny Bruce said that. This one is ready to go. When the alarm goes off, this post swings back and forth, striking the small pieces of metal that replaced the bells. I considered leaving the bells on but was afraid they might go off and ring at the wrong time." He fiddled with one of the knobs on the back of the clock and clicked the two switches. We waited for about a minute, then the striker began to rapidly click against the plates on the bell stems. "Kaboom."

"Can it go off prematurely?"

"That's why the switches are there. Nothing happens if this switch is off; in fact, I put two in as safeguards. When both are switched on—that's the green dot I put there—the alarm strike will connect the voltage in the battery to the blasting caps, then boom. Simple."

"Can the heat set them off?" I asked.

"It's possible, but right now the weather is cool. But when it's hot, those dynamite sticks can sweat, and then they are dangerous. Allanson also got blasting caps with fuses that you light—like in the movies. Those are over there on the shelf, along with the electric fuses—safety first. We can carry these around. They are safe and will fit in a shoebox. Only when I connect these wires and click on the switches will it become active. A poor man's time bomb, compliments of Mickey Mouse. And when they explode, they will mix with the gasoline, one five gallon can to each member of the Mickey Mouse Club."

I put my hand on the table to steady myself.

"You okay?"

"Still shaky. I'm going to go lie down; I'll be good. Jimmy and Barb are still asleep. Thanks for bringing me back—I need to get to my apartment. Do you need anything?"

"Spend the night here. Go to your apartment tomorrow. We'll get back together on Sunday afternoon, then we can take these to the draft boards in the early morning. Yesterday morning, I checked out the locations; what we planned will work. This will get their attention."

"Good. We need to stick it in their face, make them know we are real."

I felt like shit for two more days. I tried to push my way through it, but I must have had a lingering concussion from that nightstick. There is still a lump on the side of my head. My arm aches from the cut; the cut on my head no longer bleeds. I took off the bandage. I should have gotten stitches; yeah, that and an arrest record when they turned me in to the police. It is tough to sleep; the headaches have eased but come and go. I'm popping aspirin like M&Ms. The TV and the newspapers are still going on about the demonstrations and chaos on the streets of Chicago. They are demanding answers from Mayor Daley and the police. And hardly a word about the three hundred American soldiers killed in Vietnam during the week—three hundred men, sons, brothers, and husbands. The assholes in Washington own this war and they will pay for it. The *Tribune* newspaper, on the other hand, blames the demonstrators and that the police were the innocent victims—all bullshit. The national TV reporters tell a different story, maybe because a couple of their guys got roughed up. Hey, welcome to the revolution, Dan Rather.

Early Sunday morning, Zeke Allanson, the representative from the Students for a Democratic Society—the SDS—

called. I was at my apartment. He wanted to see me, have lunch; I thought he'd gone back to Ann Arbor. He babbled on and on about the SDS and how he was proud to be at the demonstrations. He asked about my group's future, what we were planning—just being nosy. Then he asked when we were going to use the dynamite. Soon, he hoped. "You must make a point." I wondered why he said that. Then he said that I'd make an excellent addition to the Midwest regional committee for the SDS. Not up to it, I said. I don't join organized protest groups. I like where I am, what I'm doing—I am in control of my small piece of the revolution. He mumbled something about being sorry to hear that and that the next time he came through Chicago, he'd give me a call. Thanks for nothing, you dope-smoking, short-assed, rat-faced, spongy-haired twerp. For a white guy, he had a serious drug problem. I was glad he was gone.

Later that morning, I met Debbie at the Addison Street L station, and we walked to the house. Finally, the headaches were gone. The weather was comfortable for the 1st of September. "Happy birthday." She handed me a small, wrapped box with a ribbon and bow. Inside, wrapped in cotton batting, lay a silver charm bracelet. Hanging on the chain were a heart, a small revolver, a teddy bear, and Mickey Mouse.

Debbie said, "Each of us bought you a charm. I got you the teddy bear, Barbara the heart, Jimmy the gun, and Abe the Mickey Mouse. He thought you'd get a kick out of that."

"What kind of revolutionary do you think I am accepting bourgeois gifts like this?" I said with a laugh. It was thoughtful. A revolutionary must also have a heart—not one of silver, but one that pumps real blood.

We stopped at the market and picked up a few things for dinner: hot dogs, buns, a bag of potato chips, coleslaw, a dozen eggs, and two six-packs of beer. I couldn't believe the clerk at the counter carded me. We walked the three blocks from Clark Street to the rear of the house.

Standing at the back porch, Debbie tried the handle to

the door; it was locked. Usually during the day, when somebody was there, it was unlocked—too many people went in and out for all to have keys. She banged on the door; I stood next to her holding the bag of groceries. Just as she started to knock again, the door burst open, knocking her into me. The bag split and the groceries fell to the porch. I heard bottles break. Knocked down, my knee crushed the carton of eggs. Zeke Allanson pushed his way past us; an older man immediately followed.

"Why the hell are you here?" I screamed at Allanson as he jumped down the steps, dodging Debbie.

The other man, clean shaven, white, looked back at the two of us. Hatred, pure hatred, filled his face. He began to say something, but all I heard was "fuck you." They ran to a dark blue sedan. Allanson climbed into the passenger's side; the other man fell into the driver's side. He tried to start the car; grinding the starter over and over, it screeched. Then the motor caught and roared; black exhaust exploded from the tailpipe. He floored the accelerator and fishtailed down the alley, gravel flying everywhere.

Debbie tried to put the groceries back in the bag; it was impossible. The paper had disintegrated from the broken bottles and crushed eggs. I gathered up a few things and pushed my way into the house.

"I'll get a new bag and clean up," Debbie said. "Your knee, is it okay?"

"I'm fine. What the hell was all that?" I said.

The dishes from breakfast were still in the sink. It was quiet, too quiet for a Sunday afternoon with three people living here. There should be a baseball game on. Abe was a big Cubs fan; he'd said something about a doubleheader. Debbie took a paper bag from the closet and walked outside to collect the rest of the food. The door to the basement was closed. I smelled coffee, gasoline, and smoke.

Opening the basement door, acrid smoke billowed up from below. I stumbled down the stairs. Smoke filled the upper half of the basement. On the floor at the bottom of the steps were two bodies, Abe and Barb. In the back of the basement, boxes and junk were burning; flames reached to the ceiling. I choked, and as I went to my friends, I yelled for Debbie. Abe's face was bloody, and his head had a massive cut across the forehead. Barb was still, unbreathing. I shook her, tried to wake her.

"What the hell is going on?" Debbie yelled from the top of the stairs. She started coughing.

"Abe and Barb are down here. They're injured—the smoke is too thick." Choking, I couldn't see anymore. I tried to pull Barb up. "There's fire everywhere."

"Get out of there! There's also gallons of gasoline and the dynamite. Get out."

"We need to save them."

"And die—not a fucking chance. Get up here."

A wall of gasoline-fueled fire washed through the basement toward me. I ran up the stairs and slammed the door.

"Out," Debbie yelled, running to the front of the house. I followed. "Shit." She stopped. Through the front window were two men walking to the house. One was a cop, the other in a suit.

"The back door. Go!" I shouted.

We ran through the kitchen. Smoke squeezed itself out the cracks and gaps around the basement door.

I heard pounding from the front of the house.

"Go, I'm right behind you," I yelled.

Debbie, a single step in front of me, threw open the door. Just as we reached the rear porch, the house exploded. The shock wave of smoke and heat blew us off the porch like rag dolls. Every sound was instantly muffled. I fell on top of Debbie, who was sprawled across the bottom step. As I tried to stand, my sweater caught on a piece of the shattered stairway. I yanked it off and crawled over to Debbie.

"You okay?"

"Jesus Christ," Debbie answered.

"The dynamite—the fire set it off. We need to go; the fire

is spreading. I smell gas—the gas lines are broken. Can you walk?"

"Walk? No, run!" Debbie yelled as she struggled upright. We double-timed down the alley. Halfway to the next street, the house exploded again, knocking us to the gravel. We staggered forward. I looked back; the house was completely on fire. We ran. Three blocks later, we caught a CTA bus. As we climbed on board, fire trucks raced past us.

———

Bobbie Davis / (AKA: Dorothy Cooper): Now
Grand Haven, Michigan
September 2, 2019

Yesterday, from my perch on the broad weather-worn deck, I watched the child leave tiny footprints in the sand along the margin of the lake, the soft waves gently washing them away as she tottered and squealed with delight as the golden retriever chased a bright yellow tennis ball flung by one of those contraptions that sling the ball twice as far as her father could possibly throw it. The pale-yellow sandcastle, now abandoned with its overturned buckets and shovels, stood exposed to the late morning sun in its partial collapse. Watching over them, the mother, her legs tucked tight under her bottom, sat on a red blanket stealing a cigarette. A cool breeze, foretelling the oncoming seasons, riffled the water, and sent a shiver down my back.

The family was new to this beach; I hadn't met them. For forty years I have enjoyed this strand the same as I hope this young family will. My children grew up on this golden stretch of Lake Michigan. And now, at that moment—that late summer Sunday morning—I fully realized the damage my lies had left. I slowly exhaled a mind-cleansing breath as Mitch leaned in and gently wiped the tears off my cheek and then kissed them dry.

Be forewarned, this is our family's true story—Cate's,

Joe's, and mine—another legacy, like the beach, I leave you. Being a complicated story, believe what you want of it. However, please consider that even though our stories may be similar, they are not the same. And both stories, yours and mine, are likewise filled with the same lies that we tell ourselves to get to the next day, the next week, the hereafter.

Today is September 2, the day after my seventy-third birthday. I have been hiding in plain sight from the authorities, the *man* as we used to say, since September 1, 1968. It was easier to hide in those days. Now, our modern government insists on following its citizens through the Orwellian use of CCTV cameras, digital bytes, GPS, and the self-indulgent and ever-confessional social media. Eventually the regime's huntsmen moved on to bigger game. I was no longer the trophy I once was or thought I was. Nonetheless, dismounting my disguise of the pale horse is not just hard, it is dangerous—the government has a long memory.

I was born Roberta Susan Davis, or Bobbie Davis to my family and friends. For more than fifty of my seventy-three years, I have hidden under an illegally documented name given to me by my friend Deborah Toomey. My first alias was Dorothy Childen, then, after marrying Mitchell Cooper, I became Dorothy Cooper. Until this morning, Mitch never knew my past, only a concoction I'd made up on the fly when I first met him in a bar on Highway 31 between Grand Haven and Grand Rapids. He slid over a bar stool, introduced himself in a casual way, and asked if I wanted a beer. He was handsome, thick brown hair pulled back in a ponytail, bright chocolate-colored eyes, athletic, and he carried himself with ease and projected an obvious kindness. Why he was alone on that cold January night, I have never asked him. One of my favorite lies is that God was finally giving me a fucking break that evening.

"Hi, I'm Mitch Cooper."

I smelled a hint of Old Spice—my dad wore Old Spice. "Dorothy Childen," I said, accepting the Stroh's beer while pushing the ragged strands of my blonde, now dyed brown, hair out of my eyes.

"Well, Dorothy Childen, who are you and why are you here tonight?"

At this point, I'd been hiding for a few years; his question was the same question I'd been asking myself, and the line, almost, from *Casablanca* made me smile. "Awfully personal," I answered. "Tell you what, I'll recite some facts, you can believe which ones are true, then we will see. You ready?"

"Shoot."

"I'm thirty-years-old [true]. I rent a room from a widow in New Holland [true], my parents are dead [sadly true], and I was born on the far Southside of Chicago [again true]. I graduated from Northwestern University in 1966 [true again] and have been bouncing around Europe for a few years [not true] until I finally came home and landed here in Michigan. I'm a cashier at the supermarket in Holland [again sadly true]. And I am the most alone person you will ever meet [you decide]."

He got half of them right. After that introduction, everything else I told him was a lie; it's what I did then. I also was the most sanctimonious, self-absorbed, middle-class, rebellious, self-radicalized white-girl bitch bent on fighting the system and authority you would have the misfortune to run into in a bar. I'd read all the important books and propaganda: the existentialists, the Beat poets, Kerouac, Ginsberg, and Burroughs. I was self-enlightened, anti-draft, anti-government, and at that moment didn't trust anyone over thirty—including me. I was a real piece of work. Mitch asked me years later, "Now that this is all over, what made you a radical?" I told him it was to have power, control, to be seen, to be heard—not ignored. How foolish I was, which certainly confirms the white-girl bitch part.

I love Mitch to death, but back then he believed everything I told him. He wasn't naïve, just interested and concerned, as you would be for a lost puppy. We dated for six months. To my profound shock I fell in love, and we married in the summer of 1973. Life can be simple when you lie; the difficulty is living the lie. I discovered I was a pro. I could teach a college course on lying.

Yesterday, I confessed it all to Mitch: the lies, the deceit, the fabrications—all fifty-one years of them. Then, the man I love kissed me on the cheek and said thank you. Who the hell does that? I deserved to be slapped, maybe something worse, a good beating, a leather strap if necessary. Someone else would have divorced me, dumped me on the side of the road, a marital roadkill. For most of those years, I genuinely believed that at any moment a black car with government plates would roll up our driveway, two men would exit, wave FBI credentials in Mitch's face, and throw me against the wall, handcuff and arrest me for murder, and haul my bony ass off to jail. I would be tried, convicted, and consigned to the dark abyss of the American gulag system. It could have happened—probably should have happened. I am a wanted radical who was there in 1968 when my best friends and two cops were murdered. In 2014, when dearest Debbie Toomey turned herself in to the FBI, I was certain that that black car would arrive at any moment. For five years now, it hasn't. Mitch smiled, and again kissed me on my cheek; I love this man. He must be crazier than me.

I confessed my lies to Mitch because my famous sister, and world-renowned author, Catherine Davis, appeared on national television yesterday morning. Watching her answer questions about the recent loss of her husband, her books, and the tragedies and triumphs in her life emotionally flattened me. I learned that Cate believed that I was dead—dead for fifty years. Lies and lies, piled like dark layers of a cake hidden under white frosting too sweet to eat.

Dearest Cate was elegant, casual, and obviously sophisticated. She had grown up. She is nine years younger than me and as such, missed my revolution. I have followed my sister's career for decades, celebrating each of her successes and bestsellers in my heart and an occasional bourbon. A million times I wanted to reach out to hold her, rejoice with her—but couldn't or, more correctly, wouldn't. Couldn't is a lie, an excuse; I wouldn't is the truth. For Cate, this past year has been as malevolent as 1968 was for our family. After fifty years of silence, I had to finally tell the truth.

Chapter 2
My Recurring Nightmare

Cate's Nightmare: Then
Michigan Avenue, Chicago
August 1968

There was no escape from the oppressive August heat that Chicago day and being stuck in downtown Chicago traffic only made it worse. My damp summer dress clung stickily to my teenage figure in a yellow crinoline mess. Gini, my closest friend, hid in the backseat footwell next to me. She shrieked and screamed with every slam and bang on the car's roof and trunk. Sneaking a look over the back of the front seat, I saw nothing but loud, angry demonstrators. We were surrounded. Their heads bobbed wildly above the car's windows. They hit us with signs and yelled words I didn't understand. We were overwhelmed; the demonstrators pushed us and the station wagon forward into the line of National Guardsmen. Chanting, with fists punched high, they threw themselves against the wall of police and soldiers who filled our windshield. Something or someone must give way, and I was certain it wouldn't be the National Guard.

My head ached; we were inside a steel drum; they wouldn't stop banging on our roof and hood. Mom yelled—

I'm not supposed to know those words. She regripped the steering wheel and blasphemed . . . again.

"Mom, why are they doing this? What's happening?" I yelled while shaking from panic and fear. Gini grabbed my arm and pulled herself up. Here we were, two teenage girls, in blue and yellow summer dresses, watching the battle going on outside Mom's brand-new Ford station wagon. We were going to die.

"It's okay, pumpkin. We will be out of here in just a minute," Mom said evenly, using her mom voice. "Soon, real soon." Me, I was positive we were going to be pulled from the car and killed right here on Michigan Avenue.

The soldiers, wearing helmets and gas masks, blocked Michigan Avenue from curb to curb, cutting off any escape north by the marchers and us from Grant Park. They jammed their rifles and bayonets at the car, then the tires, and then pointed them at Mom. Other soldiers, using their tear gas launchers as clubs, pressed the demonstrators against the front grille. Fear and sweat ran down the soldiers' faces. They were the same age as the protestors— they were the same age as my older brother, Joe. The crowd surged again using the station wagon as a battering ram against the National Guard's line. The car slowly rolled toward the soldiers.

"Take your foot off the brake, lady," a bearded face yelled through the window. "We're gonna push the Ford through the fascists."

Signs and posters slammed repeatedly against the car; one read *Make Love Not War*. Each bang triggered another terrified scream from Gini. God knows I wanted to scream, too—I was struck dumb. Demonstrators or soldiers blocked every way out. Nothing could leave, nothing could enter— there was no escape. I'm too young to die.

The guardsmen held—an olive drab bulwark against the crush of blue jean–clad, anti-war protestors. Like most of the crowd, every soldier was white and male. Their faces were hidden behind gas masks with googly glass eyes and can-sized air filters—it was otherworldly. Gini screamed again.

Six guardsmen advanced on the station wagon; their bayonets aimed at the front tires. It was obvious that if the car was pushed another foot, they would either shoot the tires or drive their blades into the rubber. A fat sergeant struggled forward between his men and came to the window; he banged on the glass. Mom stared back at the man. He made the motions of rolling down the window. Mom shook her head and yelled, "No."

"Lady, please open the goddamn window," he bellowed. "I need you to back up and leave the area."

Voices in the crowd yelled: "Fuck you, pig! . . . Baby killer! . . . Fascist!"

The sergeant—he wasn't wearing a gas mask—glared back at the crowd. "Stay out of this, you, you . . . hippies. I want you all out of here. Leave."

"It's a free country, man," someone yelled.

Gini was crying.

Mom continued to curse.

I tried to . . . I don't know what I tried to do; I was frozen.

Then Mom said distinctly, "Sergeant, I can't go back. It's fucking impossible. I can only go forward to Randolph Street. That's all I can fucking do." She looked to the other side of the car. "And for the love of God, tell your men to take those goddamn guns out of the window; my children are scared to death. And, you"—she pointed at a soldier with a tube-like gun—"get that fucking thing out of my face."

She continued to curse at everything. I was embarrassed. I'd never heard my mother swear like that. I was impressed.

The sergeant took the soldier by his shoulder and pulled him away. "Return to the formation, Kaminsky."

Kaminsky and the other soldiers slowly backed away but kept their weapons pointing at the open window and the other demonstrators.

"This is no place for you, ma'am." The sergeant leaned in and looked at the back seat. "And with those kids. Goddamn it, woman; whatever possessed you to come down here?"

Mom, hands still on the steering wheel, looked up—a thousand demonstrators were reflected in the rearview mirror.

"Sergeant, we came downtown to shop," she evenly said. "The girls need school supplies and clothes. We left the garage behind Marshall Field's. I couldn't turn around. The traffic is a mess. So, I'm stuck here. I can't go back, and you won't let us go forward. For the love of God, just let us through—for the children's sake."

A dozen men with cameras and handheld movie cameras now surrounded the car. Screams of "Look this way!" . . . "Hey, lady. And you too, Sergeant" bounced back and forth over the car. Mom covered her face with her hands. A car horn, from somewhere beyond the crowd, shattered the air.

"Mom, make them go away. Make them stop," I yelled. "Please."

A woman I recognized pushed her way through the crowd to the station wagon and banged on the window.

"Mother, why the hell are you here?" she yelled.

"Bobbie, why are you—"

"Look, lady, you need to get out of here," the sergeant yelled, then looked at the demonstrator. "You know this woman?"

Ignoring the soldier, my sister Bobbie leaned through the open window. "You have the girls here? Jesus Christ, Mom, what were you thinking?"

"Can you help us?" Mom pleaded.

"Mom, no one can help us," my sister said. "No one can help us now." And that was the last thing I heard my sister say.

Then, like it always did, my nightmare faded away.

I swung my thin, bare legs out from under the sheets and dangled them over the carpet, then I slowly slid off the edge of the mattress until the thick fibers filled the spaces between my toes. I unsteadily stood; my yellow nightgown, damp from the nightmare's sweat, clung to my back. I sipped from a glass of water on the nightstand. How many times had this dream shattered my sleep? After all the decades, I'd lost count.

As a teenager, the dream came almost every night in one demonic form or another—I was in the crowd, I was a soldier, I was my sister. Now, thank God, not so much. When Joe, damaged and confused, returned from the war, the dreams returned. Now, once again, they are back. God knows how much I've paid shrinks and quacks to make them go away.

Before, I had John to hold me tight until the ghosts finished their torments. His words comforted, soothed. It's so different now. Tonight, there is no safe place, no hugs, no comfort, no John—just this new nightmare that had been pressed on me.

———

Cate: Now
Carmel, California
Saturday, July 20, 2019

The bee instinctively toiled its way down one of the soft outer petals of the white rose, caressing and probing; while methodically searching for pollen—or, alternatively, some overly curious nose to sting. That thought made me smile, the first time in days. My guests aimlessly walked about in my garden; most were ripe candidates for my black and yellow toiler's bite. Oblivious to my curious eyes, the little beast pushed apart a fold in the petals and penetrated the heart of the flower. It was *Apis mellifera*, the common honey-bee. The flower, *Rosa "John F. Kennedy"*—a difficult rose, and a challenge to grow in the damp climate of coastal Carmel—was my mother's favorite. Mother excelled in raising difficult things; I was one of them. Just beyond the kitchen window, the bee continued with its passionate labors. Below the window sat the sink filled with dirty plates and glasses. Like a fervent lover, the insect slipped in and out of the petals; and then, its pollen sacks hanging like golden baskets, it crawled to the top of one incandescent petal, ran its forelegs over its head twice, and leaped into space. A moment later, another alighted and repeated the doings of the first. I smiled; the flower had taken on the locus of a botanical brothel.

I intimately knew the creature's details, solely because my mind never let go of anything—eidetic memory they call it. I call it my idiotic memory. Yes, I know what eidetic means. After publishing thirty-three novels, this idiotic thing in my head never lets me forget a story, a character, or even a scene. Maybe that's why the nightmares keep returning; they give me something to use, an idea, a horror—that and my drug of choice, Ambien. Sixty-four years of living large leaves quite a lot in its dark and turbulent wake. My life's list—we all have one—some days seems unending and itself is worth the yellowed pages of a tawdry novel.

Let me recount the tally for you: there's my Vietnam-damaged brother, Joe, and his missing leg; my sister Bobbie's bizarre disappearance and presumed death half a century ago; and the senseless death of our brother Thomas soon after his sixth birthday from leukemia. When I was fifteen—still counting here—I found Mom on the bathroom floor, dead. They said it might have been a stroke; she then fell and hit her head. The images of that day remain stuck: Mom, naked, vulnerable, alone, on the bathroom floor; the blood from the head wound, the towels I draped over the body before the police arrived; the sticky perfume mess from the broken bottles that littered the floor, the water still running in the sink. I remember my panicked father pushing through the front door yelling for Helen, Joe hobbling in behind him, one leg short. Then, less than two weeks later, the policeman standing at our door, coldly informing Joe and me of Dad's death in a car accident. They said he was probably drunk—had crashed into the abutment of a bridge near Chicago's Sag Canal, and all but hinted it was intentional. And those, mind you, were my early years, the years before my so-called fame. Private moments that sit like a pile of manure dumped by some relentless, cruel, and merciless God. At least the inheritance and insurance allowed me to go to college and get Joe the therapy he needed. It also kicked me in the ass—and later, after college, I needed to find work. I also needed to find love. Eventually, I found both.

Sneaking another look at the next promiscuous bee and the nymphomaniac rose, the tears start all over again.

"Are you all right, Cate?"

The question was inane. There is nothing "all right" about this day. Or the past week—or the last six months. Week after week of my unstoppable train ride into hell. And for the past month, no matter how desperately I wanted to throw myself on the rails, there was no one to stop its inexorable passage.

"I'm okay, Alice. It's just so hard," I said as I ripped a strip of paper towel off the roll and blew my nose. "We never thought it would end this way. Our plans never had an end; there was no final chapter." Through the window, past my reflection, past the licentious rose, I gazed into my garden. The flowers, their gay colors filling the long beds, belied the anguish infecting the house. It was a cruel anguish that extended beyond the yew hedge that hid, fifty feet below, the surging Pacific Ocean. Cruel anguish that stretched beyond the azure sky in mocking indifference to my pain and distress. I felt for the dagger in my breast; it had to be there. I felt its sharp blade in my heart—the constant source of my pain.

"John would not have wanted you this way; you know that. He would want you to be happy," Alice Pengrove said. Alice was my best friend. Tall, athletic, brown eyes, auburn hair, and high cheeks; she was all that you would not usually find in one of those recent multimillionaire emigrants from Texas. My experience was they tended to dowdiness.

"Happy that he's dead? Happy that he left me stranded? Happy that the son of a bitch left me all alone on a desert island crowded with hurt, loneliness, and self-pity?"

"You, of all people, know better than that—shame on you," Jules Wallace said while limping into the kitchen—his foot still in a boot due to the snapped ankle he'd acquired during his late spring ski trip to Tahoe. He handed me a crystal tumbler with two fingers of bourbon, adding, "For medicinal purposes."

"We bought these glasses in Ireland, at the Waterford factory. I was writing *The Eyes of Ireland* then. We stayed at a white-pillared inn that looked out over the Celtic Sea. It was all so wonderful." I shot the liquor back and handed the glass back with an expectant look.

"Catherine Wallace, how do you do that?" Alice said, leaning back against the kitchen table. "I can barely remember what to get at Safeway without a list and you . . ."

"A curse and a blessing," I answered. "A curse for the bad things, and a blessing for the good." The curse of learning six months earlier that John's persistent cold and backache were more than that, and the terminal prognosis was, at best, six months. The blessing of his "to-do list"—God, he hated the kitschy term "bucket list". Our standing on the ice of Antarctica and claiming our seventh continent; the cruise along the coast of South America; and, after spending the day hiking around the pyramids, standing on the deck of the felucca drifting down that ancient river, declaring—with a glass of fifty-year-old scotch in his hand raised to the setting Egyptian sun god Ra: "Cate, look, I'm in denial on d'Nile." The asshole, my goddamn heartbreaking-love-until-the-end-of-time asshole.

This is all in concert with the cursed mid-summer weather in Carmel. The last few miserable weeks, the cold nights trying to keep John warm, the damp fog smothering everything. And finally, on a bright sunny Wednesday—while sitting in the garden, two days after his sixty-sixth birthday—I held his thin hand while he took one deep breath and died. The Adirondack chair, John's chair, sat under a rhododendron; it and the shrub's massive flowers were both a tone of cardinal red, a color hard to find. Years earlier, I spent an entire spring trying to match the color of that chair to the color of the rhododendron's flowers. I know now why it mattered, then.

There are blessings, numerous beyond count, between the dog-eared front and back pages of my life. Our two grown children and four grandchildren, our successful careers, our legendary adventures filled one side of the ledger. The last few days broke me almost in two as our worldwide collection of friends arrived for the funeral. Most came with love and friendship, but a few, as always, sought opportunity. They uplifted me even as my shattered soul wanted to hide. The death, the Mass, the funeral, the cemetery—how many times had I written casually, and often carelessly, about funerals and death? Bang, bang, another one bites the dust. Too many—must do better. At least I'd never write about this one.

"Your garden is amazing," Jules said. "I can't keep anything green in that yard of mine. How do you do it?"

Jules Wallace was John's younger brother, who at sixty-three was John's shorter and stouter alter ego. He is a brilliant writer of thrillers, mysteries, and short stories. The walls of his library in his San Francisco Marina flat display numerous plaques and awards. His books are full of bullets, body counts, and bad guys. His backyard, on the other hand, is a postage stamp wasteland, a few scrawny plants desperately trying to survive, a floral gulag. He is well known for his insatiable readership, and he complains about their macho-tainted emails. It is all too strange. Then again, I make it a point never to criticize other writers, even one as

California quirky and Castro Street, rainbow flag–waving gay as my brother-in-law.

The work of writing is too hard. There will always be some better, and some worse, but never do I believe it is easy. To finish a novel is like finishing a painting. Some artists blend colors, and the image becomes tantalizingly real; others just slap on paint. Many paintings—novels—demand a gilded frame. Yet others write to match the chintz of the living room couch. A great painting must tell a story; in fact, an extraordinary painting must be read like an epic novel that fills the mind with abundant yet troubling dreams. Writing is always hard—damn fucking, hard.

After the funeral, a third of the people who filled my cottage were writers, another third were dear friends (and some were writers), and the remaining were tangentially connected to the literary institution of Catherine Davis through the business of publishing. They were all here to help, to support me, to curry favor, and not a few wondered about their future and financial attachments while tethered to yours truly, one of America's premier novelists, so they say. They are like the bees in my garden—life and pollinating will go on. The search for fresh flowers never ends. After the third bourbon, I fully understood that I needed to expand my circle of friends.

"Mulch," I replied.

"Huh?" Jules said as he searched for ice in the overtaxed freezer side of the refrigerator.

"Mulch, Jules. Every year I put down a thick layer of mulch that both feeds the soil and insulates the roots—black and fibrous stuff. I have a source I've used for twenty years; they are up in Carmel Valley. No redwood bark or raw sawdust, mind you; none."

Jules looked at me. He still hadn't registered my answer to his question. "Mulch?"

"Mulch." I tossed back another bourbon—that was four—and sat the tumbler on the counter. Outside, a new *Apis* landed and negotiated a fair price with the wanton flower. Through the open door, I inhaled the garden and embraced its fragrance. For the next hour, I welcomed the hugs, kisses, soft back-of-the-hand patting handshakes, condolences, and promises of lunch —if I ever got back to New York . . . "Please, Cate dear, you must call." There were a forgettable few who, even with my memory, I couldn't dredge up one recollection as to who they were. Literary mendicants, I guess. The guest book, open on the entry table, had been filled to five pages. I made a mental note to send thank-you notes. I was raised well; I'm known for sending notes for everything. However, God was not on my list today; no one gets a thank you for taking half my heart.

Outside of the doctors, only five people knew how sick John was. My brother Joe, Jules, the Pengroves, and the pastor of the Carmel Mission Basilica. The last three months, after we returned from our travels to Antarctica, South America, and Africa, were the toughest to hide the secret. John wanted to be left alone, to die in peace on his terms—not to be a bother. At this moment, walking through the garden, I am extremely pissed at John for accomplishing that. Our kids only learned of his illness during the last month. Louise would have chained John to a hospital bed and waved burning sage over him. Edward, the brainiac in my family, would have just clammed up, withdrawn, and talked for hours with his analyst. I love them, but there are times I want their DNA tested—the switched at birth thing. My family menagerie wandered off about an hour ago; they all walked together down the road toward the village. I'm not sure they knew where they were headed. I should probably organize a search party.

Jules was talking to a tall, well-dressed man in the far corner of the garden. He was one of those I did not know. I crossed the grass and Jules smiled when I reached them.

"Cate, I want you to meet Ben Taylor," Jules said. "He is from Colorado."

I looked up at the suntanned face of a strong man, a sure man, a man with a thick mustache, and a man wearing a cowboy hat. I put my hand out.

"My sincere condolences," Mr. Taylor said. "I knew John. He was a friend."

"I'm sorry but I don't recognize your name," I said curiously.

His smile was like Colorado, wide and sunny. "I knew John from some conferences we attended. I'm a writer as well. Westerns, war stories, such like."

My mind clattered like an old computer. "Now I remember . . . the High Range books. I know them. However, I am especially impressed by your military books."

"Ma'am, it is a pleasure to meet you. I am a big fan of yours. And thank you for the kind words."

His voice was warm and full. For a man as big as he was, it was soft and tempered.

"I am not an idle flatterer. You knew John?" I asked.

"Yes, from conferences and the bar—the liquor, not legal, kind. I've been in San Francisco this week; Jules and I were having lunch. We got to talking about his brother and his death—I am so sorry. He asked if I would like to attend the funeral. I said yes, and here I am."

"I'm sure John would be pleased. Are you staying over?"

"Sadly, no. I have a plane to catch in San Jose at 9:00 p.m. Jules is dropping me off."

"I'm sorry you can't stay. Returning home?"

"Yes, San Jose to Denver."

"Do you get to California often?" I asked, becoming more intrigued with the man.

"Not as often as I want, but a few times a year," Ben said.

"Let me know the next time."

"Cate, I need you to talk with someone," my brother Joe said, interrupting. "They are leaving and want a few minutes."

I looked up at Ben. "I'll be right back."

By late afternoon, the crowd had thinned to just a dozen, and these malefactors were spread around the house having intimate discussions, smoking dope, or in the case of two elderly graybeards, asleep on the living room couches. I closed my office door behind me, took in a deep breath, and gazed absentmindedly out the wide window at the Pacific Ocean.

"Cate, dear, how you write in this room amazes me," a warm and familiar voice said from the leather couch sprawled across the far end of the room. "I would be horribly distracted—not sure I could write one word."

"And that's why you paint, Joe. It permits and excuses you to waste your life wandering the world looking for what I found right here."

"It *is* a good excuse; hardly a waste, though. No one questions a crazy one-legged painter and his crusty easel. They didn't object to me in the marble and gilt of the Vatican, or on that hot, sandy desert ledge overlooking that Arizona canyon that extends out into eternity."

"Thank you for going on the trip. John needed your strong arms."

"Sis, I would do anything for that man. Did you say goodbye to Ben Taylor?"

"Oh my God, I forgot. It got so busy and then everyone was leaving. I'll track him down."

"Jules told me to give you this." He handed me a card. "All the particulars are there. Call him sometime."

I absently looked at the card, my mind a haze. "All this falderal is just crap. We know it, but shit, it's just wrong—too wrong. John should be here; this is his party."

"God's way."

"Yeah, right. 'It's God's way' is the excuse we all use to explain life and death. Most of the time, it's our damn fault. Too much of this and certainly too much of that. But isn't a full life like that—too much of this and that? It's the tasty stuff that makes life worth biting into and ripping out huge pieces. However, in John's case, God just stood out of the way like a prejudiced umpire. Sadly, we are the ones that screwed it up."

"Sis, right now, the paint is flowing, this decrepit body is marginally healthy, and even with this peg leg, nothing seems to stop me—or us. Sister dear, we are a formidable couple. Our legacy, such as it is, will be fought over by our grandkids' kids for a hundred years. I wish I could live to see that . . . it would be fun to see the little bastards brawl over the crumbs and residuals. I hope there are lawyers, many lawyers."

"You really are a pain in the ass today—thanks for coming." I kissed him on his hairy cheek. I slipped Taylor's business card into my pocket.

"I talked with Louise and Eddy out in the garden. It's good to see them," Joe said. "And the grandkids are good, all blessings. The whole family wandered down to the beach, Patty and Brant in the lead."

"I saw, a grand consolation."

"They are all good; I don't see them enough." He stood. "Like us, they have their lives."

"Your boys, they okay?" I asked.

"Yes, they keep their mother company," Joe answered. "They are sorry they couldn't come."

"It's a long way from Boston. I understand. Weddings and funerals, such are the way points now in our dotage."

"You didn't tell the kids?" Joe asked.

"Not until the last month. We told them it was a sudden diagnosis. John declared he would not be chained to our gilded prison."

"Time and tide. God knows we've carried our agonies over the last half a century."

Joe picked up a black valise that leaned against the face of the couch and sat it on the coffee table. "These are for you. You asked about them; I thought now was a good time. These are from 1968 and 1969. Back then, as you remember, I wasn't sure there would be a 1970." He removed four books and sat them next to the valise.

"You had them bound?" I said, noticing the beautiful quality of the covers.

"Just like everyone in the family has, and garnet is my favorite color." Joe looked over to the bookshelves that filled three of the walls. "Ours is a great family tradition, and you are the current designated keeper of that tradition. Those journals go back through the Kent family . . ."

". . . to 1756, when Gideon and Rupert Kent first landed in America," I added, finishing his sentence.

"More than two hundred and fifty years. Remarkable. I'll get the others to you when I can; they are in a safe place. How is the novel coming? Do you have an idea?"

"Novel or history? Not sure what it is right now. It's like a bastard looking for a father. Thank God, my publisher is staying off my back. They know about John; in fact, the president of the company is in the garden smoking dope with a young man contending for the job of my new agent. New Yorkers, what can you say? 'Come to California, smoke dope. It's the latest Disneyland ride.' They are releasing new editions of my first books with special covers and all the hoopla and marketing baloney. They tell me there's a whole new generation of readers that don't know about my books."

"Vultures and bootlickers—lickspittle all."

"The checks don't bounce," I said. "Lickspittle?"

"I've always loved that word. And the checks? Yes, there's definitely that. But 1968—you sure you want to go there? We both were handed a lot of crap then."

"Some of us more than others," I said, looking at his leg.

"The leg was so long ago I don't think about it. It's an annoyance, but it hasn't stopped me, has it?"

"There is nothing that could have stopped you. You were, and still are, a force of your own."

"Yes, but only after I got well," Joe continued. "Before that, Lord, I'm not sure what I would have done or become. A bullet to the head was on the agenda—darling Cate, you were my savior."

"Mom and Dad were never the same after Tommy's death, and when Bobbie disappeared . . ."

"None of us were—and they were the smartest of us; that was the problem. You remember everything. I slap paint on canvas for a living. Tommy was the future, rich clay yet to be formed. Bobbie saw things that we didn't; she saw the future. That's what probably fucked her up. Then Mom and Dad dying—it was like being hit by an asteroid."

"They are the cosmic hole in our family," I said. "For half a century, I have believed Bobbie's disappearance killed Mom—and maybe Dad, too."

"You may be right, but it's not something with an answer. You know my theory."

"That they were killed. I can't accept that. Back then it played into your paranoia."

"How far are you into the book?"

"Four chapters and a strange outline. Your journals will be a big help. Are you sure you don't mind my using them?"

"The story must be told. It's my story, our story—my hangover and dark inheritance, your legacy. Use my name if you want; I don't care. However, change the names of the others—no need to rile them up or get their families upset. There were good men and there were bad men. We didn't want to be where we were, yet we did our duty. So yes, start with January 1968. I recall in one of your letters that it was cold at home."

"That winter, Chicago was bitter, and the country was on the verge of rebellion," I said, remembering.

Chapter 3
A Family's Legacy

Cate: Now
Carmel, California

I turned away from the window and faced the bookshelves behind my desk. The sun, as it set, left sharp shadows from the blinds across the stacks. The house was still and quiet; only an occasional clink of a glass disturbed the peace. Joe was rummaging through the few survivors in the library's liquor cabinet. He remembered an old brandy that he and John had shared—he'd finish the bottle in John's memory. I'm glad he's spending the weekend: two lonesome kids looking out for each other—just like we have for fifty years. He was my first babysitter. Then it was my turn when he returned, torn and shattered, from Vietnam. I tended to both his broken body and his troubled soul until he could again walk and think straight. Tough for a fifteen-year-old.

I removed a green journal from the shelf; all of mine are bound in dark green leather. The spine, imprinted with gold, read: "Catherine Ann (Kent-Davis) Wallace, Book One, January 1968." Above the shelf holding my diaries are more than three hundred others. They stretch from one end of each walnut shelf to the other and then climb, ladder-like, to the coffered ceiling. Some were covered in cloth, others leather; for many, the spines are faded, just barely legible. The lives of over one hundred of our ancestors are written on their pages; all are amazing stories. Years ago, I explored them like an anthropologist. Many became ideas for my novels. I was a voyeur, a peeping Tom, even though their authors had died more than a hundred years ago. Every day I thank those ghosts for the DNA flowing in my blood and their part in making the Kent name live on. Two of my (or their) books became successful television series, another a feature film. They, like Joe's request about the names in his journals, became novels with new names—all to protect the less innocent members of our tribe.

Ours is a family made up of ten generations of ministers and brigands, farmers and merchants, lovers, and a few seriously screwed up in the head. An American dynasty to be sure—rebels, rousers, and rogues. Not a bad title for my next book.

My current project is about 1968—it was my family's chaotic and radical year. It would be our story, or more precisely, my own family's descent into hell and our climb out. It was a hell that had more tortured and descending rings than anything Dante imagined.

———

Cate: Then
January 2, 1968

Dear Diary—an excellent way to begin, having never started a diary. Mother instructed me: "There will be a time in your life when you will read this journal, and your own words will remind you that you were once a teenager and, at the same time, a blossoming woman." She said that a week ago, on Christmas morning. This diary, a present, was wrapped in a beautiful pink box with gilded edges. A golden key was secured to its top with a blue ribbon. As I thumbed through the blank pages, Mother continued: "Write down your thoughts, your dreams, your ideas, your heartbreaks, and most especially your loves. It will become your close friend and confidant." I already knew a little about our family, the Kents on my mother's side, and their tradition of journals and diaries. So that you know, I'm fourteen going on fifteen, and knowing all this history about my family intimidates me. Mother told me that my sister, Roberta, calls her diary Annie, and that Joe named his Duke. The new year 1968 is just a day old. What to write, or what not to write?

So, okay, here goes.

Dear Diary,

First, let me introduce myself. I am Catherine Ann Davis; you can call me Cate. I am almost fifteen years old; my birthday is February 2. I live in Flossmoor, Illinois. I have curly blonde hair that I wish was straight, brown eyes that I wish were blue, and I'm almost five feet seven inches tall (yes, I'm taller and more mature—and some say scarier —than most of the boys I know). My mother, who gave you to me for Christmas, is Helen Davis, and my father is Charles Davis. Everyone calls him Chip. I have a much older sister who is in college at Northwestern University; her name is Roberta Susan; we call her Bobbie, and never Bobbie Sue. My brother is Joseph Kent; we call him Joe. He's named after our great-grandfather Joseph Davis. Right now, he is a Marine, fighting communists in a country called Vietnam. My teacher talks about it all the time—actually, she complains more than talks. Vietnam is a country somewhere in the Orient; I still do not know exactly where it is.

I also had a younger brother. His name was Thomas; we called him Tommy. He's dead. Someday I'll tell you what happened; I can't right now.

Mom says I should give you a name, like Bobbie and Joe have, so that when I write it is to someone like a friend. I've thought a lot about it, and since my favorite song in the whole world is "White Rabbit" by the Jefferson Airplane, I will call you Grace, after Grace Slick. I hope that it's all right. Besides, I like the name—makes me think of God and church and all.

Since you cannot see or hear, I will try to be your eyes and ears. I hope, after we get to know each other better, you can help me when I get in trouble. And boy-o-boy, am I famous for that! Just ask Joe. We kind of grew up together since he's only five years older than me. Bobbie is ten years older, so she was in high school the first time I really remember her. Then she went away to college and is studying political science, whatever that is. All I know is that when she's home, she and Dad argue . . . a lot. That's not cool. I go to my room when they start.

Mom is a homemaker. She's always here helping, and cooking, and gardening. We have a very nice garden; I'll show it to you some time. Right now, it's just a week after Christmas, and everything is under a ton of snow, and it's freezing. The summer is when it looks the best—that's when I'll show it to you.

Dad writes for the Chicago Daily News, a newspaper. He is what he calls an investigating reporter. He tells stories about things that happen; he tells me that he tries to help make sense of senseless things. I like his writing; maybe someday I'll be a writer, too. Or a songwriter like Grace Slick or Carole King. I almost called you Carole, but I like Grace better. I still like her song "Up on the Roof", though I don't understand how you can like being up on a roof in Flossmoor with all the shingles and stuff. But it has a nice beat.

Got to go, Mom's calling.

————

Grace, I'm back. You'll get used to that. I'll write some, then leave, then come back. Maybe I'll get into a pattern or something. No school this past week. New Year's was yesterday; school starts Wednesday. Did I tell you I'm a freshman in high school? The school is very nice. And our church is enormous, with great high ceilings. Most of my teachers are Dominican nuns; some are kind, and some are, well, just ornery. That's all I'll say about that; God will probably punish me if I write what I really think.

Bobbie stopped by for Christmas dinner, stayed a while, then left. She and Dad started yelling, and Mom was crying. It was all about the war and politics. Sis was nice at one time; now, I don't know what happened to her.

Joe was here for a few days last summer around the Fourth of July; he's such a big man. He said he was being sent to Vietnam, had to be there by the end of July, and may be there for thirteen months. I miss him. He wrote a lot during the summer, now not so much. We used to have so much fun together. But there were times he wasn't in a good mood. Mom says those were his "bad" days. We all have bad days—that's so we know when we have good days. He said he'd write. I miss him a lot.

More later, Cate

———

Cate: Now

The morning after the funeral, I cleaned the house and the garden. The ghosts were the hardest to sweep out. Busywork, to be sure, but it kept me occupied. I'm mildly annoyed at how rude and thoughtless those friends of mine had been. Cigarette butts and doobies in the shrubbery, wineglasses left on the window ledges, plates of half-finished sandwiches and napkins littering the garden tables. I wondered why the neighborhood raccoons hadn't finished off the debris; they would have had a first-class party. Four full black trash bags now stand next to the bins on the side of the house, waiting for Monday's trash pickup. It was John's party . . . at least someone else should have come to clean up.

I rinsed another glass and set it on the towel near the sink. I'm an enemy of untidiness. It's almost a disease, but it did give me a chance to both clear the house and clear my mind.

Joe coughed as he entered the kitchen. He opened cabinet door after cabinet door until he found a cup, then went to the coffeemaker.

"I could have used your help," I said.

"I spent the last hour looking for an aspirin. You'd think with that pharmacy John left upstairs, there would be at least one."

"Don't be an ass. What time is your flight?" To be truthful, I was glad he slept in. John's death was almost as hard on him as me. They were, to each other, brothers.

"Noon. Just the hop down to San Diego. You okay?"

"Yeah, I'll be fine. I was cleaning up. I'll get to the remaining ghosts this afternoon after you're gone. Maybe I'll have an exorcist from the Mission stop by."

"Brilliant idea."

"And I'm having dinner tomorrow night with Alice. It seems everyone wants to distract me from all of this . . ."

"Shit? I know that stuff. I remember you wrote a book about it, starring me."

"Yes, you're right. Was that *Joe Gets His Ass Handed to Him* or *Strangers the Morning After*?"

"Hah! Anyway, at least you waited a decent time after my divorce to write that second one. I don't think Linda ever connected the two."

"Lucky for you. Teachers and students—nasty business there, shame, shame."

"They were old enough."

"Nowadays, they are never old enough—always too young, and you, too old. However, you . . ."

"Just stop. I've learned my lesson—and when to keep my pants on. And today, I can assure you that the brush *is* mightier than the sword."

"Still, if it weren't for the sad fact that people love to

read about the collapse and failure of other people's lives, I'd be out of business. It makes them feel better and superior about themselves."

"And the small triumphs and victories they score. That is until the shit happens to them."

"Short-term memory loss, always a good thing," I added.

"I was thinking . . . you need a dog."

Pulling the plug from the sink, I watched the suds recede and settle to the bottom. I took the spray and washed away the foam.

"Now why would you say that?" I countered. "One dog was enough in our house, and he was for the kids. When I want an annoying mutt around, I'll invite you back."

"Aren't we ornery? That's a good thing, I guess. I mean it —a dog would be a distraction, give you something to take care of. Go for walks, get you out of the house, be your protector, something to match your personality. Maybe a bulldog?"

"Really? A bulldog? I see myself as the English sheepdog type."

"Too much upkeep, hair everywhere. Compromise—how about a golden retriever? She'd fit your personality. Do you remember Tack?"

"And what would I do with a dog when I travel? Would not be fair to either of us. And besides, Tack was your dog."

"Until you stole his heart. I was away and he just crawled into your lap. I never forgave you for that. Think about it. I know a couple of breeders; I can get some advice."

"Joe, just leave it alone, okay? What time do you need to be at the airport?"

"I'll take a cab or Uber."

"I need to get out of the house and get food. If not, I'll be eating leftover brie and cold cuts for the next week. There are things I need at Costco and the car needs gas. All this crap doesn't change any of that. I'll drop you off, then run errands."

Late that afternoon, after I put away the groceries and restocked the liquor cabinet, I chuckled about the woman at the checkout at Costco. She never said a word as she passed the dozen bottles of hard liquor over the scanner. I was sure I heard a *tsk-tsk* somewhere between the half-gallons of rye and vodka. Dinner would be part of a prepared enchilada thing from the Costco fresh food counter; I might squeeze four dinners out of it. As it warmed in the oven, I opened a bottle of cabernet sauvignon. It came in a cute bag with a note; I'm not sure if it was a gift or a bribe. Either way, it was delicious and very expensive—I'm going with bribe. I counted more than two dozen bottles of excellent wine, mostly red, and five superb single-malt scotches left in John's honor. Sadly, I prefer bourbon or, like what Al Capone drank, Templeton Rye. Rye is for killers who use a pen.

The doorbell rang. Through the gauze curtain a man stood, a basket of flowers in his arms.

"No need to sign, Ms. Wallace, these are for you."

The flower arrangement was at least two feet wide. "Can you set them on the table there, Louis?"

"Certainly. Quite an arrangement. My mom says this was one of the biggest she'd done in a long time. I'm not supposed to comment on the delivery, but these are absolutely gorgeous."

They were gorgeous, white and yellow roses, sprigs of breath of heaven, chrysanthemums, blue bonnets, a riot of colors—cheerful and gay. Reminded me of fireworks.

The card read, "I hope these will brighten your day. Sometimes everyone needs flowers. Ben Taylor."

———

A week later, Joe's diaries still sat on the coffee table in front of the leather couch. Intimidating, I hadn't moved them. Like a bomb with a temperamental fuse, I was afraid to touch them; the slightest movement might set them off. I thought about using a long stick to crack them open; maybe it would provide a margin of safety. The house still echoed a week after Joe returned to La Jolla. He taught at the Fine Arts Institute of California at San Diego and held the lofty title of emeritus professor. That's what you get when you hang around long enough. Emeritus; i.e., Latin for "old and useless". His specialties were advertising graphics and art; his oil painting was his own. The institute also had one of the finest culinary schools in Southern California. Joe admitted that it was one of the reasons he stayed. "The excellent free food," he'd say. I would point to his boiler and reminded him of his promise to lose thirty pounds. Promises, promises.

Frankly, Joe's diaries do frighten me. All quiet and unassuming on their garnet outsides, but hit them with a stick and hell's hornets might pour forth. I'd reread my diaries from that period; it had been twenty years since I last cracked them. That was when I had them re-covered in green leather. Grace Slick? Joe told me that the singer was now a painter. Amazing—the past fifty years had sped by like a home movie on super-speed. The images flashed and flickered, the reels spun and whirred. Some memories came like the sound the end of a strip of film makes as it slaps against the metal parts of the projector. Every old song provided an ephemeral soundtrack to a moment, or an image, or a thought.

There were good songs in 1968, some even great. I have a CD somewhere with the hits from that singular year, a background leitmotif to the words I'd scribbled then in my diary. It's even on the satellite radio station in the car, 60s on 6, the ancient radio jock Cousin Brucie, presiding. Sometimes, listening, a tear backs up, waiting to slide down my cheek. It is hard not to smile nostalgically at most of the songs; a few bring serious memories, teenage loves lost; yes, there was that boy . . . Some, thank God for the balance, are just awful and numbing—really, the Cowsills?

Fifty years—good God—half a fucking century. They like

to say, "That's a lot of water under the bridge." It's more like Yosemite Falls. As I read Joe's diaries, he told stories he'd never divulged to me, or anyone else that I knew of. Short recons that turned into firefights and death, days and nights of sheer boredom punctuated by mortar rounds dropped haphazardly around the base. They were entries about fear and filial comradery all tangled together in sweat and blood. A few of the pages were smudged with what looks like water; a couple had fingerprints that could have only been dried blood. I found a lock of hair taped to one of the pages; someday, I'd ask Joe about it, assuming he remembered why it was there. There was also a running count penciled in on almost every page, 96, 97, 98 . . . I assume they were the days he'd spent in Vietnam. The numbers stopped two days before the firefight that cost him his leg.

I stopped halfway through that volume; it was hard to go on. It was so real I smelled the jungle, the cordite, the death. I set it aside. The hell that Joe had been through.

My brother Joseph Kent Davis was born in 1949. Five years, either way, make a difference between siblings. We are older to each other and younger. We did not attend the same schools at the same time, especially high school. There was a sense that each of us was just a little out of reach; my brother and sister were more managers and babysitters than mentors. When Joe, broken and lame, came home, it was my duty to be his nurse, protector, and eventually his savior.

Luck was never on Joe's side, and it sure wasn't a lady. At fourteen, he was the star on his Little League team and was quick with both the glove and the bat. He dreamed of playing for the Cubs. "I'll be the greatest shortstop they've ever seen," he'd tell me. He taught me to play catch. He practiced hard that summer of 1961, and his team was in the regional championship game. The next series, after the win, would be the state championship. Tied going into the ninth, Joe hit a line drive over the third baseman's head to left field. Joe wanted the win. He saw that the boy on first was now almost to third. He wanted the kid to go for home, for the win. Joe forced him home by rounding second and yelling at him to score. Joe would not be the last out. The kid slid into home, scoring the winning run. Joe, not watching where he was still running, stumbled into the opponent at third, caught his leg on the edge of the bag, heard a snap like a breaking tree branch, then tumbled past third. The pain was excruciating; the win was divine.

By the time the doctors finished putting rods and pins in his right leg, Joe knew that his career as a professional ballplayer was in serious jeopardy. His team lost the next round of games. The rest of the summer, laid up in bed and away from sports and almost all other activities, blackened his soul. He became moody, restless, angry. He withdrew. I tried to make him happy; he told me to get lost. Later, he didn't join sports in high school, and even though the limp was gone, he could feel its ghost when he tried to run. He liked to draw and sketch; there were many scribblings spread through his journals. He took it on with a passion. Mom—seeing something that would hopefully distract the boy from the turmoil in his head—encouraged him to take summer classes in art.

In high school, he emerged from his shell, and by his senior year was back to his old self. He had a steady girl-friend, average grades, and no desire to go to college. One month after leaving high school, with the war in Vietnam on everyone's mind, he was drafted. He opted to join the Marines instead, the same military branch our father, Charles, had been with during World War II. The Marines helped to repress the dark days that hung along the edge of Joe's horizon. Maybe it was the friends he made, solid boys his age. Perhaps it was the discipline, the regimentation, the daily goals, and the camaraderie that helped turn him around. When he was home, the war was always on the edge of our conversations. Mom, still recovering from Tommy's death three years earlier, was stoic. Looking back, I don't understand how she managed it.

We were a model family, as if painted for the cover of *Look* magazine. All curly blonds, bright faced, brown eyes, with roundish comfortable faces. Mom and Dad looked so much alike they were once mistaken for brother and sister, not a committed pair of husband and wife. Our English heritage, with its amalgamation of a dozen other northern European tribes, shone through even though our lines had fled England before the Revolution. The Kent and Davis tribes were always a pain in the ass of some government.

"The rumor is we are going to Vietnam; my battalion has been reassigned," Joe said, as he pushed the spaghetti around his plate. "We aren't going to Germany, as we were told. I leave in a week. First Japan, then I don't know where, but I suspect Vietnam."

Mom took Joe's hand in hers. "You'll be fine. You'll do well, I know it."

For the second time in Mom's life, she was sending one of her men to war. She and Dad were dating when the nineteen-year-old Marine went to California for basic training in 1943. This time the ache for her son was deep in her life-giving belly. *"Goddamn fucking government,"* she would say. *"It's not their children who go; it's my son, my flesh and blood, my Joseph. And for what?"*

We said goodbye on an overcast and cool summer day in 1967. Bobbie and I joined them. We drove Joe to Midway Airport. At the gate, Mom in tears and Dad stiff and proud, stood tight to Joe. Bobbie handed him a small package.

"Open this on the plane—you'll know what to do with it," Bobbie said and then hugged Joe.

I gave Joe a small brown teddy bear. "Keep this in your pack; his name is Yogi. He'll protect you."

"Yogi's my guy, Cate." He gave me a hug and a kiss.

Later I asked Bobbie what was in the package.

"It's a camera. Maybe he'll send some pictures."

I don't remember Joe sending any photos home.

———

February 3, 1968

Grace,

I turned fifteen yesterday, and to spoil the party, my little friend—as we call it—also arrived. So, my stomach hurts and I had my girlfriends over for dinner. It was Friday night, but Mom made sure the girls didn't stay too late. It was going to be a slumber party, but I didn't feel well enough. Even after a couple of years, I'm still not used to it. At least it's not as cold as it was at Christmas.

The girls gave me a locket; Mom and Dad gave me a blue cashmere sweater. I hoped that I'd hear from Joe or get a letter, but nothing. Bobbie sent a card, that was a shockeroo. It also had five dollars in it. And Grandpa and Grandma Davis called and wished me a happy birthday. Grandma Kent sent a cute card with a dollar.

The sweater is beautiful, and it does show off my "expanding" figure a little.

———

February 4, 1968

Mid-afternoon, two days after my birthday, two Marines arrived here at the house. I answered the doorbell but kept the storm door closed. Tack, the sizable tan and black mutt that Joe had found three years earlier—as a puppy in the nearby woods—stood in the hallway growling.

"Can we talk with your parents, miss?" the sergeant asked. Then he saw Tack. "He okay?"

"Yes, as long as you stay there. Would you like to come in? I'll put him in the garage." I was still unsure why the two soldiers were standing at the front door.

"Thank you, but we will stay out here. Are your parents at home?"

"Yes, I'll get them." After I put Tack in the garage, I walked down the hallway to the family room where Mom and Dad sat. A hockey game between the Blackhawks and Philadelphia was on the television.

"Mom, there are two soldiers at the door. They want to see you and Dad."

Mom screamed. Dad ran to her.

"What's the matter?" I asked.

"Cate, tell them we will be right there," Dad said. "And ask them to come in."

The Marines stoically stood as they waited in the foyer.

"What happened, Sergeant?" Dad asked.

"Mr. and Mrs. Davis, we are here to inform you that your son Corporal Joseph Davis was wounded last week in a battle near Khe Sanh. He is now in a Navy hospital on Okinawa. He is expected to recover." The sergeant handed Dad an envelope. "All the particulars are in the telegram, Mr. Davis."

Father took the letter and placed it on the table. Mom was crying. I held her with my arm.

"Thank you, Sergeant. Is there anything else? Would you care for some coffee?" Dad asked.

"Thank you, sir, for the offer, but we have a couple of other stops. I'm glad that your son is okay."

Helen glared at the two men. "Glad? You're glad that he was shot? For God's sake . . ." She began to collapse again. Dad put his arm under hers to hold her.

"I'm sorry, gentlemen, thank you," Dad said.

The two men silently closed the door behind them. As my father slowly walked Mother back to the family room, I went to the window and watched the soldiers climb into a dark green Buick, US MARINES on the door.

What an awful job. At least Joe's alive. I have a friend at school whose cousin was killed in Vietnam. I picked up the envelope and carried it into the family room. Mom was still crying, and Dad was trying to comfort her.

I gave the envelope to my father. He removed the telegram.

4:15A CST Feb 3 68
MR AND MRS CHARLES DAVIS
367 SHADY MAPLE LANE
FLOSSMOOR, ILL

THIS IS TO CONFIRM THE REPORT THIS HEADQUAR-
TERS RECEIVED 30 JANUARY 1968 THAT YOUR SON
LANCE CORPORAL JOSEPH K DAVIS USMC UNDER-
WENT A SURGICAL AMPUTATION OF THE RIGHT LEG
ABOVE THE KNEE AT THE STATION HOSPITAL,
DANANG. HIS CONDITION IS SERIOUS, AND HE HAS
BEEN RELOCATED TO THE SURGICAL STATION IN
OKINAWA. HIS PROGNOSIS IS GUARDED. WE UNDER-
STAND YOUR CONCERN AND BE ASSURED THAT HE
IS RECEIVING THE BEST OF CARE. YOU WILL
CONTINUE TO BE KEPT INFORMED OF ALL SIGNIFI-
CANT CHANGES TO HIS CONDITION. HIS MAILING
ADDRESS REMAINS THE SAME.

LUCIUS P STREELMAN GENERAL USMC MEDICAL
STATION OKINAWA

"His leg. Oh my God, Chip, they took his leg," Mom
screamed.

"He's alive, Helen. My God, please think of that," Dad
answered.

I took my mother's hand. "He will be okay; he's coming
home."

Mom took a deep breath and fell back into the couch.
"Yes, there's that. We need to find out more. The naval
hospital in Okinawa? Who knows where he is? We need to
find out when."

"We will find out as soon as we can. Right now, we must
be thankful it's just his leg."

The doorbell rang again.

"Would you get that, Cate?" Dad said.

At the door were our neighbors, Delores and Bob Debolt. They followed me to the family room.

"Is everything okay, Helen?" Mrs. Debolt asked. "We saw the car and the Marines' name on its door. Is it Joe? Is he all right?"

"He was wounded, lost his leg," Dad said. "He's in Okinawa. That's all we know."

"Jesus, all hell is breaking out in Vietnam right now. They're calling it the Tet Offensive," Mr. Debolt said. "All over the country, it's horrible. We're glad Joe's okay."

The Debolts stayed for an hour. The Symingtons from directly across the street also stopped by; they also saw the dark green car. I excused myself and went to my room with Tack.

"Tack, I know Joe will be just fine. He'll get over the leg, I know he will," I said as I looked into his brown eyes and scratched the back of the dog's head. I knew he knew something was happening. I wrote Joe a letter, my twentieth since he left.

That evening the house was quiet. The TV was off, and after dinner, the family huddled around the kitchen table. Dad tried to reach Bobbie at school but could only leave a message with her roommate.

"He will be just fine, Mom," I said. "He's strong. I know he will."

"Cate, Joe's going to have some real problems," Dad said. "He has a lot of issues to deal with—and you are going to have to help him."

"I can. I know I can," I said.

Chapter 4
The Jungle

Joseph Davis: Then
Khe Sanh, Quang Tri Province, Vietnam

January 28, 1968—Diary Entry

Duke,

Weather report: It's fucking raining—again. No time for a full entry tonight. We're off the ground at daybreak, all the ammo and rations we can carry. Rumors are everywhere about the VC; something's going on. No one can figure what those fuckers are doing, no one. But every day brings new rumors and dead Marines; that's the way it works here. That means that Tiny will also have double the dope he carries in his pack. That asshole would leave his rations behind just to take extra weed. More when I get back.

Right now, I wish, and in fact pray to what God there is, that I was dead. I'd welcome it. But to help the reaper? Put a bullet in my head? I won't give the VC the satisfaction. Do you know Hamlet's line about being or not being? Fuck, that's the question, a damn good question right now. The agony deep in my right leg burns like it is roasting over a fire. The desolation surrounding me is real and the stench, overpowering. The misery, the agony, the dying, the dead—the fucked. Those that could have heard me *are* dead; their shattered and burned bodies lay strewn about in the darkness. Upward, to the stars and to no one, I prayed: "Please, God, take all this, take this pain, take this wretched soul. I am totally, completely, and holistically fucked. I am yours."

I slowly and quietly draw my poncho over my head, hoping to help the night hide me. If I can't see, maybe I can't be seen. To be seen is to die. The nauseating stench of the waxed canvas is more than the smell of the bodies. My right femoral artery throbs; the twisted belt tourniquet tight around my upper leg has kept me alive. It keeps time like a clock pounding one beat after another as my heart tries its hellish best to push past the constriction and spill what is left of my life across this ripped and charred hillside consecrated by dead Marines. My right hand is slippery and sticky; the sharp iron odor of blood fills the air. I lick my fingertips; they taste like rusted metal. I know the stench; it is part of the life here: sweat, blood, guts, and death. The odor of burned flesh mixed with the sticky air, ripe with the rotting jungle and human shit, drifts among stripped and blasted trees. I wave my invisible hand past my face—hell could not be blacker. I don't care about the stench or the darkness; all I care about is the thumping of my heart trying desperately to bleed me out.

A cough.

"Shut the fuck up," I mutter. Someone three feet away couldn't hear me.

"Fuck you."

"Jonesy?"

"Who's that?"

"Joe."

"Yeah. Which one."

"Davis, you fucken asshole. The other Joe's up the hill, a hole in his head."

"You okay?"

"No, my fucking leg's been ripped open. You?"

"Good, real good. Don't know the fuck why—I should be fucking dead."

"Maybe the fuck we are?"

———

A few days earlier, in the last week of January 1968, our squad had been dropped on a nameless hump of mud and grass ten klicks outside the base at Khe Sanh. It was all a part of strengthening the perimeter defense of the base. Below us, along an almost dry riverbed, lay a collection of huts. It had no name on the map. With no name, it simply didn't exist—the lieutenant called it gook-town. It wasn't large enough to be called a city—hell, not even a village. Upper echelon poetic license, I guess. That morning, we searched it thoroughly before climbing the hill. It was empty except for the few pigs that grunted and snorted through the garbage. They showed no fear and acted as if they couldn't care, which was probably true. We searched the huts and banged on the ground, looking for trap doors. In one of the huts, the sergeant found some Viet Cong propaganda and a rosary hung on a hook next to a picture of Jesus Christ.

"What the fuck is this doing here? I thought they are all Buddhists or some other fucking gook religion," the sergeant said.

"The French converted a lot of them to Catholicism," I answered, trying to enlighten the idiot.

"So you fucking say. Burn it."

"No need to do that, Sarge," I said. "Let's get the fuck out of here—too open. We're like ducks on a pond."

The sergeant looked at me and my two stripes. "You a gook lover, Corporal? I said burn it." Then he pushed past me and headed toward the far end of the tangle of huts. "I said fucking burn it down—burn 'em all down . . . too close to the hill . . . a place for cover. Burn it."

I slipped the rosary into my pocket and pointed to the others in the patrol. "You heard the sergeant, burn 'em."

Fifteen minutes later, the village was like a gate to hell had opened. The heat created its own wind, and the flames curled upward as if the devil's hands were reaching into the green overhead canopy. The fire and heat first toasted, then set fire to leaves and branches. We still had not seen one human—VC, ARVN, or native—since we humped in from the drop zone.

For the next two hours, we slogged a single-file track, twenty feet between us, along the narrow footpath at the top of the dry riverbank that led into and out of the village. Above us, the distant hilltop hid behind the trees. A thousand VC could hide on that hilltop. The point man studied the ground for thin spider wires and discolored dirt that might give away tripwires and anti-personnel mines—bouncing Betties that would explode three feet upward and, after emasculating you, shred your legs so you would bleed to death. A hundred feet behind the point walked the sergeant and our interpreter from the South Vietnamese Army. His name was Cao Phan or something. I can't remember for sure, as if it makes any difference now. The top of the gook's helmet barely reached the sergeant's shoulder. The Vietnamese all looked the same to this kid from Chicago. I apologize for being an asshole, but that's what happens out here. You become an asshole with no soul or become dead—which is one and the same thing.

It was to be a three-day patrol looking for Viet Cong. The orders were simple: try not to engage; see what you can find, recon. After the helicopter inserted us on the flats between the river and a dry hummock of razor grass, we'd trekked in. As far as I was concerned, we were suppositories looking for an asshole. This, like an asshole, meant Injun Country, as we politely called it. It was in front, in back, and all around us. I was positive the gooks were under us as well, wiggling around in their hidey-holes and tunnels just waiting to jump up and stick an AK-47 up our ass. Somewhere to the west, across the boundary with Laos, was the Ho Chi Minh Trail. As far as I and others in the patrol were concerned, it was an unreachable river of gooks and guns flowing south from North Vietnam.

At every rest break, the bugs hovered in thick clouds, trying to find openings in our mouths and noses and ears. The bug spray didn't stop them. I was positive that the little fuckers liked the shit.

"If only this oily crap would keep away the VC," I complained.

"What did you say, Davis?" the sergeant asked.

"Nothing, Sarge—nothing."

That was the day we burned the village.

On the second day of the climb, two men out front had been too close to the point man. The point man was now dead, the other two—badly shredded by the land mine—managed to climb into a helicopter while we provided covering fire. None was needed, but we shot up the jungle anyway. It was mostly to impress the pilots and the medical aide in the chopper. We rolled the point man's body onto the steel deck and then watched them disappear over the hills that flanked our right. Every one of us wished they were on that chopper. If there were VC, we never saw them. Only sporadic sniper fire that cut through the jungle told us they were out there. Could have been one man or a thousand—who the fuck knew? The direction of the gunfire was hard to figure; the jungle absorbed everything.

By nightfall of the second day, the sergeant was dead. The right side of his face stove in by a bullet, and the radio lay worthless where a lucky slug had punched a hole entirely through the steel case. Most of my squad were also dead, some mercifully quick, others slowly, bleeding out from missing arms or legs from the mortar shells that dropped on our position. The survivors—yours truly, Corporal Joseph K. Davis, and Private Jonathan Jones—sat with our backs to each other, waiting for God to send us to perdition. The blackness, only the blackness, hid us from the VC.

"You still there, Jonesy?" I whispered.

"Fucking A, Joe. Just us two Marines waiting to go to hell."

"Oorah!"

"Why the hell don't they come in and finish us?"

"Maybe they went for chow, some of that fucking fish and rice balls and raisins."

"And drowned in that oily shit they call fish sauce."

"Maybe that'll kill 'em," I said. "Give 'em the runs until their insides lay all over the ground. That would fix 'em." Something slithered over my good leg, then left.

"Fucking A, Joe, fucking A. Just thinking about the Cubs and wondering whether they will finally make it to the Series this year."

"You know damn well they'll never get there with Durocher as manager, no fucking way," I answered. I'm a Cubs fanatic. "It's just the way it is. They'll never win the pennant with that shit of a team and manager. Just saying, Jonesy, just saying. It will be fifty years before they make the Series."

"Sacrilege, Joe. That's just fucking sacrilege. I know it in my heart this is the year. Ernie Banks will carry them, and with Santo's bat, they gonna do really well. I just knows it."

"You're hopeless. Besides, we won't even care, since we'll be very, very fucking dead and the fucking leeches and snakes will be sucking our souls out of our assholes. Yes, dead, soulless, and the Cubs still won't win the Series."

"Maybe, maybe not," Jonesy answered. "We'll get picked up when it's light. I believe that; don't you, Joe?"

"Maybe, maybe not."

The jungle slowly emerged ghostlike with the sunrise, and with the light came the suffocating heat. The gloom of early morning separated the brown ground litter from the trunks of the trees and the bodies of my brothers. Finally, the dark green canopy overhead materialized. The dead appeared like apparitions rising from the mist that covered the ground as daylight punched through the trees.

"Just you and I, Joe. Just you and me. How's the leg?"

"Hurts like there's a fucking fire burning its way up my leg to my balls. Thank God the tourniquet's stopped the bleeding or you'd be talking to yourself. Goddamn—it still feels on fire."

"Good, fire's good. If you didn't feel nothing is when I'd start to worry."

"Thanks, just fucking thanks."

The firefight caught us by surprise—not a great surprise, but anyway a surprise. The Cong found us after the land mine rang the dinner bell, and the VC headed toward the blast like flies to a corpse. I lost count after thirty mortar rounds. Now, out of the original twelve, only me and Jones were left, sitting on the hard ground, back-to-back, each silently praying that the Cubs would win the pennant this year.

"Where the fuck are they, Joe? We sit here with fucking targets painted on our backs. Why don't they just shoot us and put us out of our misery?"

"Don't know. Maybe we're not worth a bullet. That dead asshole sergeant over there said we're not worth shit; now he's dead—serves the bastard right. That sergeant would have been fragged at some point in his fucking career. Now we won't have to waste a grenade. Should tell the VC they did us a favor."

"Some favor. We sit here and watch the son of a bitch rot —while we wait to die."

Through the jungle's buzzing came the predatory *whomp-whomp* of a Huey's rotor. Far off but coming louder. It came from down the valley.

"Jonesy, you got a smoke grenade?"

"One, green."

"Pitch it; maybe we can hitch a ride before the gooks decide to kill us. Jesus, my leg hurts."

The green smoke drifted up into the trees; the whole area around us turned a bilious yellow green, helping to hide us from the VC. The noise grew louder and, for a moment, hung directly over us. The downdraft blew the smoke away and into the trees. We again were exposed.

"Fucked," Jonesy grunted.

"Couldn't have said it better."

The pounding sound moved away up-valley. Five minutes later, ten Marines emerged from the forest. The sergeant looked around the small clearing and crossed himself.

"Jesus fucking Christ," was all he could say while looking around the clearing. "Can you two get up?" he asked, seeing us sitting on the ground. Jones still held his M16 on the approaching men.

"Old Jonesy can, Sarge. I'll try—my leg's a fucking mess," I said.

"Get them to the choppers," the sergeant yelled. "Gooks here any time. You three start moving the bodies. We are angels as soon as the bodies are onboard."

No one wanted to touch the bodies. They tied the men's bootlaces together and dragged them a hundred yards up the trail to the LZ. Another soldier placed the body parts in a bag. Whose was what didn't matter; they'd sort them out later. As he provided cover to his squad, the sergeant collected what had fallen out of the dead men's pockets. I hobbled up the trail with Jones holding me upright; the pain was unbearable. When I hit the chopper, a medic jammed me with a morphine syrette. The bodies filled the floor of the Huey. To make room for us, we had to sit on the dead men for the thirty-minute flight to the base at Khe Sanh. The air blowing through the open side of the helicopter was the first breeze I had felt in three days. I closed my eyes and let the morphine wash away the pain.

"Hold tight," the copilot yelled through the open door. "The VC have lit up our LZ, fighting everywhere. No options. We land hard, you roll out and run for whatever hole in the ground is near. Leave the dead; they don't fucking care."

The two Hueys banked in a wide arc that circled out to

the relative safety over the river. Then they dove hard and swept in toward the airport and the base. Out the open door, I saw explosions rising out of the jungle and gray-yellow clouds of smoke wash across the complex of buildings and the airfield. Two jets screamed past; sheets of napalm roared up from the jungle. Another Huey appeared and swung in close to us. I watched mesmerized as its massive M60 tore into the jungle below. On my left, the corporal who had helped load us into the helicopter fired his own weapon mercilessly into the dark canopy.

It was surreal, dreamlike. I drifted in and out from the world, angel-like from the morphine. The helicopter twisted and turned, trying its best not to be a target. The noise deafened and dampened all the senses. I tasted gunpowder and salt; my left hand gripped one of the strap handholds. The dead, held down with canvas straps, moved like they were alive. Without the straps, all of us—the living and the dead—would have tumbled piecemeal out of the aircraft. I looked at my hand; it was bloody. I found the rosary and fingered the beads. "Hail Mary, full of grace, the Lord is with thee. Blessed art thou amongst women and blessed is the fruit of thy womb, Jesus . . ."

The Huey slammed into the soft ground, almost tipping its tail over its nose. It plowed along on its skids for a hundred feet until it settled hard. As the rotor spun down, a dozen men rushed from the surrounding bunkers and helped me out. They put me in the back seat of a jeep as Jonesy climbed in the front. A truck arrived; I watched as the dead were quickly transferred. As we bounced across the airfield, I could feel the concussive *whoomphs* of outgoing mortars and the *thumps* from the howitzers.

We stopped outside a massive tent.

"This is where I leave you, Joe," Jonesy said as he hiked his rifle to his shoulder. "They'll take care of you."

"What the hell is happening? I can't hear a thing," I yelled.

"It's Tet, the first day of the gooks' fucking New Year.

Guess they decided to give us a party. The sergeant said the VC and ARVN are attacking across the whole of this shit-hole of a country. From what the pilot says, it's a wide-open offensive. We've been caught with our pants down, taking a dump. Got to go, gotta find a new platoon, new sergeant, new fucking bullshit. You take care—see you on the other side."

"Been there, Jonesy. Be safe; don't die."

Two men in clean fatigues lifted me from the back of the jeep and helped me onto a stretcher. We headed to one of the sandbagged huts aligned along the runway. All I could see through the smoke and haze were dozens of trucks and jeeps racing across the open airfield.

"We're going to take good care of you, son."

"What?" I mumbled.

The man's face in a gauze mask hovered over me. "Relax, I'm going to give you another shot for the pain, and then I'll look at that leg."

I stared up into the man's brilliant blue eyes. My shot was almost gone, then a sharp pain. The world slowed and quieted; the lights dimmed like the setting of the sun. ". . . Jesus. Holy Mary, Mother of God, pray for us sinners, now and at the hour of our death. Amen."

Chapter 5
Oorah

Joe: Then
Okinawa, Japan
February 16, 1968

Dear Duke,

I'm stuck in a hospital bed in a room full of shot-up, wounded, and brain-dead Marines. What could be worse? Yeah, my leg, the right one, is gone above the knee.

I'm writing this on a notepad. I'll transfer it to my diary when the damn thing finally finds me, along with all my other gear. I hope someone remembers to get my guitar from that kid in the mess; he borrowed it just before we went into the jungle. If there is one thing I want in this world, other than my leg back, it's to never see that fucking jungle again.

My life could be crueler; I could be wearing a diaper with no control, no input, no leg—just pain. Good God, the pain. I got what happened to me from a nurse. She makes sure I get fed my drugs through an IV; right now, she is the only person I truly love. When she walks into the ward, I smile, mostly because she's going to put a new bag with a morphine drip on the rack above my bed—the nectar of the gods.

The right leg is gone; there's a void where my future with the Cubs should be. Looking back, I ought to be batshit crazy over the loss—very angry, kill someone angry. That's when my problem with morphine began. First it was for the pain, then for the healing, then for the ability to forget. The rationalizations were the easy part; they became lies, then they became a habit. Later, when I got out, I found the good stuff, heroin. But I'm getting ahead of myself. There are worse things than being stuck in a hospital bed in Okinawa; I could be brain dead like the poor kid next to me. No, there is nothing fun about being in a ward in a Navy hospital; nothing.

As soon as I'm well enough to stand on my one good leg, they are flying me back to the States. The nurse says it will probably be Great Lakes Naval Hospital near Chicago. They need the bed here—one out, one in. I'll be close to the folks and the girls. They say you don't know what you will miss until it's gone; not true. I miss my family. I never had the angst issues and combative teenage thing with my parents. Sure, I had some tough times in high school, but that's on me. My folks, I love them to death. Same for Bobbie and Cate—love them.

I miss my leg and all that it promised. But the government, the politicians—I will not miss them. After months on the ground in Vietnam, I never understood why I, or we, were supposed to be there. Orders? Fuck orders. Every Vietnamese officer I met, or South Vietnamese politician that walked through the camp, made my ass tighten. One guy waved around a riding crop like he was George S. Patton or something. I didn't get it. We were there to save their country from the communists; why did I have the feeling they were using us? I miss my buddies, the Marines —Oorah.

———

US Navy Hospital, Okinawa
February 25, 1968

Dear Duke,

It's Sunday, and finally, all my gear caught up with me from Khe Sanh. Got to love my guys; they even replaced the rubbers I lent them, not that I need them here. Tommy K also returned my second baseman's glove, but no guitar. I hope someone puts it to good use. I could use the guitar; not sure I can ever use the second baseman's glove. And my journal was in the duffel; I can't believe it has been two months since I last scratched something in it. A lot of fucking shit has happened, Duke.

The Tet Offensive—even the guys here in the hospital, are calling it that. From what I hear, the VC got hammered, thousands of the gooks dead, shot, or blown to hell and gone. That'll teach them. There are more than three dozen guys in my ward here, row after row of busted, shot-up, and damaged men. Seeing some of them, I feel lucky. Losing my leg was nothing compared to what's been ripped off some of these sons a bitches: eyes, limbs, faces. Goddamn all this. Every day a general or admiral wanders through pinning medals on guys. Most of them would trade the ribbon or Purple Heart for whatever was blown or torn off. They tell me that if I'm good, in a few days they are going to get me up and walking or whatever you call getting around on crutches is. They showed the movie Thirty Seconds Over Tokyo the other night. When Van Johnson lost his leg, I yelled OORAH, from my wheelchair. A lieutenant told me to be more respectful; I gave him the finger. Shit, that poor asshole could have died and been buried in a Chinese rice paddy full of shit—leg missing and buried in a country no one had ever heard of. A lot of similarities, I tell you.

The good word, as good as it can be for a poor son of a bitch like me, is that I'm going home Thursday. They tell me it's first Hawaii, then San Francisco, Denver, and finally Chicago. I'm going to hold them to it. One deviation, and

I'm getting off the fucking plane the first place it lands on American dirt.

––––––

March 23, 1968

Two months after the start of the Tet Offensive, and after weeks of being bounced around half the world, Dad and Mom finally met me at Great Lakes Naval Hospital. I'm in the rehabilitation ward along with a couple of dozen Marines that all share one thing, a missing body part. When I finally looked in a mirror, I saw a pale and broken Marine, in desperate need of a haircut and shave. For a kid about to turn twenty, I look old, crazy old. My hands shake. When the folks saw the void of my missing leg, both began to cry. Me? I am fucking angry. The tremors in my hands and body feel like small earthquakes that foretell exploding volcanoes. Only Cate, my darling Cate, can quiet me, a hand on my shoulder, her hand in mine, a kiss on the forehead. When she does that, everything slows, even the beating of my hard heart. I cry when I run my fingers through her golden hair.

The war won't leave my head; sleep is the worst of it. Explosions and screams fill my nightmares. I awaken drenched in sweat, mouth dry, hands and body tense. I vibrate. The leg has mostly healed, but there is some pain in a spot halfway between my missing knee and foot. It is as if my brain still hasn't realized that the leg is gone. They told me it would be months before I could be fitted for a pros-thetic leg; the leg had to heal entirely. Me? I am at a point where I don't care. One day drifts into the next. In time, I began to dread Mom and Dad's visits.

"Joe, we brought a visitor," Cate said one Sunday. "It took a lot of convincing to get him past security."

"Who?" I hate surprises.

"A guest, someone who has missed you even more than me. Mom?"

Tack led Mom and Dad into the room. The dog looked confused, even frightened. He looked everywhere, sniffing, almost whining. Then something caught his nose, his eyes brightened, and he spotted me. There was nothing that any of them could do to stop that mutt. He pulled so hard against the leash, his feet almost spinning on the floor, that Dad had to let him go. Tack slammed his whole body into me; the wheelchair slid backward across the linoleum until it smashed into the bed. Tack, paws to my chest, licked my face and then buried his snout under my arm. He squealed and cried; nobody could stop that dog from climbing up to my shoulders.

"Oh my God, Tack, good boy. Calm down. I'm good. Slow down." I looked at Cate and Mom. I was smiling, the first time since I came home. "He's lost some weight."

"After you left, he would do nothing but mope around," Cate said. "His appetite was gone. He'd eat so little. We were afraid. He came out of it, but he still doesn't eat like he used to."

I rubbed the back of the dog's head and hugged him tightly. The dog still squirmed and tried to fold himself up like a huge puppy into my lap.

"What's going on here?" a nurse demanded as she rushed into the room. "And what is that god-awful racket?" She stopped when she saw the dog. She pointed a finger. "Who brought that thing into my ward?"

"Nurse Kane, this is Tack, my dog," I said.

"He needs to leave," Nurse Kane said with a harrumph. She was dressed in a brilliant white nurse's uniform and white cap; short black hair, no makeup, and an gold oak leaf on a lapel. Her white shoes made a distinctive tapping sound when she walked.

"Are you going to be the one to make him?" I asked, as I wrapped my arm around his neck.

Nurse Kane looked at the dog and me. She took a deep breath. "He can't stay, you know that. You can't walk him or feed him." She looked at Cate. "But he can come and visit. Are you, young lady, the dog's keeper?"

"Yes, when Joe left, he left me in charge," Cate said. "He so missed Joe. I think they are both better now. When can Joe come home?"

"It will be at least a month." The nurse turned to Mom and Dad. "They are getting him used to the crutches, and it takes time. There's a lot of therapy to go through. But today, the dog has done more than any medicine I've got. So, bring him along, but if he has an accident . . ."

"I'll clean it up, but Tack's a good dog. He knows his place," Cate said.

As Nurse Kane left, I heard her say to Dad, "Damn, that's the first time the kid has smiled since he rolled in."

After their third visit, the nurse invited Mom and Dad into a meeting with me and the psychologist, Dr. Lewis. Cate waited in the lobby with Tack.

"Joe is doing well; the leg is almost completely healed," Dr. Lewis said. "However, Joe has some genuine problems, psychological ones. He knows this; we are working on them. We are also beginning to understand the trauma that this war is having on our soldiers. What they've seen, and even done, keeps coming back. They can't stop it. We are doing what we can to help. For some, time will be the best and, maybe, the only healer. Even your other daughter coming to see Joe didn't help as much as I hoped."

"Roberta came to see you?" Dad asked. He looked at me. "When?"

"Last week, she stopped to see how I was doing," I said.

"Mr. Davis," the doctor said, "I do not think it would be a good idea for your daughter to see Joe for a while. Please ask her to wait until he's better." He looked at me. I know he wanted to talk to them without me there. I made sure he understood that was not going to happen.

"Joe became agitated while she was here," he said. "She told me to my face that I was a quack and that I was glossing over the damage that the military was doing to the soldiers—mental damage. I cannot have her here upsetting my patients, so if you could, please ask her not to visit."

"We're sorry, Doctor, we didn't know. Our daughter has strong opinions about the war. And she doesn't live with us."

"I gathered that. That is why I can't have her visit. Would you tell her?"

"Good luck with that," I said.

"We will," Mom said. "We understand. This war has driven a wedge in our family."

"Helen," Dad said. "Dr. Lewis doesn't need to know our family's business."

"Amen to that," I said.

"Yes, he does," Mom answered, "if it will help to make you better. Chip, you and Bobbie have been fighting about this for more than a year, long before Joe left for Vietnam. And now that he's back, we will have to confront all of this. If Dr. Lewis can help, all the better."

"And what can you do, Doctor?" Dad said, looking at him, then me. I hate it when he puts his father-face on. "Can you make this all go away? Can you make our son whole? Can you make any of these men whole? In a few weeks, you will discharge him and make it our problem."

"I'll do my best not to be a problem," I said. "Mom's cooking will fix everything."

"You are not helping," Dad said. "We don't know what to do. I read it every day in the papers. Doctor, I work for the *Daily News*. I know what's not printed. And to tell the truth, I'm beginning to think my daughter is closer to the reality of what's happening than what I see and hear from you, the Marines, or Washington."

"I understand . . ."

"Do you? Do you understand what this is doing to families across America?" Dad looked pleadingly at the doctor; there was no response from Dr. Lewis. "Helen, we need to get home. The traffic will be a mess in this weather." Dad stood and took Mom's hand and headed to the door. I sat there and watched. I felt like the guy in the third-row balcony seat. Dad turned back to the doctor. "When will Joe be discharged?"

"I will let you know. It will be soon."

"Thank you."

I followed in my wheelchair as they gathered up Cate and Tack. Two guys, ward mates of mine, sat in wheelchairs next to my sister and the dog. One of the men, with both legs missing, stroked the back of the dog's head. Tears ran down his cheeks.

"Can I see him next week, Catherine?" the soldier asked. "He reminds of Butch, my old dog."

"Of course. We will be here at the same time," Cate answered.

"Thank you."

I learned later from Cate that they never told her that Bobbie had visited me.

Chapter 6
A Dog is Cuddlier than a Goldfish

Cate: Now
Carmel, California
July 2019

A dog? Really? Laughable. A dog would be fun, certainly a lot cuddlier than a cat or a goldfish. It might even be a comfort; God knows that's something that I need. But it would be unfair to the animal. For three months, John and I had traveled while he could. And that was all for John and his insatiable need to fill out that damn to-do list. It had been exciting, fun, diverting. However, during the whole adventure, it was like standing in a Midwestern prairie watching a tornado coming straight at me. Until it hits, everything is fine. There'd been two dogs in my life. Tack, when I was a teenager, was Joe's dog and a sweetheart until he died while I was away at college. And there was King, a mixed breed of some kind (mostly Labrador). We brought King home when our oldest boy, Edward, was eight. The boy did an excellent job raising and caring for the mutt. When Ed went to college, he took King with him. They stayed together for fifteen years until, as all things must, King died. *No, I do not need a puppy.*

Twenty years ago—it was the summer of 1999—John and

I packed up our East Bay collections of family mementos and personal debris and moved to Carmel, California. Edward had just completed high school and was headed to Caltech, and Louise was a senior at Cal in Berkeley. Louise joked that we were moving to Carmel to get away from her. We smiled and protested, but not too emphatically. As we drove the two hours south, the death of John F. Kennedy Jr., in an airplane accident off Martha's Vineyard, was announced on the radio. Why I still remember that? As I said, an idiotic memory.

John was an intellectual rights attorney; he could work anywhere. He was damn good, always in demand, and his clients included writers and inventors. That's how we met in 1976; it was while I was writing my second novel. My agent —who had hunted me down after reading a draft of novel number one—was not comfortable with me, a brash, twenty-two-year-old, would-be, full-of-herself author. Until she met me, she'd thought I was much older. Yes, I was young, and to be honest, cute in a tall, blonde, and buxom Midwestern sort of way. I had moved from Illinois to New York City then. I lived in the Village, a basement unit, as a writer should—or so I thought. However, within a few months, I was quite sure the publisher she hooked me up with was intent on screwing me over, in more ways than one. Fed up with my protests, physical and literary, my agent passed me on to a New York law firm for advice. An equally young, aggressive, and nervy lawyer named John L. Wallace was assigned to me. In the space of one month, he nullified the publishing contract, helped me find a new agent and publisher, took me to Paris, and took more than my innocence. Short story: We fell in love, married, bought and packed up a beat-up, irides-cent green 1974 Ford LTD station wagon, left New York City, and drove cross country by way of Chicago, Iowa, Denver, Santa Fe, and Las Vegas to San Francisco. And three weeks before our second anniversary, we produced the next chapter in our lives, Louise Helen Wallace. Edward John came a couple of years later after we moved from our Filmore Street flat to Piedmont in the Oakland hills. My life in one paragraph, dot, dash, dot, dash, dot.

The day we walked through our first Carmel cottage (acquired with my royalties), John said, "Cate, the love of my life, you deserve this. Hell, we deserve this. After twenty novels and more than forty million copies, we deserve all of this."

"Don't be so cocky. Maybe the well will dry up?" I answered.

"Don't you be a spoilsport—I'll be dead long before your well dries up."

And how do you like that, John? You son of a bitch, you win again. I took my bourbon out onto the terrace. Summer is winter in Carmel. The fog was busting in, and a mist fell, like rain, from the overhead cypress trees. It was strangely comfortable, the cold and damp. It fit my mood. A rare summer front was moving in. The surf, high from the faraway storm and the tide, pounded the rocks. Some winters the house vibrated from the big waves. I'd let those tremors wash into my writing. Great waves of emotion, tsunamis, and floods would roll over my characters. Someone once wrote, in a review, that I made rain fall on the pages. I remembered the wet spots and runny ink in Joe's diary. To be honest, I prefer warmth and sunshine.

I pulled the buzzing phone from my jeans; it read *Alice Pengrove.*

"Hi, Alice . . . yes, I'm doing okay, or at least as well as expected . . . Dinner? . . . That would be nice—anything to get out of the house. At Pebble Beach? . . . See you at seven."

I met Alice and her husband, Derek, at a Carmel zoning hearing ten years ago. They were concerned about a remodel a few blocks away. In Carmel, everyone worries about remodels. The new owner, a Silicon Valley executive, wanted to double the size of the existing cottage. Eventually, he relented and kept the house in scale with the neighborhood, and the Pengroves became our friends. She referred to herself as the trophy wife when it was Derek who was the trophy. He'd sold his company to a conglomerate the year after his first wife died. It was his way of shedding everything that reminded him of his past. They met at a country club outside Dallas. Alice, a successful businesswoman in her own right, fell for the massive Texan. It was her second marriage; the first had been to her business, a travel agency that focused on the extremely wealthy. She sold her business soon after he'd sold his. They were relatively young, played golf, and wanted out of the Texas heat. Pebble Beach and Carmel suited them.

I was in the Terrace Lounge when Alice strolled in, the maître d' in tow. She pointed to a table at the window.

"I'll take your drink to the table, Ms. Davis," the bartender said.

"Thank you, Frank. And you might bring a Stoli on the rocks for Mrs. Pengrove. I think she needs it." The table looked out over the 18th green and Carmel Bay.

After the usual hugs, we sat. We had dined at this table a hundred times, sometimes with our husbands, most often just the two of us.

"News, great news," Alice said as she settled in and brushed her auburn hair away from her face. Her drink arrived a minute later; I noticed that Frank had refreshed mine.

"And the news is what?" I answered.

"Derek and I are going to London. There's a revival of *Guys and Dolls* at the Palladium. We're going for two weeks . . ."

"And?"

"We want you to come along, get you away from here. Recharge yourself. You have always loved London. It will be fun."

I sipped my drink. John and I had been to London five months earlier, a stop before Egypt. "Sounds delightful, but

I can't. The book is working; I can't take a break in the middle of it. Besides, John and I were just there."

Alice took my hand. "John would understand. He'd want you to go."

"That's not it; it really is the book. I never take a break while I'm writing, or at least I try not to. I need to get this done. Sorry."

"Well, if you change your mind, let me know. And I will keep pestering you."

"You are good at that."

"Part of my charm. Can you tell me about the book?"

"Too early; still trying to get the kinks out. I'm not sure where it's going right now. Lots of painful memories."

Alice looked at the waiter and pointed to her now empty glass. "So, you are now finally going to write the story of 1968. John and I discussed it, wondering when you'd attack it. But London is so delightful in the fall."

"Yes, I know. But right now, I must beg off. And besides, I've got this reporter from *Hello America* coming by in a couple of days."

"Reporter? I hope it's not like one of those past arrangements your publisher had worked out. If I remember, some of those were okay and—"

"You don't have to remind me . . . especially about the ones that didn't go well. They start pushing, and I get my back up. But this is just a one-on-one. The network said they received letters about me from some of their viewers. They want to know how I'm doing after John's death. My publisher's gotten the same thing. John was my agent; together, we handled all the business. I guess I owe my public something."

"They are the ones that keep you going. Millions love your stories. I can certainly believe that, when they heard about John, they felt sad—for you. Do you know the interviewer?"

"I met her once in New York. Seems fair, not out for a scalp. God, I've had it with those kinds. John put together a list of reporters that I should never talk to—it's a long list. Her name is Marsha Templeton, fortyish, quick-minded, and too damn thin. It's just her and her cameraman; I don't want a huge production. They want to see the garden. And thank God, it's not live. I hate those. They will splice it together, probably make a mess of it."

"Any idea about the date for the broadcast?" Alice asked while she pointed to the bottle of wine she'd brought. The waiter nodded.

"It's on Sunday morning, September 1. I can't believe I'm doing it. Seems too soon after John's death."

"Then tell them to wait."

"The publisher wants it out front of the new book release. It's okay."

"Please think about London."

"Alice, right now, no. I have no idea what fall is going to be like. Too much up in the air."

"Ooh, I see a chance. I will keep pestering. Besides, it's more than two months away. Derek is finishing some financial consulting, and he has a board meeting as well; he'll be in Dallas next week. I'm going with him. Are you sure you're all right?"

"I'm fine," I said, lying.

Chapter 7
How to be a Spy

Cate: Then
Flossmoor, Illinois
March 24, 1968

Dear Grace,

My heart is near to breaking. Joe is so tired and in so much pain, I wish there was something I could do. He's in a hospital on the North Side, Great Lakes Naval Hospital. When we visit, he seldom talks, just stares out the window. It takes us almost two hours to drive to Lake Forest—that's where the hospital is. We spend an hour or two, then Joe tells us to leave; he says he's exhausted. Then we come home. But yesterday we brought Tack. Joe was so happy he lit up like a light bulb, and so did Tack. I'm going to bring him every time. Makes Joe brighten up. The doctor told Mom and Dad that Joe could go home in a few weeks— there are no complications with his leg, and it's healing well. He will need therapy. Maybe being in his room will help. Having all his posters and baseball trophies, perhaps it will make a difference.

There is some good news; I met a boy. I've known him for a long time. We've been in school together since we were nine, but this is the first time we've talked to each other. His name is Adam. He's cute, and I mean gorgeous cute. We were talking about the Beatles and the Magical Mystery Tour album; he said the music is so cool. He said he was also a big fan of the Rolling Stones. Me, I'm not so sure. Mick Jagger is not anywhere as good looking as Paul McCartney. What do you think?

————

Cate: Then
March 1968

After one of our visits with Joe at Great Lakes hospital, I spent the afternoon cleaning his room. During the past nine months, while Joe was deployed in Vietnam, I never once entered it. To be honest, it scared me. What secrets my brother had put the fear of God into me. However, as I dusted off his baseball trophies, and straightened his posters of the Doors and Jimmy Hendrix, I began to realize that he was just a guy, older yes, but still a guy, my brother. I didn't know why he had a poster of Steve McQueen on a motorcycle, but I was beginning to understand. His albums are so different than mine: the Doors, the Rolling Stones, the Velvet Underground, Bob Dylan, someone called The Mothers of Invention, Cream, and the Kinks. Not one of them was in my collection; mine revolved around English bands, starting with the Beatles. I know that the Stones and Cream were English, but they are so different than the Beatles and Chad & Jeremy.

"Find anything interesting, or are you practicing your spying?" Dad asked, sticking his head in.

"I am not spying," I answered.

"I would be, Joe's a complicated guy. You can tell a lot about someone from what they have in their room. Those albums of his are all done by radical singers on the social and political edge. I'd even say some of them are socialists, or worse, communists. Joe took his guitar when he left for

Vietnam. I asked around at the VA; no one knows where it is. He probably left it there."

"He was terrific, I remember."

"Good enough—just needs more practice. Maybe that's something you can help him do when he comes home. He'll have the time. Ask him to play for you."

"He doesn't have a guitar."

"I can fix that. What do you think?"

"It's a good idea. Maybe he can teach me a little."

"That's my girl."

There were stacks of sheet music on a shelf in his closet; more Dylan, and Peter, Paul and Mary; even a couple of songs by Buffalo Springfield. I can read music a little, but when I read the words to the songs, they strike a hard note. Little about love and relationships; more about government and fear. I could hum the songs; many I recognized. Dad was right about Joe and his complications. Yes, maybe that would be something that I could do with Joe. He could teach me to play the guitar.

Tack curled up in the corner on a bed of old blankets that Joe had stacked up for him. While Joe was gone, Tack would come into the room, curl up, and stay for a while, almost like he was waiting for Joe to come home.

———

April 6, 1968

Grace,

Joe came home today. Even though I saw him in the hospital, he still looks way too thin, and he refuses to use a wheelchair. He fumbles around on his crutches. Tack was ecstatic. He ran about and bumped into Joe, knocking him over. The dog just enveloped him and sat on him. Joe tried to push him away. Tack wouldn't stop. Mom had to take the dog by the collar and drag him away. Joe couldn't stop crying.

He stays in his room. I brought him a can of Coke. He said thank you and then said he wanted to be alone. He seems angry. He sits in his big chair in the corner, his good leg up on the desk chair. I can't look at where his other leg used to be. He smiles, then a tear rolls down his cheek. He looks so much older than I remember. I asked if he wants anything, and he just shrugs. After I left, I asked Mom what I should do. She said to give him time.

————

Cate: Then
April 1968

"Give him all the time he needs, pumpkin," Mom said as we finished washing the dishes. I hung the towel over the long handle on the door of the stove. "The doctors said that he would have good days and bad. We need to be there for both."

"I wish there was something I could do."

"Go talk to Tack. He's upset, doesn't understand what's happening. Then again, we are all in the same spot."

At dinner that night, we sat around the table. Joe hobbled from his room to the dining room on his crutches and leaned them against the wall behind his chair and took his seat. Mom had made a pot roast. Joe smiled, said it smelled wonderful, and then picked at his dinner.

"It's good to have you home, Son," Dad said. "This pot roast never tasted as good when you were away."

Joe looked at Mom. "Thanks, it is good. Sorry, my appetite isn't what it used to be. Then again, there's a lot that's not as good as it could be."

"It will all be good again," Dad said. "You just need time."

"If there's one thing I have, Dad, it's time."

————

Cate: Now
Carmel, California
August 2019

I opened one of my diaries and thought about the man Joe had become. Much can change in fifty years: a redwood grows from a sapling to a monster a hundred feet high with a trunk that would take two men to encircle; a man matures, marries, and has children, then grandchildren. A man's reward, if he's lucky, is to be considered successful—Joe's reward was survival. The turning seasons bring a bright spring and fruitful summer, then a colorful fall pause, then in the dead of winter, rest. That was Joe's past half-century: youthful growth, chaotic change, dark personal winters, and finally a blossoming rebirth late in his life.

"I'm in the summer of my life," he'd grouse. "Fuck that autumn thing. Spring is continually being reborn in this old carcass." He was now seventy years old, had had a bypass, took a handful of pills each day, and sucked everything he could out of life. There was a divorce and a few near misses in love. He had painted serious commissions and seen his work hanging in museums, and many artists claimed him as their mentor. Even a few claimed to be his friend. "Better to hang in a museum than from the courthouse oak," he said once. No one was sure whether it was a joke or some political statement. I'm sure even Joe didn't know.

Joe's marriage of twenty-five years ended when he walked out after the two boys were in college and old enough to fend for themselves. There was something that pushed him away from his wife and over the edge. Joe never discussed it. I was sure now, more than twenty years after the fact, that he'd tell me if I asked. I didn't; a man needs his secrets.

After the breakup, he filled his Chevy van with artist supplies, fled Boston, and escaped to San Diego. "I need a warm place for my bones," he'd said. "I prefer to paint outdoors where my fingers don't freeze and the snow doesn't stick to the canvas." He was always a self-centered ass.

He was offered and took a faculty position at the Fine Arts Institute of California at San Diego; his fame as a graphic artist and businessman didn't hurt. And after a few heated and dramatic faculty meetings, he learned to keep his politics to himself. The man was a cultural conservative in a state chock-a-block full of flaming retarded liberals—at least that was his opinion. I never believed that being a Reaganite defined you as a Nazi.

"To advance in this world," Joe said once, "a civilized man learns when to keep his opinions and his pistols to himself." I used that line in one of my books. I took the literary flack; not him.

The five years after Joe returned from Vietnam were the hardest. When I wasn't at school, I was his constant companion and aide. Tack, God bless the soul of that sainted dog, saved him.

One evening, about three months after his return, and at the end of an agitated day, we were sitting in the family room watching television. Joe was in his room. Mom told me to leave him alone. The dark shadow days, I called them. An episode of *It Takes a Thief* was on; we could also hear it on the TV in Joe's room. Then Tack began to bark, loud and furious. The dog ran into the living room, then back down the hallway, barking the whole time.

Dad chased after the dog to the bathroom. Joe lay in the bathtub, his wrists slit. The dog howled and couldn't be moved out of the way. He kept lunging at Joe, knocking his head against the tub. Joe's eyes would flicker open after each hard nudge. After the ambulance arrived, they stabilized him. The dog calmed after Joe stroked the dog's back as they wheeled him out. I tried to understand, but it would be years before I fully understood. Joe never again attempted to kill himself, and he never talked to us about it. That was one day in a year full of one days. Tack would have taken a bullet for him; I'm glad he didn't have to.

The trauma of the war, his lost leg, his lost friends, slowly abated. In the mid-1970s, Joe was accepted into Loyola and, in time, graduated with a Master of Fine Arts. His first job was in the art department of one of the largest marketing firms in Chicago. He was good, damn good. Eleven years after Vietnam, he married a woman he'd met during therapy. They both would learn that two broken people do not make a whole; later I learned about the heroin. After their boys were born, Joe traveled for his graphics job; his wife resented it. The boys took their mother's side. I was surprised the marriage lasted as long as it did. He was a better father after the divorce, even from two thousand miles away. John and I were married then and living in California.

"I'm an asshole," he'd tell me. "Self-indulgent, self-righteous, self-centered, and self-serving."

"You are right about the first," I said. "But the others, don't be so hard on yourself."

"You've always been my guardian angel."

———

April 28, 1968

Grace,

School is exciting. I am taking French classes, and in English we are learning to write and construct complicated sentences. It's a lot more interesting than math. Boy-o-boy, I-do-not-like-math.

Joe comes out of his room more and more. That's good. He even takes Tack out into the backyard so he can do his business. Dad bought him a guitar. I can hear him strumming—nothing fancy, but it's good to hear. He also started sketching again. He's excellent. He did a few sketches of Tack; I have one pinned to my pegboard.

All Mom and Dad do is talk about politics. The president said something during a speech tonight. They talked about it way after I went to bed. Dad said that Johnson's not going to run again for president. When Joe heard, he said good riddance.

Dad is writing a story about the election; he doesn't talk much about it. He flew to Washington, DC last week for research. Someday I'm going to go to Washington.

Bobbie came by for Sunday dinner. To my shock, she and Dad didn't argue. They were civil. Maybe it was because Joe was home, and she didn't want to upset everyone. Anyway, when I went with them to the train station, she even kissed Dad on the cheek. They both were in tears.

Chapter 8
I'm Marsha Templeton

Cate: Now
Carmel, California
Late August 2019

A month has passed since John's death. I was in the kitchen puttering about, expectant puttering, nervous puttering, killing time puttering to be sure. The clock, high over the door to the outside, seemed frozen. Five minutes after ten o'clock, the doorbell chimed. A striking woman, about my height, stood on the stone stoop. Her straw-colored hair was neatly combed and fell straight to her shoulders. The haircut was expensive and looked casual, too casual, and there was an aura about her. Maybe it was the straight cut across the forehead a measured quarter inch above her sharply lined eyebrows. She wore a dark pants suit with a white blouse and sensible red flats. Her blue eyes twinkled mischievously. Damn, I can be so catty when I want to. Besides, she looked like a Nordic beauty queen. All she needed was a sword or an axe—I'll stop for now.

"Good morning, Ms. Davis, I'm Marsha Templeton. We met in New York."

"Of course, welcome. Call me Cate," I said and extended my hand. Behind Marsha stood a lanky, bearded man about forty. Black T-shirt, black jeans, and belt. His shoes were black canvas—Ninja cameraman. In one hand was a massive camera and a suitcase-like bag in his other.

"Cate, this is Curt Jefferies. He's my cameraman and sound guy. You asked for a small team; this is about as small as I can get."

"Perfect." I led them into the house. "Have you been to Carmel before?" I asked as we reached the large living room with its view out to the Pacific Ocean.

"Once, years ago. I have to say it hasn't changed much," Marsha said.

"One thing that *has* changed is the prices. They are stratospheric right now and will probably remain that way. Then again, that's the California lament. Housing is way too expensive. We like to blame the Texans and New Yorkers, but it's really our own fault. I have some goodies on the table in the garden. We can strategize there."

The two New Yorkers followed me around the cottage, saying nice things about the collection of paintings and antiques.

"John and I collected what we liked," I said, still thinking of them as ours. "We were in and out of fashion many times when it came to art; we didn't care. However, I do remember why we bought each and every piece. Mostly traditional, they each have a story. That's why we acquired them, a time stamp in our lives. There came a time when I believed we were living in a museum. Each is personal."

"Is that a Mary Cassatt?" Marsha asked, looking at a bright painting of a mother and child in soft pinks and butter yellows.

"Yes. We found it many years ago—way before the current insanity in the art market. Someone liked my novel *Children of the Light*. They offered it to us during the sale of their family's estate; it is from a home in Virginia. It was John's favorite." I looked at the painting; a thousand thoughts flashed through my mind. I'd named the child in the painting Jacque. The woman was his mother; her name was Nicole. Only John knew this.

We continued through the house to the stone terrace that extended out into the garden. Marsha had a dozen questions about the house. Who designed it? How long had I lived here? The garden was in full midsummer color, the long beds luxurious with tall, flouncy delphiniums, vivid roses in the sunny spots, yellow daisy-like coreopsis, and loose perennial pink geraniums. A sculptural, red-leafed Japanese maple dominated the far end, while azaleas with their crisp brown depleted flowers filled the bed underneath. Under the shade of a lime-green Japanese maple, I'd prepared a table crowded with cheeses and fruit. Two bottles of wine, buried to their necks in a large bucket of ice, sweated in the comfortable shade. Above, a cloudless blue sky held forth like a magical azure hand blessing everything that it passed over.

"My God, how perfect," Curt said out loud. "I may never go back to the West Village."

"The West Village?" I said, sorting out the glasses. "I lived there for a few years. That was when I was in my twenties; it was a strange place then—the 1970s."

"Still strange, but I'm sure different," Curt said. "This is about as far from New York as you can be and still claim to be an American."

"There are those with doubts about any of us, on either of the coasts, being truly American, but that's for a different conversation," I offered.

"And that is certainly being tested this election cycle, especially by that Maryland candidate, Jeanne Ellen Talant."

"Marsha, ground-rule one: no politics."

She gave me one of those mischievous looks that seem to be patented by many who live and breathe politics. "Got it, no politics—we'll see." Then she changed the subject. "Your house and garden are spectacular. Have you ever done an *Architectural Digest* story or Martha Stewart?"

"No, and that's why we will be doing the interview out

here. John and I insisted on keeping our personal lives . . . personal. Please, sit. Curt, which way do you want the light?"

Marsha looked at Curt; he shrugged. They understood now that they were in the lair of a master. I'd done a dozen shoots in this garden.

"Whatever works for you, Cate," she said.

"I'm sorry, I get a little carried away," I said and took a sip of wine. "Please, however you two are comfortable is good with me. And you must try this Chardonnay; it's from a friend's vineyard up the Carmel Valley." I handed them glasses.

"I'll hold off until we are done. May we stroll through the garden while Curt gets set up?"

"Absolutely." We walked out across the lawn to the far perennial beds. I heard the clattering of Curt setting up the tripod and extending the shades, screens, and lights. A squirrel up in the live oak chattered away at the intrusion.

"Those beds are for the spring—azaleas, rhododendrons, and pieris," I said, pointing to the shrubs under the Japanese maple. "Those on the end of the bed are deciduous azaleas; they came originally from the Appalachians. The English hybridized them until I'm sure there isn't a leaf you could call American in them; the colors are intense. Those long beds over there get all the sun this garden can trap; they are my perennials. John planted most of it; he was always pleased with his artistry. He was like a symphony conductor, he'd say. His job was to have all the flowers play in concert with each other."

"I'm in awe. Successful writer, gardener, teacher," Marsha said.

"If you live long enough, you can accomplish a lot. Survivor's benefits, I guess. Were my requests acceptable, Marsha?" I asked, turning the conversation formal.

"Yes, but they were so few. I've had interviews that had pages of subjects that were off-limits. Yours were easy—just your children and politics."

"They didn't ask for my fame," I said. "And politics is never a subject that comes out clean in any kind of conversation. No matter what is said, somebody gets upset. Is that okay?"

"Completely. I just want to be sure that you are comfortable."

"I will let you know if I'm not."

"Understood. Your reputation for being candid is well known."

I clipped a half-dozen yellow roses and snuggled them into a blue glass vase on the table. I surveyed Curt's handiwork and smiled. "Good job."

"Thank you, Ms. Davis."

"We ready, Curt?" Marsha asked.

"Five by five," the cameraman answered and peered into the monitor that extended out from the camera. "I've two lapel microphones—please clip them on your blouses. We'll do a soundcheck."

Five minutes later, after a few adjustments, we were good to go.

Marsha smiled, nodded, and turned to the camera.

"Good morning and hello, America. I am Marsha Templeton. This morning, I am here in the spectacular Carmel, California, garden of America's favorite novelist, Catherine Davis. Good morning, Ms. Davis."

The camera shifted. "Good morning, Marsha, and welcome. It is a beautiful day."

"Catherine Davis has written over thirty-five novels that, in one form or another, have told the story of America from revolutionary days up until the years following World War II. Her novels are known for their depth and vitality, and especially strong female characters. A few have found their way to television, and her incredible novel *Two Souls Lost in the Woods*, about Michigan in the 1930s, was made into a critically acclaimed movie."

"That, unfortunately, didn't make any money at the box office," I offered with a laugh.

"And why do you think that was?" Templeton asked.

"I didn't have flying men in iron suits or women with magical powers. It was too sedate for today's movie audience."

"Have you ever thought about writing a novel about the future or fantasy?"

"There is more than enough fantasy in my books. I just leave out the magic beans and Harry Potter wands."

"The literary community was saddened by the death of your husband, John Wallace. I extend my heartfelt condolences. Many of my colleagues knew John, and they, too, extend their respects."

"Thank you, Marsha. We were together for more than forty years; he was my other half. We complemented each other, and besides being my agent, business partner, and drinking buddy, he was my best friend. There is a large hole here in my breast; I miss him every day."

"Your life has had its great successes. You have sold millions of copies of your books. They can be found in fifteen countries—"

"Twenty-one with the newest release in Romania."

"I stand corrected, twenty-one countries. There are television shows and movies. What do you attribute to your success?"

"You've made me blush, Marsha. Until last month, I blamed it all on my husband. He pushed me; he was my sounding board, my muse. Now I'm on my own, feeling a little adrift, and for the first time I think I'm getting old. But success wasn't always the road I was on. When I was a young woman, I confronted problems that most of us face at one time or another. My brother died from leukemia, another brother suffered from Vietnam issues, the disappearance of my sister, and the loss of our parents, all within a few years. I had my faith and friends to help me but growing up was complicated and difficult. Then John walked into my life, and as they say, the rest is a fairy tale. I wrote my books, raised a family, and never looked back. I know this is not a fashionable thing to say, but we had a great life. That was one of the last things John said to me, and he made me promise not to stop. 'Keep moving and the bastards can't get you,' he used to say. Oops, sorry, I didn't mean to say that."

"I'm sure your readers wouldn't mind. You mentioned your sister."

"Roberta Sue; we called her Bobbie. She disappeared in the late summer of 1968. Our family can only conclude that she died; we have nothing else to prove otherwise. It was a difficult time for my brother and me—Roberta disappeared, then Mom died in an accident, and within a few weeks, our father died. It was tough on a fifteen-year-old."

"All within a few weeks?"

"Yes. He died in a car accident." I looked out into the garden. After a moment I said, "Nonetheless, my brother and I soldiered on. I lived in New York for a few years, got lucky with an early book I wrote about a tough woman during the Revolutionary War. I had issues with the contract with the publisher. The law firm I was working with assigned a young attorney to help me; that was John Wallace. I won the legal battle, found a new agent and publisher, and kept the attorney."

"After all the darkness, it does sound like a fairy tale," Marsha said. "Tell us about your wonderful garden."

For the next five minutes, we talked about the design, the plants, and, of course, mulch. Curt then asked for a break.

"I'll have some of that wine if you don't mind," Marsha asked.

I watched Curt as he walked through the garden filming the beds. He stopped and took close-ups of the flowers, even the hummingbirds that argued and bickered at the feeder. The squirrel was joined by his partner somewhere above us.

"I can't think of anything as perfect," Marsha said.

"It would be if John were here—that's my reality." I

sipped my wine and looked at Marsha. "What else do you want? There's something else going on. I've done too many of these not to notice. What's your angle?"

"I admire you too much to spring this on you, Cate. And I will not bring it up unless you accept."

"Accept what?"

"That you won't bite my head off. You do have a reputation."

"I don't like to be blindsided. What is it?" I looked at the mic on her lapel; I removed mine. She removed hers.

She took a deep breath. "My Washington sources say there is an FBI agent asking questions about your missing sister. It has to do with an explosion in Chicago fifty years ago."

"Who told you this?"

"A reporter for the *Post*; he's a close friend. He mentioned it when I told him I was interviewing you. He said that it's a cold case, and the agent has ties to the explosion. Sounds like a deep-sea fishing operation."

"Is this the explosion in 1968 on Chicago's Northside where four people died? Is that the one you are talking about?"

"Yes, I believe so."

"Good God, Marsha, it was fifty years ago. I was a teenager. My brother was going through a tough time; my family, like thousands of others then, was on the edge of chaos. Hell, I bet your parents were still teenagers themselves."

"Yes, they were. I wouldn't appear on the scene for another twelve years, so this is all ancient history."

"I remember it like it was yesterday. So, thank you for the heads-up, but I would appreciate it if we didn't talk about it in the interview. And I would also hope that you will keep this to yourself. I'm certain the FBI wouldn't like this to be out there. Besides, I'm guessing your friend may already be looking to put together a story. I wouldn't step on his lead."

"Have they contacted you?"

"No, and that's the truth. And that's all I'll say about it." But the fuse had been lit; my head was spinning. The FBI, five decades; all the crap was coming back.

The rest of the interview lasted about ten minutes, a chill had moved in, and it was obvious. We discussed my newest novel, now with my publisher and editors, *A Summer of Change*, and the rerelease of the earlier books. Even Curt sensed there was a change in the tone of the conversation. Templeton was true to her promise, and we did not discuss Bobbie or any of the events of fifty years earlier, not that I could or would contribute anything.

Their rental car left and weaved its way along the narrow road above the rocks and beach across from the cottage. A lone white vehicle sat along the road; it was pulled off to the side in one of those parking pockets that lined the narrow lane. The ocean beyond tumbled up and over the sand. It's easy to spot a rental in this town. I looked down the beach; no one walked along the water. The wind had shifted, and a thick fog bank was sliding across Carmel Bay toward the village. The mist had already engulfed the hills above the Pebble Beach golf course. I glanced again at the ghostlike car; a dark shadow sat in the driver's seat. After I was back in the house, I looked out the window. The car's headlights switched on, and it slowly pulled out and passed the house. I couldn't see the driver's face. I shivered; it would be a chilly night.

————

Looking back, I believe we were never the same after Tommy died. The family lost its cohesion; we seemed adrift. There was no fault, yet it *was* Thomas's fault, not that he deserved the honor. I was ten and he was six. One day my brother had a fever. Mom was concerned and took him to the doctor. Soon, and after stumbles and falls, the bruising and pain began. Within a month, he was diagnosed with leukemia. Mom and Dad told me that he was very sick and did not want me too close to him, as if he could pass it on to me. The doctors said it couldn't happen, yet they were afraid —we were all afraid.

Looking back fifty-six years, I didn't know how sick Tommy was until a rainy Sunday morning when they told me that he had died the previous night in the hospital. Bobbie was heartbroken; she knew everything that was going on. I found out later, so did Joe, and I was upset. They never let me say goodbye. Today, leukemia has a higher survival rate, especially with children. Then, in 1963, nearly every child contracting the disease died. Tommy was a fighter, yet some wars can't be won, at least with the weapons available. A few years later, I was about twelve, I learned about the disease and understood what had happened to my brother. A ten-year-old can't comprehend a lot; there is a lack of knowledge and comparative scope. However, I do remember the house being dark and quiet the weeks after his death. I went where I was taken, stood in the church. I remember a funeral, my mother crying. Later, after my success and a novel that included a sick child, our hearts and money went to the research hospitals that fight this horrible disease.

I said that the family was never the same. Of course we weren't—what family would be? Mom and Dad, during the next few years, turned their efforts to Joe and me. Until he broke his leg, Joe had his sports. I was a tomboy until I blossomed into a woman, then it was fashion, clothes, and music. By the time I received my diary from Mom, I already had written pages and essays about the Beatles and Johnny Mathis. Mom kept her eye on me. I was popular, and she didn't trust the boys in my school. I had no idea then about how perverse and yet entertaining the dear things could be. The following summer—I was eleven and Joe was sixteen— naiveté would have been my headline. The spring Tommy died, Bobbie was at Northwestern. She had been awarded a scholarship through the efforts of Dad's newspaper. I believe to this day that she should have been the writer in the family, not me. Mom talked to me about making sure that Bobbie got the diaries and journals when the time was right. That day, I didn't understand what she meant by "the time was right." Years later, long after Bobbie's disappearance, I finally understood the magnitude of the charge and responsibility to care for my family's past. That was after my heart, that summer, had not just been broken but slaughtered.

Fifty-six years later, that period is a fog. Some nights, those nights when the ghosts come and talk to you, I think about Tommy and wonder about what could have been. I conjure up a man, strong, decisive; he'd be sixty, married to the love of his life, four children, five grandchildren. I believe he is a successful architect, a builder of cities. Then again, looking back, the losses piled up in our family so quickly, it's a wonder that Joe and I even survived.

Those same ghosts conjure up images of my finding Mother on the floor of the bathroom. They are the ghosts that opened the door to the policeman who tells me that my father is dead. They are the specters that stand in gray silence when our grandparents—all four were alive when their son and daughter died—are so stricken with grief their own lives seemed to shorten, and they passed before their time. All taken by those ghosts of the tragic Kent and Davis family past. I become maudlin when I drift into that dark realm. With John gone, I'm not sure there will be someone to stop me from wandering off with them some night.

Chapter 9
Time and All It Takes Away

Cate: Now
Carmel, California
September 1, 2019

Joe flew up on Saturday morning to join me to watch the Sunday morning interview with Marsha Templeton. He'd stay if I needed him, even though I had no idea what I'd do with him for three days. We spent most of the previous day and night going through our diaries and Mom's. I was finally getting an idea of the structure of the book. What I did not tell him was Templeton's comment about the FBI snooping around. There was no reason to get Joe all juiced up about something that would probably not amount to anything. But it did gnaw on me; fifty years was a long time to have a wound reopened.

"Do you know that today would have been Roberta's seventy-third birthday?" I said as we sat down in the family room. I placed the tray with the coffee on the low table.

"Your memory, as always, astounds me," Joe said. "Yeah, three years added to my age—she would have been seventy-three."

"She was twenty-two when she disappeared, and now all

our children are older than that. Damn time and all it takes away."

The show went well; I admit it. Templeton was her cute self and introduced the five-minute piece. I was charming, radiant, and for an old broad, even perky. Book sales would soar. Joe said my publisher would be pleased.

"It's all about units sold," I said, going to get more coffee. "I told them that I'm not up for a book tour. Not right now, maybe late in the fall. This little puff piece will have to do."

"It was worth a hundred bookstore signings," Joe yelled from the study. "And cheaper."

The next piece on the show was about the gaggle of Democratic candidates running for president. When Joe saw the promo, he asked if I wanted to watch. Before I could turn it off, the face of one of the candidates appeared. It was Jeanne Ellen Talant, the junior senator from Maryland. The screen then went black.

The doorbell rang. Through the living room window, I saw an unfamiliar white car parked against the curb. It screamed rental. The shadow of a man stretched across the sheer drapes and glass of the front door. I pulled aside a corner of the curtain. He was clean-cut, tall, in a dark suit and tie, no hat, middle forties, dark red hair, and handsome. He was turned sideways and looking out to the Pacific. Joe walked up behind me.

"May I help you?" I said, opening the door.

"Mrs. Catherine Wallace?"

"Yes."

He raised his arm and in his hand a billfold opened, a badge, and the letters *FBI* appeared. "Please excuse the intrusion; I am Special Agent George Talant. I'm out of the Washington, DC, office. Do you have a few minutes to talk?"

"On a Sunday morning?" I answered as I stepped back into the foyer. "I guess so. What's this about?"

"It's regarding your sister, Roberta Sue Davis. I have a few questions."

I took another step and stumbled into Joe. I gave him a quizzical look. "Agent Talant, this is my brother Joe Davis."

"Joseph K. Davis? Excellent, this saves me a trip to San Diego. You were next on my list."

"And what list is that, Special Agent Talant?" Joe asked as he shook the FBI agent's hand.

"The list of people who may know where Roberta Davis, your missing sister, might be."

Joe had a strange look on his face. It likely matched mine.

"Come in." I stood to one side as the agent walked past and down the hall. He held a small valise under his arm. I looked outside; he was alone.

"Coffee?" I asked. "The pot's fresh. Why don't we go into the living room?"

"Yes, thank you. Beautiful house, Mrs. Wallace."

"Thank you, Special Agent Terrance," I said. "Joe, why don't you and FBI—"

"It's *Talant*, ma'am," he said, correcting me.

I remembered his name; I was just being a jerk. It's fun to occasionally poke the bear, especially if you have a long stick on a Sunday morning and basking in the warm sunshine of five minutes of international fame. Nonetheless, why was the FBI here and what did this have to do with my dead sister?

"Joe, would you direct Special Agent Talant into the living room? I'll bring coffee."

"I've actually worked with a few writers over the years," I heard Talant say as they went into the living room. "I answered technical questions and others about Bureau procedures. They wanted to get the jargon right, the process, what's my day like, the usual stuff. Even spent time on a movie set once. Maybe I'll give writing a shot; it's always an option. Right now, I have bills to pay, so it's the Bureau."

As I filled the tray, I heard nothing more from the living room. Entering the living room, I said, "I still have some pastries. We just finished breakfast, Special Agent." I handed Talant a porcelain cup decorated in violas, still poking the bear—big man, little cup. "So, what do you want to know about our sister? She died fifty years ago."

"Do you know if she might be alive?" Talant asked.

"As far as I know, and I think I can speak for Joe, she's dead."

"Can this be confirmed?"

"No," I said. "We haven't heard from her since late 1968 when she disappeared a few weeks after the Democratic convention in Chicago, the one with the police riot. That's the last time I saw her. I was fifteen. It was during the riot. My mother and I were stuck in traffic caused by the demonstration. Bobbie just appeared, then left."

The agent gave me a peculiar look. "And you, Mr. Davis, when was the last time you saw her?"

"Why the questions about our sister?" Joe said.

"It's a case I've been assigned. So when?"

Joe looked at me, a defiant look on his face. "About a week before that, I think. I was recovering from the wounds I got in Vietnam. She stopped by the house to say hello. I had no idea it would be the last time I would see her." For emphasis, Joe pulled up the cuff of his pants. The titanium shank of his lower leg flashed in the sunlight.

"I'm sorry, I didn't know. And thank you for your sacrifice."

"That's okay, and thanks."

"May I take some notes? This is all unofficial."

"Your questions all seem very official—" I stopped and thought for a long moment, recalling Templeton's warning. I remembered an entry in my diary that I read to Joe. "Special Agent Talant, in the fall of that year, when Bobbie disappeared, I remember two men in suits coming to the house. I had to go to school. Mom told me they spent more than an hour with the men. Don't you remember that, Joe? Didn't they ask you questions, too?"

Joe looked at me and tilted his head. "Yes. But after fifty years, I can't remember why."

"Yes," Talant said. "Our files show that your family, among dozens of others, was interviewed about the events in Chicago."

"The police riot and the demonstrations?" I asked. "Why would we be of interest? We lived thirty miles away."

"Some of the questions were about the demonstration, but this particular interview with your family concerned the explosion of a house and the deaths of four people on the Northside of Chicago, three days after the demonstrations. Two were civilians, and the other two were law enforcement officers, one an FBI agent."

"Fifty years, my God," Joe said.

"There's no statute of limitations on murder, Mr. Davis. This is a cold case that I'm investigating."

"But why now?" I asked. "What caught the attention of the FBI after all this time?" I didn't volunteer anything. Joe also held back. We both waited for the explanation.

"Technologies have advanced during the last fifty years, and most especially the last twenty," Talant said, opening the valise and removing a manila file. "It was found that dynamite caused the explosion, possibly a case of dynamite. It was never determined whether the explosion was accidental or intentional. Two people outside the house, both law enforcement officers, were severely injured and then later died from their injuries. Two inside the house died instantly. Their remains were identified from dental records. One, Abraham Klausnick, was a known anti-war radical and had been on the radar of the FBI for more than six months. He was an honorably discharged Army soldier with experience in explosives. He was twenty-four years old. The other was Barbara Dumas; she was twenty years old. Another man, James Abbott, was found severely injured outside the house. He was later convicted for criminal conspiracy and manslaughter. We were able to identify others in this group, or cell as it was called then. Our investigations concluded that most of these suspects were nowhere near the explosion and could not be placed at the house during the week before the explosion. During the post-explosion search of the premises, a woman's bloody sweater was found. The blood type did not match either of the deceased. There was suspicion that one of the women in this cell was Roberta Susan Davis, a grad student, a known agitator, radical, she had been seen at the house, and was possibly the ringleader. She is your older sister."

I studied the agent for a long time, then said, "Could you excuse me for a moment?" I left the room.

"I like your sister's books," I heard Talant say as I reentered the living room a few minutes later. I carried one of the journals.

"She is good, but I can't say that to her. She gets all—" Joe started to say.

"All what?" I asked. "Telling stories while I'm out?"

"No, just that I admire your books," Talant said. "I'm a history buff, and your books certainly bring a special significance and life to the stories. I especially like your series about the Revolutionary War."

"Thank you." My finger was stuck between pages in a dark green book. I looked at the agent. "How old are you?"

Talant smiled. "I'm forty-four. I've been with the Bureau since I was twenty-six. I joined just after the towers were hit. I was in the Army before that, officer, military police. Another reason I like your books—many of the characters are Irish immigrants."

"Well, Special Agent Talant, I'll bet there are stories to be told," I said.

"Too many; I could write a book."

"And that's how it begins," Joe said, with a grimace.

"I thought I recognized your name." I held up one of the journals. "This is my mother's journal. She wrote back in 1968, September 6, to be exact, that two FBI agents visited them that week. One was named Michael Talant." I looked up at the agent. "Any relation?"

Stunned, the agent adjusted himself in the chair. "Really? Fascinating. That would have been my grandfather, Michael Allen Talant. The Talants are well known in the FBI; I'm the third to serve. In fact, my grandfather, the man who interviewed your parents, is still alive. He's ninety-seven."

"An amazing and a bizarre coincidence," Joe said. "So, Agent Talant, why are you really here?"

Talant took a deep breath and let it out slowly. "This is a cold case I'm following. It has been on the shelf for the last forty-five years, but in the FBI no murder case goes completely cold. Especially when it involves one of our own and when new evidence appears."

"There's new evidence?" I asked.

"Yes, Mrs. Wallace, new evidence that is old evidence. It concerns your daughter, Louise Nevis."

"My daughter? What in God's whole world could my daughter have to do with Bobbie's death? She died decades before Louise was born."

"This unsolved case has bothered my grandfather for years. He pursued it off and on, hoping that he would find the murderer of his friend who died when the house exploded. It has been the story we talk about on holidays. It's sort of the Talant family's ghost."

Joe looked at me. "See, there *is* more."

"More what?" Talant asked.

"Please continue, Agent Talant," I said as I gave Joe a sour look.

"My grandfather tried for years to find the other people involved, he was sure there were two others. About five years ago, a fugitive by the name of Deborah Toomey turned herself into the FBI office in Charlotte. She said she was tired of hiding. She was sixty-eight then and was one of the people we had been looking for. According to our files, she was linked to the radical cell that was connected to this house. There were also tangential connections to the SDS, the Students for a Democratic Society. The speculation then was that it was the same group your sister was involved with. Toomey admitted to being part of a radical group, a group that held meetings at the house that exploded, but not the SDS. However, she would not give up the names of anyone connected to the group. She denied knowing Klausnick and Dumas.

"Toomey was ill, pleaded guilty, and was given a three-year prison sentence. The sentencing judge waived the jail time to time served. She passed away just last year from lung cancer. So, I'm doing this as a way to hopefully clear it all up for my grandfather, the assignment came from my boss. As I said, the FBI doesn't like to leave any case unsolved, especially one that involves the death of an FBI agent."

"Your family's legacy?" Joe said.

"One that I'm hoping to solve before we lose him."

"There is more, isn't there?" I asked. "The sweater? My daughter Louise?"

"Yes, the sweater. We had it tested after the case was dropped on my desk," Talant said.

"Being your family's legacy, I assume you have some involvement in it being dropped on your desk?" Joe said.

Talant smiled. "Maybe. I reviewed all the documents and evidence and had the sweater tested for DNA. It had never been done. The FBI lab was able to create a good profile."

"And that led you here? How?" I asked. "Louise, our DNA? It's not in any criminal database that I know of."

"No, not specifically. The connection came through an entirely different route. We compared the sweater's profile to the millions of others out there in the public domain. And we got a hit. A profile from a person in Connecticut had familial matches. The match was to a fourteen-year-old girl who had done DNA research on her family. It came through the National Geographic genetic site."

"Remind me never to leave my DNA anywhere," Joe said.

"I went to Connecticut and interviewed the family. Louise, your daughter, was shocked that there was a match. Her husband, Luke Nevis, was outraged at the intrusion. Your granddaughter is Patricia Nevis. I asked Mrs. Nevis not to talk with you due to this being a federal investigation."

"But it is perfectly acceptable to invade their privacy. Good God, Agent Talant, this is incredibly wrong and unfair on your part. And the point of this infringement was . . . ?" I demanded.

"We were pursuing a lead, the DNA."

"More like a fishing expedition. Louise and Luke were born years after that explosion," Joe said, standing. "They couldn't have had anything to do with this. And you already believe that my sister is who you are looking for, DNA or not. This is all bullshit."

"Such is the way of an investigation, Mr. Davis. I asked if they wouldn't mind having both her and her husband's DNA tested. I could not seek a warrant to compel them for a sample of their DNA; there was too little to go on."

I looked at Joe, hoping that he'd stay quiet.

"What?" Joe said, looking back at me. There was a sharp edge to his question.

"Continue, please," I said and gave Joe a smirk. I was waiting for him to go ballistic. He is so good at it.

"They said they would think about it. Mr. Nevis said they would be talking to their attorney. While I was talking with them, I noticed a collection of framed photos on a shelf behind them, above the couch. One of those photos matches the one on the shelf behind you, Mrs. Wallace. I assume it is of your family, fifty years ago. The tall girl is Roberta. Her face matches photos my grandfather took before the explosion."

"What photos?" Joe asked.

"Surveillance photos taken at the house."

"And this means what?" I said.

"It corroborates that the woman, whose blood is possibly on the sweater, was in the house, and that woman was your sister, Roberta Susan Davis. May I get a sample of your DNA to verify it? Either one of you; I'm not particular." Talant began to reach into his valise.

"This requires more than coffee," Joe said and went to the bar. "Sis?"

"Two fingers." I asked the agent. "Agent Talant?"

"Just the coffee."

"So, all this 'evidence' alleges is that our sister, Roberta Davis, was in the house sometime before the explosion and left a bloodstained sweater. That's all you have? And her even being in the house, at some time, hardly proves she was there to set off a bomb." I took the tumbler from Joe.

"Yes, thin evidence at best," Talant said. "But it does lead me to speculate that you and the Davis family may, and I emphasize *may*, have been hiding her these past fifty years. Aiding and abetting a felon is a serious crime, and a federal officer died. This is a federal crime. And lying to an FBI agent is also a criminal act."

"Agent Talant," I said slowly. "I am a very public person and have been for the last thirty years. Never once has the subject of our missing sister ever come up. The same for my brother. We are not good at keeping secrets, and if Bobbie had been under our control, or part of a cover-up or some form of a charade, I just don't see how we could have done it—especially for fifty years."

"Bobbie? You mentioned that name before."

"That is what we called her," Joe said. "The only one who believed she was alive after the riots was our father."

"Your father?"

"Yes, he told me that she was all right and safe. But both our parents died within weeks of her disappearance," I said. "Bobbie, if she were alive, didn't come to their funerals; we know she would have if she were alive. For fifty years we've heard nothing. That's why we are certain she's dead."

Talant reached again into his valise and removed another folder, opening it, he removed a sheet of paper. "Both your parents died within weeks of her disappearance. Your mother in an accidental fall in the bathroom, and your father in a car accident. It notes here that he may have been drinking," Talant said as he looked at the papers.

"Why the hell do you have that information? You people never change, sticking your governmental nose into everything—even after fifty years, damn you all," Joe said.

"This information was collected during the investigations into the Chicago Seven trial. During follow-ups, the FBI investigators found the information about your parents, in fact, some of it was in a news story in the *Chicago Daily News*, the paper your father worked for." Talant paused and looked at me. "I'm sorry for your loss. And you still believe that your sister is dead?"

I thought that Joe was going to assault the agent, he was livid over this intrusion. I looked at him, nodded a little, and watched Joe slowly inhale and relax. We knew each other all too well.

"Yes. We have nothing else to go on, nothing," I said. "For fifty years there has not been one breath of news or communication . . . nothing. Yes, the sweater may have belonged to Bobbie; the DNA may prove it. But it does nothing to confirm that she was even there that day, was responsible for the explosion, or that she is still alive."

"I understand. How did your parents die?"

"You don't have that in your little packet?" Joe said.

"I only have a summary, not the complete file," Talant said.

I was well beyond annoyed by this time. Boundaries had been crossed.

"Mom fell in the bathroom, hit her head on the sink. Cate found her," Joe said. "They said it was a stroke or maybe a heart attack, or she just stumbled climbing out of the tub. No one knows. They did not perform an autopsy; it was declared an unfortunate accident. That was a couple of weeks after I last saw Bobbie."

"It was Monday, September 16, 1968," I said. "I came home from high school and found Mom on the floor. By that time, she was gone. The dog was in the garage—a strange thing since Mom never put the dog in the garage. They also found the back door was slightly ajar, but that door always stuck. In those days you could leave your doors unlocked."

"I'm sorry that you went through that," Talant offered, then turned to Joe.

"I was in the hospital," Joe said. "I was recovering from a half-ass attempt the week before to kill myself. Dad came to the hospital to take me home; I remember it like yesterday. When we arrived, the street was filled with fire trucks and police. Cate was standing on the lawn with our neighbors, crying."

Talant looked up and directly at Joe. "There's nothing in this file about any of that. Only that they died."

"And there shouldn't be. It was none of the government's goddamn business," Joe said. "Nonetheless, Mom tragically died alone. Her death hit Dad hard; then we lost him in a solo car accident a few weeks later."

"I'm sorry."

"Thank you, I guess," I said. "When it comes to tragedy, Joe and I have seen way more than our share. That's why I'm concerned about Louise and her family and this intrusion. Joe and I will talk about the DNA thing; I will let you know. Agent Talant, I want you to do everything you can to keep my family, and Joe's family as well, out of whatever this, this expedition, is."

Talant made a few mores notes in his wire-bound tablet, reinserted the tablet and folders in the valise, then stood. "Thank you for your time. If I may, you can reach me any time at this number." He handed both of us a business card, the FBI insignia boldly printed on the front.

Joe looked at the card. "Talant. Irish, I assume. Rare spelling. It's the same spelling as the senator from Maryland running for president. Coincidence?"

The agent paused, then said, "Jeanne Ellen Talant is my younger sister. As I said, my family goes way back in government service. Without a doubt, she's the brightest of all of us."

"Quite a dynamo, strong speaker, and cute," I offered. It was an attempt to make up for my earlier bitchiness.

"She is that—an anomaly in our family that is full of dark Irish. Why she turned out the way she did had a lot to do with our mother and grandfather. Our father died in the line of duty when I was eight."

"I'm sorry for you and your family. It's tough growing up without parents, we know," I said.

"Thank you. This has been a bizarre morning."

"Agent Talant, you don't even know the half of it," I said.

We stood at the door as the agent took another long look out to the ocean and then climbed into his rental car. He waved before closing the door.

"What the hell was that all about?" Joe asked as I closed the door.

"I don't know, but I have a feeling these are the first clouds on the horizon of an approaching storm."

Chapter 10
The Past is Prologue

George Talant: Now
Carmel, California
September 1, 2019

I left the Wallace cottage and parked a few blocks away. This was the second time I was here. The first was a few weeks ago when that television news reporter, Marsha Templeton, stopped to interview Catherine Davis. Interesting people. Catherine is strong, well educated, and obviously successful. Joseph, while a little rough around the edges, comes across as experienced, confident, and not too little arrogant. I like them. Through my contacts in the media, I heard about the scheduled interview by Ms. Templeton. I let it slip to a reporter and friend of Templeton in Washington about the reopening of the fifty-year-old Chicago case, hoping it would get to the TV reporter. What I'd hoped this morning was to see some of the effects. If there were any, the brother and sister are good at hiding them. I would take time when I returned home to review the interview.

My grandfather had talked about the explosion for as long as I can remember. It was the crime that got away. He likened it to a big game hunt. He knew the quarry, the terrain, but could never find a trail or even a scent. What I was doing was hoping to bring him the trophy, to solve a cold case, and bring to justice a killer—the killer of his best friend and fellow FBI agent, James Overfeld.

My grandfather, Michael A. Talant, is ninety-seven years old. He has come to the point in his life where he feels entitled to a few proclivities and blasphemies, and he humorously chides us grandchildren that we should kowtow to his wishes and whims. He is more than twice my age, and has led an admirable life and career, even envied by some in the department—though that number is now down to just one or two retired agents. Nonetheless, he still complains about how the goalposts are continually moved. "How can you win the game if you don't know how to score?" he once said. On his eighty-fifth birthday he confided that he was amazed that he had lived so long. "Maybe it's time to ignore the goalposts," he said with a snort.

Gramps was born in Hell's Kitchen, New York City, in the early 1920s. The Kitchen was one of those close-knit Irish neighborhoods on the West Side of Manhattan. As he told it: "I was a sub-average student with a promising career running numbers for the local Irish gang run by Owney Madden. When Da died, he left Ma with my three younger sisters, me, and jack shit. That was 1935. If a city bus hadn't hit him, I'd have probably beaten him to death. I had it all worked out: he'd come home drunk as usual, all his money gone, looking to pick a fight with Ma, the usual shit. I was ready. I'd clock the son of a bitch over the head with a sock full of lead shot, drag him down the stairs, and out to the alley—let the locals take care of him. He saved me the trouble by stumbling out of Landmark Tavern into the front of a city bus. It took me three days to find him in the morgue." That conversation happened while he, my sister, and I killed a bottle of Jameson Irish Whiskey back maybe twenty years. How much of his story did I believe? Enough to know that most of it was probably true. His legendary years in the FBI attest to that.

Gramps's nickname is Red. It was pinned on him because of his thick head of red hair, a proud color he said—so Irish. My dad also had red hair; I'm guessing the same as Gramps (which has now faded to thin gray). And my sister and I carry on the genetic tradition. We are both redheads. Hers is long and thick; mine is a buttoned-up military style. Even my kids, Colleen and Sean, have red hair; they call it ginger. At least we were spared the freckles.

Red grew up fast and mean, then the war came to America, and it saved him. He was drafted in the late summer of 1942, and two hard years later found himself a sergeant in the 8th Infantry. He was a leader of decent men who were butchered as they pushed the Nazis across France, the Ardennes, and back into Germany. It's a story he's proud of, and he is pleased he was part of the greatest liberation in the history of Western civilization. He wasn't a saint and could handle himself. A boy of twenty-three grows up fast on the beaches of Normandy and in the forests of Belgium.

He lives in a studio apartment in a retirement village overlooking Chesapeake Bay near Annapolis, Maryland. He is a proud man, a successful man, and loved by his children and grandchildren. I know he feels like he's been rewarded for his life by being put in a prison cell—solitary confinement.

My phone rang. "Hi, Gramps," I said as I left Carmel and headed back toward San Francisco. "Did you have your lunch?"

"Yes, I did, vegetable soup and fruit—yuck, I could use a burger. Did you talk to that Davis woman? I saw the interview on the TV. There's something wonky about her, too damn perfect, something dodgy. You said you were going to talk to her? She knows something, I know it."

"I don't want you excited," I said. "We can talk next week when I come down for lunch. Does that work for you?"

There was a long pause. There are a lot of long pauses

when I talk to my grandfather. "Yes, we can talk then. She may be cute but be careful."

"Who, Gramps?"

"Roberta Davis. She will lie to you, I know it."

"Catherine Wallace believes that her sister, Roberta, is dead."

"Who's Catherine Wallace?"

It was my turn to pause; yeah, losing it. I took a deep breath. "We will talk next week. Go take your nap. The news is on in a few hours, okay? Maybe there's a golf tournament on. I'll call you when I get back to Washington. Bye, Gramps, love you."

It had become more and more like this during the last year. At times, he's more lucid than men half his age, but time is finally wearing him down.

I did like Catherine Davis's books, and it was because of Ireland. Gramps would talk about my great-grandmother Nora Jones—I could see her in some of Davis's books. On the wall, over his bed, hangs a crucifix she carried from Ireland in 1905 when she emigrated from County Kerry. Unfortunately, it couldn't prevent her from marrying the devil, and Gramps said she had the most beautiful red hair.

Gramps has lived at the Annapolis complex for ten years. We begged him to sell the house after Grams died, but it took ten years for him to finally make the move. He retired from the Bureau at sixty, and was there to take care of me, my sister, and our disabled brother when our father was killed the next year during a raid on a militia camp in Idaho. There were times he was as much a father as our own would have been. His awards, citations, and war medals fill the wall opposite the crucifix. He is my hero.

On my desk back in Washington lay dozens of files I dug out of the archives. The tab on the top file, worn and torn, reads "Deborah Toomey". The other files are for Abraham Klausnick, Barbara Dumas, and James Abbott. I can recite, from memory, the content of every page. They are all dead. The bodies of Klausnick and Dumas were in the basement of the house that exploded, their remains discovered under the shattered and burnt ruins. Abbott, severely injured, was found on the front sidewalk; he'd stumbled out of the exploded house before the fire.

Deborah Toomey died last year from lung cancer, fifty years after the explosion. At my grandfather's insistence, I followed her case through the trial and conviction. I interviewed Toomey to press her into finally telling us about the others in the group. There were three interviews; Toomey never revealed any other names, and continued to deny knowing Klausnick, Abbott, and Dumas. When I showed her pictures of a woman we identified as Roberta Davis, Toomey just smiled. Roberta Davis's file is the last one in the pile.

I paged through the Davis folder. Gramps believes she's still alive. She would be in her early seventies now. I was going with dead; but after the interviews this morning, I'm not sure now. If she is alive, she has done the best job of staying off the radar I've seen.

Before I flew to California, I looked again through the Klausnick folder. I disliked the man's face; the photo was from his Army file. Abraham Klausnick was born in a Chicago hospital in 1945 and grew up in Joliet, Illinois. His grandparents were Polish immigrants from a village south of Gdansk. They left Poland after World War I. An average student and good football player, Klausnick enlisted in the Army a day after his nineteenth birthday and was sent to Vietnam in 1965. He was injured in a firefight with the Viet Cong while transporting munitions outside the Da Nang base. He returned to the United States in late 1965. After his recovery from the damage to his left hand, he was honorably discharged. He settled into a house on Chicago's Northside, the same house that exploded. The post-incident investigator's notes say that he became friends with Abbott and was dating Dumas. They also were friends with a group of students from Northwestern; Davis and Toomey were part of that group.

He and some of that group had been photographed and identified at anti-war rallies in Chicago by other FBI agents planted in the crowd. Every demonstration photo of the bearded Klausnick has him wearing Army fatigues with no insignia or patches; he was one of the dozens of confirmed ex-soldiers protesting the war. He was pissed with the Vietnam War, and it appears he was the technical brains behind the operation.

Barbara Dumas was twenty. The picture in the file is a blowup from her 1965 Peoria, Illinois high school yearbook: cute, sharp-eyed, dimples, dark hair nicely coiffed. I still don't understand why she was there with Klausnick and Abbott. Even though the files say she was dating Klausnick, fifty years later, I'm not sure. Two people from opposite sides of the tracks. Abbott, in the notes taken during his recovery and trial, never gave up any information about the personal lives of anyone in his group. Dumas, like Klausnick, was burned beyond normal recognition. Dental records were used to confirm both, and that's only because the investigators knew where to start. When her parents were interviewed two weeks after the explosion, they were shocked to find that their oldest daughter was involved in radical politics. She had been an honor student in high school. They blamed Klausnick, a man they'd met once.

The government came down hard on Abbott. In his interviews, he confessed to the group's political intentions. They had targeted three selective service draft boards on Chicago's Southside; they also had a list of others in northern Illinois. The first bombing was going to happen on September 2, Labor Day. A package of ten sticks of dynamite was to be placed near the rear entry, next to the trash and the gas meter. A simple clock fuse was to be used. Five gallons of gasoline were also to be placed next to the bomb. Abbott gave no other information. The records also say it took two months to get him off his heroin habit. Because of his intransigence, attitude, and lack of information, he was eventually convicted for manslaughter in 1969, and sentenced to twenty-five years in the federal prison in Marion, Illinois.

My grandfather gained a strange friendship with Abbott. In follow-up interviews, Abbott continued to refuse to give out any information about who else was involved. Fifty years later, I feel sorry for the kid; he was twenty-two when the explosion killed four people. The government wanted the death penalty, but his defense attorney was able to get that taken off the table. Abbott eventually blamed Klausnick and Dumas for everything. He claimed not to recognize pictures of Toomey and Davis. He was shown pictures of Black Panthers who were also seen at the house a few weeks before the explosion. He claimed never to have seen them. He spent twenty years in prison and was paroled in 1989. He died a year later in a Joliet halfway house; the heroin needle was still in his arm when they found him.

During one of our conversations, Gramps said, "We thought we had a chance to nab her at a restaurant a few weeks after the convention. Turned out not to be either Davis or Toomey. It was Davis's father, a reporter with the *Chicago Daily News*, and one of his associates; it was a setup. I believe to this day we were played. Eventually, we were pulled off the case and put on other investigations. We had the indictments of the Chicago Eight underway—you read about that at the academy. Now that trial—what a clown show. The only black guy, Bobby Seales, was severed from the trial of all white guys, then it became the Chicago Seven. We had to track down a new set of witnesses for Seales. And there were hundreds of witnesses to interview and process —a nightmare. It was only after the White House changed to Nixon that the trials happened, and they were a farce. The judge, an Eisenhower appointee, tried to rein in these radicals—they were disrespectful and insolent. Eventually, they were all let off on appeals. Maybe they were guilty, maybe not, maybe just stupid. My bosses wanted heads; we tried to give them heads; it was a fucking fiasco. Unofficially, I was told to link the house explosion to the group; there wasn't anything to use. Hoover said, to my face, 'Make it stick; make something stick.' They pushed it, then it stopped. I found out later that what happened to my friend Jim Overfeld and that Chicago cop Thomas Belden was not politically important enough. Still pisses me off."

"Two or three of those radical defendants are still alive," I told my grandfather.

"Hard to believe, Buddy. We tried but could not connect any of those eight radicals directly to the explosion or to our Northside gang of anti-war protestors," Gramps said. "Hell, the radicals in the house were so insignificant we didn't even give them a fancy label. There was the Chicago Eight, Students for a Democratic Society, Yippies, Black Panthers, Vietnam vets, and feminists. I, still to this day, believe the Catholic Church was involved, considering all the priests and nuns that showed up at demonstrations. Buddy, I've said this before, it was one giant cluster-fuck all around. No one person or group shouldered the blame or took the responsibility."

Gramps told me that in 1968 he supported President Johnson and the enlargement of the war—a lot of it due to what he saw in Europe after World War II, the expansion of communism. As a result, he and his fellow agents were spending a lot of time and resources looking over the shoulders of the demonstrators, taking names and photographs, compiling dossiers and folders. He said that Hoover knew there was a direct connection between Russian communists and the college demonstrators. Hoover ordered everyone to find the evidence. The history of this ill-fated program was taught at Quantico; internally it was called COINTELPRO (Counterintelligence Program). The program was set up by the director. It required the FBI to follow every lead that appeared to undermine the United States, whether it was the communists, the Negroes, the anti-war protestors, feminists, even animal rights.

In the early 1950s, my grandfather was involved in the investigations for the House Committee on Un-American

Activities. Then, he said, they looked at Hollywood actors, even civil rights leaders. "You want to get on one of our lists," Gramps said, "just publicly denounce Director J. Edgar Hoover." The year 1968 was just like the 1950s. The Bureau took photos, set up wiretaps, even planted informants in the organizations to collect intelligence on the hundreds of dissidents and radicals throughout the Midwest. The radicals were in universities like Michigan, Wisconsin, even Kent State. The eastern and western schools, like Columbia and Berkeley, were watched by their local FBI offices. Everyone was looking for connections, threads that tied those organizations to each other. It all came to a head that summer in 1968.

After a few whiskies, Gramps would lean back and say, "George, looking back, as a country, we dodged a bullet. There were some sad things to come, Kent State and Jackson State College in May 1970, to name two. The press, always on the anti-war side, even tried to pin the 1969 shooting of that black radical Fred Hampton on the FBI. But right then in 1968, it was as bad as it could be. Crazy time. That's what I called it—crazy time."

"What happened to this informer, Zeke Allanson?" I asked him. There was little in the file. "He shows up in a few of the reports, but there's no picture or other information."

"Zeke Allanson was an FBI agent from the Detroit office," Gramps said. "He was ordered to work his way into the Students for a Democratic Society, the SDS. He was deep undercover, became one of their organizers. We made sure that his name did not come up during the Abbott trial. Allanson was sent down from the University of Michigan to help us with the Chicago demonstrations. He'd made a connection to someone in the house. But it was never written down; I assumed it was Davis, but never confirmed. He took off and went back to Michigan a week before the convention. As far as I knew, and I later confirmed it, it's there in the files, that Allanson was in Michigan when all this happened. No one ever blew his cover. He helped us in Michigan for the next year or two, then went back to the Detroit office."

"Is he still alive?" I asked. There was nothing in the files.

"I have no idea," Gramps answered. "He had serious problems, problems that I learned later led to his resignation from the agency."

"Problems?"

"Dope and smack. I've believed it was from his undercover days in Detroit. When he got out of his undercover work, it became a real problem. The Bureau asked him to leave, retire; he'd keep his pension. I think he worked for a private security company for a few years, then claimed disability. As I said, he's probably dead."

As I was nearing San Francisco Airport (my flight was a red-eye), my phone rang again. I pushed the speaker button.

"Hi, Gramps."

"Hey, Buddy. Where are you?" Gramps was the first to call me Buddy. It stuck.

"Almost at the airport. I'll be home in the morning."

"How's the Davis investigation going?"

I slowed on Highway 101; I was nearing the exit ramp. These conversations with him were becoming more and more confused. I'd just talked to him two hours earlier. "You know I can't talk to you about it."

"That's okay . . . I'll squeeze you when we have lunch."

"Saturday, Kindra's got some things going on at the high school with Colleen and Sean, so I'm free. I'm buying lunch —how about Carrol's?"

"Deal," Gramps said. "Besides, the Nationals are playing that afternoon. They have a chance at the playoffs."

"Might be too exciting for you, and this year they could go all the way," I said, teasing him.

"It's the Nationals. I can only wish."

I made the exit and disappeared in the massive rental car garage.

Chapter 11
I Do Not Suffer Fools

Cate: Now
Carmel, California
Late August 2019

I looked at the area code. I did not recognize 970. Probably a call center. "Hello," I said.

"Hi, Cate, Ben Taylor."

I paused. "Colorado!"

"Ah, yes, Colorado."

"I didn't recognize the area code, then . . ."

"Covers the western part of the state—that's a lot of ground."

"How are you?" I asked, growing both curious and excited. "I'm sorry I didn't say goodbye after the funeral—it got so busy as people left. I was rude."

"I am good, in fact damn good, and no worries about the reception. I watched you work that group—remarkable. With all the concerns that afternoon, you managed to brilliantly smile and be incredibly accommodating. I know a few of those people; you are a lot more generous than I would have been."

"I try. Joe says I don't try enough. I'm noted for not suffering fools—and thank you for the flowers."

"I got your note—you are welcome. And not suffering fools? An admirable trait. And wonderful job on the Sunday interview. The press can be such fools when they want to be."

"Thank you. Where are you? You sound like you're in a crowd."

"Denver airport. I'm off to a conference in Chicago. Had a few minutes and thought of you."

I paused. Joe walked through the kitchen, coffee cup in hand. He looked at me. I pointed out of the room; he immediately turned and went the direction of my finger.

"You okay?" Ben said.

"I needed to clear some riffraff out of the kitchen—you thought of me?"

"Yes, I've even started rereading a couple of your books, especially the one about the Civil War. Wonderful writing. I'm trying to get back to California. Is there a chance I can leave a standing order for a date? Don't know when, but just wondering."

"I have no plans for the near or long term, Ben. I will put you on my dance card; just give me a day or two notice." I heard a loudspeaker announce a flight number.

"That's me—I'm off. We will talk soon."

"Again, thank you for the flowers. That was nice."

"Anything for a pretty lady. You needed them . . . you always need them."

————

Joe stayed two more days after the broadcast and the subsequent visit by FBI Special Agent Talant. The next morning and after my coffee, I hiked up the hill and retrieved my mail. The exercise did some good; the tension in my back got stretched out by the climb. Carmel does not deliver mail to its residents; it must be picked up at the Post Office. Most drive. Besides the usual junk and a few nicely addressed fan letters, a USPS standard box was included in the haul. The ten-minute wait in line was a chance to get caught up with the local gossip. Mostly the issues were remodels, the latest restaurant to fail, and tourists. The box wasn't heavy, and whatever was inside slid around. My curiosity wanted to open the box right then. I told it to be patient and wait—it's a risk-reward thing.

I placed the three-inch-thick rectangular carton on the table in the foyer. It was one of those *all you can pack for one price* boxes from the post office. The return address read: Grand Rapids, Michigan.

Who do I know in Grand Rapids? I flashed on a bookstore somewhere on one of its downtown streets, tight aisles, tall stacks, beautiful sitting area, packed with readers waiting breathlessly for my pearls of wisdom and a signature in one of my books. The carton had the heft and thickness of a couple of paperbacks. Grand Rapids also brought back the memory of driving with my family north through Michigan to a cabin Mom and Dad rented on Lake Michigan somewhere near Petoskey. Memories of deep pine woods, the glass-like lake, and campfires tickled my mind. Surprisingly, all these were soft and pleasant memories covered with fifty years of mental moss.

The marine layer had slid in during the night. A melancholy haze carried out into Carmel Bay, and at some indistinguishable point on the horizon, it changed from sea to sky. Soft swells on the Bay's surface surged the thick rafts of kelp up and down. Seagulls busied themselves in the open water between these dark green islands. Along the far horizon's thin edge, the ghostly shape of a container ship, heading north to Oakland I guessed, imperceptibly traveled. A dozen locals, tourists, and a few dogs explored the tidal debris on the sand.

Pushing aside the Windsor Castle coffee cup stuffed with pencils and pens, I placed the box on the long table in front of the window in my office. As I positioned it with the taped seam up, the items inside shifted. I removed the stiletto from the cup—the blade was bought in Toledo, Spain—and slipped its tip into the gap on the package's cover and began to cut the clear tape. I stopped. What if this seemingly innocuous package were a bomb? Here I am, cavalierly opening an unexpected package with what could be a fake return address glued to its top, and in a split second sever a thin circuit wire—boom. I cautiously placed my head to the side of the carton, expecting a ticking, the usual sound that bombs make. Not that I'd ever heard a bomb ticking in my life. I stepped back and sipped my coffee; it looked harmless enough, a white and blue printed USPS box, one of billions delivered every day—I guess.

I picked it up and tilted it. The contents inside did shift. I assume that bombs don't usually shift inside boxes. I gingerly reset it on the table, took a breath, said a quick prayer, reapplied the point of the stiletto against the tape, slipped it along the plastic seam, and then cautiously raised the flaps. No boom. Inside the box was a bundle of clear bubble wrap. So far, so good. I slowly and deliberately lifted the bundle, popping a few bubbles in the process. The first pop nearly stopped my heart. Through the wrap I could see three books. After more knife work, I freed the volumes from their wrapping and read the spines of the wine-red, cloth-covered books: the top read 1959–1964, the second 1964–1967, and the last 1968–1970. Above the dates, in gold leaf, the name Roberta Susan Davis was neatly embossed.

Stunned, I dropped the books back onto the table. In the process, I knocked my cup of coffee off the table; it missed the carpet and shattered into hundreds of bits of white English porcelain. I looked at the mess and then the books. Then, as if in both a blessing and a revelation, I whispered, "Oh my God."

Unnamed ghosts rose from the diaries; they hissed their moldy breath on my face. No—not true. They were more than ghosts; it was as if a world dead to me for fifty years had risen from the grave. Chills and a flash of sweat washed over me from a surge of adrenalin. I examined the inside of the carton for a letter or some type of note—it was empty. From the top book, a thin strip of folded paper extended out from between the pages.

Outside, in elegant cursive handwriting, it read: *For Catherine Davis-Wallace*. I guardedly opened the neatly typed letter.

Dear Catherine Davis-Wallace,

We have never met. In fact, until a few weeks ago, I never knew that you and your family were connected to me. My name is unimportant. For the last forty-five years, I have been married to a woman whose name, I believed, was Dorothy. When we met, she told me her last name was Childen. This note is quite a shock, I assure you. And will be to you, too, and from what I've learned, to your family as well.

Dorothy and I watched your interview on television last Sunday. When it was over, she left the room. I heard her crying. Why was she in tears? It was something I'd never seen her do in all the years we were married. I didn't understand. She handed me these diaries and told me to somehow find your address and send them to you. You have no idea what it took to find your address. Finally, someone at a publishing house in New York gave in. Please don't be mad at them.

I have only known this woman as Dorothy. I never knew about these diaries, or journals as she calls them. I didn't know her real birth name. She tells me that these volumes are about her life before we met. She told me that she was an orphan. During our years together, she never said anything about her family.

There are additional diaries, but they include information about our family and children. I have kept those. These three diaries start in 1959 and go through 1970. Someday I'll see that you get the others. There are currently ten of them. There are gaps, months without entries, and in fact, during the years we were raising our children, few entries at all. That's sad, I guess. But they contain personal information; I'll keep those for now.

We were married in the late summer of 1973; it was on a beautiful beach along Lake Michigan. A small ceremony, just my family and a friend of hers, a woman, who soon after the reception, left. I don't remember her name; maybe it's in the diaries. I never saw her again.

We have three children and five grandchildren. One of the children was named after you; I didn't know this until last Sunday.

We owned our own business. We did well, and the kids all received excellent educations. Dorothy raised them. They are strong and have their own families.

Mrs. Wallace, I am sorry about the loss of your husband. Our condolences.

I fully realize that this is as much a shock to you as it was to me. Dorothy tells me that you and your family have believed that she has been dead since sometime late in 1968. I can assure you that she was not and is a loving wife and mother.

How Dorothy hid you and these diaries from me all these years is a mystery. But then again, she kept the house, and I'm not that inquisitive. I worked to keep our household strong, and the kids fed, clothed, and educated. We each have our secrets, though in her case, once she told me, I could see a great easing in her.

She has asked me not to include our family name or where we live. She says that there may be some who are still looking for her. I have not read these diaries and she has only generally told me what was in them. Some secrets are best kept secret. I'm sure that you have a million questions. Lord, I sure do. However, our children do not know about any of this, and with these diaries now out of the house, hopefully, they will never learn.

There was no signature or even a name of the author, only the name Dorothy Childen. As I finished the letter, my whole body was shaking so hard that I had to sit, afraid I'd faint. I took deep breaths trying to slow my racing heart. My tears blurred the edges of the letter I held.

I folded the typewritten letter and placed it back in the first journal. Another slip of paper had been inserted into the second diary. It was handwritten. Even after all these years, I recognized the elegant cursive style of my sister.

Dear Cate,

I asked my husband to forward these diaries to you. I have kept them hidden from him. It was your television interview that finally pushed me to contact you and Joe. I wish I could have met your husband, one of many wishes and what-ifs in my life.

There is no way I can apologize to you for disappearing. For the past half a century, I have selfishly believed that by hiding, I was keeping you and Joe out of the mess I put myself in. I assume, after I disappeared, the FBI stopped by with questions. Mom and Dad could only tell them that they didn't know where I was. I wanted it that way. Then your career took off, and Joe got better, and soon the two of you were something. If I had come back, the press and the trial would have destroyed everything you'd worked for—the sins of the sister and all that.

I wish to God I could have been there when Mom died. I was told that you found her. I'm so sorry. And then Dad, even though we once had our differences, his death so soon after Mom's tore apart my heart. We were closer than you might believe. But that was years before I met and married my dear husband. He never knew. I'm so good at keeping secrets, even now I believe who I've become. In fact, during the last ten years, there were months I never thought about my other life. Then the diaries would call me back, and I would return to that other reality—that other me, that other time.

Every few years I would rewrite this letter in case I was hit by a bus or something. Now, even though in excellent health, I'm feeling my age and now count down as opposed to counting up. Even as a fugitive, I've lived a strange, yet surprisingly full life. Yes, I guess that I did beat the "man".

Give my love to Joseph; I am sure he will be very pissed.

All my love.

She didn't sign the note. After rereading the letters, I picked up the phone and called Joe.

"Joe, pour yourself a drink, get comfortable. I'll call you right back. Our peaceful little world has just been turned upside down."

Twenty minutes later, my hands still shaking, I called Joe. He said he was sitting down and *did* have a glass of bourbon in his hand.

"So, what's got you all in a twist?" he asked.

"Bobbie has been alive for the last fifty years. Her husband just sent me her diaries."

"What the hell?"

I read Joe the two letters. He was beyond shocked.

"She is alive?" Joe said. "I can't believe it. In fact, I don't believe it. This has to be a trick, a scam, maybe something the FBI is doing. It's that Talant guy—he's doing this."

"All I know is what's in these letters," I said. "I don't know what to believe. From the few pages I've read, the diaries are hers. I can tell—they're full of her. I was fifteen when she disappeared; then Mom died, then Dad. You were . . ."

"Twenty, one leg short, and still riding my demons on the sharp precipice between reason and insanity."

He asked me to read the letters to him again.

"We survived," Joe said. "For years we've talked about Bobbie until we knew that she was gone. That whole year after the FBI and Mom and Dad, we talked about it: Was she still alive? If so, where was she? Why didn't she try and contact us?"

"You and I were lost at sea, adrift," I said.

"For the past fifty years? That's a big fucking ocean," Joe exclaimed. "Goddamn her, why didn't she let us know?"

"You heard the letter; there has to be more in the diaries. Joe, this changes everything. Everything is all bent. I just don't know how much."

"You needed this, Sis. It's her gift to you. They saw your interview. It made an impression; if not, she would have stayed missing, stayed hidden."

I paused and swirled the bourbon in my glass. "Maybe."

"There were no names?" Joe asked.

"Just the names 'Dorothy' and 'Childen'. There was a return address in Grand Rapids. Lake Michigan is mentioned; it was where they were married. I checked; the address on the label is a city park near the center of Grand Rapids. No last names, not even her husband's, nothing. Bobbie's isn't anywhere either. Only you or I would believe it is her."

"She says this is to protect us, right?"

"That's what she said. All I have are these three diaries. I read the first few entries from the summer of 1968. She was troubled, disturbed; it all read like a drug-addled haze."

"Nonetheless, she survived, married, and raised a family," Joe said. "Read the diaries, understand why all this happened. Maybe she was involved in that explosion like the FBI said. Right this moment, that's your first *maybe*. If there is anything I can do, call me."

I clicked off, refilled the glass, and stood at the window. How many times, during the troubled middle of a novel, have I stood here and watched the sea? The mist was tenderly swallowing the headlands above Pebble Beach and Stillwater Cove. How many afternoons has the weather's panoply pushed its way across Carmel Bay? A hundred, a thousand, countless times, and always different. Sometimes winter storms, the slashing rain, and the pounding surf drove me gladly into the arms of John. Or he would stand behind me, his big arms wrapped around me, his breath in my ear. And in summer, the quiet, cat-like, marauding fog did soothe my soul. Today the wild swirls and grays were akin to the goings-on in my head. Bobbie had been alive for more than fifty years, damn her. She had been hunted, she had been called a traitor, and yet was she a defender of the right, even a hero to some? My sister had become the fog.

I ran my fingers over the burgundy cloth, then picked up the books and carried them to the living room. I set the bottle of Iowa's finest rye next to my glass and poked the smoldering fireplace into flames. It would be a long afternoon and evening.

Chapter 12
It Was Not the Summer of Love

Bobbie: Then
Chicago, Illinois
February 27, 1968

Dear Annie,

I had another argument with HIM last night and stormed out of the house and went back to my apartment. He needs to see how wrong he is about the war and the president and those fools that are killing my friends and my generation in Vietnam. And Joe is coming back, missing a leg, and he'll be so fucked up in the head he probably won't even know us. One of the girls in the house told me that she just heard that her brother was killed in one of the battles around Hue. It was just two weeks ago, right after Joe. What the hell is this world coming to? If those assholes in Washington want a war, I will give them a war.

I'm spending more and more time at the house now. There are all types crashing, mooching, or just bumming. It's near Wrigley Field. A couple of the kids play Tom Rush's album *The Circle Game* over and over; it's killing me. I'm going to snap it in two one of these afternoons. At least we can count on somebody bringing dope. Unfortunately, when most of these kids left their cozy homes and mothers, they forgot how to wash their clothes or even shower. Some afternoons the house is rank with the revolutionary stew of sweat, tobacco, dope, and patchouli oil. I don't even try to sleep here; the bedrooms are appalling.

One of the girls brought photos of that South Vietnamese cop blowing the brains of that Viet Cong prisoner all over the street. Freaked her out. I told them I'd enlarge them to poster size, and it would be in the front of our next march. That will show the bastards.

I am a true believer, a revolutionary, a visionary—I can see the future. The war in Vietnam is wrong, and the politicians know it but are afraid to be wrong. When Johnson escalated the troop counts, I marched and demonstrated— even poured my blood on the steps of the Selective Service office in Chicago. For three years, I've played my part. I've berated university presidents and administrators and spit in the faces of the police. It's all mashed together, like some narcotic brew of dope and cocaine. I've been disgusting and righteous. I've had police put a gun to my head. I've heard "Commie Bitch" so often that I'm beginning to think that they are right. Whatever it takes to end this racist, genocidal war. The dope is real, the lids of acid are real, the mushrooms real. All real, until it all becomes unreal.

————

March 8, 1968

Annie,

Mom told me Sunday that Joe would be home at the end of the month or early next month. What hell he must be going through. The old man is still ranting about the Tet Offensive. Hundreds of Americans are dead. Lord, how many Vietnamese slaughtered? They say thousands. He said it's got to be a win for us—shit, no one is going to win this. Lies, lies, lies. I'm getting to be as crazy as the next doped up and paranoid fool. There're days I must just get away from those people. I ride the L, walk the parks, stroll along the still-frozen lake. School can wait; I am a soldier in this fight against the war.

Good news, there's a rumor going around that Bobby Kennedy is going to run against Johnson. Right now, everyone is behind Gene McCarthy. I want Bobby; he will be our salvation. And the Republicans? Rockefeller and Nixon? Are they serious? Those fascists will destroy us.

And, astonishingly, a pamphlet sent out by somebody in Canada got picked up by the Feds—everyone in the house is pointing fingers. The pamphlet came out of Toronto. The FBI says it was going to be sent to 327 anti-war groups. Lies, lies. The Chicago Tribune reports that it gave instructions on bombing draft boards. Shit!! I wished we knew about it, but it's not a bad idea. Me? I believe it was the Feds who put it together, faked it all. I'm not sure anyone could come up with a list of even fifty genuine radical groups, let alone exactly 327. The Tribune also says Johnson's sons-in-law want to go to Vietnam—the assholes, let them go.

———

April 1, 1968

Dear Annie,

The son of a bitch did it. Johnson quit, won't run for reelection. Good riddance—he built this war on lies and deceptions, and now he's become its latest fatality. Johnson is a coward, not a hero. May he rot in hell . . . forever.

The fallout from his quitting is worse, and in some ways, even more toxic than the anti-war demonstrations that run every night on the news. The paranoia and outright fear of the American people fills the half-hour news programs and the front pages of the newspapers every day. I watched Johnson's speech on a television in a bar off Rush Street. He believes in his righteousness and the war. The fool—he is on the wrong side of history.

That's what I've been saying about politicians; they are worthless. And Humphrey, good god, what the hell can he do? McCarthy is shit, an old man, the last generation, old blood. It's all Bobby Kennedy's now.

I was beyond thrilled when Bobby threw his hat into the ring just a few weeks before Johnson's about-face. It is a three-way race for the Democratic presidential nomination: Hubert Humphrey, Eugene McCarthy, and Robert Kennedy. Two old men and Bobby, the future of America.

For two years the radical political groups have coalesced around the civil rights and voting rights factions. They've marshaled their followers into a wave of anti-anything movements. Feminism, through the speechifying efforts of Betty Friedan and Gloria Steinem, joined the front lines of the anti-war demonstrators on college campuses. Me, I can't trust them; I won't trust them. They are in it for themselves and book sales—Marxist-capitalists in tie-dyed Brooks Brothers skirts. With every escalation, more follow us—not them. Nothing helps recruitment like being told you are 1-A, going to be drafted, and die someplace you can't find on a map.

This war must stop and I will see that it does.

Mom told me that Joe is coming home this week.

April 5–6, 1968

Dear Annie,

My heart is broken. Martin Luther King was killed yesterday, murdered. He was the last decent man in America. I can't believe that the March on Washington was almost five years ago. His dream for the blacks in this country is the same for all of us now, freedom. But then again, right now, the only black people I know carry guns, have Afro haircuts, and scream about black power. I met one guy, real smart, smarter than all of them together, and he's a Black Panther and from Chicago. His name's Fred Hampton. He's going places, he's a leader. The others—none of them would cross the street to shake Martin Luther King's hand. Some even call Reverend King an Uncle Tom.

Where I grew up, there were no blacks in our church and none in my school. When I came to Northwestern, it was the first time I even had a conversation with a black man, and the whole time he was checking me out. The riots and burning cities are all over the television. I don't see the purpose of burning down your own house to prove a point.

We went up on the roof of Debbie's apartment building last night and watched the revolution begin. Flames and smoke rose in black columns against the night sky from the Chicago neighborhoods to the west and south. The skyline glowed red in spots; you could see the flames. The never-ending wail of fire trucks provided the background noise to the chilly night. In the distance, we heard the occasional popping of gunfire; it sounded like firecrackers. There were reports of many dead. Detroit; Washington, DC; and Los Angeles are also burning. This is what is needed to show those in power that what they sow, they now must reap.

Richard J. Daley, Chicago's mayor with the most political power over any city in America, has lost control over the black neighborhoods. He's taking it personally. When he speaks, he looks like he's going to explode. This politician from the Irish neighborhood of Bridgeport has no clue what is happening in the black communities just sixteen blocks away.

He ordered the police to shoot to kill any arsonists they find. Un-fucking-believable.

————

May 15, 1968

Dear Annie,

My paranoia has increased since the raid on the New York City print shop, the one where they found the pamphlets. And I'm also guessing that the FBI has raised its level of surveillance at the marches and the rallies. The assholes are so damn visible, it's almost laughable. Who the hell shows up at an anti-war demonstration in a crew cut, dark suit, and tie? Might as well hang a sign on them that reads "FBI". It's the others I worry about, the ones that look like us, act like us, smoke dope like us. They are the ones that will cause the greatest harm.

Help from the SDS arrived this afternoon—two from the University of Michigan. I'm not sure about them. They seem all buttoned up, tight. I could almost use the word conservative. The man looks like a kid, younger than any of the those in the house, bushy black hair, thick black beard—Che Guevara thing going on. The woman, blonde and hard-core, looks a year or two older than the guy. His name is Zeke Allanson; the woman, Susan Appledour—I kid you not.

Allanson made some remark about my people in the room. "This is it?" he said. "I came all this way for this shit? We should have stayed in Ann Arbor. What the hell can you offer us?"

Abe stubbed out his cigarette, stood, and walked up to Allanson. When he was three feet away, he punched the man in the mouth. Allanson spun around, stumbled. Appledour grabbed him to keep him from falling to the floor.

Abe told him to stop acting like a pussy. He wanted to throw them out. I probably should listen to Abe—he's a good judge of people. Hope I'm not wrong.

Later, after Allanson and Appledour left, I told Abe to stay away from them.

Abe smiled. "You the boss."

———

June 10, 1968

Annie,

I am so fucking mad; I'm screaming and going completely insane. I was in Los Angeles last week when Bobby Kennedy was assassinated, murdered. I thought about what happened to King, and now Bobby—I can't stand it. They say a Palestinian immigrant shot him, Sirhan Sirhan. I don't believe it, not for one minute. Bobby was a threat to the old guard of the Democratic party. They put a gun in this moron's hand and made sure he'd take the fall. I wouldn't be surprised that they cover it all up, just like they did for Bobby's brother John. Hoover and the FBI must be involved, have to be. If this killer lives for a year, I'll be surprised—they got to Oswald.

I was there at the hotel. I wanted to be a part of what Bobby was doing in California—be there from the beginning. I took the train from Chicago and crashed at a USC girl's apartment. I met her and a couple of other Californians at a May Day rally here in Chicago; they offered me a place if I went west to help with the primary. I was there that night, the night of the primary win, when the crowd was chanting, "We want Bobby! We want Bobby!" After his acceptance speech, he turned away from the microphone and with his entourage, walked toward the hallway that led from the Ambassador Hotel's ballroom to the waiting cars.

I stood to the side of the crowd, watching and smiling. I was thrilled; he was a bigger hero in person. His parting words rang true in my heart: "On to Chicago and let's win there!" I was thinking, I'll be back in Chicago before the Illinois primary on June 11. Bobby Kennedy will win, I'm certain. It will be the turning point of this cultural war and will be a change from politics as usual. My heart pounded with joy; I was glad I came.

At the far end of the room, the crowd shifted from the dais and toward the doors leading from the ballroom. Random, exuberant shouts came from the audience. Their faces, like mine, were bright, smiling, and happy. For most of us, it had been a long day. I volunteered to get out the vote that morning. Later I helped at a polling station and grabbed a bite to eat when I could. Now late in the warm evening I was famished. I gathered with others at the hotel to watch our savior accept the support of California Democrats to replace Lyndon Johnson as president. It was a narrow but decisive victory; Bobby won the nomination by four percentage points.

The crowd followed Bobby from the stage and disappeared through the back doors. Then came the gunshots—it could only be that—snapping over the crowd. Then the yelling and the screaming. The people running back into the ballroom. More yelling and shouting. Those in the ballroom stopped, expectant, anticipating. More cries from beyond the hallway—a chaotic noise of a hundred voices.

Then a man ran to the podium, seized one of the microphones, and asked if there was a doctor in the house. I knew that Bobby had been shot. The man who would lead the world to peace had been shot. I knew it. I slid slowly down the wall until I sat on the floor. My hands to the sides of my face, tears ran down my cheeks. I pulled a cigarette from my shoulder bag and, with hands shaking, I lit it and took a long drag and watched the chaos. My world collapsed until I was alone in a sea of bodies and legs.

"Out of the way," someone yelled. "Move."

Black wheels appeared and rolled past my feet. The feet and legs in front of the wheels moved aside, and the gurney continued its way until it disappeared in the forest of legs. I didn't move; I couldn't move. More yelling; words flew over the heads of the crowd. "Shot . . . Bobby . . . Dear God . . . No . . . I can't believe it," filled the room. Minutes passed, then the black wheels reappeared and parted the legs of the crowd once again. The gurney rolled past. I felt a sharp pain as it banged into my shoe. I looked up and saw a bloody hand hanging over the side of the gurney. Shoes left bloody footprints across the linoleum in the wake of the gurney's passing. A women's hand, small with a gold wedding ring, held tight to the larger hand; both were bloody; small black beads hung from between Robert Kennedy's fingers. I saw a crucifix attached to the beads. Then the gurney, the hands, and the bloody shoes disappeared.

I sat against the wall; I was physically paralyzed, yet my mind raced. I grew angry, and in time I slowly stood. The ballroom was almost empty. A few people still comforted each other; many wiped away tears. The camera crews were loading their equipment onto wheeled carts. It was surreal. The dais was empty, except for one man methodically winding microphone wires around his arm. I looked down at my canvas shoes. A crimson spot of blood sat on the white cloth. My shoes were now a religious relic to the martyrdom of America's future.

I left the hotel and spent the rest of the evening in a haze walking the miles west on Wilshire Boulevard. As the morning sun rose behind me, I reached Santa Monica and the bluff that overlooked the Pacific Ocean. I climbed down the stairs to the pier and boardwalk. If I could have, I'd have walked right into the ocean. A lone surfer drifted on the swells, waiting for the sun.

Two days later, I arrived in Chicago at the Dearborn Station, and for a week, I went through the motions of living. I slept, ate, and got drunk on a succession of bottles of bourbon.

―――――

July 10 to 18, 1968

Annie,

I am completely fucked. Daryl knocked me up. I'm pregnant. My guess maybe three months. I've been so busy with the marches and California; I thought my period was just late. I'm sick, puking, and there's no doubt anymore. They tested me at the clinic. Talk about awful bedside manner. The nurse, a condescending bitch, just shrugged and asked, "Do you know who the father is?" Sure, I know who the father is, a useless bastard who hangs around with the local Black Panthers, smokes dope, and has mental issues. He even managed to get himself shot in the leg trying to steal a case of vodka after Martin Luther King's assassination.

Nausea overwhelmed me; mornings were the worst. I'm pissed at both Daryl, who has been missing for almost a month, and myself for getting into this predicament. What a sorry piece of work I've become.

Debbie stood in the door of the bathroom and asked if I was going to keep it. She knew I was pregnant. She told me I was seriously messed up. No shit.

She said she could help with the abortion if I wanted one. Like she knew about abortions. Then she told me she'd had one the year before. It was a mess, she survived, still could have kids, but was lucky. I was stunned—abortions were wrong.

The morning sickness got worse. Two days later, I came to the only conclusion. I would go through with the abortion. I'd spent the last two nights at Debbie's; she was in the kitchen with a cup of coffee. Anti-war flyers filled the tabletop. Debbie lit a cigarette and asked if I'd decided. I told her yes.

The best and safest place is in London, England, she said, better than some back room here in Chicago. England made abortions legal; it was the place to go. She helped me get my passport. I had to borrow some money. Debbie told me what she thought the cost of the ticket would be, plus a couple of days in a hotel, and miscellaneous expenses.

A week later, I sat in the middle seat of the last row in the economy section of a United Airline 747. For someone who is always in control, I was adrift, lost in both my head and my body. At least being in the last row allowed me easy access to the toilets. That was about the only benefit. Everyone around me smoked. Even for a smoker, the air was sickening. Somewhere over Iceland, I threw up in the toilet, again.

At Heathrow, Debbie told me to look for a woman. She

would have red hair and be holding a sign for Roberta Davis. I have never seen a woman with hair as red as hers.

The woman, maybe mid-twenties, was thin, tall; I would describe her as angular. The hair was red, her complexion was brilliant white, and her eyes were like green marbles.

She held up a sign that said "Bobbie". She said her name was Sarah Toomey, a cousin of Debbie. She was all business; I was at a complete loss. I did what she told me. Sarah said I was too trusting—probably why I got preggers, she said.

Sarah's long strides through the airport were challenging my stiff legs. At one point, she stopped and waited for me, an anxious look on her face.

I dropped my bag as Sarah walked back to me. I was mad and told her to drop the fucking attitude. She laughed; told me I was the boss. I followed her to the car.

Everything was confusing. The roads and cars were going the wrong way. The signs were different. Even the air, for some reason, seemed strange. Sarah was waiting across the access road at the entry to the garage, a smile on her face. Screw it, I said to myself, crossed the road, and followed Sarah into the carpark.

July 20, 1968

Dear Annie,

I guess that I'm going to hell. It's over. It was all so clinical, so cold, so not right. But it was the only option. Talk about a lonely decision. I've never had to make one like this, ever. I only have Debbie. She understood, she's been there, she knows. I had time to think about it flying home. The stewardess asked me if I was all right; I was crying. I told her I was okay, that I had a breakup just before I left England. She nodded, she understood. Lies on lies. I feel pain; it must be imaginary; they said it might happen. Lord, what have I done?

August 27, 1968

Dear Annie,

We are ready to move. Allanson got the package. It's more than enough to make our statement. Next week is the convention; a hundred thousand of us will be here to show the world that we demand an end to this war. There are reports that Mayor Daley will have the National Guard and the Army here, along with the police. Perfect.

The way I figure it, the week after the convention we can attack at least five draft boards, blow their damn doors off, show them that the people are tired of their shit. Klausnick complains and wishes it was a stronger explosive, C-4. I told him we do not need to blow up the world, just put a little fear in it.

I was surprised when Allanson had offered to acquire it —then again, no one else volunteered. He said he knew a place in Indiana, near Warsaw, a feed store that carries dynamite and caps. We paid him out of the donations we've been getting. Abe's keeping it in a cool place in the basement; he knows how to handle it.

The Friday before the start of the convention was a kick. Some of the Yippie organizers, Jerry Rubin, the folk singer Phil Ochs, selected Pigasus, an actual pig, to run for president. Later, as they marched the pig around, the police arrested them, including the pig, for what I'm not sure. But the pig did look a lot like Mayor Richard Daley—maybe that was the reason, professional jealousy. Another guy, sounded like he was from somewhere around Boston, was also there, Abbie Hoffman—smart, funny. I was pissed because these guys came into my town and tried to take over. We'll see how that goes.

Sunday, we put together a simple demonstration in Lincoln Park—it turned into a warm-up session for the police. When there were enough people, they fired tear gas and began to swing their billy clubs against heads and backs. Many were arrested. It was a fucking circus.

During the next few days, it got serious. Demonstrators at the International Amphitheater, where the convention was held, were bombarded with tear gas and mace, forced to run when the police pushed through. On Tuesday night, we marched up Michigan Avenue. By this time the National Guard was holding the perimeter. The Chicago cops waded in, grabbed who they could, all the time looking for the leaders. I saw one girl—cute thing, couldn't have been eighteen—screaming in the face of one of the cops. He was maybe her father's age. Then he jammed his nightstick into her gut. After she doubled over, he knocked her over the head, grabbed her hair, and savagely dragged her to the open back of a police wagon. Then with a smile on his fucking face, he waded back into the chaos.

Seeing my mother and sister Tuesday afternoon baffled me. Why Mom was in her car on Michigan Avenue in the middle of all this shit, I don't know and still don't understand. She said she made a wrong turn; she was going to pick up Joe from the VA. She's damn lucky they weren't hurt.

It was on Wednesday that the worst of it came down. The night before, the world had caught fire, too. The Russians invaded Czechoslovakia and seized its capital—no one knew what to think. On TV, images of Russian tanks rolling through Czech cities were followed by people marching in Chicago. Many were confused; they believed they were the same news story. Later, the papers said that 15,000 people rallied in Grant Park. They lied—there had to be more. When we marched, all I saw ahead was a wall of police and soldiers.

Debbie grabbed my arm, and we pushed our way through the growing riot. She pointed to a group of reporters. From behind me, I heard the chant, "The whole world is watching." It continued as we marched down Michigan Avenue. Then the lights went out.

―――――

September 14, 1968

Dear Annie,

I am so screwed. Sorry it took so long to get back to you. It's been two weeks since the house exploded; Debbie and I have been hiding at a motel. A couple of days ago, I snuck back into my apartment to get you and a few other things. I can't believe they are dead—Abe and Barb at the house, the policemen. All dead.

I called Dad; he was frantic. He'd been trying to find me. Joe tried to kill himself, cut his wrists, and then a few days later they found Mom dead in the bathroom. An accident, he said. I just talked to her; it was three days ago. We talked about Joe; she said he was doing okay. I called to tell her that I was all right, nothing to worry about. She was afraid, said the FBI had been there, they talked to her and Dad and Joe. I knew that; Dad told me, I said. He's working on a story; he's investigating what happened. I know, Mom, I said. I gave him the photos Debbie took. He said they show who blew up the house. But Mom is dead?? How the hell could that have happened? Dad said that it looks like an accident. She fell in the bathroom, cracked her head, Cate found her. Poor Cate. There are too many things happening.

―――――

September 26, 1968

Annie,

Dad is dead. It was in the newspaper, his newspaper, a car accident. Jesus Christ, this has all gone way too crazy. I'll fill in the details someday when I know what happened. The paper doesn't say much, just that he was found dead in a single car accident. He may have been drinking.

I went to Mom's funeral. I hid from everyone, watched

from far away. God, I am a worthless shit. Right now, we are running. Debbie says she has a place in Michigan where we can hide. Won't say where until we get there. I'm confused, shattered. I want this to all go away; make it like it once was. What the fuck have I done? I know all this is my fault.

Chapter 13
The Set Up

Bobbie: Then
September 1, 1968

After the house exploded, there was no one that afternoon who Debbie or I could turn to for help. We aimlessly rode city buses for two hours; we changed three times. We didn't talk. We got off the last bus in Skokie and walked through a residential neighborhood for a half hour watching to see if anyone was following us. Three hours after the explosion, we slipped into a bar on Lincoln near Main Street and took seats in a booth in the rear. The news was on the television; baseball scores filled the screen. We took turns in the restroom cleaning up; luckily neither of us was seriously hurt, just a few bruises, skinned hands, and knees. The gauze around my arm, under my shirt, was loose. I took it off and threw it in the trash. There was no blood; but, holy goddamn, my attitude had taken a severe hit. I had no idea what went on back there at the house.

Finally, Debbie looked at me. "Are you sure it was Abe and Barb in the basement?"

"Yes, I didn't see Jimmy. I don't know if he was there or not. Maybe he was upstairs, asleep, or maybe he's dead. I don't know—there was so much smoke. It was awful; the two of them were lying there on the concrete floor, eyes open. I tried to see if they were alive, but Abe's head was smashed in, there was blood all around, and Barbara was lying next to him. I'm sure they were dead. Jesus Christ, I don't know, I just don't. I've never seen a dead person—I'm freaking out."

"Why was Allanson there?" Debbie asked. "Did he kill them?"

"I don't know. I don't know why he was there—he was supposed to be back in Michigan," I said.

"Do you know the guy he was with? I've never seen him before. Do you think they killed them? Did they set off the dynamite?"

"I don't know, I don't know," I repeated, over and over. My hands were shaking. I'd never seen Debbie this confused. She was our rock, the thinker; she still hadn't figured this out, whatever *this* was.

"What else do you remember?" she asked.

I'd had hours to go over what I'd seen, I pieced it together. "You went to the porch to get the food that was spilled from the ripped bag; I opened the basement door and smoke exploded out. I went down a few steps and saw Abe and Barb on the floor. I yelled; there wasn't an answer. I was choking; I went down a few more steps. There was fire. Abe was lying on the floor; he had on his Army jacket. Barbara was to his . . ." I paused and thought. "To my right, on her back, eyes up to the ceiling. My eyes were stinging. I went down to them, tried to help. That's when I yelled, ran up the stairs, to you at the door. We ran—then the house exploded."

Debbie reminded me that she saw two men coming to the front door, one in uniform.

"Any idea why there were the cops at the door?" Debbie asked.

"I have no idea," I muttered.

"The one in the suit looked like a Fed; he had to be," Debbie said.

"A cop and a Fed? What the hell? Allanson and that other guy must have killed Abe and Barb and set the fire. Allanson knew the dynamite and the gasoline were there. They must have—it's the only explanation."

"Lucky, we were damn lucky," Debbie said.

"No shit." I looked up at the girl behind the bar and caught her attention. "Two Stroh's." I held up two fingers.

"Got it, honey," the girl answered.

"We've been on the freaking edge of disaster all summer," I said. "The riot, the beatings, all the crazy shit." The bartender dropped two beers on the table.

"Glasses?"

"No, we're good," I said and watched her return to the bar and the two guys sitting there. I leaned into Debbie; I'd given this a lot of thought during our escape. "What if this is all a setup? We've had too many people coming and going —those Black Panther assholes, Allanson and those SDS shits from Michigan. Way too many. Any of them could be undercover Feds—how the hell would we know? Now, this."

"Bobbie," Debbie said looking at me, "we have been set up to be the biggest patsies I can imagine. They will pin all of this on us, and if those cops were hurt or, God forbid, worse, they will be coming for us."

"Worse, fucking worse? Allanson and that other guy killed them and blew the place up. It must be them."

The bartender walked to the end of the bar and asked, "You girls want some food? Menus?"

"Menus would be good. Did the White Sox play today?" I asked.

"We are Cubs people out here. They beat the Astros 2-0. Don't know the White Sox score; they are on the road. And then all that excitement of that house exploding a couple of blocks from Wrigley—what a mess. They said you could hear the explosion in the park."

"A house? Explosion?" Debbie asked.

"Yeah, just as the game ended, the fire could be seen from Wrigley. Some thought it was fireworks. The guy on the TV"—she pointed to the box over the bar—"just now, says two cops were at the door when it blew. Guessed it might be a gas explosion. The cops are at the hospital, hurt bad. They are still looking for anyone who might be inside. They did find a guy in front. Not sure who he is. Not much else. Strange about the gas. It's warm now, no need for the furnace. Anyway, I'll bring you girls menus."

I leaned back in. "Cops? And Allanson and that guy running out the back door—Deb, we are fucking suckers. We were set up. If we're caught, we will spend the rest of our lives in prison."

"Or worse."

———

Debbie and I rented a motel room off Chicago Avenue near the Northwestern campus. We prepaid with cash for four nights; whether we'd be there that long, neither of us were sure. Debbie was beginning to run short. I had thirty-two bucks in my pocket.

There was only one man I could talk to and that was my father. Lord knows we have had our issues, from my boyfriends to the Vietnam War. His current criticism is: "Roberta, what are you going to do with your life?" And the corollary: "When are you going to start?" Right now, I'm probably wanted for the deaths of four people—and my options are shit. He's an investigative reporter for the *Chicago Daily News*.

Four days after the explosion, I called my father at the newspaper.

"Thank God you are alive. Are you okay? Where are you?" Dad asked. "Your mother is frantic. Somehow she knew you are involved in this."

"I'm fine, and I can't tell you where I am. It's better if you don't know. And tell Mom I'm okay," I said. "I need help; I need money."

"There were two people from the FBI at the house

yesterday; they scared your mother," he said. "They had questions about the demonstrations last week and a house exploding."

"The FBI?" I answered, shocked. The Feds knew I was involved; this had gotten all out of hand. "What did they want?"

"They said you are one of the leaders of the demonstrations that caused the riots, and that you were seen at that house that exploded. They have questions about the deaths of four people, two of them law enforcement. What's going on?"

"It got out of hand, Dad. Things needed to be done; Americans need to wake up. That's all we were trying to do. Debbie and I were there, just before the house exploded. We didn't do it—it wasn't us."

"Who's Debbie?"

"A friend. Right now, she's the only friend I've got. We've been together for six months; she's helped me out of a few scrapes and troubles I got myself into."

"Scrapes? What troubles? The house explosion, were you involved? Good God, Bobbie, what's happening?"

"We were just going to scare them, show them that we meant business."

"Damn, what have you done?"

I explained about the dynamite. Told him that Zeke Allanson, the guy from the University of Michigan SDS, got it for us. That he was running from the house just before the explosion. He was with another man, an older man. I stared straight into his face. He had red hair, but I knew Allanson. They may have murdered two of our friends, set fire to the house, and are responsible for the policemen that died. I told him I was sure it was them that set off the dynamite.

"Where are you now?"

"Dad, I won't tell you. I don't want you and Mom involved. This is my problem."

There was a long pause on Dad's end. "Dad, you still there?"

"I'm here, Bobbie. I took some notes after the FBI left; I didn't want to forget any of their names. You said the man running out of the house was Allanson, Zeke Allanson? He was with the Students for a Democratic Society?"

"Yes, I thought he'd gone back to the University of Michigan," I said, then repeated, "They ran out of the house, the two of them. We believe they killed Abe and Barb. They were dead. They were lying on the floor in the basement; I saw them on the floor."

"And Allanson is the one that got the dynamite?"

"Yes." I told him about Allanson getting the explosives from Warsaw, Indiana.

"Can you describe the other man?"

"Yes, taller than Allanson, maybe six feet, twenty years older, mid-forties, athletic looking, wore a dark gray fedora, short red hair under the narrow brim. He had a ruddy, bright complexion. Allanson was wearing a blue Michigan sweatshirt. The older guy had cold gray eyes, wore a dark suit, no tie, and come to think about it, gloves, black gloves. They ran to a car in the alley next to the house, a Ford sedan, I think. Late-model. It was dark blue."

"Gray eyes?"

"Yes. I only saw him for a second, but they were color-less, ice cold. He glared at me then jumped down the steps to the car. When he hit the ground, his hat flew off—his hair was bright red. He was the driver. Allanson climbed in the passenger side. I'm sure he was a Fed; maybe Allanson is one, too. I'm so screwed."

"Why do you believe that?"

"Allanson was too clean-cut, didn't fit the radical look, a little too buttoned up. He tried hard, had the beard, the messy hair. He and Abe got into it at the house once; wasn't a fair fight. Allanson backed down quickly, like he didn't want any trouble."

"Abe? Who's Abe?"

"Abraham Klausnick. He was another of our group. No one knows, maybe they will find out. But I knew them, the woman is Barbara Dumas. I saw them in the basement, they were on the floor, dead."

I could hear Dad writing. "I'm going to make a few inquiries and phone calls. Your description fits the FBI agent that stopped by the house yesterday, especially the bit about the red hair. This isn't good. You and your friend need to stay low for a while. There's a pay phone at the entry to the Lincoln Park Zoo; the number is 555-7862. Be there tomorrow afternoon at four. I'll call you. It's almost impossible to tap the phones here at the newspaper. Don't call home; I'm not sure who might be listening. I'll get some money to you somehow. You stay safe, pumpkin."

"You haven't called me that for years, Dad."

"You have never been out of my thoughts. Just stay safe. We will talk tomorrow."

"Tell Mom I'm okay."

"I will."

———

The phone rang precisely at four, and Dad and I talked. I was in tears; I've never been so afraid. Debbie and I decided that she was safe; maybe they didn't know about her. Among all the people in the house, her name hadn't been mentioned on the news. When I asked Dad if any of the photos the FBI showed them included a tall, Irish-looking woman with short red hair, all he could say was that the photos were black and white, and no one looked like who I described. All the women in the photos had long hair. And, he added, the television news never showed any of the same photographs that the FBI showed them during the interview. None of anyone crossing the street, and most notably, none of me.

I should have been all over the news; I was a suspect in a terrible crime. Yet now, five days later, the story had begun to fade. By midweek, nothing more was reported about the explosion. Sure, the demonstrations continued. The police and the Feds started to make arrests of the supposed ring-leaders of the Michigan Avenue riots, holding them for questioning—probably hoping they would turn on each other.

I stayed in the motel room. Debbie brought in sand-wiches, pizza, and beer. And she cut my blonde hair; I dyed it dark brown. Dad sent money to the Skokie post office, general delivery, care of Debbie Toomey. I was worried to death about the FBI stopping at the house. That afternoon, I took a chance and called Mom. We talked. She was in tears. She said that Dad had been working long nights on a story in his study. When she brought him coffee, she said she saw some photos on his desk of a restaurant. I told her we took them and that I'd tell her about them later. She said she loved me and to be safe—it will all be over soon. That was the last time I talked with my mother.

A few days before I talked with Mom, Dad had an idea. He wanted me to confirm the identity of the older man, the man I saw. He'd gone to the FBI office in Chicago to ask some ques-tions about the riots and arrests. There he talked to the agent who had come to the house. This was an official visit, he told the agent, and that he was working on a story for the *Daily News* about the demonstrations and the riot that followed. It was to be a multi-part series that looked at the events from all sides, including the house explosion, and he was asking for help from the FBI. The agent remained silent for a long time; Dad believed he didn't like that the tables had been turned, his interviewing the FBI. The agent said they were still inves-tigating the explosion and that he had nothing to add. Maybe in a week or two he would have something. Dad wanted to leave enough suspicion to ensure that he would be followed.

Later, during another call, Dad said to me, "Late tomorrow morning, around ten, I'm going to the restaurant on North Street off Wells—you know the place. There is a coffee shop directly across the street. Get a seat in the window and watch if anyone follows me that looks like the guy you saw. All I'm trying to do is confirm that he's the man you saw running from the house. Can you do that? Write down this phone number." I wrote it down. "Call the number, tell the person who answers that I have a call; they know me. Can you do this?"

"Anything to get out of this room," I answered.

Debbie and I both went. She had a 35mm camera. We took the L to the Sedgwick stop and walked to the coffee shop and found two seats in the window. Thirty minutes later, Dad walked past. He never looked, but I'm sure he saw us. Then he crossed the street at Wieland Avenue. Behind him, a block away, strolled the man who had escaped the house before it exploded. He was in a dark suit, white shirt, and black tie. A gray fedora covered an obvious fringe of red hair. The look screamed "federal agent". He passed by our window; he was so intent on Dad, he never looked at us. Debbie took his picture.

"That's him; that's the son of a bitch," Debbie said.

I went to the pay phone in the coffee shop, entirely amazed by the intrigues my father had conjured up. Coffee shops, restaurants, the zoo, pay phones, and phone numbers —a whole world that I never knew. Dad was seated in the restaurant window; I could see him from the pay phone. I called and I asked for Mr. Charles Davis. A waitress walked up to him and said something; he stood and walked back to the entry.

"Was I followed?" he asked.

"He's standing outside near the restaurant door, he is wearing a gray hat and has red hair, and yes, that's the man we saw run out of the house. Debbie also recognizes him; she took his picture. She'll shoot the whole roll of film. I will get it to you."

"Yes, that's all I need from you. In a few minutes, if I'm right, all hell will break loose. You can stay and watch or leave through the back of the coffee shop. I'll be fine. Soon, I hope, there will be a shocked and embarrassed federal agent."

We decided to stay. A woman, about my age and size, and with long blonde hair, walked past the FBI agent and into the restaurant. After hanging up, Dad went back to his seat. The woman walked with him, his arm around her. At the table they hugged, and then they both sat. The agent, still outside, raised his right arm and rotated his hand; three dark green sedans appeared and skidded to a stop in front of the restaurant. They mustered in front, then the man from the explosion led six men in through the single glass door. We watched as he stood over my father, barking something. Dad just raised his hands in submission; the woman went crazy. She threw water at the agent. The other FBI agents tried to pull them from the booth. Dad held up what looked like his business card, pushed it in the man's face. He was yelling. Eventually, the men hustled them out of the restaurant to the sidewalk and to the waiting cars.

"I'm out," Debbie said. She rolled the film back into its canister, opened the back, and handed me the film. "Get this to him."

The north end of Wells Street, near North Avenue, is part of the hippie and flower children neighborhood called Old Town. During the past three years, I'd spent many summer nights eating and drinking on this part of Wells Street; the best pizza in Chicago was at the end of Piper's Alley. The sidewalks throughout Old Town, even in the middle of the day, were still filled with kids of the counter generation, many hopped up and wasted. A few still had bandages around their heads, all worn as badges of honor. As the FBI dragged my father and his cute decoy to their cars, the kids started yelling and screaming. The decoy, about my age, screamed and pushed back at her abductors. Three more Chicago police squad cars pulled up; traffic began to back up on North Avenue. In minutes the area became a demonstration itself; people chanting and singing.

Through the glass of the coffee shop's window, I heard, repeated over and over, "The whole world is watching."

"Time to go, Bobbie. Your dad is a big boy; he knows what he's doing," Debbie said. I looked across the street. My father was standing there arguing with that FBI son of a bitch. Later I realized that was the last time I saw my father.

I mailed my father the film canister; it was sent to his office. I learned later from Dad that the day after the restaurant sting, my brother Joe cut his wrists, and then five days later my mother was dead. And then I read in the newspaper that my father died in a car accident.

Chapter 14
An Ominous and Dangerous Tone

Cate: Now
Carmel, California
Late August 2019

Exhausted, I closed Bobbie's journal. I had assumed that my sister was into something dangerous and political, but she was gone, I never knew. Now, after what I read, I was upset and brokenhearted. I was fifteen again, and dark, mysterious stories were being told. I am certain that Bobbie never told anyone, especially our parents, about the abortion. Joe has never said anything. I remember her coming into my room after one Sunday dinner that summer when I was listening to my records, and before Dad would take her to the train. She asked about my boyfriends, school, and other stuff; then she walked down the hall to Joe's room. He never said what they talked about. She never said anything to me about the marches and the anti-war protests—never. Dad wanted to know what was happening with her, what she was doing, who her friends were. I didn't know. That's when their arguments would begin. Someone at the *Daily News* told Dad that she'd been seen at the demonstrations. Dad wanted an answer; she walked out of the house. Early that summer, Bobbie's visits home became fewer and fewer. It is still a jumble in my head; her diary entries only confused me more. All I can believe was that they must have had some type of reconciliation.

After I punched in Joe's number on my phone, a soft female voice answered, "Hello." There was a smokiness about the sound that wasn't objectionable, just unexpected.

I confirmed the number; the line on the screen read *Joe D.* "Is Joe there?" I asked, a bit confused.

"Is this Cate?"

"Yes, and you are?"

"Mitsi, Mitsi Treharne. I'm a friend of Joe's. He's taking a shower and told me to answer any calls."

"He did, did he?"

"Yes, I know it's strange. I understand. We've never met, but it is a pleasure to finally meet you, or at least over the phone."

"I assume that you are one of Joe's associates . . . at school?"

"Oh no. We've been dating four months now and I know what you must think. I am not one of his students and I know all about his reputation. He is a legend around here. I am, as I said, an associate of his. I work in the admissions office. I have been there for now, let me think, for thirty-two years."

I did some arithmetic in my head. "So, you aren't one of his students?"

"Oh, God no, Ms. Wallace. I understand what you're thinking. Joe said that sooner or later we would talk, and you would immediately try to sort out our relationship. He said that's what you do. I understand. If one of my kids kept secrets and didn't tell me everything, especially about my grandchildren, I'd sure as toot'en would let them know about it."

"Children . . . grandchildren?" I asked.

"Two grown children, and between them, five grandchildren. I started when I was young. We Treharnes are like that; my sister Grace has six grandkids, and she's only sixty-two. But I do go on. I'm sorry about that."

"Ms. Treharne . . ."

"Please call me Mitsi."

I heard Joe's voice in the background. He took the phone.

"Good morning, Sis. I'm glad you met Mitsi." I could hear the grin in his voice. At times, his tone was endearing. Right now, it was annoying.

"Mitsi?"

"We've been dating since spring. We've known each other for more than a year; we like each other. She puts up with all my shit, and she even laughs at my jokes. And besides, she's a lot closer to my age than some or even all of the other ladies I've dated. We can talk about things."

"Like pre-cell-phone days and when gas was less than a dollar?"

"Cute. No, like what someone goes through when they lose someone. That's where we met, at a PTSD meeting. In her case, it was a husband. He was killed in Afghanistan; he was a Marine officer. She was going through a tough bit. I needed a tune-up, as I call it. We met, hit it off. It's been good for each of us."

"You could have told me," I said.

"With all you were going through with John?" Joe said. "There would be a good time; it just wasn't then. But now you've met—that's done, and we can move on. I'll bring her up to meet you someday."

"Someday? Really. How about sooner than someday? I'd like to meet the woman that could finally break down those fortifications you built."

"Okay, got it. Is there a reason you called? It's early."

"It's ten in the morning, Joe."

"It's early for us. We were out late."

"I called because of Bobbie's diaries. There's an ominous and dangerous tone to them," I said. "I'm trying to understand what was going on back then; some of it is muddled. Did you know about any of what she was doing back then?"

"Only that she was demonstrating and protesting the war . . . and that Dad was pissed at her. But I was out of it a lot that summer—you know that. A couple of times when she came home for Sunday dinner, she tried to get me to join her in her marches. I told her no fucking way; it wouldn't be right. No matter what I believed, I wouldn't dishonor the men I knew in Vietnam. She said it would honor them. Then we'd get into it. But each time before she left, she'd give me a hug—so many contradictions. So, no, I didn't have any real idea about what was going on with her. I had enough troubles of my own."

"Did you know about the abortion?"

Joe's breathing was all I heard for almost a minute. I heard Mitsi's voice asking Joe if he was all right.

"I'm fine, Mitsi," he said. "No. I didn't know. Was it in her diaries?"

"Yes, she went to London. Good God, what she was going through."

———

Joe: Then
September 5, 1968

Dear Duke,

Damn, it never ends. Two FBI agents, Michael Talant and Louis Cartwright, stopped by the house and grilled us about Bobbie. They wanted to know where she was, what was her involvement in the demonstrations, and who were the other people in the SDS that she was meeting with. They showed us photos and newspaper articles. They kept coming back to an explosion. It had been on the TV news for the last few days. Mom and Dad are panicked; they have not heard from Bobbie. God, I hope she's not involved, but then again, considering what's going on, I would not be surprised. They said there is an unidentified body, a woman's. Mom's worried sick, terrified.

Agent Talant said a lot of people were hurt during the demonstrations, and that the explosion of the house was a part of an effort to build a bomb or bombs to kill police. A result is that a policeman and an FBI agent are dead. He warned us that if we learned anything and did not inform them, we would be breaking federal laws—screw them, I say.

It's been more than seven months since Khe Sanh. Every day, I relive it. I still see my buddies in pieces across the jungle floor. I still feel the pain; I can't sleep. God, for just one long night of sleep.

Chapter 15
Time to Grow Up, Catherine

Cate: Then
Flossmoor, Illinois
September 16, 1968

Dear Grace,

I'm so heartbroken I can barely write this. Mom would have said to tell you what happened, tell the truth, put my thoughts and feelings on paper; all for later. It's so hard—Mom's dead. Dad's downstairs with the police and Joe. He picked up Joe from the hospital. They are answering questions; I can't talk to them anymore. I'm so exhausted.

I came home right after school; the house was quiet. Tack was in the garage barking; he's never in the garage; it was all strange. I yelled for Mom and there was no answer. She's always here when I come home from school. I went to the bathroom to wash up; she was lying on the floor. There's blood everywhere . . . I can't write anymore.

———

Cate: Then

I want to block it all, refuse it, tell it to go away. I want to believe that it didn't happen, that this is all a dream. But it's not. Yesterday, Mom died. The police say that she may have slipped on the floor of the bathroom as she climbed out of the bathtub, stumbled, and as she fell, hit her head on the side of the sink. There's a bloody spot where her head hit. Then, as she lay on the floor, the cut on the side of her head bled until she died. I still can't believe it.

I did what I could. I tried to pull her up. She was limp. Her blood was all over the floor and my hands. She was naked; I laid a towel over her. I went to the phone in the hall and called the police and then the fire department, then I ran next door to the Debolts. That's when the police arrived, then the fire department. Mrs. Debolt tried to get ahold of Dad, but he was not at work. I was crying; I didn't know what to do. That's when I heard Tack howling; he was in the garage. I don't understand why Mom put him there. He always stays in the house when we are home. When Mom's taking her shower, he lays in the hallway, like a guard. I can't understand why Mom put him in the garage.

I'm numb. Dad spent a lot of time with the police since he and Joe came home. He was late because he had to pick up Joe from the hospital. Mr. Debolt and Mr. Symington stayed with him. I was with Mrs. Debolt. I heard Dad; he was angry with the police and their questions. Joe sat in the big chair in the living room, his wrists wrapped in white tape. He just glared at the police and the ambulance people when they came and took Mom away. After the week he'd been through, I was afraid for him. Tack sat on the floor next to Joe, his head on Joe's shoe, protecting him. It was last week when he tried to kill himself, the week after the FBI interviewed Mom and Dad. Mom and I spent the next day in the hospital with Joe, helping him through his crisis. She held his bandaged hand. So much has happened in such a short time and Bobbie is still missing.

The funeral is next week, Tuesday. Father Ignatius, from

the church, stopped by and talked for hours with Dad. Then he sat down with Joe and me.

"Time to grow up, Catherine," Father Ignatius said. "I wish you were older. I can't sugarcoat this; it is an immeasurable tragedy. We all face losing a loved one at some point in our lives. I just wish for you and Joe it could be later in your lives."

"I've seen a lot of death, Father," Joe said.

"I understand, Joe," Father Ignatius said. "A couple of other boys from the parish are in Vietnam; they are in the Army and the Marines. If you need anything, let me know. I will be back tomorrow to help you and your father. There's a funeral home that we can have your mother sent. Your father said that Helen has a sister?"

"Yes, Aunt Sue. She lives in Michigan," Joe said.

I like Aunt Sue. I've spent summers at her house; actually, it's a farm. She lives there in a small house she rents from the owners of the farm. Mom said she likes her independence, and since she's a writer of gooey romance novels, I've always liked her.

"Could she come down and help?" Father Ignatius asked.

"I'll call and ask," Joe answered. "She could take some of the tough stuff off Dad's shoulders."

"Joe, we can take care of ourselves," I said.

"Yes, we can. But I need help getting around for the next few months. They have me going to a shrink, and there's my therapy. Aunt Sue can help, and Dad still needs to do his job."

I knew this was all true. Yes, as Father Ignatius said, "It's time to grow up."

———

Cate: Now

Yes, there's a time in our lives when we must grow up. Before Mom's death, I believed it would be when I went off to college, and looking back, I thought I had a good three or four years before I had to deal with the big stuff. Death is as big as it gets. I'm reminded of how big it is with John's death. Then, during Mom's funeral, I didn't understand how big things would ultimately get. A lot of my friends and their parents came to the wake and burial; they offered to help as much as they could. I wasn't sure what kind of help I needed.

I remember Dad being preoccupied during the next week. He held his own during the wake and the funeral. I've never seen him so strong, yet every minute it was apparent that he was doing everything he could to hold himself together. He loved Mother so much. He held us close, talked to us about what was happening; he was a rock. How Joe pushed away his suicide attempt, I'll never know. His mind must have been a jumble. But honestly, I believe from that moment at the cemetery, Joe understood what he would have put us through if he had succeeded. I later learned what he had buried in his soul was scary. It took years to satisfy those ghosts. Growing up was hard for both of us.

Two nights after the funeral, I went into the family room; it was in the middle of the night. I couldn't sleep. It was dark, and Dad was sitting in his chair, a bottle of bourbon resting next to him. He was asleep, or so I thought. As I turned to leave, he said, "Come sit next to me, pumpkin."

"I don't want to bother you," I said.

"These days, you are my greatest bother . . . and love. Sit there." He pointed to the couch next to him, Mom's place. "We need to talk."

I sat on the couch. Tack jumped up next to me.

"How much have you had to drink?" I asked.

"Enough and not enough," he said. "Enough to ease the pain, not enough to make it go away. I miss her so much. We planned so much. We are young, a whole lifetime ahead of us. This is wrong; she didn't need to die this way."

"Is there a better way to die?" I asked, wondering where such a question came from.

"You are right; there is none. We are never prepared for the surprises that life throws at us from out of nowhere, and Helen's . . . death is the greatest of shocks."

"I wish Bobbie were here—she should be here. I'll never forgive her for running away."

"I miss her, too. She is headstrong, so sure of herself— and then this. Cate, Bobbie needs to do what she's doing; I know that now. Someday you will find that out. Like you, I want to blame someone; someone must be at fault. It's that damn war, Joe's leg, Bobbie's disappearance, now Mom; it's all wrapped up together in my head. There are sinister and evil forces at work. I need to sort them out, to help—to stop them."

He took another sip of his drink, then a long, deep inhale, which he slowly let out through his pursed lips.

"Evil forces?" I said.

"Not to worry; I'm dealing with it. Cate, just remember this: I know that Bobbie loves you and loves all of us. She is in trouble and trying to find a way out. I shouldn't be telling you this, but you need to know."

"That's okay. I understand. I am fifteen, you know." I reached out and put my hand on his.

"And now, after this week," Dad said, "you are going on twenty-five. Do me a favor and don't grow up too fast. I want to enjoy all the time I can with you."

Two weeks later, I was standing next to Mom's grave. The grave's sod hadn't had time to root. And next to her was an open grave—sitting over it was my father's casket, waiting to be lowered in the hole. I hadn't wanted to grow up that fast; I didn't want to be there; I didn't want any of that. Joe sat on a chair, staring into that abyss. Our friends and neighbors were standing near to us. Behind them were Dad's fellow newspaper men and women. I stood behind Joe wondering if I'd be next.

Aunt Sue stood next to me. She held my hand so hard it hurt, as if she were keeping me from tumbling into that grave. Behind us were our grandparents. Grandma Louise,

Mom's mother, hadn't stopped crying since she left the church. Grandma Ann, Dad's mother, stood next to her, holding her around the shoulder. Grandpas John and Al were stoic; they stood shoulder to shoulder. A parent never wants to outlive their child.

It happened five days after Mom's funeral. Dad told me that morning he would be late that night; he was working on a story that could not wait.

"Are you sure you are up to it? Is it necessary?" Joe asked as Dad got ready to head back into the office.

"Joe, I need to do something, and this is incredibly important," he said. "I'll know in a few days. I've some follow-up interviews with the police, an interview with a person who lives near the explosion, and maybe even the FBI."

"What is it about?" I asked.

"The demonstrations and the house that exploded. That's all I can tell you right now. When the time is right, you will find out what happened. Maybe you can make it right." He smiled and put his hand on my cheek.

"Be careful," I said. Those were the last words I ever said to him. That night—it was two o'clock in the morning—the doorbell rang and woke Joe and me. Tack was going crazy; he ran back and forth down the hall. I put him in the garage; in fact, I had to drag him.

"What's the problem, Officer?" Joe said as he leaned against the wall of the hallway on his crutch. Outside, the lights of a squad car flashed up and down the dark street. The rain had left everything glistening, and the lights reflected, clicking off and on, from every surface.

"Is this the Charles Davis residence?" the policeman asked. He was a local cop, Officer Jim Dowdy. Joe recognized him.

"Yes, he's our father. Why?" Joe said. Aunt Sue stood at the end of the hallway. She held her robe tight to her body.

It was apparent that the man did not want to be here, especially at two o'clock in the morning.

"I'm sorry to report that Charles Davis was killed in an automobile accident," the officer said. "His car slid off the wet road; it was near where Western Avenue crosses over the Calumet Sag Canal. The reports say that his car slammed into the abutment of the bridge. It was about eight o'clock last night. They found the car; he was inside. He was dead at the scene."

When Aunt Sue heard, she screamed and collapsed. I stayed with her, not sure what to do.

The officer said, "I knew your dad—that was back in your Boy Scouts days, Joseph. I took over as scoutmaster after he left. He was a great guy, and so was your mother. Everyone at the station is heartsick about this. I'm sorry for your loss."

"Are you sure it was our dad? He was supposed to be working. He was on a story—you must be wrong," Joe said.

"He will have to be identified. We can do that tomorrow, but it all points to him," Dowdy said. "They found his wallet; it was with him. I saw your Dad last winter. He said you were in Vietnam." He looked at Joe, then his crutches, then Joe's one leg. "Jesus Christ, I'm sorry. I didn't know. Damn, what a sorry mess."

The next week is why I've hated funerals my whole life. After Mother's funeral, I swore I'd never go to another, and yet there we stood, in the rain again, putting Dad in the ground next to Mom. It was also about then that I stopped believing in God; it would take me a long time to find Him again. During the service, I looked for Bobbie, and just like for Mom, she didn't show at the wake, or the church, or the cemetery.

Our grandparents looked as broken as Joe and I felt. Two funerals in less than a month—no one expects that. When they asked about Bobbie, I couldn't answer. Joe told them what he knew; she had disappeared. The police had identified the female found in the house after the explosion; it was not Roberta. I was afraid of what was going to happen to me. It would be impossible for Joe to take over the responsibilities of taking care of me. I knew it, and Joe knew it. I was fifteen, a sophomore in high school, with friends and teachers I liked.

Surprisingly, Grandpa and Grandma Kent said they would move into our house from their condominium on the Westside, near La Grange. Later, Joe told me the insurance covered the mortgage and tuition for my Catholic school, as well as a chunk of money to cover college when I graduated. I didn't learn this until two years later, when I graduated from high school. Thinking back—I remember it all—but the edges are blurry, and the timelines now tend to mash into each other. But I remember that day at the cemetery, the rain dripping off the roof of the canvas tent over the grave, the dozens of people standing under umbrellas, the priest giving the sign of the cross, and Joe leaning over to me and whispering, "It's just you and me, kid—just you and me forever."

———

The shock of rereading my diaries, with both Joe's and Bobbie's to fill in the blanks, made for the first of many sleepless nights. The most significant shock was learning that Dad and Bobbie had grown closer that year than I'd imagined. Something was going on and I didn't know about it. For most of my life, they had been two Type A personalities butting their heads against each other and the world. Dad dealt with it with words. Bobbie, at that time of her life, used violence, or at least the threat of violence. I am confused, hence the sleepless nights. I realize now that they were not just perpetrators but possibly victims. My writer's curiosity scrapes at the mortar between the bricks, the story hidden in plain sight between the lines. What adds to my curiosity and confusion are the newspaper articles, both from the *Daily News*, that Bobbie had cut out and taped to the pages of her journal.

The FBI's point man in all this was Michael Allen Talant.

They'd tricked Talant into revealing himself when Dad had Bobbie positively identify him as the man who ran out of the house before it exploded. And the only one who could confirm this identification was a fugitive, my sister. A few lines in a journal is hardly proof. I'd sat through enough trials for research to know that.

Did Talant also set the fire in the basement? Did Talant or the other guy kill Bobbie's friends? How far would they go to cover up the crime? When I thought that, I feared what I might discover. A fear that, fifty years ago, was close to home.

Both articles had Dad's byline.

August 30, 1968
Senators McGovern and McCarthy Hang on to the Bitter End
by Charles Davis

George McGovern and Eugene McCarthy stayed fast to their dream of becoming the nominee of the Democratic party to the very end. McGovern, late to the process, admitted that he was a supporter of the late Sen. Robert Kennedy, and would not even have considered running if the senator had not been assassinated. McCarthy, the staunch anti-war candidate, said the nominee Vice President Humphrey "has the same decisions and attitudes as Lyndon," referring to President Johnson's Viet Nam policies.

While McGovern wanted Ted Kennedy to pick up the gauntlet of the Kennedy family and run for the nomination, Kennedy could not overtake the support given to the vice president. This may leave open the opportunity for Ted Kennedy in four years. McCarthy said that his greatest regret was his failure to those in the youth brigades who had been at his side for the last eight months since his surprise showing in the New Hampshire primary. Their impossible dream would never be realized.

How much the old guard of the Democratic party turned away from its young people, many new to politics, was evident in the support given to the platform plank backing Johnson's Viet Nam policies. During the convention, they booed, shouted, cursed and sang "We Shall Overcome," all to obstruct and interrupt the proceeding. Support for Humphrey was given even in the face of the anti-war demonstrations, delegate protests and those strenuously against the vice president's nomination.

The delegation from Illinois gave 112 votes for Vice President Humphrey. They gave only three votes for the nomination of Eugene McCarthy, and three votes for the late entry, George McGovern. Mayor Richard Daley announced the count after a two-hour, closed-door caucus of the Illinois delegation. There were boos from the McCarthy supporters when the final tally was announced.

The California delegation, chaired by California Assembly Speaker Jesse M. Unruh, bitterly complained about the high-handedness and oppression by Mayor Daley. Their support for the nomination of Ted Kennedy, their anti-war peace plank and their alleged mistreatment by the convention brought serious recriminations by the California delegates. As Winfield Shoemaker, a delegate, complained, "We came here to pick a president, not sit at the feet of Mayor Daley."

September 2, 1968
House Explodes—4 Dead—Anti-War Protesters Suspected
by Charles Davis

On September 1, late in the afternoon, a house on Byron Street near North Clark on the near north side of Chicago exploded.

It was reported by neighbors to the fire department and the police that there were two explosions; the first was loud and blew out windows on nearby buildings and destroyed much of the structure. About five minutes later, a second explosion, assumed to be fueled by gas from damaged lines, set the building on fire. When the fire department arrived, they found three men sprawled on the front lawn of the house. One was Thomas Belden, a Chicago police sergeant. The second was FBI Special Agent James Overfeld of the Chicago office. Both were severely burned and suffered from massive injuries caused by the explosion. They both died in the hospital late last night.

The third man was presumed to be a resident of the building. He was also injured. He is in critical condition but is expected to survive. He has not been identified yet. After the fire was extinguished, two more bodies were discovered in the basement. Both remains are unknown.

Initial police reports are that the two found in the basement and the man on the front lawn were residents of the house and were connected to the radical anti-war movement. It is also speculated by the police that the initial explosion was a result of a dynamite detonation. Police estimates are that it was at least a case of dynamite.

The FBI reports that the house had been under investigation for the past three months, and the two officers, Police Sergeant Belden and FBI Special Agent Overfeld, were there to serve an arrest warrant for persons in the house. They have not released the names of these suspects, or whether any of the victims in the house were on the arrest warrant.

The explosion occurred three days after the bloody

confrontation on Michigan Avenue between the anti-war demonstrators and anti-Democratic convention pickets and the Chicago police and the Illinois National Guard. Scores were injured, and thousands suffered from tear gas fired into the crowds. More than 200 demonstrators were arrested during the riot in Grant Park. In the middle of the melee and chaos, a mule train sponsored by the Southern Christian Leadership Conference, with three covered wagons each pulled by two mules, was stalled on Michigan Avenue. No one was injured, and the convoy was successfully allowed to pass before the crowd closed in again on the police.

Convention delegates who were staying in the Conrad Hotel directly in front of the battle said they were appalled by the actions of the police. There were reports that some of the hotel's guests threw toilet paper, bags of water, and even ashtrays on the crowd below. By early Thursday morning, much of the rioting and chaos had faded away. The National Guard took back control of the streets. Since Thursday, both the political and physical war between city hall and the groups of demonstrators, the Yippies and the hippies has continued.

It is not known whether any of the residents of the house that exploded were involved in the demonstrations. The house was five miles north of the Conrad Hotel and the demonstrations on Michigan Avenue. Other than generalities, the FBI has been silent about the explosion. We have repeatedly asked for information about the dead special agent. They responded by saying the incident is an ongoing federal investigation. The Chicago Police Department has been more forthcoming. Sergeant Thomas Belden, 36, the policeman killed, had fought in Korea and was a decorated policeman with 12 years of service. He is survived by his parents, a wife and two children. Funeral services are pending.

Reports from the residents in the area say that two men and two women were seen in the alley behind the house fleeing the scene just prior to the explosion. The men left the house in a blue sedan, make unknown. The women were last seen running down the alley toward Grace Street. Police are continuing with their investigations.

I find it hard now to understand how my father could have written the second article. One of the unidentified women might have been Bobbie, his daughter. The articles also reveal an apparent cynicism that I'd never known about my father. Then again, that's not unusual. I adored and idolized the man, and during the last fifty years have learned nothing to change that faith. I wish I'd have known him better. Another idea was growing, one that scared me: How far would the government go to protect itself and its interests during those radical days? Did they go beyond arresting and charging America's children with sedition? Did they kill Americans to hide the facts of the government's involvement? And now, after fifty years of cover-ups and lies, I was beginning to believe in the possibility that they were involved in my parents' deaths.

Chapter 16
To Be Young Again

Dorothy Cooper: Now
Grand Haven, Michigan
September 2019

The summer heat and humidity produced a flickering to the late afternoon air above Lake Michigan. The white-headed and gray-backed seagulls dipped and coursed through the transparent waves of heat as if surfing. They would disappear, then, as if by magic, reappear a foot or two to one side or the other of the shimmering air. Their screeching declared they understood their magical transformations. Then, from high above, they dove straight and true, like feathered missiles, and hit the lake with a smack. Dozens of silvery smelt and shiny fish exploded from the aerial attack. Then, winged brethren of the first attacking force followed in rapid succession, making the scene a frenzied massacre.

Up the beach, toward the inlet where dozens of children and families played, umbrellas stood in irregular and indiscernible patterns, coolers and blankets spread across the hot sand, almost naked bodies laid about on aluminum lounges. The soft blue riffling of the lake's surface matched the sky. My children had grown up on this beach, and now my grandchildren play here. The views from our deck, when the air is clear and dry, are easily twenty miles each way. Muskegon lay to the north and Macatawa, with its pincer-shaped outlet to the lake, to the south. The famous Grand Haven lighthouse stands close by.

In winter, thick layers of wind-shaped ice transform this ancient phallic structure into a vengeful ice god more than fifty feet high. After some winters, the beach changes from a benign sallow strip of fine sand into a massive jumble of blue-tinged ice plates, some as large as a house, tilted against each other like giant cards thrown against a wall by some crazed card dealer. Other winters the ice will grind its way inland across the beach, like a slow-moving frozen tsunami. Today, though, the only ice on the beach fills my highball glass.

Mitch and I have lived in this house for forty-two years. The saplings we planted are now mature guardians that embrace the house; they soften and blend the structure's hard edges into the soft, rolling dunes that climb up behind us. After leaning my cane against the rail, I took a sip. Dad drank Kentucky bourbon, and even though we had issues, we both loved our bourbon. I set the sweating glass back on the top rail; the water quickly evaporated off my fingers. After my family, my greatest love is this house. It is a natural part of me; it gives me strength, inspires me, and provides refuge—a sanctuary, and at the same time, a prison.

Mitch cupped my shoulder with his hand. I tilted my head against those fingers that have caressed me, held me, and have been my strength.

Mitch paused. "It is the right thing to do."

"I know, but it will be a shock. More than that, it will shake their lives," I said. "I knew it would come someday. It might as well be now than come as a shock after I'm dead."

"Don't talk like that."

"We all die; it's nature's way of clearing the way for others and getting rid of the deadwood."

"There is no one that can take your place."

I kissed the back of his hand. "I'm sorry I never told you."

"I knew you would tell me someday. I knew you held secrets when we met."

"Some secrets fester, like a wound, if not open to the sun. This has festered far too long. It was time, and Cate's interview ripped open that wound. I hope to God that she and Joe understand."

Earlier, Mitch, with a mug of coffee in his hand, had walked into the family room while I watched the interview of my sister on the television. When it was over, I turned off the television and, with tears streaming down my face, looked at him and patted the seat on the couch. He sat and wiped the tears from my cheeks.

"What's wrong?"

"My life has been a lie."

"I've known and loved you for almost fifty years. We have raised three wonderful children and have five grand-children. We have built a business from nothing and are a known and a valuable part of this community. We have been through tough times and wonderful times. There is nothing that I don't know about you. So, why do you believe that your life has been a lie?"

It all came out in a confessional rush of pain, tears, and revelations.

"When I was twenty-two, in the fall of 1968, on this day, my birthday, my actions led to the deaths of four people."

I told him everything. No other living person knew the secrets buried deep in my heart. Mitch listened; his eyes never left me. He held my hand, and at times, squeezed it so hard, I winced. I didn't pull it away. It was part of my penance, even though I knew there was no forgiveness for what I had done. There are only retributions and indict-ments left; someone will want justice. Someone will want my head.

"How could you endure this for so long?" Mitch asked when I was done.

"I don't know. It was always there," I said. "I would look at you and the children and believe that it was to protect you. As the years passed, I began to tell myself that it had been a nightmare. Foolish, I know, but we construct all sorts of things and excuses to hide our actions. I even began to believe that it was someone else who did those things. I'm not asking for forgiveness; God knows I don't deserve it. I don't know what to do. When this comes out, it will destroy the children."

"They are strong; you made them strong," Mitch said.

"*We* made them strong. But they will not understand. It was all so crazy then. I was such a coward. And it killed my mother, and I don't know what it did to my father. For all I know, it killed him, too."

"You can't think that way. You don't know."

"I know. In my heart, I know . . . And Cate and Joe need to know; it is the least I can do."

"It will cause them pain. Is that what you want?" Mitch asked.

"But they don't know. They don't deserve what will come."

"Will it make a difference?"

"I don't know."

I showed Mitch my diaries and journals. He knew I kept a journal about our lives; he never knew about the three before we met. He wouldn't read them but said that I must send them to Cate. I told him I bound them myself twenty years before.

————

Dorothy: Now
Late September 2019

Three weeks have passed since we sent the diaries to Cate from the post office in Grand Rapids. I wished I could have sent them from Timbuktu. I guess my secret is still safe; no one has knocked on the door inquiring about Roberta Davis. Mitch and I sipped our wine, an open bottle of cabernet standing on the teak table between us. Up the beach, in this last warmth of summer, a bonfire blazed; shadows danced past the flames. When the breeze blew toward us, we heard the laughter and smelled pine smoke.

"To be young again," Mitch said. "Remember the fires we used to have? Grand things—the sparks almost reached the stars."

"And the kids, they loved those nights," I answered. "Did we spoil them?"

"God, I hope so," Mitch said. "It's tough now, but then again, the times were never easy for any of us. I wish they weren't so far away. Why couldn't they stay here? We could have found something for them at the store."

"You know that wouldn't have worked; they needed their space," I said.

"You are so sixties, my love. They went where there was work. Twenty years ago, this state was a basket case. We managed to keep the business alive, and most of that was due to you. Now, the new owners of the store are paying us on time, even expanded. It's a nice annuity. However, I do miss the daily contacts with friends."

"Already getting tired of me, is that it? Maybe I should send you out to get a job so that you wouldn't be so lonely. Walmart is always hiring."

We sat quietly for a while.

"Since your sister's interview, I've had this foreboding. I think of ghosts," Mitch said.

"I did the right thing, didn't I?" I again asked.

"Yes, we did," Mitch said, emphasizing *we*. "You had to release the demons; your brother and sister needed to know."

The phone on the table chimed. The screen read "Marie", our middle child.

"Good evening, Marie. Dad and I are on the deck. The evening is a delight . . ."

"Mom, it's Steve. I'm using Marie's phone."

There was something in Steve's voice. I knew it. "Steve? What's the matter—is everything okay?" I put the phone on speaker.

Steve Ingalls, Marie's husband, took an audible deep breath. "No, Mom, not right now—nothing is okay. It's Susan. Marie is with her; they are at the hospital. I'm home with Helen and Tom."

"What's happened, Son?" Mitch asked.

There was another deep breath; the tension in Steve's voice was palpable. "Two weeks ago, Susan seemed to develop the flu. She was miserable—chills and exhausted. Marie said she told you about it; we thought it would pass. After a few days, when it didn't get any better, Marie took her to our pediatrician, Dr. Franco. He also thought it was the flu; it's going around here in Boulder. He said if it didn't get better to bring Susan back in three days. He drew some blood, said it was just precautionary. Two days later he called back—that was the day before yesterday. Susan was miserable; she was getting nosebleeds. We have been in the hospital since yesterday. Our little girl is very sick, Mom."

"Do they know what it is?"

"The tests are pointing to acute lymphocytic leukemia," Steve choked out the words.

"My God," I said and looked at Mitch. I took his hand. "We'll be there tomorrow night; we'll do anything we can to help."

"Mom, no. Marie and I talked about this. My mom and dad are just an hour away; in fact, Loraine is with the kids now. They are all fine—confused but doing okay. I must split my time between my job and the hospital. At least Marie can be there full-time or as much as Susan needs us."

"They won't give you some time off?" Mitch asked.

"They are great. Being county administrator does have its perks, and that's with medical leave, and I have a great staff. But it's Marie I'm worried about; she's at her wit's end and completely exhausted. The hospital is doing everything they can. I'm supposed to ask you a few questions; they might help with therapies."

"What's that, Steve?" Mitch said.

"Mitch, did anyone in your family have leukemia or something similar? I know that you, Dorothy, are an orphan. But I was wondering, Mitch, if there was anything on your side that might help them. The doctors say there might be some genetic connection to the disease. They are asking me to find out what I can. My family is doing the same thing, trying to see what they can remember."

Mitch watched as horror now replaced the concern that had been on my face. Even in the thin light of the setting sun, he had to see my face twist in pain. He tilted his head and mouthed the words, "What is it?"

I nodded at the phone. "Steve, are you at the hospital?" I asked.

"Heading back right now."

"You drive carefully. We will call you back later. Is that okay?" Mitch said.

"Yes. In fact, that's better. There's a summer storm blowing through right now and I need to pay attention to the road."

"In an hour, Son. Please give our little cowgirl a hug," I said.

"Will do." Again, Steve paused. "Is everything okay there?"

"Yes, just drive safely. Call you in an hour." Mitch touched the phone. He looked at me. "What?"

"Oh, how God does come back to punish me," I said. "There is so much I haven't told you; in fact, some things I have forgotten, things that I forced myself to forget. I guess if we remember everything bad that happens, we will go crazy, and I know what crazy means. So, yes. God is doing this to punish me."

"That's not the way God works, and you know that."

"Then whatever it is, my sins have come home. The world knows all about Cate, especially now after the interview. I haven't told you everything. At one time, there were four of us: a sister, two brothers, and me. The youngest, Thomas, died in 1964. It was . . . leukemia. I was away at college; it was my senior year at Northwestern. His death put my mother into a deep state of depression. That was what I've called the beginning of the worst decade of anyone's life, especially our family's. It started with Tommy's death, Mom's depression, then the war, Joe's loss of his leg, Mom's accident and death, and Dad's death in a car accident. It was all so terrible, especially for Cate and Joe. And I wasn't there."

"How can you blame yourself for any of this? And all that was fifty years ago," Mitch said as he gathered his wits about him. "We have done so much since then, the kids and the grandkids. Marie and Steve will get through this. They can do so much more to fight this disease than when your brother was sick."

"I know, but it is all my fault."

"Really? You think this was *all* your fault? *None* of this is your fault."

"They are my fault."

"Are you talking about Susan, or your brother, your parents, or that other thing?"

I stared out into the blackness over the lake. The bonfire was just a glow against the lights that strung along the beach until they disappeared in the haze. "All of it. All of it is my fault."

———

April 10, 1964

Dear Annie,

I just left Mom and Dad at the hospital. They are a wreck. Tommy passed away this afternoon. He seemed to fade away. Mom held Tom's small hand; she wouldn't let it go. I'm concerned about her and Dad. It's easy to see that their hearts are broken. I sat in the corner, watching, my heart also breaking. Joe waited in the small sitting area, as there wasn't enough room for all of us in the room. I have to tell Cate when I get home. Tommy is so small; the disease just stopped his little body from growing. He was strong, but not strong enough. I'm not sure I could deal with the last eight months as Tom did. The funeral is next week.

Chapter 17
We Were All Lost

Cate: Now
Carmel, California
September 2019

My legs are tucked under me on the window seat in my office, Bobbie's first journal next to me on the seat. I wiped away the tears of Tommy's death. It was as real now as then; I've played that movie in my head maybe a thousand times. Tommy, on the bed, almost hidden amongst the sheets; Mom and Dad standing next to him, the nurses quietly walking in and out; Joe, looking around like he was lost; and me sitting on the chair, smoothing the wrinkles out of my yellow dress. I remember it all. And I remember it being cold. He'd be a strong, smart, sixty-two-year-old man today. His birthday was June 3—I never forgot it. I sent him a card on his thirty-sixth birthday: Thomas Davis, 36 Celestial Drive, Heaven.

His laughter was infectious and mischievous. He loved bugs and butterflies. The world is a wonder to a child of six. Every day a new page, something to be explored and poked. Something to be held in the hands and studied with the fresh eyes of a child that are open to all the things life offers. When Tommy died, my young faith was tested; it came away bruised. Later, it would not survive. I'll carry those scars until—probably forever. How can I miss someone so much —someone I barely knew?

Mom and Dad were stoic, yet I knew underneath they were shattered. Recently, I haven't thought of Tommy. That's on me. He deserves more than a passing comment in a diary or journal. I was ten when Thomas died. He became an empty place at the table, a hole in our collective soul, a friend that didn't come home from the hospital. What it did to Mom and Dad, I can only now imagine. There isn't anything about Tom in Joe's journals; I will have to ask him someday why. Joe was a teenager then, fifteen. Bobbie was heartbroken—that was obvious. If I remember, she was eighteen, on her way to Northwestern. Her journal opened a small door to the room that held Tommy's death; until now it was a room I never went into. Nonetheless, for the past fifty years, Joe and I have never talked about Tommy. That is on us, too.

The death of a child is a loss to everyone, but to a parent, it's more than an amputation, it's a forfeiture—it is the loss of expectations, the loss of a future, the loss of new memories. I thank God that John and I had not had to endure such pain. Our kids are healthy and hearty; they come from sturdy stock. Louise's children add spark to my life; Edward's boys remind me of Tommy.

I remember we were at Brookfield Zoo, the whole family, maybe six months before Tom became sick, and now that I think about it, it may have been the last time we were all together doing something fun. It was a day that runs like a movie. Short scenes and no words—all emotions. It's strange how the mind works; it's selective, too. Polar bears wander unhindered through memories; so do lions, tigers, and elephants, zebras, and rhinoceroses—all are quick flash-cards of images and recollections. My oldest memory is Tommy astride the bronze lion at the zoo's entrance, like a modern Edmund in the C. S. Lewis tale. He magically waves his imaginary sword over the lion, Aslan, as he looks for enemies to defeat. If only his sword could have cut the cancer from his body. Aslan returns from the dead. Sometimes I wish that Tommy could have performed that miracle for my parents. Maybe it would have saved them.

My parents lived with the loss of Tommy for five years, then we lost them. That's when Grandpa and Grandma Davis came to stay with Joe and me. They lived near us. They had retired, sold their house and farm, and moved to a condominium complex in La Grange. I missed the farm Dad grew up on, but it was great having them nearby. After they retired, they traveled a lot. I guess that's where I got the bug. They moved into our house. There was an insurance settlement that made it easier for everyone. The death of their only son greatly pained them. Once, when I was older, we spent the evening talking about Dad, his career, and even World War II. They died within a few months of each other; they were in their late eighties and lived to see their great-grandchildren. That was a miracle in and of itself.

Mom's parents, John and Louise Kent, lived in Evanston. They both were high school teachers. The journals and diaries were a tradition maintained by the Kent family. Grandpa continued the tradition, but it was our great maiden aunt, John's sister Amanda, who continued the tradition of the diaries. This tradition, mostly through the women of the Kent family, has somehow been maintained for more than two hundred years. Their thoughts and our family's history sit on those shelves in my office.

———

I steadied myself. The slight jolt and the rolling aftershock of the earthquake barely rattled the dishes on the Irish sideboard. Beyond the dining room window, the Pacific Ocean benignly swelled. The kelp beds still drifted aimlessly. I thought about the tsunami that had washed over northern Japan a few years ago. This placid ocean could, at certainly an inopportune moment, swell to unimaginable heights and wash away everything along this measure of the coast of California, equally pulling rich and poor alike into its depths. Thinking about it would make you crazy. My mother, a fatalist, would have said, "It will be God's will." Mother would have also added something about dissolute California, righteous damnation, and God's flashing sword of justice—all for color. Mom seldom left things to chance; all was fate and preordination.

I stared at the cove and wondered if the tsunami sirens would blare after this small tickle of the earth's crust. Would I have time to scramble to the car and drive to a high spot—and would it be high enough? Would I float away and be consumed while stuck in a traffic jam—so Californian? I speculated that the quake was in Hollister or maybe Gilroy, somewhere to the east. There had been tremors a few weeks earlier along the crotchety San Andreas Fault to the east. California was always trying to find a way to rip itself in two, physically and politically.

The front doorbell rang.

Standing at the door was an older woman; I guessed her to be maybe ten years older than me. She had a thin, drawn face, sharp gray-brown eyes, and an elegant haircut. It was silvery gray-blonde, a bit short, but fashionable. She wore a dark blue pants suit with a white, black-striped shirt. A soft sack-like tan handbag hung over her shoulder. On the street sat a car, a Prius, an Uber sticker stuck to the front windshield.

"May I help you?" I asked.

"Cate, I think it is *you* who can help *me*."

Stunned by the sound of her voice, I studied the woman and, from deep in my breast, poured out: "My God, it's you." I took my sister in my hands and pulled her to me. Bobbie did not resist. From her uncertain response, her stiffness, she wasn't sure what my reaction would be. She was prepared for the worst: total rejection.

"For God's sake, please, come in." I looked past her to the car.

"I'm alone. I just have one bag in the car. May I get it?"

"Of course," I said, dumbfounded by the arrival of my sister. The woman, a cane in her left hand, spritely maneuvered down the steps to the curb. The driver removed a small suitcase from the trunk and carried the bag to the porch and set it down. Bobbie followed and said thank you to the woman. I picked up Bobbie's bag, and standing to one side, allowed my sister to pass into the foyer.

"I hope I'm not interrupting anything," Bobbie said.

"I doubt that after fifty years, there is anything more you can do to interrupt my life." I dropped her bag on the wooden floor. "For the love of God, where have you been?"

She didn't answer the question. She continued down the main hallway, past the living room, and to the kitchen. She looked around—an amazed look on her face.

"I always wondered what kind of a woman you would become, pumpkin. You are beautiful and successful, and Joe is, too—or so I've read. This house fits you; in fact, it *is* you. I am so sorry about your husband. I would have liked to have known John. My home is the same; it's like me. I've lived in it for more than forty years. A house will mold us as much as we shape it. I know it's not yet nine o'clock—I flew all night. Do you have any bourbon around? I could use a shot of something."

Stunned, I mechanically walked to the bar and poured two glasses of Old Grand-Dad. "Ice?"

"No, this is just great." Bobbie took the drink and, in one swallow, finished the glass. "Now, please, with some ice."

We studied each other like two feral cats meeting for the first time, circling, squinting, each trying to pull the past into the present. We took our drinks out the French doors into the garden. The marine layer held overhead, but the garden was warm. The sun was a diffused bright spot in the gray sky.

I sat first. Bobbie slowly walked around the terrace, studying the garden. "Mom would be proud. I do remember your green thumb; even for a punk kid you had a way with things, plants, and dogs if I remember," Bobbie said and then took a seat opposite me.

I blurted, "Where the hell have you been, fifty fucking years? Good God, Roberta, you could have said something, a note, anything. Mom's death, Dad's death, the unanswered questions. And you were a part of that. It all fell in on her. You didn't even come to the funerals. Jesus Christ!"

"I'm sorry, pumpkin."

"And *you* can't call me that. We are older, much older. Dad was the last one to call me pumpkin; no one else can. The time for pumpkins and Bobbies and Joeys and other endearments is over. There's too much pain, too much time. No funeral, not even a memorial service—you left us nothing. Now, a half-century later . . . What the hell? You ripped us in two. And now you appear, as if risen from the dead."

"I understand. I really do understand. And I was at Mom's funeral. I hid among a landscape crew; they were filling a grave a few hundred feet away. I watched. I saw it all; you and Dad did a beautiful service. I cried. Good God, I cried."

"Then why all the secrecy? Why hide? Why are you here?"

"Because I was afraid that the police would be there at the funeral. I was a fugitive. I was in hiding; in fact, it took everything to force myself to go. My friend Debbie told me not to go to the funeral. She was sure the FBI and the police would still be watching. Who knows, maybe they were, but they didn't find me."

"But why now? Why the diaries? Why risk it all? You've come back into our lives. Good God, why?"

"The reasons are more than I can count. Because I—I mean, we, my family—need your help."

"Really? What could we possibly do for *you*?"

"Save the life of my granddaughter."

I stopped and stared at her. A million thoughts bounced

around in my head, but to save a life was not one of them. "What?"

"Catherine, for forty-five years, I have been married to a wonderful man. He, until a few weeks ago—in fact, it was the day of your Sunday morning interview—only knew me as Dorothy. We have three perfect and healthy children. Wesley, he lives in Kansas City. Marie, she's married to Steve; they live in Colorado. And my most creative and progressive girl is Catherine. She lives in Chicago. She has a partner, Laurie. I named her after you—only I knew why."

I listened; the morning could not have become more surreal. Then it did.

"Wes and Jane have two children, a boy and a girl, both bright and inquisitive. Marie and Steve have three children. Cathy doesn't have children though they are talking about it, or so they say. Cate, I'm a proud grandmother and will do anything to protect them. That's why I'm here."

"After all these years, what can I do?"

"It's the youngest of Marie and Steve, a girl. Three weeks ago, she was diagnosed with leukemia, acute lymphocytic leukemia."

"My God, I'm sorry," I said. Tommy's face appeared.

"We need help."

"All I know about leukemia is from research for a book I wrote," I said. "The disease is insidious, hard to pinpoint the origins, maybe even DNA related."

"Yes, the doctors are doing everything they can."

"Good." Then I remembered: a donor, bone marrow, white cells.

Roberta took my hand. "In some cases, a donor might be found that can provide healthy bone marrow to boost the body's fight against the disease."

"Yes, but those matches are hard to find and rare. The odds increase when the donor is a blood relative. Joe and I, even if we match, are too old. For transplants, they have their age limits and targets."

"I know. But maybe your children, maybe Joe's children.

Cate, we're desperate. I will do anything to save my grand-daughter. I was there when Tommy died; I will not let that happen to my granddaughter."

"I understand."

"I know you do. I left for reasons that are in the diaries, and there's so much more that is not in them. But all that is irrelevant. I've done everything to keep that past away from you and Joe. My family is in trouble; my sins are mine, not theirs. If I'm exposed, arrested, the pain and embarrassment will destroy our family—my family—and maybe even yours. So, I'm asking for your help. But, God knows, I understand if you refuse. I'll leave, and you will never hear from us again."

I walked back into the house. A few minutes later, I returned with a tray, coffee cups, and the pot of coffee I'd made an hour earlier. Sitting on the tray was the bottle of Old Grand-Dad.

"That's a pretty charm bracelet," I said. "I still have the one that Mom gave me for my eleventh birthday."

"A friend gave it to me a long time ago; I wear it all the time. It has charms for the kids, and grandkids; almost every important event in my life is here." She held up her wrist and jingled the silver charms.

"Have you had breakfast?" I asked.

"No, I came straight from the airport. I flew through Las Vegas; I was lucky to get the early flight this morning into Monterey. So far, it's about the only thing that's worked for me this week. Mitch, my husband, stayed home. We are going to meet in Boulder when I leave here—that's where my daughter lives. Breakfast would be wonderful. Thank you, Cate."

I showed her to the upstairs guestroom. While I made breakfast, she took a shower. We ate on the terrace. The sun, by this time, had burned away the thin clouds; the day showed a benign, yet sunny, promise. I couldn't keep my eyes from my sister I hadn't seen for more than fifty years.

"Should I call you Dorothy or Roberta?" I asked.

"I'm not sure I would answer to Roberta or Bobbie; it has been so long since anyone called me either name. Dorothy was a name given to me by my friend Debbie Toomey."

"Then it's Dorothy, for now. That name Toomey—wasn't she a fugitive? She was arrested a few years ago for something that happened in Chicago."

"Your memory still astounds me. Yes, it was after the demonstrations. I haven't seen her since the summer I married Mitch. We said our goodbyes and never talked again, not even a letter. Even after she turned herself in to the FBI, I didn't try to contact her. I loved her like a sister. She died keeping our secret."

"Were you involved with what she was charged with? It had something to do with an explosion and people dying."

"I won't say anything about what happened. It is in the diaries. Even my being here puts you in jeopardy; you could be called an accomplice after the fact. The FBI has a long memory, as Debbie found out. She was sick with lung cancer. That's what killed her. As far as I know, she said nothing about me."

"The FBI was here a few weeks ago," I said. "Evidence was recovered, they said. DNA testing had been done and they are trying to make a connection to you. They have contacted my daughter; it was through a DNA sample my granddaughter supplied for a school project."

Dorothy slowly pushed her plate away and inhaled. "I hadn't expected that. Not that I'm surprised. They are tenacious. Did you know that they visited Mom and Dad a week after the explosion?"

"Yes, Joe reminded me. I'd made an entry in my diary. Joe was here at the house when the FBI agent stopped by. Joe remembered the day of the interview; he was there for that one, too. The agent who interviewed us is the grandson of the agent who interviewed our parents."

"Unbelievable. May I ask what he asked and what you said?"

"No, I don't think so. The less you know, the better. And how did you know about the FBI and Mom and Dad?"

"Mom told me. A week after I left, I called. She told me about the FBI and that Dad had told her everything that happened, especially the involvement of the FBI agent who may have killed my friends. She said I should give myself up; it all could be worked out. I told her it couldn't; I wouldn't. America was in the middle of two wars, one here and the other in Vietnam. I believed they would arrest everyone, you and Joe, and everyone—all because of me. Then Mom died, then Dad. That, too, was on me."

"They were declared accidents."

"To this day, I am positive that neither was an accident. I believe Dad was murdered because he knew too much. He was investigating the explosion and the FBI agent involved. He met him and interviewed him. It was for a story he was writing—one he never finished. It took a lot of years for me to get past all that, then it was too late. I couldn't come forward; no one would believe me."

"Murdered? Dad killed?" I said. My suspicions were becoming real.

"And I honestly believe our mother, also. I'm sure that something happened in the house that day, someone was there. Her fall was not an accident."

In the space of an hour my life had been completely upended. My sister returns, and my fear that Mom and Dad were murdered confirmed.

"I remember Tack being in the garage; Mom never put him in the garage," I said. "One of the policemen said the back door was unlocked—it was often unlocked. Someone said there was a car no one recognized parked down the street. The police said it could have been anything."

Dorothy took my hand. Her fingers were thin yet strong —the hands of someone who'd worked her whole life. They were also cold.

"Yes, I've thought about this a long time. After all these years there's nothing we can do now."

"And your granddaughter?"

"I will do anything to save that child, anything—even if it means going to prison."

"Mom and Dad knew about you? They never said anything," I said.

"They both knew I was alive and in hiding. They did not know where; they never did. If they had lived, Dad would have done something; I would have come home. Then they were gone. I wasn't sure whether they said anything to you or Joe. I know now they didn't."

"They never said anything. All I know now is what I read in your diaries, and I had trouble believing them."

"I understand. Early in the war, Dad and I had our differences, but after Joe came back from Vietnam all busted up, his mind changed. He was working on a story about the demonstrations and their impact on the American people, fathers and sons, parents and children, war and anti-war. About that time, the house a group of us were using exploded. Four people died; two were friends of mine. Dad told me he was building a multi-part story, and he wanted to know more about the house, anything I remembered about the FBI or the man I thought may have been an informer, maybe even a spy. I told him everything. Dad was beginning to see it differently. We talked a lot. He thought that a lot of what was known was being manipulated by the government. It was being made to look like the radicals were bent on destruction."

"How did you talk with Dad?" I asked. "It would be dangerous to call the house. They may have bugged the phones."

"We set up pay phones around downtown where I would call him, and we'd talk. I did have a phone call with Mom just after Joe tried to kill himself; that was a couple of days before she died. It was breaking my heart. After that, Debbie and I went deeper into hiding."

"It had an impact on him," I said. "After Mom died, Joe and I took care of Dad. We were sure he was headed toward a breakdown. He blamed the politicians for Mom's death. Then he rallied, made a comeback—he even smiled. I remember that smile. He said he was finishing that article; he was obsessed with it. Joe survived his suicide attempt."

"I remember. Dad told me what happened. I wanted to see him," Dorothy said.

"I wish Dad had told us. That afternoon when I came home from school, Joe was there. Dad said he was going to work late. We waited late for dinner, but he didn't come home. Early the next morning—when the police came to the house—they said that someone called in the accident along the canal and the police found the car. Dad was in the driver's seat, dead. Nobody else around. The coroner called it an unfortunate accident. Dad's blood alcohol was high; they said he was drunk and probably slipped off the road and crashed into the abutment. I know he'd been drinking; some nights, that was the only way he could sleep. He and Joe would get into the bourbon. I tried to get them to stop or at least slow down. It was hard; they were two dark souls."

"I'm sorry you had to go through that. It was unfair. Dad said I should turn myself in; he would help make it right. I told him no. He was working on that article. I asked if he needed help; he said no. He said it was too dangerous. Ever since the FBI visited him at the house, he was certain they were following him. He'd become paranoid. All he had was his job at the *Daily News* to keep him sane. One of the last things he said to me was that if there was a subpoena served at the newspaper for his notes, he didn't want them there. He said he kept a lot of the notes and photos at home."

"Photos? There were photos?"

"Yes, we did a sting-like trick on the FBI to identify one of the agents. I assume that you read some of the diaries?"

"Yes, I know about the restaurant on North Avenue."

"Debbie took photos, a whole roll of film. I sent it to him. I hope he got them, had them processed."

"I wouldn't know."

"I've thought a lot about that day, that day Mom died. I may have been at fault. I called her; we talked about Dad's notes. If the phone line was bugged, someone could have gone into the house to find them."

"In 1968, I was fifteen. Dad was only forty-eight. Mom was forty-seven," I said. "They had a full life ahead of them. Dad's death ended what Joe and I call the devil's decade."

Dorothy looked at me with heartbreaking eyes.

"That series of articles was never published," I said. "Months later, when Joe and I cleaned the house, we put a lot of Mom's personal things in one box and Dad's in another. We added personal mementos that the newspaper said came from Dad's desk. I've had them. I've never opened the boxes; they are on shelves in the attic area of the garage. Mom's diaries are on the shelves in my study. I just looked at them; they were up to date just a few days before she died. Dad's diaries are missing. Joe and I aren't sure he was keeping them." I picked up the dishes and placed them on the tray and took them into the kitchen. Dorothy followed. "Are you still keeping your diary?" I asked.

"Yes, I try. And I convinced the children to keep theirs. I used bribery in the beginning, but they keep them up, or at least they say they do. Do you and Joe?"

"Yes. Joe gave me his early journals through 1968," I said. "Then yours arrived. All a coincidence."

My phone rang, the ringtone particular to one man.

"That's Joe," I said. "We have a dilemma; how much can I tell him?"

"You decide."

I clicked on the speaker. "Hi, how are you this fine and glorious day? And how is that girlfriend?"

"Am I in trouble?" Joe said. "You sound happy this morning; that doesn't bode well for me. And the girlfriend is just fine, thank you very much. Surprisingly, she likes you. I told her everything, yet she still wants to meet you. That's why I'm calling."

I looked at Dorothy; she shook her head. I mouthed the words, "Okay."

"Mitsi has a conference in Monterey at Cal State next week; it's with a bunch of administrators. I'll be bored out of my mind, so I thought I'd hang out with you, maybe spend a few mornings on the coast painting, then dinner. What do you think?"

"That sounds wonderful. Hold a second, I've another call." I muted the phone and turned to Dorothy. "When are you heading back to . . . Colorado?"

"Tomorrow."

"You know we have to tell him. He must know, especially if he can help."

"I know, but . . ."

"Joe, hold on a second. There's someone you need to talk with." I handed the phone to Dorothy.

"Hi, Joe. It's Roberta."

"Roberta who?" Joe said, then stuttered. "Oh my God, Bobbie? Is that you?"

"Yes, Joe. It's me."

Joe never answered. After a long pause, the phone clicked off.

"That went well," Dorothy said. "I hurt him more than anyone."

"He'll be fine. We've talked about your diaries and what you did, where you might be. Yes, you did break his heart. He loved you—we both did. Give him time."

That evening, after I put a log on the fire to cut the chill of the summer evening, my phone rang again with that particular ring.

"Hi, Joe, you okay?" I waited as Joe answered. "Can I put you on speaker?" I sat the phone on the table between Dorothy and myself. "Joe, she goes by the name Dorothy."

Joe cleared his throat. "I'm sorry about this afternoon. I was stunned and felt ambushed. I know that you didn't mean it, but your being there surprised me. Why are you with Cate?"

Dorothy explained the difficulties with her granddaughter. She talked about the DNA and the need to find a donor match. Joe listened patiently.

"Where are you living now?" Joe asked.

"I will not tell you. It's better if you don't know anything more than what I've told you. I've been a wanted woman for fifty years. If I'm caught, it will bring immeasurable harm to you, your families, and mine as well. I am only concerned about making my granddaughter well. When that is accomplished, I will talk with my family, tell them what happened, and seek their counsel. I will not do anything that will jeopardize their families and reputations. The same for you two. It's as simple as that."

"I've learned that plans, no matter how well made and designed, can and probably will go to shit," Joe said. "I want to see you."

"That's not a good idea, Joe. In fact, I can't allow it. I am leaving on the early morning plane; I'm meeting my husband in Colorado. I need to be with my daughter and granddaughter. As much as I want to see you, I can't. I took a chance with Cate, and it's been good, so far. I've gone over everything with Cate. She will talk to you about the DNA samples and what we need."

"I don't care. Whatever you need. Cate and I will work it out. What time is your flight?"

"Early morning."

I gave Dorothy a questioning look. She put a thin finger up and touched her lips.

"I can be there by ten o'clock," Joe said.

"No, Joe. Please don't. Cate will explain everything."

Dorothy stood and walked out of the living room. I heard the sliding door to the garden terrace open, then close.

"Dorothy?" Joe said.

"She left the room," I said, clicking the phone off the speaker. "She is troubled and in a lot of pain over her family. I'll call you later in the week, okay?"

Chapter 18
I Have the Scars to Prove It

Joe: Now
Mission Bay, San Diego
September 2019

For a long time, maybe decades, I blamed myself for Bobbie leaving. It was easy, one more brick laid on my pity-me wall. I believed she left because I was the real-life version of what she fought, the Vietnam War. I was a constant reminder; I was broken, and I believed it was easier for her to run away than deal with me. Hell, I was having enough trouble dealing with me. I tried to disappear—permanently. You know how that turned out; I have the scars to prove it, I see them every day. And now, fifty years later, those days are as sharp and bright as the edge of the bloody razor blade on the floor next to the bathtub. My Cate held me together. Don't tell her that, especially now with John's death creating its own hell. I'm not worried. She's noble and has a brave heart; she will pull through. However, I'm still here—Bobbie's not. Or at least was not—she's back. I don't have an answer to the question: Why did either of us survive?

A few years after America extracted itself from that shitty war, I found a group of guys that were facing the same demons I was. This was in Boston, before I moved to San Diego. Two were legit alcoholics, two others had marriages that made a freeway accident look like a birthday party, and almost all of us managed to push it all so deep that our favorite word was *denial*—denial of the denial. I fit in between them. My drinking hadn't gotten all that much worse, and I'd shaken the drugs. Soon, I found a woman who would put up with me. We went twenty-five years before that bell rang; as I said, two broken people don't make a whole. My personal refutations were on my wrists. Fifty years later, five of the original seven are still among us. One died so long ago I can't remember his name; it was Bob something. We've concluded that Bob was already a stat when he joined our group. Still, his face appears occasionally, one of the ghosts, like my brothers in Khe Sanh. Al Getz died just a few years ago, colon cancer. He was our de facto leader for the first ten years or so.

When we get into our cups, the five of us who remain, we wonder about all that history. Over the years, there were maybe a dozen others who came and went; there were no dues, no rules, and this is the God's truth, no excuses. Sure, most of us (maybe all of us, the truth be told) saw therapists and head doctors; the VA picked up the tab for all of it. But it was the hand of your buddy, when you were down, that helped keep you from being sucked down into the mire. Chet, Jimmy, Jose, and Jonesy, my brothers until the day I die.

No rules, just show up. Chet and Jose haven't had a drink in forty years, and both are still married to their sweethearts who they met after the war. Jimmy has an autobody shop outside Boston and five grandkids. Jonesy—he was the one that survived the firefight that day—is a lot like me. DWK: divorced, with kids. And, honest to God, he's the lucky one. Jones followed me to California, bought a one-dollar lottery ticket at a 7-Eleven in Oxnard, and scratched off a million dollars. And the SOB still has most of it. I said we were a sad lot, but not stupid. Compound interest and twenty years of Apple stock can make a guy happy. And we are alive—no small feat these days.

I was the first to get out of Chicago. No, that's not right: Bobbie was the first. I didn't know it then. Like Cate, I didn't know she was a fugitive. After Mom and Dad died, I spent the next three years self-sequestered in the house. With our grandparents there, I managed to get the right people to believe that even I, with one good leg, could take care of Cate. That responsibility was my therapy. The grandparents just made sure we didn't set the house on fire. To think that Cate would be hustled off to a foster home of some kind, that would not happen on my watch. The grandparents and I raised her until she went off to college; at that point, she was the oldest eighteen-year-old woman I'd ever met. Dad had done well for a man who had hardly made a lot of money. He had insurance on both Mom and him, the house was paid for (that was a shock when I learned that), and their social security benefits helped a lot. Eventually it ran out, so other arrangements had to be made.

I married, left Chicago and went to Boston, raised a family, failed, then ran off to California with paint embedded in my fingers—my life in a sentence. Cate secured a full scholarship to Mundelein College and made a success of herself. That's the short version. She will tell you the long, early painful first few years and the wonderful reward named John. As I said, she was and is the one person I never worry about.

"What are you doing?" Mitsi asked.

I was sitting on our balcony that overlooks Mission Bay. I had just hung up my call with Cate and Bobbie. Far out to the west of San Diego, a wall of haze hung over the Pacific. We Davises need our view of the water.

"Sit, join me," I said and pointed to the opposite chair.

"What are you drinking?"

"Nothing at the moment. Maybe a martini later."

"Gin? A special occasion?"

"No, more like the end of the world as I've known it for the last fifty years."

"Ominous. Will there be flying sharks? If you don't mind, I'm making one for myself."

"Seriously, I'm good—and yes, maybe flying sharks."

A final note about my guys. We try to see each other two or three times a year—that's the way these things go. New Orleans is a favorite, Las Vegas, even Montana—I've become a reasonably decent one-legged fly fisherman. Phone calls and text messages, then a weekend or dinner somewhere. We're good, don't worry about us, and besides, it's more like a medical conclave when we get together. All the infirmities and surgeries are noted, then the serious partying begins, and fresh bottles of Rolaids and Maalox are cracked.

When Mitsi returned, I'd resolved that if I didn't tell her, I'd explode. "I've told you about my sister Bobbie; she is the one who disappeared. We believed that she died many years ago. A few weeks ago, she reappeared, alive and seemingly well. Talk about a kick in the ass. I just talked to her."

The look on Mitsi's face was priceless. She had had more than her fair share of problems, and she knew me.

"You have got to be shocked," she said. "Are you sure that it's her?"

I was bemused by her question. "Interesting that you ask that, and to be honest, it never occurred to me that she might not be Bobbie. I'm certain she is, but you are right to ask. Talk about wishful thinking."

"You should try and verify it. I don't know how—before this goes too far. What happened—why now?"

I told her everything I knew (she'd watched Cate's interview at her home when I was in Carmel), the diaries arriving, and Bobbie's sudden appearance at Cate's. But I kept a few things to myself. Someday I'd tell Mitsi, but there was no need to know her name was now Dorothy or the reasons she left. Cate never gave me a last name; I'm guessing that Bobbie never told her. I told Mitsi about the fall and winter of 1968, the last time I saw her, our family's trials and losses, and the vast emptiness that grew around Cate and me. If anyone knew about loss, it was Mitsi. By the time I'd finished, I was one martini ahead and a handful of Kleenex behind.

"And she appeared because of her sick grandchild?" Mitsi said. "I know this sounds brutal and so un-Christian-like, but that's awfully self-serving after all these years. To keep away from her family and only come home when she needs something."

"I had the same thought. Hard not to. Cate says she's sincere; maybe the self-serving need worked. We do what we do to protect our own, especially when it is a matter of life and death."

"I'd do the same for my kids, and don't even think about what I'd do to protect the grandkids. Didn't you say that Jules, the brother of John, writes thrillers? If someone were to go after my kin, even Jack Reacher would have trouble stopping my resolve."

"I bet," I said.

"You mentioned that there was an explosion? People died?"

"Yes, a house on Chicago's Northside, near where the Cubs play ball. It was my dream as a kid to play baseball in that park one day. She disappeared soon after that; I was in a fog then. It was eight months after I lost my leg. It took me a year to get my head around it. I blamed myself for her leaving. I know different now, but back then there was a lot of shit piling up."

"And this FBI agent? His showing up right now, after all these years—strange, don't you think?"

"Yes, too strange."

"Does he know more than he told you?"

"Probably. That's the nature of the secret police."

Mitsi rolled her eyes at me. "Cynical?"

"At my age, cynicism is a virtue. Keeps you from making a fool of yourself."

Another eyeroll. "Fifty years is a long time to hold a

grudge or, in this case, the potential of an arrest for murder," Mitsi said. "The FBI is a busy bureaucracy these days, lots of stuff out there, and to spend the resources on a cold case like this—something else must be going on, someone pushing. I've worked in big bureaucracies; I know them. There is more here than Special Agent George Talant has told you and Cate."

"Talant wasn't even born when this all went down," I answered. My head was trying to get itself around the thoughts that Mitsi had just jammed there. "He is directly connected, as bizarre as that is. There's too much of a coincidence."

"You think?"

It was my turn to roll my eyes; my expression must have struck a nerve.

"I'm sorry. I didn't mean it to sound like that."

"But you are right; there is more here than just a cold case. Talant is hunting; he's not fishing. He can see his quarry—us. He is beating around the edges to see if anything flushes from the brush. He is laying traps."

"Did he say anything about his grandfather or even his family?"

"Other than the fact that Jeanne Ellen Talant is his sister?" I said with not too little irony.

"No shit! The presidential candidate from Maryland is his sister and the granddaughter of the original FBI agent on the case? The one that may have blown up the house?"

"Yes."

"Well, mister, I would suggest that here is an excellent place to start."

Chapter 19
After All Those Years

Cate: Now
Carmel, California
September 2019

There are good reasons for my office window to look out on Carmel Cove: the view, the changes in the weather, and most especially watching children run up and down the beach. A not-so-good reason is the lane below. When I'm in the office, it's hard for anyone to sneak up on me. Today, the midsummer sun had burned away the morning mist, and the tourists had taken over the beach. It was full of dogs, joggers, and children. And near the walkway to the beach, an unannounced George Talant had parked and was headed my way. Time to suit up.

"Good morning, Special Agent Talant," I said, not the least bit snarky. "Coffee is hot."

He held up a bag. "I splurged on some of those raisin snails from that bakery on Ocean Avenue. Can you be bribed?"

"And by a federal officer, no less."

We took chairs on the terrace.

"It's a lot more pleasant here than when I left Washington, DC, two days ago," Talant said. "The change in seasons, it's getting cold, and there's a chance that a late-season hurricane may sweep up the coast. Typical for this time of year; nonetheless, this is considerably nicer."

"Some days, when the fog is in, you might change your mind," I answered, then dropped the bomb. "I heard from my sister."

Talant stopped in mid-snail and looked at me. I thought he was about to choke. Either he wasn't expecting me to be so forthcoming or I'd really surprised him. Joe and I had discussed this little bit of honesty. Tell most of the truth, shade it some, leave the door open a little. "Put it out there," Joe said. "Maybe with some chum in the water, he'll rise to the bait."

"How?" Talant said. "Why did she contact you? After all these years, she just shows up?"

"How do you know that she showed up? Maybe she called, sent a note, a letter?"

"I'm sorry, an assumption. What I mean is why, so soon after we talked, did you hear from Roberta? Strange coincidence, don't you think—especially after all these years?"

I poured coffee. I was beginning to enjoy poking this bear. I also reminded myself what Joe also said: "That bear has very long claws."

I did understand. I was being watched, or monitored, or even bugged—possibly one, or all the above. "Her family has a health crisis, and she hoped that my brother or I might be able to help. The disease is leukemia; it's her granddaughter. She is very sick."

"Where does she live?" Talant asked as he removed a notebook from his pocket.

"I honestly don't know," I said, pissed because he didn't ask anything more about the health of the granddaughter— the bastard. "She contacted me, asked for our help. She did not give us her new name, or an address, or the grandchild's name. I assume that for the last fifty years she has lived under an alias of some kind."

"When did she call you?"

Thinking back, we never talked on the phone. "She didn't call me; she came to the door; it was a few weeks back. She was desperate. Joe and I are too old, and we can't be donors."

"Why didn't you contact me? You know you could be involved in aiding and abetting a felon."

"And you for bribery," I said, taking a bite of the pastry. "This is delicious. This is a game to you, isn't it? I'm hoping to save the life of a child. Roberta stopped here, spent the night; we talked. She told me nothing about her past life, and then went home."

"You have to tell me the exact day she arrived."

"My memory suffers these days," I confessed. "Between my books, John's passing away, all the people coming and going, I can't remember a lot of things. And besides, threatening me about a supposed crime from fifty years ago—that happened when I was fifteen years old—shame on you. I had enough trauma that year. I don't need more."

"Trauma? You mean about Joe, Vietnam, your parents."

"Yes, all of that."

"Was there anything else?" he asked.

I wasn't sure if Talant was trying to draw me out, or that he didn't know. I hit him between the eyes.

"That isn't enough," I stood. "I told you that the last time you were here, all within weeks. So, Special Agent Talant, within a month our world—Joe's and mine—collapsed. I wouldn't wish that on anyone."

He looked past me out into the garden. "I understand, more than you can imagine. I mentioned that we lost my father when I was eight. He was killed in an FBI shootout in Idaho—militia, free-staters. Eleven died, including my father."

"I'm sorry. We both have our traumas to deal with."

"Like for you and Joe, it's been a long time, but he's the reason I'm in the FBI—like my grandfather. A family legacy."

"I get it. I'm a writer because of my father." I slowly sat.

"So, we both have our histories. Roberta told me the same thing; the deaths of our parents hit her hard."

"Where is she?"

"As I said, I do not know. She said she flew in. She didn't tell me from where; I assume somewhere back east. She left the same way. She said to me, 'the less you knew, the better.'"

"And her granddaughter?"

"She is very sick, needs a bone marrow transplant. That's why she was here. She was hoping for a match."

"And you and Joe didn't?"

"We don't know and besides we are too old. Sixty-five is the cutoff. A girl never tells her age."

"You could have surprised me; you don't look that old."

"Thanks for that. Plus some of the medications I take make it all problematic."

"Was it one of your children? Did they match?"

I was stuck. He knew all about Louise, her family, the DNA. But not about any medical issues, so they weren't watching that close. "A match? I really don't know." I went on offense. "So here we are, two damaged and traumatized children of events that no child should ever endure . . . and you want me to turn over my sister to you so that you can make your grandfather happy."

"That's unfair."

"But true. I have a prosperous and lucrative career writing about crime, families, history, and the interactions of people with law enforcement. I've sat in more courtrooms than you probably have. I interviewed cops and criminals for almost forty years. I've spent months looking through old newspapers, journals, and histories trying to understand the criminal and sane mind. And after all those years, I'm just beginning to understand motivation and human desires. You, Special Agent George Talant, are doing this investigation not out of some lofty desire for delayed justice, but to provide closure to your family, especially your grandfather. And I assume that time is of the essence. And maybe there's something here about your sister as well. What a coup to have this drop in the news cycle right now. I see the head-line: 'FBI closes fifty-year-old case of murder; brother of presidential candidate solves radical bombing.'"

I was extremely snarky and from the expression on Talant's face, hitting close, maybe below the belt.

Talant stood and glared. Families, especially families with power or access to power, can be like that. We mortals must fight with the tools we have.

"Ms. Wallace, I thought, for a moment, that we shared a bond—I see now that I was wrong. You have broken the law. You have abetted the flight of your sister, maybe harbored her. You have failed to inform us of what you learned in an ongoing federal criminal investigation. Be very careful. If you are involved in this, I will personally handcuff you and make sure that—"

"What? That I'm trying to save the life of my grand-niece? Doing what I can to protect the life of an eight-year-old child—the same age you were when you lost your father? Is that how you want this to play out? And with your sister a presidential candidate—really? Furthermore, and I want you to understand this, so listen carefully. What you have in your files about what happened that day in 1968 —when that house exploded—is wrong, dead wrong. They are lies, piled on with more lies. It is a fabrication. So, Special Agent Talant, be careful. I suggest that you look for the truth instead of my sister. I know that families will do anything to protect themselves."

"Do not threaten me, Ms. Wallace."

"Threaten? How can I threaten you? I am warning you. I am telling you to be cautious, to learn the facts, *all* the facts. And most of all, realize that what's in your files, and what you believe might be wrong. And keep this in mind: you may be being used by your grandfather and maybe even your sister."

He started to say something, stopped, then turned away. He stuffed the notebook in his jacket pocket and walked through the kitchen to the front of the house. I followed in his wake; I wanted to make sure that he didn't punch in a wall or leave a secret listening device stuck under a plant or something.

He stood on the outside landing and turned back to me.

"Please contact me if you hear from your sister. Thank you for the coffee." He handed me a card. "In case you lost the other one."

"And thank you for the pastry, Special Agent."

Talant crossed the lane to his rental, climbed inside, and slammed the door. I'm sure he was pissed on many levels—that was his problem. I felt sorry for the man. He carries the same trauma; it is evident that both he and his sister overcame that loss, just like Joe and me. And they probably don't know what their grandfather did fifty-one years ago, a bloody act that binds both our families together. When I told Talant that what he knows could be lies piled on lies, I shivered and had an epiphany. My heart seemed to stop; my breath caught. What had happened to our parents was more real than I imagined. I don't know what Talant will do—finding the truth will be hard, if not impossible.

Chapter 20
Families Will do Anything to Protect Each Other

George Talant: Now
Annapolis, Maryland
Late September 2019

Carrol's Crab Shack is a true survivor; I've been eating and drinking here my whole life. Gramps would talk about having lunch, back in the day, with Dad and my two aunts, Bridget and Cecily. Then, growing up, I'd sit here on the deck with Jeanne Ellen; our autistic brother, James; and Gramps. We'd watch the Naval Academy boats train on Chesapeake Bay. Gramps brought me here for my first legal drink, Jeanne, too. It was a rite of passage. We'd take James from the home he was living in, just to get him out of the place. Gramps loved the adage that age gives you two things: great memories and poor bathroom habits. Now my sister is running for president of the United States; you have to love the dream. Gramps said that he would do anything for us—anything.

After I picked him up from his "old folks' prison," as he calls it, we drove across the peninsula to the restaurant on Spa Creek. It's on a pleasant, tree-lined street just fifteen minutes away.

"One drink," I told him after we sat. "I know you, so just

one Maker's Mark."

The waitress, Delila, stood with pad and paper over me. I flashed on a schoolteacher I had thirty years ago; then, I think, she held a ruler.

"The usual, Mr. Talant?" Delila asked.

"Make it a double Maker's,"—he looked at me with a smile—"in one glass. On the rocks."

"Cute," I said.

"Counts as one drink," he said.

"Whatever. Iced tea for me, Delila."

"If I were fifty years younger," he offered, watching Delila as she walked toward the bar.

"She wasn't even born then, and her mother was in grade school, Gramps—and you would still be too old."

"How's Jeanne doing?" he asked, changing the subject.

"She is going crazy; debates every month, and the convention is still a year away," I said. "Nothing left to chance: she's in California banging on doors this week. I talked to her last Monday night. When she's back in Washington in a couple of days, I'll see her."

"I assume doors with money?" he said.

"The big doors, as she put it. Only the big doors," I said.

"Money and politics, nasty business."

"That's the system. Nothing I can do about that."

"Such pessimism. I taught you better."

Delila set the drinks on the table. I ordered fish and chips, Gramps a crab roll.

"Did you follow up on that woman, that writer, in California?" he asked. "After your first interview, you thought she and her brother might know something. Can't remember her name."

"Yes, I saw her again last week," I said. Gramps was aware I was looking into the cold case. "It took some finagling, but the deputy director assigned me the case and has given me a little room because of Jeanne. I'm not pushing it; I was able to string it along with some other work. Her name is Catherine Davis Wallace. She shocked the hell out of me—told me her sister, the missing Roberta Davis—came to visit her a few weeks back. Out of the blue."

Gramps stopped, took a slow sip, and stared at me. I thought he was going to choke on his bourbon. "Roberta Davis is alive?"

"Seems to be, at least according to Wallace. Said she didn't know where she lived or what name she'd lived under the last fifty years. Just showed up at her door, asked for help."

"Why the hell would she do that?"

"Her sister needed help finding an organ donor for her granddaughter," I said. "The child has leukemia, needs a bone marrow transplant. Wallace said Roberta wanted to find out if any of the family might match."

"Damn, after fifty years, she reappears," he said absently, looked out the window to the harbor, and stirred his drink with his finger. "So, you don't know where she lives? You didn't check the airlines? Chase her down?"

"We are checking; we are trying to narrow it down. We don't even know what day she was there. Obviously, there isn't any surveillance. It's hard to chase down the route she might have taken. We assumed she flew in from somewhere; Wallace didn't say. There are four airports in the region; on any given day, there are a quarter of a million travelers. Not easy—probably impossible. And the assistant director flat out said that he isn't going to throw people and resources at this fishing expedition, even for me—or you . . . or Jeanne. Roberta Davis had to go through one of those airports, but for fifty years, she has remained hidden. She's probably good at this."

Gramps again turned his head toward the water. He was fading, I was sure of that. His body was reasonably healthy for someone ninety-seven years old, but his mind, I wasn't too sure.

"Gramps, you okay?" I asked, trying to punch through his thoughts. "You keep drifting around—eat your sandwich."

"Sorry, Buddy. I have been doing that a lot lately. Don't worry; it's not dementia—just that I'm easily distracted these days. I get what you're saying about chasing Roberta Davis. It's like chasing a rabbit down the rabbit hole. Too many options, easy to get lost—you need to be careful."

"Wallace said something about what happened that day. She said that what's in the files is not true. In fact, she said they were lies. Then she said something that's troubling. She said I was being used by you and Jeanne. I have no idea what she meant."

Gramps sat there, picking at the crab pieces with his fork. "She's using an old interrogation technique. Confuse the interviewer, make them question the evidence. I was there, I saw the house explode, I saw the men on the ground. It's like a photo forever in my head. If someone is lying, I say it is her. She is defending her sister—families will do anything to protect each other. Obviously, her sister is getting at her, she's the one making it up."

I didn't tell him that Cate Wallace had said almost the same thing.

"There were a lot of investigations not pertinent to Roberta Davis going on then, especially in Chicago," he said. "The Chicago Eight, a year later Fred Hampton, the riots, even the feminists. The Bureau under Hoover was a different place than it is today. So just be careful, Buddy. Okay?"

"Have you talked to Jeanne about this?"

Again, a pause. "No, she has enough on her plate. No need to worry her."

"Worry her about what?" I asked.

"Any of this—it was so long ago. It means nothing now. Don't forget that I told you not to mess with this. I wish you would just drop it—it's one of those cases that will never be solved."

"People died. Your friend died—an FBI agent died." I couldn't believe what I was hearing.

"Then leave the dead alone, okay, Buddy? Just leave them be."

"One last thing," I said. "The files have an FBI agent and undercover guy working for you, Ezekiel Allanson. The reports are referential, little detail. What happened to him?"

Gramps took a bite out of his sandwich, and slowly chewed. After a minute, he said, "That name still in the files? Zeke Allanson, now there's a guy I'd forgotten. Zeke was an FBI agent undercover in the Michigan SDS. We brought him down to Chicago to use him to get what information we could from this radical group. I understand he was gone when the house blew up. They were a paranoid bunch in Washington; they kept him on the outside—they did not want him to get too involved. I later heard he had a substance abuse problem."

"There's not much in the files."

"I wouldn't know about that. If he's still alive, he'd be in his seventies, mid-seventies. He was from Michigan, smart kid, looked five years younger than he was. There were dozens like him across the country, men and women. Chicago had their undercover cops and so did the Illinois State Police. That's why they were sent inside the radical groups; they looked the part—college age. They just fit in. One was a cute blond, I remember that."

"Seems tame by today's standards. Some of our people nowadays are deep into international gangs, especially from Mexico."

"Yeah, back then Hoover and the Bureau were trying to save the United States from communism and anarchy." Gramps took in a deep breath. ". . . how are the kids? I haven't seen them in months. And Maria, she still teaching?"

"Gramps, you really are drifting about today," I said. He'd done this before. "Maria's not taught in two years. You okay? What's wrong?"

"Nothing, Buddy. I'm good. Things get jumbled more now . . . Just thinking about that kid, Allanson. You could maybe track him down through personnel. I don't know the circumstances of his leaving the Bureau, not even sure how long he stayed in. He might have remained in touch with some of the guys in Michigan. They might know where he is, SSI, pension, the usual. Keep it on the down-low, though. As I said, he didn't have much to do with what happened, probably won't be much help. He's probably dead, anyway."

———

A few days later, I was sitting in my sister's outer office in the Hart Senate Office Building. The door was open to her office; I heard her voice. As always it was strong and forceful; she'd always been a leader. I'd walked over from my office at the FBI Building on Third Street. She said she was free for lunch. With her travels and schedule, other than phone calls, it was only the second time we'd gotten together since Christmas—nine months is a long time. I am so proud of Jeanne Ellen; my heart could just burst. She is two years younger, and I've thought, in many ways, twenty years older.

Her assistant, a striking young woman who'd attended Vassar (I read the FBI background reports on her staff), sat behind her desk diligently banging away on a keyboard and glaring at the screen. She wore headphones and a mic.

"Soon, Agent Talant; she'll be off the phone, soon," Beth Ellington said.

I smiled and nodded a thanks.

The outer office walls were covered with trophy photos: Sis with President Obama, standing next to both Clintons, holding a plaque with Joe Biden, and one with Reverend Jesse Jackson. Centered in the collection was a large reproduction of a painting of President Roosevelt—Franklin Roosevelt. The last Republican senator, her predecessor, from Maryland retired more than thirty years ago.

"You can go in, Agent Talant."

Jeanne was standing in the window looking down on C

Street; the better views were for senior senators. She turned, walked to me, and gave me a hug. She looked tired, but good; she was always a stylish dresser. These days she was being graded on more than her policy stands; her hair and clothes were fair game. I like the new color of her hair. She'd darkened the Talant bright copper to a more auburn tone—but still an Irish girl through and through.

"First, how are the kids?" she asked.

"Colleen is starting at William and Mary, but you knew that," I said, "and acting just like a freshman. She needs to call home more often—Maria is concerned."

"All mothers are. Remember how Mom acted when I didn't call? I thought she'd send in the police to watch me. Sean?"

"Studying hard, wants to play basketball this winter—we told him only if his grades are good."

"He'll be fine—he's smart. And you?" Jeanne asked.

"Good. The current politics have the Bureau in an uproar. We hate to be caught between the sides, but it's hard not to be. Washington is nothing but politics."

"Maybe I can change that," Jeanne said.

"Easier to turn an oil tanker."

"We don't have a firm position on oil tankers—at this time," she said with a laugh.

"Like this every day?"

"Three and four times a day." The phone on her desk buzzed. Jeanne put up her finger. I waited while she talked—mostly yeses.

"Sorry, I have to cancel our lunch. There's an impromptu meeting with the leadership; it's at two. Rain check?"

"That's good, no problems," I said. "But I want you to promise that we get together soon, maybe take Mom out to dinner. She'd like that."

"Absolutely. Just tell me when. I had some time last week and stopped to see James. He's doing well. They keep him engaged. They found some computer games that he's good at."

"Good. Mom calls him all the time. It's good for both of them—I'll see him next week if I can."

"The rest of my day is crazy. There's a Senate vote at four. Then a plane to New York, a donor thing at eight. I might get home by midnight. And I have to prepare for the debate in Colorado that is coming up, and I may be going back to California in a few days."

"In for a penny, in for a pound," I said.

She took a few seconds and looked through some papers on her desk. "I understand that you're investigating that case of Gramps that he never resolved." She pulled out a sheet of paper and handed it to me, then walked to her office door and closed it.

"What's this?"

"Some friendly intel."

I quickly scanned the paper. It was about my travel itineraries to California and Connecticut.

"This is proprietary information—why do you have it?"

"Does this have anything to do with that missing killer, the woman Gramps has talked about—that case from the sixties?"

"This does not concern you. It's an FBI cold case we are hoping to close. Why do you ask?"

"Don't do that, Buddy. Everything that happens in the Talant family concerns me right now. I am an open book—everything is out there. This is Gramps's case, right?"

"Who told you?"

"A little birdie, that's all you need to know. Can't this just go away, for now?"

"Excuse me, are you telling me to drop a legitimate case?"

"No, not at all—heavens no. It's just the timing, hell it's fifty years old, a few more days won't make a difference. Someone might get the hint that there's an investigation going on—I don't need the questions right now. There will be better transparency later, I guarantee it."

I couldn't believe what I was hearing. "As in when-the-primaries-are-over time, maybe the election? You and I should not be having this conversation. This could be considered stepping over the line."

"I am in no way suggesting anything like that," she said. "You will be upsetting Gramps about this; it might cause him problems. You know how he feels."

"You've talked to Gramps? What did he tell you?"

"No, nothing about this. He's becoming more confused. I'm just concerned."

"Well, just stop. Getting involved in this, nothing good will come out of it, trust me," I said.

"Have you found this Roberta Davis?"

Eighteen months ago, when Jeanne decided to run for the presidency, she asked my permission. We were at Carrol's. To say it's been a whirlwind since then would be an understatement. Now, the party was into the debates, one a month, each in a different part of the country—a dog and pony show at best. The convention was a lifetime away. Her campaign had momentum and could not withstand any shock, and Roberta Susan Davis could be the shock. Jeanne knew about the explosion and now my investigation. Gramps had squawked, maybe she had someone in the Bureau. I glared at her.

"Yes, you should have told me she is alive," she said. "One of your interviews turned her up. She appeared at her sister's house in California."

"He should not have told you."

"That's the writer, Catherine Davis, right?" Jeanne asked. "I will only ask you once and this is important. It will never leave this room—what does she know?"

This is so wrong; this is how careers explode. "You cannot ask me this, and I will not tell you."

"I know everything; I need you to confirm it, Buddy. You are family, you understand. Should I make a call?"

Jesus, I felt like I'd been kicked in the nethers, I folded. "Yes, that's the name she uses for her books. Her last name is Wallace, Catherine Wallace. She says there's an issue about a sick grandchild. Roberta is her sister. She showed up asking for help to find a donor. The child has leukemia."

Jeanne stood there. I wondered what was churning, then she said, "It had to be a sick child—that's not good for optics. Damn, we need to find a work-around for this."

Optics? Work-around? Whatever this is had just morphed into a personal political threat and was getting out of hand. It was all in the past, the long-gone dead past, and besides, it had nothing to do with her or her campaign. If it came to light, the voters would understand—yet she was going full-blown paranoid.

"Do you know why I'm concerned?" Jeanne said, pointing at herself. "Here is an example: One of the other candidates—I will mention no names—a smart and ambitious congresswoman from upstate New York, was outed by an unfounded claim about a party she attended when she was an eighteen-year-old freshman at NYU—eighteen years old and twenty-five fucking years ago. A coed died at the party. When the firestorm and finger-pointing was over, the candidate stepped away from the campaign. There was no evidence about the candidate's involvement with the girl, a known drug user, or with any of the others at the all-girl sorority party. But innuendos, and more to the point, the complete and immediate collapse of funding, killed her campaign. I am not going to let that happen to my supporters. I am here for them."

"You are asking the impossible," I said. "Stay away from this."

"You have no clue as to what this can do. Sure, it was long ago, but there's blood in the water, and the opposition would love a red meat story. And the possibility that the FBI was caught up in the anti-war movement, the marches, and four deaths at an exploded house full of radicals is just that kind of story. Drag it all back, put it on the front page again. And my grandfather, our grandfather, a decorated war hero and FBI special agent during the J. Edgar Hoover regime, was involved? This is a story that must not get out, you need to put a cap on it."

"It is out; you put it there," I said. "I told you to leave Gramps out of that memoir; there was nothing to be gained." I pointed to the stack of books on the coffee table. "But it's out there now. It is your narrative. I'm not blaming you; you wrote what you knew." We'd had this conversation a few times a year ago when the autobiography was under development. Jeanne never shared the final draft of her memoir with me. That was at the advice of her then campaign manager, the one before the current manager. I'd have run my pen through whole paragraphs, her ego just had to have it all in there.

"According to you, Buddy, only one person, other than Gramps, was alive that knew what happened," Jeanne said. "Roberta Davis—and until a few weeks ago, I would have bet that she was not alive."

"She is. It would have been a bad bet."

"That's why Gramps said he's taking care of it."

I was stunned. "Gramps is taking care of it? How the hell can he take care of anything? He can't take pee without help." Then a thought. "Who is taking care of it for him?"

"You do not need to know. In fact, forget this conversation even happened. Gramps says he is very good at what he does. Buddy, I want you well away from all this. Deniability might be necessary. I'm taking care of it. It is important for the future of the country."

Jeanne looked up at the tap on the closed door. "I know, Beth. I'll be right there. Get everyone saddled up—we're going to the Speaker's office."

I stood there. I felt embarrassed and mortified by what I'd heard.

"Do we have an agreement?"

"I need to think about this," I said.

"Don't think too long. Events and history are overtaking us, Buddy."

Chapter 21
The Lion that Came Back from Death

Dorothy: Now
Boulder, Colorado
Late September 2019

I went directly from the Denver airport to the hospital; I talked to Mitch three times during the return trip. Steve met me in the lobby of Boulder's pediatric hospital.

"How is she?" I asked. Steve was the anchor to this storm-tossed ship. A broad-shouldered, dark-haired, fifth-generation Coloradan, he'd met my Marie at a summer music camp more than two decades earlier.

"There's been no change, and that's a good thing," Steve said. "Susie's resting; Marie's with her. My mom and dad are taking care of Helen and Tom. They are coming by later. Susie misses them. How are you doing?"

I looked at Mitch. I had told him what happened in California on the phone when I was in the San Jose airport. We had agreed not to tell Steve and Marie about why I was there and who I saw.

"Steve, I'm doing okay," I said. "I'm sorry I haven't been here for the last few days. There were a few things I needed to take care of. At least Dad was able to be here." I leaned in and kissed him. "Let's go see our baby."

We walked through the hospital. The children we passed were in wheelchairs and sitting in the waiting areas with parents and families. Most seemed happy, or at least as happy as they could be, considering. There were children with taped-up ankles and casts, and some maneuvered unsteadily on crutches. Others wore bandages or brightly knitted caps. I wished to God that Susie's problems were nothing more than a broken leg, instead of a body that was trying to kill her.

Our girl was sitting on her bed, holding an iPad. Her blonde hair was neatly combed, her brown eyes warm; the pink hospital gown was much too large for the small child. For a moment, all I saw was Tommy. Next to her was an attractive blonde woman in her early forties, my daughter Marie. Susan looked almost identical to Marie when my daughter was the child's age. She was knitting. I stopped at the door and tapped on the glass panel.

"Grandma," Susan said with a hoarse voice. The oxygen prongs and various wires connected to the child took an instant toll on me, like being slapped on my heart. I took in a deep breath.

"How are you, pumpkin? I've missed you so much," I said and looked at Marie. She put down her knitting and answered with a weak but affirming smile. The men held back in the hallway. I took a seat on the stool and rolled up close to the child and took her small hand.

"I'm doing much better today, Grandma. I even ate my cereal."

"That's a good girl. It's important to eat your lunch, too."

"I know, but I really would like a peanut butter and jelly sandwich. Where have you been? Grandpa's been here— where were you?"

"I had to see some people about helping you get better."

"Can they help?"

"I think so, but it will take some time. What are you playing?" I looked at the iPad.

"I'm not playing. I'm reading. Miss Braun has a couple of books she wants me to read. They are really good."

"Then what are you reading?" I looked at Marie.

"She's reading the first book you had me read, Mom," Marie said. *"The Lion, the Witch, and the Wardrobe*. It's a good distraction."

"I love this book," I said. "When I was your age, it was one of the first books I read, too. You know there are other books after this one?"

"Yes, and I have two of them on my iPad. Mom bought them. She says when I finish these, I can start the Harry Potter books. Mom thinks I need to be a little older. But these are just fine; I especially like Aslan, the lion."

I held the thought for a moment. The lion, the lion that came back from death, and I gently squeezed Susan's hand. "Yes, he is one of my favorites, too."

"I think that I am like Lucy. We are about the same age."

"I think you are exactly like Lucy. She is strong, loves animals, and is magical. She believes in miracles."

"Yes, I do love animals. Do you believe in miracles, Grandma?" Susan said.

"Yes, I believe in them. And the older I get, the more I believe in them."

A tap on the door interrupted us. A nurse stood in the doorway.

"Time for our medicine." She held a tray.

Marie and I left the room and met with Steve and Mitch. Outside, in the corridor, Marie turned to me. There was a fire in her eyes.

"What's going on, Mom? Where were you?"

"I was taking care of some things, important things that may help Susan," I answered. "She seems better."

"Yes, she does. But nothing has changed. She is still very sick, Mom. Steve and I are going crazy."

"We understand. I was meeting with some people your father and I know who might be able to help. They are people you do not know. The doctor talked about a bone marrow transplant, and they are helping us to find a match."

"And who are these people?" Steve asked.

"We are not at liberty to say, but they can help," Mitch answered.

"This is our daughter, your granddaughter, we are talking about. What do you mean you can't say?"

"You know what the doctor said about the Be The Match people; everything has to be in secret to protect both the donor and the recipient. I'm not sure that anything will come of this, but I am hoping for a miracle. Please let Dad and I handle this part of it. The hospital is pursuing its connections; I'm just adding ours."

"The doctors say that a match from someone in the family is best," Marie said. "They have already checked Wes and Cathy, and they don't match. Cathy was close but still not a ten out of ten. They just don't have all the markers. Maybe Steve's older sister . . ."

"Marie, you know she's probably too old," Steve said. "We talked about this. And besides, all the medication she's taking for her heart problems would make it potentially dangerous. We are trying to involve some people we know; Be The Match is great. We have talked with them; they are onboard. Just give us a few days."

"I hope to God we have a few days," Marie said.

Steve and Marie took turns staying the night at the hospital. Mitch and I stayed at a nearby hotel. Helen and Tom, Susan's siblings, stopped and stayed for a few hours. The hospital scared Helen, even at fourteen. It was a strange place, foreign to a girl on the cusp of becoming a woman. The only time she had been in the hospital was for a broken leg received in a tumble on the soccer field. Tom was interested in all the machines and wires. Susan tried to educate him the best she could.

The day after I arrived in Boulder, Mitch and I drove out to a park overlooking the mountains that flanked the western side of the city.

"Why do I have this feeling that this is all my fault?" I confessed. "The sins of the mother and my past."

"Please stop this guilt," Mitch said. "That's just stupid thinking; you are better than that. Anyway, you don't believe it. There is no heavenly retribution scale that must be balanced. What you did in the past is separate and apart from this, and has nothing do with Susan, or Marie, or anyone in our family. I won't have you thinking this way. It's tough, I know, but what's going on with the child has nothing to do with anything you did. Our little girl is sick, and we need to do everything we can to make her well. Your brother Thomas and his disease are in the past. The doctors and the science are different now; so much more is known. They will find a solution. I believe this with all my heart."

I leaned over and kissed him. "It's so hard. I have to tell Marie and Steve."

"And what would that do? It would only pile on more concern and pain. We will do what we talked about: Find a match for Susan, get her well. Then we will see what we need to do when this is all over."

"The FBI visited my sister and brother. It's only a matter of time. They will find me. I took a great risk going to see Cate. Hell, they could have been watching her house."

"They've had fifty years and they have found nothing. I seriously doubt they had someone staking out the place; this isn't a movie. They will do what they do. But I do know that Susan can't be confused and upset. Anything you do right now that might distress her is unfair to her and Marie. So please, we must keep this to ourselves."

The setting sun filled the western sky; shafts of brilliant orange and gold light filled the horizon. The mountains beyond glowed. It was all so different than the sunsets over Lake Michigan.

"I can understand why the kids love it here," Mitch said. "We have our lake; they have those mountains. It takes your breath away."

"I'm going to call Cate," I said.

"And what can she tell you?" Mitch said.

"I don't know, but anything will help."

"Hi, Cate, it's Dorothy." The car's speaker kicked on.

The pause was measured. For a few beats, my sister said nothing, then, "How's Susan?"

"She is doing as well as we can expect. She has her good days and bad. The doctors are doing what they can. It's so tough, and she's so small."

"I understand, Bobbie. Even John, as strong as he was, couldn't stop his disease. It just ate him up. I'm sorry, I didn't mean to say that. If I never enter another hospital . . ."

"That's the hardest part, hospitals," I answered. "Everyone tries to be helpful and say they understand. Yet, they build walls to protect themselves. There is another child on the floor with the same disease. He's a fighter like Susan, but the nurses must keep some separation. It would drive them crazy if they got too close."

The conversation paused. Mitch cleared his voice; his emotions had taken hold.

"Are you alone?" Cate asked.

"Mitch, my husband, is with me. We are watching the sun set behind the Rockies."

"Hi, husband, I'm Cate."

Mitch said, "Hi, Cate. I'm a big fan—was even before all of this. Now I know why Dorothy has all your books."

"Oh God, I called you Bobbie. I'm sorry . . . Strange, isn't this?"

"The last few weeks couldn't get any stranger, Cate," Mitch said. "Thank you for helping with Susan."

"You're welcome. After all, even as difficult as all this is, we are family."

"Someday, I would like to meet you," he said.

"And I you, and Joe would also like to meet the man who took such good care of our sister." There was a long pause.

"Are you still there?" I asked.

"Yes. FBI Agent Talant stopped by the house again. I told

him about you and your granddaughter. I could tell him nothing else; I don't know anything else. But I did tell him that what he knows about what happened is incorrect, and to be careful. And you need to be careful."

I wasn't sure what to say. I'd been outed by my own sister. I understood; I just wasn't prepared. "I think I understand. I didn't want to drag you and Joe into this."

"We're big boys—we can take care of ourselves. You take care of the little one. And, Mitch, take care of her."

"Sometimes, I think she took more care of me than I her," he said.

"Can I call you at this number?" Cate asked.

I looked at Mitch; he nodded.

"Yes, I'm sure if this phone were on somebody's radar, I'd have had visitors by now."

"I understand. Our love to the little one, and my love to you, too," Cate said. "Goodbye."

I took a deep breath and watched the last light of the sun disappear. Stars began to appear in the purple sky. Mitch took my hand and squeezed it. I cried on his shoulder.

———

Two weeks later, I sat with Mitch in the small conference room next door to the doctor's office. Sitting on one end were Jim and Donna Ingalls, Steve's parents. Marie and Steve sat between us. Marie held my hand. Across the table sat Dr. Isaac Bloom, and the chief pediatric nurse, Jill Norris. They had been with Marie and Steve since the day Susan was diagnosed.

"We have wonderful news," Dr. Bloom announced. "We have found a donor who matches Susan. All the markers and all the necessary traits are there. The donor is a woman who lives in Connecticut. She is about your age, Marie. Right now, that is all we are at liberty to say. She had been contacted and is excited to help in every way she can."

Steve put his arm around Marie and hugged her. "Finally, some good news."

"When can this take place, Doctor?" I asked.

"There are more tests to complete on the donor's side," Nurse Norris said. "These tests will help learn more about her health and ability to withstand the procedure. Even as minor as this is, for her, there is always some risk. The Connecticut hospital says that the donor should be ready next week. And there's a lot we have to do here to prepare Susan."

Donna took the arm of her husband and squeezed it. "What is it that you need us to do?"

"This is the hardest part for Susan," Dr. Bloom said. "She has been through all the chemotherapy we can administer. Her body has not responded the way we would like; you know that. As we've discussed, this bone marrow transplant is the next step in her recovery."

"You said there's a lot to do with Susan to prepare her?" Steve asked.

"Yes, we first eliminate the unhealthy cells. We will start with an aggressive type of chemotherapy; then, there will be radiation to ensure these diseased cells are destroyed. This takes about four days of intense therapy. It will be tough on Susan, but she will be fine. Then the donated bone marrow cells will be intravenously placed into Susan. These healthy cells will migrate into her marrow and replace the diseased cells. This is called engraftment. It will take a few months for the new cells to fully replace the lost bone marrow cells. It will be hard on Susan, but when they do their job, she will get better."

"Will it cure her?" Marie asked.

"We hope that it will," the nurse answered.

"And what are the chances of recovery?" I asked.

"For this type of leukemia, with a bone marrow transplant, it is about sixty percent. We have had better results here at this hospital; we have a seventy percent survival rate. There are no promises; I wish I could be more optimistic."

"And if this is not done?" I asked.

"The prognosis is not good. This is why we are recommending the transplant now. Susan is strong, but she is still just eight years old. The other therapies will continue to wear her down; we need her as strong as she can be. We would like to do this procedure sooner than later."

"How will you know?" Donna asked. "She's in so much pain."

"When her white blood cell count rebounds, this means that the transplant is making new blood cells. We will know in three months, but it may take a year to understand the transplant's success fully. She will be home during this time —that's a good thing."

"How soon do you need an answer?" Steve asked.

"Mr. Ingalls, the sooner the better," Dr. Bloom said. "I wish I could tell you otherwise, but time is not our friend here. Her body is doing what it can to fight the disease. This should be initiated as soon as we can. I would like to tell the donor what's happening so they can proceed. The donated marrow can be kept viable for many days, but the sooner it can be transported and transplanted and into Susan, the better. Timing and coordination are everything."

"I think we all understand," Mitch said. "Can you give us some time?"

"Mr. Cooper, please take all the time you need. I have surgery this afternoon, but Nurse Norris is available. Just let her know, and we will start the process."

Dr. Bloom stood, collected his papers on the table, and left. The nurse followed him out.

Marie started to cry; Steve held her tight. I felt helpless.

Jim, who looked like an older version of his son, turned to me. "Steve tells me that you went to visit someone before you came here. Can I ask who that was?"

"Where I went, Jim, is irrelevant," I answered. "But I can tell you that it was in the interests of Susan. There are people I know, from a long time ago. I asked them for help; they said they would do what they could."

"And this person who is a match, did this have something to do with them?"

"Jim, Donna, we've known each other for a long time. I love your son and our grandchildren beyond any measure you can think of. However, in this case, I ask that you just leave this alone until our child is well. Please, nothing will come of it. Just be grateful that we have a donor and someone who can save the life of our grandchild. Can you—can you do this for me?"

"Dad, please," Steve said. "Marie and I have talked about this; we knew this day would come. We knew that the only answer would be this transplant. We will deal with all this other stuff later. Right now, the only person we care about is Susan. The rest can, and in fact, must wait."

"Steve and I will talk with the nurse," Marie said. "This is our decision; we appreciate everything that is being done and your concerns. But it is our decision. We will proceed with the transplant. We will talk with Susie about it. She needs to understand and know what to expect. She is a strong and bright girl; we are proud of her. Mom, whatever you did to help with this, we are grateful. And someday maybe you will tell us what happened. Right now, I don't care. If it saves our little girl, we are eternally thankful. Steve?"

They both stood. Steve took my daughter's hand, and they left the room. The door remained open.

A week later, Susan, exhausted from days of chemotherapy and radiation procedures to clear her body of the diseased cells, slept fitfully in her room. I watched my grandchild do everything she was asked. It was the unquestioning trust of a child who believed, deep in her soul, that Mother and Father knew what was best. Susan showed heroism that most people never could or would understand. If it were possible, she seemed even smaller. Intravenous fluids flowed to her body; she kept nothing in her stomach.

The fluids were doing their best both to prepare her for the transfusion and keep her alive.

She'd been relocated from her room to a floor of the hospital that was for patients with compromised immune systems. The various chemo and radiation therapies had destroyed her immune system; a simple infection might kill her. On the fifth day of the process, she was brought into a room, secured to an intravenous pump, and over the next few hours, an orange mixture of preservatives and bone marrow cells was slowly transfused into her body. She felt discomfort but no pain. Her eyes looked expectantly at her parents; they were the only ones, other than the nurses, allowed in the room. They were dressed in hospital scrubs and wore surgical masks. Through my tears they looked like angels. The only person smiling was Susan. I stood in the hallway, desperately hoping for a miracle and the comfort of Mitch's arm. I felt like I was cut in two.

Later I learned that Susan told Marie, "Mom, I feel it. I feel my body getting better. It's working."

The nurse looked at my daughter and son-in-law. The brightness in her eyes said that she believed it, too.

Chapter 22
The 'Man' Comes to the Door

Cate: Now
Carmel, California
October 2019

Two weeks after Dorothy returned to her family, my phone rang. It was my daughter, Louise.

"Good morning, honey. Is everything okay? The kids, they good?" I asked as I put the phone on speaker and popped a pod in the coffee machine.

"Yes, Mom. All the usual—colds and scraped knees. What's that noise?"

"The coffee machine; it's burbling. It is only eight o'clock here. You know me, I need my coffee."

"You should watch how much coffee you drink. You know what the studies say—I sent you those articles," Louise said. "And those pods are filling up the landfills."

"Studies have also shown that if I don't get my coffee, someone might get hurt." I opened the machine, removed and threw the pod in the garbage, took the cup, and went to the table.

I waited as my daughter digested the remark. Humor, especially the mordant kind, was not her strong suit. Louise Nevis has a huge heart; she and Luke gave us two strong and independent grandchildren. But in an argument about whales, turtles, bees, or climate change, she is easily swayed. She was a sweet china doll.

"The weather here has abruptly turned hot for October; climate change and the chance that another hurricane will come up the coast," Louise said. "Hot and humid. I miss the softer weather in California. After the winter we had, it's what you can expect from climate change."

"Yes, dear. It's way too early."

"I know, I know," she answered sharply. "You'll see, someday. Right now, there's lots of dust in the air. Luke's practice is busting at the seams. And everyone has problems with their eyes—it's all so late. The clinic can't find enough experienced people, especially now with schools reopening. I help where I can; the kids are old enough to take care of themselves for a few hours."

"They will be fine. What's the problem?"

There was a pause in our conversation. I didn't want to remind Louise that we'd had a similar conversation a few months earlier while she and Luke spent a few days helping with the funeral. My daughter makes important decisions at a glacial pace.

"Two things. I wasn't supposed to tell you this, but Luke and I talked about it and it's really important to talk to you about both of them. A few months ago, the FBI stopped at the house and had a lot of questions."

"The FBI, about what?" I asked.

"Something to do with your dead sister, Roberta," Louise said. "They tracked us down using a DNA sample that Patty submitted for a school project. We didn't think much of it when she submitted it; she was chasing down the ancestry of our family."

"I have shelves full of our ancestry, Louise. Did you remind Patty of that?"

"Of course, but this was to better understand the technical aspects of genetics. That's what her teacher said. And now we have the FBI at our door. I knew nothing good would come of it."

"And they wanted what?"

"Whether we knew where Roberta Davis was. Mom, I have no idea, other than a photograph or two, who Roberta was. That was way before I was born. The FBI agent was insistent. Luke started getting upset. Then he began to ask Luke about his family."

"Did he give you his name?"

"Yes, and a business card. Special Agent George Talant."

"There's nothing to worry about, Louise. He contacted your uncle Joe and me a few weeks ago, also trying to find Roberta. We knew nothing about where she is then, even if she is alive. And we told him that."

I hated to lie to my daughter; it was breaking my heart. My rationale: I didn't start this; we did not start this. My family and Joe's know almost nothing. And what little we do know is none of the FBI's damn business.

"They want a DNA sample," Louise said.

"They will need a court order, and they may have difficulty getting one. What they want is to tie your aunt to something that happened more than fifty years ago. They will need a lot more than their suspicion to get that order. I wouldn't worry. What's the other thing?"

A pause, then Louise said, "I'll tell Luke what you said; he is of the same opinion." Another pause. "Remember a few years back when you were writing that book about transplants and medical procedures? I think you talked to a couple of clinics and associations?"

"Yes, it was a good story, one of my best," I said.

"And you asked Edward and me to get our DNA on some of the donors' lists, especially the bone marrow one."

"Yes, and if I remember, you were a bit hesitant. Your brother didn't object."

"He is too trusting, but that's his problem."

"I'm glad you did."

"Yes, you eventually convinced me, and now with this FBI agent . . ."

"Focus, Louise."

"Well, I wasn't sure how safe it would be or if the government might use it to track us down for something. But we did, even though I wasn't clear on how they would use the information. Well, they contacted me."

"Who contacted you?"

"Be The Match Registry; it's the association that helps to match those sick with leukemia with donors that have DNA that matches them. That's where you asked me to place my DNA. They can then transplant my healthy bone marrow in them. It can save their lives."

"You matched someone?"

"That's what they say. All they will tell me is that the person is a minor and has leukemia. They want to do a few more tests."

"My God, that's wonderful. Do you know where they live?" I was certain where, Colorado, and I knew why—I pointed Susan's doctors in her direction.

"No, it's all confidential. This is the first of several steps. If, after more tests, and it looks like I'm a match, they will take my bone marrow and pass it on to the recipient. Simple, really."

"You will be saving someone's life. That's special, honey," I said.

"And scary, too. I have to give them all this information, and another sample of my DNA to verify the sample already in the database. Maybe the FBI got the DNA from them."

"I am sure that Be The Match controls and protects their DNA samples, even from the government. So no, they did not get the match from them. Are you concerned?"

"Yes, very concerned, Mom. Luke says not to worry, and the kids are excited that I will be helping someone, but . . ."

"I understand. It's like a part of you is out there and you have no control over it."

"Something like that. It's spooky. I didn't give it much

thought back when you asked us to submit our DNA—no big deal, just that swab inside the cheek. Now, they tell me it will take a while to go through the process, interviews, blood tests, exams, and consent forms."

"Can't be any more difficult than when Patty and Brant were born. You'll be fine, and with Luke being a doctor, he can help as well."

"He's an eye doctor, Mom. Not a real doctor."

"Don't tell him that. Just don't worry, okay? You will do great. We seldom get a chance to help someone; I'm proud of you."

There was a pause, then, "Thanks, Mom. I just needed to talk to you about all this."

"Tell you what—when the time comes to take the bone marrow, I'll be there with you. Is that okay? Luke will have his hands full with the kids and the practice; it will be just the two of us. How does that sound?"

"Thank you—it sounds great."

The morning before Dorothy left for Colorado, I told her about my children being in the database for Be The Match. It gave Dorothy's doctors someplace to start to find a donor for her granddaughter. I assume it had paid off. My kids would not know where the idea came from. It would be better for them, or that's what Joe and I told ourselves. It was our form of rationalization. I also knew, in my heart, that this could not be kept a secret forever; it would come out someday. What would happen then, neither of us had any idea.

During the next week, I talked to Louise every day. She had up days and then down days. A dreamer, Louise takes after me a little, at least the part about arts and letters. She took literature classes at Yale, and in keeping with her father's desire, she tried the law. It was an unmitigated failure, not that Louise cared; the law was just not on her radar. She wrote poetry and a few short stories that were printed in a few literary journals. I was impressed and concerned; she reminded me of Roberta. The drive, the fire, the need to make the world right; it was all there. Then, Louise attended a dinner at a friend's house, where she met a young and extremely handsome ophthalmologist just out of Johns Hopkins. For the next few months, she never left his side, and one year later married him in a big, celebrity-thick wedding here in Carmel. My friends came from all over the world; many were friends who'd watched her grow up. Between ours and the Nevises' friends, they filled the old Mission church to overflowing. Even for Carmel, it was quite an event. The reception was held at The Lodge at Pebble Beach, quite a reversal for the blonde academic from Yale. Louise never said anything directly, but I learned through my New York publishing contacts that Louise's celebrity wedding pissed off more than one eastern radical publisher, who had thought they might get their nails into the daughter of the staid old novelist Catherine Davis. Well, fuck them.

Today, my daughter is the mother of two brilliant children, wife to one of Danbury's leading physicians, and involved in at least three charities that I know of. And she is anxious about having a small procedure to save the life of a child that she might never know. And is also being stalked by the FBI. I love her to death.

———

"Do you need that much?" I asked as Louise wrestled with her small suitcase. "It is just overnight."

"So they say. I want to be prepared," Louise said. We walked down the hallway.

My two grandchildren, Patricia and Brant, sat on the couch in the living room. Luke, the car keys jingling in his hand, stood behind them.

"You two be good," Louise said. "Dad will be back in a few hours. Grandma is staying with me at the hospital until tonight."

"We'll be fine, Mom. I read all about the procedure, and

it's quite simple, in fact," Patricia said. She was the preco-cious and inquisitive one of the two. "You have nothing to worry about. They give you localized anesthesia in the hip, then use a needle to withdraw the bone marrow from your pelvis. It's very simple."

"How big is the needle?" Brant asked. "Is it really big?"

"Big enough, brat," Patricia answered.

"Cool."

"You two are a big help," Louise said. "It's difficult having a bright and curious child, and another who watches horror movies all day. Luke, where did these two come from? By now, Patty probably knows more about the proce-dure than the doctors."

"There was a time when you were that child," I said.

"You do not have to be there overnight," Patricia added. "There should be few or no complications."

"I'm taking a mini-vacation," Louise said.

"Thank you for the clarification, Patty," I said.

"How big is the needle?" Brant asked again, a big smile on his face.

"Big enough to drain your eyeballs, brat," Patricia said. "And maybe turn them into raisins."

"I've asked you a hundred times not to call your brother a brat," Louise said. "It's not nice."

"Yes, Mother. But I do call them as I see them, and besides, I like the alliteration: Brant the brat."

"See what I have to deal with, Mom?" Louise said. "Yes, a mini-vacation, from all you guys."

"All right, you two, homework—now," Luke said. "When your mother gets home, we are all going to the shore for the weekend. It may be the last time this year. That work for both of you ladies?"

Even me, the staid old Californian, enjoyed the cottage my daughter and son-in-law owned on the beach near Misquamicut. A peaceful village that reminds me a little of Carmel in the winter—especially now that the summer crowds are gone. During the past few years, Luke spent a lot of time rebuilding it after Superstorm Sandy. The storm decimated the whole strip of beach and thousands of buildings and businesses. Homes entirely lost, hotels and apartments washed away, all a way of showing us humans how insignificant we truly are. Nonetheless, Luke was not going to lose the vacation home that had been in his family since before World War II. He took what was left of the building, drilled two dozen concrete piers thirty feet into the sand, and lifted the house twelve feet above the beach.

John and I were there the day they finished.

"It may not withstand the full wrath of God; that's up to Him. But, by all the powers that I have, it's going to withstand the next damn storm," he announced. He stood on the deck that faced Block Island Sound and yelled, "Come, Poseidon, do your worst!"

Louise added that with global warming coming and sea levels rising, this would all be washed away before their kids could inherit it.

Luke mumbled something about being able to then tie his boat up to the deck that surrounded the house, instead of keeping it in the marina a mile away. It would save a few dollars in slip fees. Louise looked at him; she didn't understand what he meant.

The drive to the hospital was quiet. Louise, usually chatty, said almost nothing. All three of us were deep within our thoughts.

"This is a good thing you are doing," I finally said. "It will help someone, probably save their life. Have they told you anything more?"

"No, just that it is a child with leukemia," Louise said, repeating things that I already knew. "The doctor said I am a perfect match, which is unusual. Not rare but unusual. I know about the procedure, but Patty didn't need to remind me. The doctor says that immediately after the donation, the marrow will be on an airplane. From there, directly to the recipient. I'm amazed at how organized this all is."

"It's the same in my world," Luke said, watching the

road ahead. "Corneal transplants can repair the sight of those with a dozen different injuries and sicknesses. In many cases, they travel long distances if there aren't donors in the local eye bank. It's all a wonderful world, Cate."

"I know some people who could use a brain transplant," I added. "The trouble is finding qualified donors."

"Oh, Mother, that's just sick."

"I agree, Cate. It's a short list," Luke said with a laugh.

I enjoy the company of my son-in-law. He is athletic, sails, smart, gregarious, successful, and deeply in love with my daughter. He reminds me of a young John; maybe that's why Louise loves him, that father-daughter thing. They have been married for seventeen years. Luke, with financial help and investment from his family, bought into an existing ophthalmology practice in Danbury. After ten years, he assumed control of the practice when the founder retired. He is well respected in the community. I'm not sure what will happen if, or when, all the drama and chaos about Bobbie becomes public. The claims of tricks, betrayal, undeserved compassion, forgiveness—all these bounced around in my head. I desperately tried, during the last few days, to come up with a scheme of how to keep a lid on all the damage that might flow from the eventual revelation or, God forbid, arrest and prosecution of my sister. It will not be easy.

The nurses spent the next few hours doing final checks and inserting IVs and monitors. Louise was surprisingly stoic. The patient in Colorado needed bone marrow, and Louise would donate some of hers. As Patricia had described, a needle would be inserted through the hip and into the back of the pelvic bone. Bone marrow would be extracted. Louise would be under anesthesia and would feel no pain. For a few weeks after the donation, there might be some localized aching and slight soreness, but no lasting effects. If Brant had seen the needlelike core device the doctor used to penetrate the bone, he would have been impressed.

That evening, I was with Louise as she recovered in her room. Luke had gone home to be with the kids. He would be back in a couple of hours to pick me up. Louise had asked to stay the night.

"How are you doing, pumpkin?" I asked.

"Mom, I'm forty years old. Do you still have to call me that?" Louise answered through pouting lips.

"You will always be my pumpkin; my father called me that. It's a family thing. We'll keep it just between the two of us. I won't embarrass you in front of the kids."

"Thanks, I think. My butt's a little sore—that's about it."

"That's good; you did well. They tell me that the bone marrow is almost to Colorado. It will be placed tomorrow. I'm so proud of you."

"It's you that made me do it. Not sure I'd have done it on my own; this is all too scary. But after all this, it's not so bad. And someday, I'll hope to find out how much I helped that child. It'd better do what it's supposed to. Besides, it would be special to know that you saved the life of someone, even if they are a stranger."

"Yes, it would, pumpkin." I rearranged Louise's long blonde hair and, with a damp cloth, wiped her face. Louise slowly closed her eyes and drifted away in sleep.

Forty years flashed by in an instant. The broken leg in elementary school playing soccer, the mice from the science experiment that mysteriously got loose in the house, the boyfriends—God, the boyfriends—the perfect grades in high school, a piano, the short-lived radical environmental turn at Yale, and meeting Luke for the first time. Such unknown roads we send our children down. She so reminds me of Bobbie, the lost body and soul of the family.

Decades ago, I decided that Roberta did die, gone like Tom, and Mom and Dad. It made it easier to remember her —we humans are strange this way. Only two people in my world know the truth, or think we know the truth. Know the truth; it will set you free—such bullshit. Lies are the opposite of truths; same coin, two sides. We build our lives on secrets, secrets we keep to ourselves, and secrets others keep from us. After Louise went in for the procedure, I called Joe.

"How is she doing?" Joe asked.

"Better than I hoped," I said. "I've been guilty of seeing her as a fragile child—she is hardly that. She is tough. Good God, where has all the time gone? The doctor doesn't see any problems; we'll know in an hour. She wants to stay the night. We'll take her home tomorrow."

"Good. And the FBI?"

"Nothing more than what Talant told us. She and Luke have not been contacted again. So, I'm not sure what his game is. Maybe now that we are on his list, he won't be bothering them."

"Good. Those two kids of theirs, still little pains in the butt? I didn't have time to talk to them much at the funeral."

"It was intentional. Louise didn't want you to influence them. You know she thinks you are weird and a social deviant—the crazy uncle in the basement."

"And I wear those badges with distinction, but those two are a strange pair. Reminds me of the kids in that family that lived in a horror house."

"The Addams Family, Pugsley and Wednesday."

"How do you do that?"

"It's a gift."

"No, it's not. It's really an annoyance."

"Joe, the kids are fine. Patricia is a beautiful young lady; Brant is as much of a pain as you were at that age. So, the family tradition continues. Patricia is like me; Brant is like you."

"Cute, something I have to live with. How is Bobbie?"

"I call her Dorothy now; it helps me to keep them separate. We talked a few days ago. All things being what the doctor says, the transplanting of the bone marrow will be tomorrow or the day after. Hopefully, and with a lot of prayers, it will save the child."

"It's all so different now, isn't it?" Joe said. "Two months ago, we hadn't a clue about Roberta. Now, my kids legitimately want to know why I asked them to put their DNA into the data bank for bone marrow. I used you as the excuse; they've always liked you."

"Smart skipped a generation in your family; I like them, too."

"I told them that a friend of yours needed their help. It was a good excuse."

"I'll keep up the cover. Lord knows, we may need it in the future."

"Not hearing from that FBI agent bothers me," Joe said. "He is a man on a mission, and with his grandfather so old, I'm sure he wants to chalk one up for the old man before he kicks off. And the connection to the presidential candidate, even more so."

"You have such a sympathetic attitude."

"Thanks, I try to understand. For us, we need to help the child first. Did . . . Dorothy tell you what she would do after all this?"

"No," I said, looking at Luke on the phone across the waiting room. "But whatever it is, she will protect her family, and I think ours as well. Besides, it may take months to fully integrate the cure into the child's little body."

"You and I will be fine; we'll just tell everyone to bugger off. Wouldn't be the first time."

"True, but our kids don't deserve it," I said. "And besides, we need to cover ourselves as well."

"Ah . . . now the conspiracy part of our evil plans begins —the lies, the deceit, the false clues. I wonder what Mom would say about all this."

"She would say: 'Family comes first.'"

Chapter 23
The Only Real Cowboy in the Room

Cate: Now
San Francisco, California
October 2019

The month had been a blur of phone calls, hospital updates, reassurances, and lunches with Alice and a few friends. I even sat down and began working out the next ten chapters of my book. I was amazed how much Bobbie's and Joe's diaries helped. One early October afternoon, after I returned from errands, medication pickups, buying printer ink cartridges, and picking up a takeout dinner from one of the Italian restaurants in town, I collected my mail at the post office. The stack held catalogs, a few fan letters, a small buff envelope, and the usual junk and claptrap. One was an Orvis catalog for men, John's name on it. I took in a breath on that one. The junk and the catalogs I eighty-sixed in the trash. I saved the fan mail for later, hoping it *was* a fan letter and not some obnoxious twit trying to correct my position on mulch or gardening or communist rule in some country somewhere. The remaining letter brought a smile, a small envelope with a well-known return address in exquisite penmanship.

It was from Jules Wallace. John's brother lives in a

charming flat in the Marina District of San Francisco. It has a postage stamp backyard that he wants me to design a garden for—never is too soon, as far as I am concerned. I'm a writer, not a landscape architect. Jules and his partner, James Dillon, have been together for twenty-two years and married for the past fifteen. They were two of the first to declare their love for each other publicly and apply for a marriage license. When the San Francisco mayor unilaterally declared that gay marriages were acceptable, the two were among the first in line. Jules never saw himself as a radical, rainbow flag-waving gay. As he put it, "I'm just an old fag who loves one man and does not want all this political goody-goody shit to mess up a good thing."

Inside was an invitation to dinner at Jules's house. My first thought was to say no. It was two Saturdays from now, a hundred miles away, and after the past emotional weeks, I'm both tired and in no mood to deal with his friends. And sometimes, to be honest, his guests could be bores. Jules and James love to collect people: painters, writers, agents, and even a few publishers. Jules would, as only a supremely gay host would, announce a topic and design the party around it—his events were almost always theme parties requiring costumes. The first clue was the drawing on the envelope of a cowboy on a bucking bronco. Really! And the requirement of western wear? In San Francisco? My first thought was the song "YMCA". Again, I considered refusing; everyone would understand. And besides, I didn't want to answer questions about John.

John has been gone more than three months; the time just escaped. The tears had faded—almost. I was sure, some mornings, I could hear John fiddling about the house—every strange noise reminds me of my loneliness. All the concerns of Bobbie are spread out in front of Joe and me; we still have no idea what to do. The issues of Susan's transplant are over there, just beyond the horizon, the cells doing their thing. Louise is fine, no complications. In time, the past might all come out—but that's in the future. Friends, especially Alice and Derek Pengrove, stop by, and others call just to make sure I am all right. More than once, I was positive they rang me up just to hear me answer the phone, make sure I hadn't offed myself, or had fallen in the bathtub and was dying of hunger. Alice again mentioned London.

"Derek's business required us to push back our trip. We are going after Thanksgiving," Alice said. "We are spending two weeks. Think about it. Christmas season in London can be so wonderful and special."

"Let me think about it, no plans yet," I said. "There are issues that I'm dealing with right now."

"Anything we can help with?" Alice said.

"No, but thanks. It's good to know you are there."

————

I RSVPed, splurged, and hired a limousine. It was a guilty pleasure that allowed me a few hours to listen to a book I'd wanted to read. As always, when in San Francisco, I stayed at the Fairmont Hotel on Nob Hill. It is a ten-minute ride to Jules's house in the Marina; I used the hotel's house car. I went all out Big Valley, a Mexican silver belt that cinched a long silk turquoise shirt over black jeans, well-worn and comfortable cowboy boots, and a simple squash-blossom necklace. Turquoise earrings matched a massive silver ring on the finger next to my wedding ring. A thin, dark blue wool wrap—I'd bought it in Santa Fe—hopefully would be enough to keep me warm this October evening. The shock was that it turned out to be one of the warmest nights of the year—it does that in San Francisco: cold summers, hot falls. The day had reached ninety, and for San Franciscans the heat was shocking.

To the surprise of the Fairmont driver, a wrangler stood at the bottom of the stairs to the upstairs flat. He was twirling a rope. The driver looked at me, then the man in leather chaps.

"Early Halloween party, ma'am?"

"Surprisingly, no. This is normal."

The driver wasn't sure how to answer. "Shall I come back to pick you up? I don't see a stagecoach."

"Good one. No, I'll catch an Uber or a cab. Thank you, pardner."

The wrangler asked if I wanted a bourbon and branch. I said yes. *Surreal* came to mind as I looked up and down the narrow street—yes, only in San Francisco. Then Jules and James appeared. We hugged and climbed the stairway to the second floor. Their place was one of those cheek-by-jowl affairs that fill the flatlands of the Marina District, garage down, flat up. Others were gathered in the living room. Fans had been set up in the corners to pull the barely cooler air from the front of the house out the back. I recognized Jules's brilliant agent, Roxanne Rostov, dressed in a full American Indian ankle-length skirt with tassels and turquoise. Across the room, a couple that I swear I knew but couldn't place from where were chatting with a well-known, yet questionable, publisher and bookstore owner in from New York. However, beyond the guests, standing in the window looking out over San Francisco Bay, was a broad-shouldered man in a suede jacket, jeans, and black boots. His silver hair combed back. I smiled and wondered where his Stetson was.

"You look marvelous, Cate," James said from behind. "We were so afraid that no one would show up in costume. You know you plan these things, and people can be so stubborn. But here we all are. It's a small group, just the twelve of us and this fucking heat. You know Roxanne, Jules's agent, and the Sloanes; Dinah has a new book out next month."

That's why I recognized the couple; she writes Western thrillers that have Indians and vampires and other monsters. One read was enough. James and I wandered through the remaining guests, shaking hands and passing French cheek-to-cheek pecks. The men were unsure what to do, with this whole "Me-too" movement thing hanging over their heads.

The man in the window never moved; he just continued to stare out the window.

Jules rejoined us; he handed me a tumbler. "I know you like your bourbon cool."

I smiled at the remark. "How's your foot?" I asked.

"A million times better, and finally no pain. It leaves me plenty of time to get ready for this winter." He looked across the living room. The setting sun was streaming up the street; the south tower of the Golden Gate Bridge was visible. "Benjamin, will you join us?" Jules said to the man at the window. When he turned, I took in a breath. Ben Taylor. Even though I knew, it was a pleasant surprise. Still darkly tanned but I'd not remembered the deep blue eyes. They twinkled in the room's lights and candles. The shirt was black under the fawn-colored suede jacket; the buckle to his jeans was the head of a buffalo. I'd forgotten how tall he was, at least six inches taller than me. I damn near choked on my next sip.

"Cate, dear, you remember Ben Taylor. He was at John's funeral," Jules cooed.

"Of course." I extended my hand.

"Ma'am, it is a pleasure to see you again."

His voice sounded like the rumbling of thunder in a far-off canyon.

"I'll leave the two of you alone," Jules said with a smile. "I see that the Emersons have arrived. She is working on a book about zombie clowns. Be nice, Cate. Both of you have a similar story."

I watched my brother-in-law scamper across the room to the entry. A reed-thin couple stood at the door. Jules's housekeeper was taking their jackets. Both were dressed in Johnny Cash black.

"It's wonderful to see you again," I said, my tongue trying to enunciate the words correctly.

"And you as well." His smile quickly cleared up my tongue issues.

"What did Jules mean, we have a similar story?" I asked, looking up.

"I lost my wife two years ago—cancer. Knocked me for a loop. And John, I'm sorry—he was one of the good guys. He will be missed."

"You said you knew John?" Remembering our past conversation.

"Yes, we met at publishing events in New York. In fact, he came to a conference in Jackson Hole a few years back; we spent an entire evening talking. That was the year I retired; all he did was talk about you."

"That was the 2014 Western Publishers Conference. I couldn't go. I think it was a deadline I was on, my book about the Revolutionary War. Book four in the series. Retired?"

"Damn, woman, they say you have one of those memories. That just proved it. Yes, that was it. And I had stepped away from my job as Colorado's attorney general; ten years was more than enough. You were a lucky woman; John was special."

"I am sorry I didn't find you that day. It was all such a . . ."

"Please, I understand."

"I was lucky; then, I wasn't. It seems like only yesterday. I'm sorry about your wife. What was her name?"

"Vera—we were college sweethearts. We met at Colorado State, which was back in the early '70s—interesting times. I had just returned from Vietnam; it was at the end of the war."

"My brother was there in 1968, Tet. Lost a leg."

"I met Joe at the funeral. Jules introduced us. He's doing okay?"

"Yes, he's great, but there were tough times back then. Today, he's a terror with a paintbrush."

"I understand all too well. Many of us vets fit that same saddle. Years of therapy and two books on Vietnam helped me a lot. And Vera was there for me, too. I loved your novel *Willow Bend*. I've not read a Civil War novel as remarkably correct and thorough. Good job." He clinked his tumbler against mine.

"Is this a mutual admiration society forming? I'm game if you are. So, attorney general?"

"Yes, I was the district attorney for Boulder for a spell, then when the state politicians needed an attorney to fill the spot left by my predecessor's premature death, I stepped up; was reelected twice. That was more than enough. For a while, it helped my book sales but cut seriously into my production. Walked away; now that felt good. Spent two great years with Vera before she got sick; it's been a hard road since. I love your stories. They are real; you get a feel for the places and the characters. Someday you must tell me your secret."

"Someday, I might just do that," I said. "You have given me a reason to go back and read yours."

"Thank you. We all need a little boost sometimes; our egos are our weakest step on our ladder. May I ask what you are working on? I understand if you don't want to say. Some writers believe it jinxes the whole thing."

"Not me. Truthfully, I've stolen a few good ideas during conversations about work. It's a story about 1968, or I'm hoping that's what it turns out to be. A strange and brutal year—assassinations, the war, student protests, political chaos. It was a time of broken hearts and shattered minds. I was fifteen; my brother and I lost a lot that year. Our parents died within a month of each other."

"Damn, I'm sorry to hear that. I was eighteen myself, facing the draft and a bleak future. My dad had just lost his ranch in central Colorado to the bank, and he was sick. Mom did what she could. My sister was pregnant with no prospects. It couldn't get much worse for us Taylors."

I looked at his glass and tilted my head toward the bar. "No one is permitted to wallow in pity with an empty glass; it's a rule. And God, I should know."

We talked with the other guests, and surprisingly, when

we sat at the table, Jules had put me at the opposite end of the table from Ben. We were the only two without a partner or spouse. I had a good view of the man as he talked with the woman to his right dolled up as Annie Oakley. She was next to the skinny Johnny Cash impersonator. His black clothing was about as western as he got. He told me he was from the Bronx and had immigrated to San Francisco twenty years earlier. All he did was talk about New York City. All I did was study the only real cowboy in the room.

During the dessert, we managed to find a corner.

"Why are you here, Ben Taylor?" I asked.

"My publisher is in town for the digital book conference. I needed to go through the next couple of years' worth of dates and appearances. He's got me booked two years out. I'm learning to write on airplanes, something I hate. I've just had a signing this afternoon in Marin County. Thankfully, tomorrow night I'll be back at the ranch. I love it there."

"You own a ranch?"

"Yes, ma'am. Just south of Vail, near a town called Red Cliff."

"I understand that the winters can be brutal."

"They are. That's why I stay in Cabo San Lucas during the worst of it. I'm no fool. Vera and I have a great villa that —" Ben stopped; a faraway look flashed across his face.

"That's okay, I understand. It happens to me; it's like it all never happened," I said.

"Sometimes, I'm positive it hasn't. Then, I reach across the empty bed . . ."

I touched the back of his hand; he smiled. Then I looked at my brother-in-law and his husband. "Those two, when did you meet them?"

He laughed. God, what a great sound. "I met Jules and James at a Western writer's conference a few years back. It was in the Black Hills. Jules constantly talked about you; he is your greatest fan. Do all the men in your life go on and on about you?"

I started to turn red. "He's a bit of a pain in the ass, but I love him. So, are you leaving tomorrow?"

"You look good with a little color," he said. "I finished up with my publisher this afternoon. Yes, tomorrow, then home for the rest of the month, then to Florida for a mystery writers thing. Florida—I just don't get it. Strange place."

"A mystery to me."

"And how is Carmel?" Ben asked.

"An expensive fairy land for adults and tourists. John and I raised two kids here in the Oakland Hills, across the Bay from here. When they were on their own, we moved to a cottage in the middle of Carmel. The current cottage, the one you saw, is our second; John had it completely rebuilt and modernized. My daughter is in Connecticut, and my son is here in Burlingame. And I have four grandchildren, and don't you say anything about youth and grandchildren. Some days I do feel like a grandmother, an old grandmother."

"I promise I won't. But you do look—"

I put my fingers up to his lips. "Do not say anything. It will jinx the whole evening."

He smiled and took my fingers in his and kissed them.

A perceptible jolt of electricity coursed down those fingers; I took a short breath. Damn!

As we were leaving, Ben asked if he could drive me home.

"Carmel?" I said with a laugh.

"Jules told me you are staying in the city."

"How did you know I didn't drive?"

"I watched you arrive in that hotel limousine. I assume that you're staying here in the city," he answered.

"I'm staying at the Fairmont, and yes, I would appreciate the ride. Let's walk a little; I can use the exercise. The Marina Green is just at the end of the street," I said.

He set his Stetson—yes, he wore a Stetson—and asked if I would mind if he lit a cigar. I said I did not.

"John loved an occasional Cohiba. Nasty things but even I enjoy the aroma."

The night was one of those exceptionally rare San Francisco evenings: no wind and delightfully warm. We strolled across the expanse of green grass to the breakwater that fronted the Bay. A massive container ship silently slid past, heading toward Oakland.

"A couple of years ago, I took one of those beasts in a complete loop around the Pacific," Ben said. "Got more writing completed in six weeks than I have ever done on the ranch: Seattle, Yokohama, South Korea, Shanghai, then back to Vancouver and then Seattle. It was six months after Vera died. Helped me get my head back together. It's not for everyone, but I enjoyed it."

"A ranch?" I asked, dumbfounded by the thought. "I don't know anyone who *owns* a ranch."

"Yes, small spread, twelve hundred acres. Last time I talked with the ranch manager—his name is Pete—he said we had about five hundred head of cattle, and some elk. He is also sure there is a wolfpack. The ranch lets me keep my boots in the game, as they say."

"So, you *do* have a big hat and cattle."

He smiled. "Something like that. I like it because it's quiet, like the ocean. Someday you should come up. We can go back in the hills, camp out. I have some of the greatest trout fishing you can imagine." Ben looked at his watch. "Need to get you back to your hotel."

"No rush."

We strolled through the Marina to his rental car. I put my arm in his. He drove up California Street to the hotel.

"Can I offer you a nightcap?" I asked, surprising myself and not knowing where the question came from. We both stood at the base of the steps to the hotel. The fog had just begun to return, breaking the heat wave. It capped the tops of the surrounding buildings; they glowed with an iridescent white aura.

"Not tonight, Cate. My flight is early—five o'clock to

drop the car at the airport," he said and leaned into me. "But that offer of a fishing trip is always on the table. Call me anytime." He slipped another of his cards in my hand-bag. "In case you lost the last one. My bona fides are on it. I may be a cowboy, but I do have internet, ma'am." I stood on my toes and kissed him, then left him at the curb and climbed the steps. At the landing, I stopped and turned. Damn, the man was still standing there looking at me. He tipped his hat, smiled, and climbed into the rental.

Chapter 24
A Political Debt that None Can ever Repay

Joe: Now
San Diego, California
October 2019

I'm about as unpolitical as a guy can get. I sit on the sidelines, like most Americans, eating popcorn and watching the political clowns make fools of themselves and occasionally looking in my wallet to make sure they left me some money. Our presidential election seasons are now multiple years long; they come as close as we can get to must-see reality TV. Honestly, most totalitarian systems are missing great stuff here. Imagine the dictators of China or Russia or some South American country parading their potential opponents in front of their citizens, and each one of these candidates believes they have a chance to throw the bum/dictator out. Then poof, they are gone. Yes, we have a unique and, at times, brutal system—but does it work? Better minds than mine can debate it; we, the average Joes, just have the right to vote. And with that, strange things can and do happen. The past twenty years attest to that.

I have my issues with all politicians; my missing right leg is a political debt that none of them can ever repay. It was their scheming—back sixty or seventy years ago—that eventually put me in that jungle. I didn't want to be there; no sane man would have wanted the honor. Yet, there they all were: Dwight Eisenhower, John Kennedy, Lyndon Johnson, Richard Nixon, Ronald Reagan, the George Bushes, Bill Clinton, and the others in the pantheon of presidents, making these decisions ostensibly for their citizens. Politics first, the people second. That day, a few months back—when I stood next to Cate watching Special Agent George Talant walk to his rental car—the thought that he was the brother of a candidate in this current horse show intrigued me. Jeanne Ellen Talant, the junior senator from Maryland, early forties, widowed-single, Irish red hair, sharp-tongued, and ambitious. Her face has graced the covers of a dozen magazines, even the *Wall Street Journal* monthly. She has the poise and the looks to win.

Nonetheless, yesterday I was at my favorite art store in north San Diego buying my usual quarterly allotment of paints, thinners, and canvases. Afterward, bags in hand, I stopped at the bookstore across the street. Both stores are a dying breed, and it's a damn shame. I've known Liz at the art supply for going-on twenty years, and her folks before that. The store is half the size it used to be, and Liz says that Mexico is her next stop, San Miguel de Allende. It's her turn to paint. I wished her luck, and to be honest, she's good. It's the online stores that are killing her; in that regard, she's fatalistic. She could have joined in, gone online, hired people to do the marketing and the order filling, fought the thin margins, and in the end—still end up in Mexico. She said it just moved her decision up. It's the bookstore I'll be sad to see fold. The margins are tight, always were. I believe that Doobie and Lin are the longest employed there. Others have come and gone over the years; there's been many. It is a stopover on their literary paths, and the chance to meet a few cool authors at signings. Cate always stops on her tours.

I walked into the bookstore with my two bags of art supplies (the canvases would be delivered), ordered a seriously dark roast Americano, found a spot on the couch, and collapsed. After thumbing through the endless and worthless postings of emails and junk on my phone, I studied the stacks of books on the table in the center of the lounge. A sign read: HOT TOPIC TABLE! Don't you love marketing?

Most were political autobiographies that included past, current, and prospective presidential candidates, their wives (or husbands), and even a couple by their children. It was a curious and even notorious collection of stories, revelations, and tall tales. George Washington and the claims about the cherry tree come to mind. In today's tribal politics, he would come under investigation as an attempt to parse his public proclamation: "I cannot tell a lie." He'd be called names, trashed on Facebook, and twittered to death. Rude cartoons would be printed about his teeth. Environmentalists would attack his fatal interaction with said cherry tree. And don't even start with his employees at Mount Vernon. Such is our world today.

A dozen copies of Senator Jeanne Ellen Talant's autobiography, *Once More into the Breach*, were stacked to the left among other fellow Democrats, old and new. Many were memoirs, or more precisely, polemics. The choice of which is left to the readers, I guess. The Talant cover had the tagline "The Story of a Family's Service to America"— catchy. I procured a copy and retook my seat on the couch. Nice cover, good headshot, well photographed. My years in marketing and graphics gave it eight stars out of ten. All it was missing was a dog—hefty, over three hundred pages, no bibliography or endnotes. Since I've been in the book business through Cate, tangentially and brotherly for over forty years, I've become accustomed to the flyby analysis and review. The preface took me on a short ride through the senator's life and general family structure.

I scanned the table of contents. The Talants have been in public service since her New York–born grandfather stormed the beaches at Normandy. After World War II, the family moved to Baltimore as the center of American power shifted toward the region around Washington, DC. All in all, an impressive pedigree for a family of poor immigrants from Ireland. Then again, almost every American family has a record of accomplishment of some kind, ours included. About a third of the way through, I came to the chapter headed "My Grandfather, Michael A. Talant." I thought of Cate and our conversation about Special Agent Michael Talant. This man was one and the same. I skimmed through the chapter; it was a dozen pages long. There was no photo.

Michael Allen Talant

Special Agent, Federal Bureau of Investigation

My greatest hero is my grandfather. I am who I am because of this incredibly honorable man. When I was eleven years old, we lost my father, Donald, to an armed right-wing militiaman during the siege of the Seeley Lake compound of the Warriors of Freedom. He was shot and killed by one of the ultra-conservatives as the FBI and Montana State Police surrounded the extensive complex of cabins and militia fortifications. Ten nationalists died, a dozen more injured, and eventually over twenty men and women went to federal prison. My father, Special Agent Donald Talant, was the only law enforcement officer fatality injured; six other law enforcement personnel were wounded, two severely. The right-wing press has called it the Seeley Lake Massacre. No specific individual was brought to trial for the murder of our father. Two of the men arrested said that shooter died in the assault on the compound. I'm not sure that we will ever know who did kill my father; the siege took place during one of the bitterest winters in Montana's history, February 1989.

It was our grandfather Michael Talant who took my brother and me under his great arms and cared for us as we grew older. In every way, he helped our mother through those tough times. Gramps became the father we would never know. He was there for our graduations, praised and celebrated our triumphs, and helped us during our college days and guided us through our later lives.

Michael Allen Talant landed on the beaches of Normandy with the 1st Army on D-Day, June 6, 1944. At the time, he was a twenty-two-year-old kid from the Irish neighborhood of Hell's Kitchen, New York City. The story goes he was a tough kid. His father, Donald, who my father was named after, had a difficult life, and died accidentally. When the war broke out, Gramps was just nineteen. He eventually joined the Army, and throughout 1944 and into 1945, fought his way across France and into Germany.

In 1947 he was recruited by his Army captain, James Overfeld, to join the Federal Bureau of Investigation. Gramps would serve professionally and diligently until his retirement. During his career, he was involved with investigations for the House on Un-American Activities in the early 1950s and assisted in the inquiry by the Warren Commission into the assassination of John F. Kennedy. And later, the notorious Watergate break-in. To say my grandfather had an exciting and thrilling career as an FBI agent would be an understatement. He often told us that he was just doing his job protecting America from its enemies from within and from without.

His most disappointing investigation, he's told me this more than once, was the inability to find and arrest the people responsible for the death of his oldest friend, FBI Special Agent James Overfeld. It was Sunday, the 1st of September, a few days after the anti-war riots in Chicago during the Democratic convention in 1968. The FBI and his Chicago task force had been investigating a house on Chicago's Northside that was suspected to be the headquarters for some of the most radical protestors and agitators that had been marching and eventually rioting in the streets. During those riots, dozens of police

officers had been injured, and even more of the demonstrators had been hurt and arrested. He was charged by
the director, J. Edgar Hoover, to find and arrest those
believed to be behind the conspiracy to shut down the
convention and to foment revolution on the streets of
Chicago and the nation. Please remember that during
the previous six months, before the convention, Martin
Luther King and presidential candidate Robert Kennedy
had been assassinated. Riots had burned neighborhoods in every major city across America. While others
in the FBI were investigating these assassinations, our
grandfather was trying to stop additional deaths perpe-
trated by these revolutionaries.

He later told me, when I was in high school, "Jeanne,
we had been observing this house in Chicago. We were
sure that it was one of the bases for these radicals. We
watched them for weeks before the convention, and
immediately after the riots, we were ordered to arrest
everyone we found in the house. Special Agent Overfeld
and Chicago police officer Thomas Belden—I'll never
forget their names—approached the house. I stayed
back at the car with the radio in case they needed
assistance. When they reached the porch, the house
exploded. The blast shattered windows in the
surrounding blocks, and with the fire that followed, the
structure was almost completely leveled. James and
Thomas were severely injured; they died the next day.
Inside the house, we found two bodies, a man and a
woman. The coroner says that they died from injuries
caused by the explosion; their bodies were burned
beyond recognition. Another radical was found on the
sidewalk in front of the house; he was injured and
survived. We had other suspects, but they were not at
the house. The investigation showed that the explosive
was dynamite and acquired from a feed store in Indiana
by a college-age student. The clerk described the dead
man in the basement as the one who bought the dyna-

mite. Two women were also seen at the house that day. We asked for arrest warrants for two Jane Does. We had their photos. It was more than forty years later that one of the women turned herself in. She was Deborah Toomey. She never identified who the other woman was; however, we had our suspicions."

Gramps never told me who this suspect was. He would only say that she was critical to the overall investigation into the riots and the trials that went on over the next few years, especially the Chicago Seven trial. My family hopes that the investigation can be brought to a conclusion before my grandfather, who has led an amazing life serving this country, grows too old to appreciate that justice can be served for his friend and those others that died.

I was stunned. Right here was the story of our family. There was no mention of her grandfather Michael Talant interviewing our family, no mention of any of what went on at the restaurant with Bobbie and Dad, and no identification of Michael Talant as the man who ran from the house just before it exploded. In fact, he says that he was on the other side of the house, parked on the street. Bobbie says he's the one who killed her friends and set the house on fire. There was no mention of Zeke Allanson at all.

I strolled over to the cash register and placed the book on the counter and smiled at the young woman.

"Don't you just love her?" she said as she passed the book over the scanner. "And it's signed inside the cover. She was here a few months ago; I got to shake her hand. She's wonderful."

"Thanks, Lori. No, I didn't see the signature. It might become a collector's item someday."

"What? A collector's item?"

"If she wins—if she becomes president."

Lori looked at me for a second, then connected the dots. "Oh, yes, of course. Maybe you should buy two copies."

"Thanks. One copy is more than enough."

Outside, I walked over to the small Italianesque plaza that had been recently built on India Street, set my bags next to one of the benches, sat, and called Cate.

"Are you in tonight? We need to talk."

Chapter 25
The Walking Wounded

Cate: Now
Carmel, California
October 2019

I was in my office working on the book's outline; the last three days had been exceptionally productive. And considering my latest interview with George Talant, I had busted through the slight block that had developed. I saw a story developing: One side of my brain said fiction; the other side said nonfiction—maybe true crime. To be determined. To be honest, if it went either way, my readers would still not believe it. The thought that my parents were murdered seriously distresses me. Mom on the floor of the bathroom, blood covering the tile from the cut on the side of her head. The door partially open. The forensics classes I taught for writers made me a disbeliever of what I remembered. Did someone surprise her? Was she pushed? Did she accidentally fall? And to this day I still don't know why Tack was in the garage. And the unlocked, yet ajar, rear door?

The same could be said for Dad. Why was he out along the Calumet Sag Canal? It's seven and a half miles from the house. During a college break, I went to the spot where he died. It was all confusing; I could not understand how my father, possibly drunk, could have ended up driving into an abutment maybe fifty feet off the road. Behind where the car hit the abutment, next to the canal, was a gravel paved clearing. Maybe he was coming that way. Most of the expressways weren't built then. Was he taking a shortcut? Did he stop for a smoke? Did he intentionally drive into the abutment—a suicide? Or was he there to meet someone; did something happen? There was a deep wound on the side of his head. He had a broken neck; the coroner said it was caused by the accident. I learned all this years later by going over the police report.

At the time, that fall and winter, I was trying to keep Joe from being his own car wreck. I remember helping him from the living room to his bedroom. He was never an angry drunk, just a troubled one. The grandparents were there to help. They were great. As parents this was as much a terrible shock to them as one could imagine.

By the time I went to Mundelein College, I'd developed a thick emotional callous over all the traumas. Joe, with the help of a shrink who'd taken on Vietnam War vets, accomplished much of the same. Walking wounded, we called ourselves. We were survivors of the war. Later it was described as post-traumatic stress disorder, PTSD—we both suffered from it.

Sitting on the table in front of the window were two cardboard boxes. Each about the size of one of those white banker's boxes sold in twelve-packs at Staples. On the sides were written "Charles Davis Effects" and "Helen Davis Effects". The use of the word *Effects* caused me to try and figure out who wrote them. It was cold, like how insurance covers "personal effects". Maybe it was Aunt Sue; my memory fails me over this. They were both dated 1969.

I started with Mom's box. Inside were letters in bundles secured with twine, all from Dad while he was in the Pacific during the war. He wrote for *Stars and Stripes*. There were two small boxes filled with black-and-white photos of the two of them and us kids. The ones of Tommy forced me to stop. Memories washed over me; I swear my preoccupation with ghosts was proven while I sorted through the personal things of a woman dead for fifty years. They were as revealing as her journals. I felt chills wash over me as if spirits were hovering.

Dad's carton was a treasure trove. There were a couple of small sports trophies, a gold-plated statuette of a baseball batter that read "First Place, Newspaper Guild". I never knew he played softball. There was a box that held Boy Scout paraphernalia, badges, a sash with merit badges, camping mementos, including a small penknife. I was stunned to find a small case with a Purple Heart. Dad was a writer; how did he get a Purple Heart? There were two bundles of letters, all from Mom. I promised myself I'd read these; they were important. There were framed photos, the small kind you would keep on your desk. The first was a group of men in Marine fatigues, then he and Mom, a couple of the whole family, and then one of us kids with Tommy, and one without. On the bottom were framed documents: his high school diploma, his college diploma, and under those, a Pulitzer Prize for investigative journalism; something I never knew—a goddamn Pulitzer Prize! Under the plaque was a manila envelope; it was thick. These had to be the notes that Bobbie talked about.

At my desk, I opened the envelope and for the next hour went through the pages of notes, newspaper cuttings, photos, and three spiral steno books. Every page was a revelation, especially the notes from two interviews he'd taken.

I called Joe.

"I'm sure you don't remember someone putting Mom and Dad's personal things in boxes the year after they died," I said.

"Not really. I expect that Aunt Sue or Grandma Kent may have done that," Joe replied. "I've never really thought about it."

"I have been carrying them around since we took them out of the house in Illinois. That was forty years ago, ten years after Dad and Mom died. Then Grandpa and Gramma Kent moved, and the house was sold. These boxes, and all the journals, were about the only things I took with me."

"That was enough—the boxes weighed a ton. Why?"

"I've been going through them. In the bottom of Dad's was an envelope. It held photos, notes, some of his steno books from interviews."

"And these were about the explosion?" Joe asked.

"Yes, but more than that. There are notes about the FBI and politicians relating to the demonstrations, the riots. These are the notes that Bobbie thought Dad had at the house, and the photos are the ones she took."

"Anything helpful?"

"There's an interview with a woman named E.S. Dad only used initials; my guess, if these notes were found, no one would be able to confirm who he talked to. I'm guessing he had a separate list of names somewhere, but not in this envelope."

"Probably doesn't make any difference. E.S. is most likely long gone," Joe speculated.

"E.S. says that she was watching out the window of her room, which faced the alley behind the house that exploded. There's a lot he took down, but the most important notes are that she saw two girls walk up to the back of the house, girls that lived there. She'd seen them many times. Then two men knocked them down as the men ran out the back door. Groceries flew all over. E.S. described one with black shaggy hair and a beard—she called him a hippy—and the other was taller, wore a suit, and his hair was bright red. When the house exploded, E.S. says she was knocked down and cut on her face by the window glass."

"You're kidding. Those are the descriptions that Bobbie gave for Allanson and Michael Talant. Bobbie wasn't lying."

"You thought she was?" I said.

"I don't know what to believe, after fifty years—but I believe Dad. What were the other interviews?"

"One with SAMT; I'm guessing that's Talant. It's in

shorthand. I need to sort through it, but it looks like Dad talked to Michael Talant. He knew the FBI agent . . ."

". . . and Talant knew him. Maybe he knew what he was. What was the other?"

"An interview with the manager of a feed store in Warsaw, Indiana. That's about two hours east of Chicago," I said. "It's about buying the dynamite. The manager identified a photo of Allanson that Bobbie gave Dad as the man who bought the dynamite. The notes say Dad was surprised, because the FBI, when they interviewed the manager, didn't have a photo. They based their ID on the manager's description of a guy with a beard and wearing an Army jacket."

"The FBI blamed Klausnick, said he was the one identified by the manager," Joe said.

"From just a verbal description. Anyone could be wearing an Army jacket."

"And a beard. When was the interview?"

"The date was September 12," I said looking at the notation.

"Four days before Mom died."

Joe and I talked for an hour. I told him I'd scan everything and email him. I also told him that I came to the conclusion that the day Mom died, someone had to have been in the house looking for these notes and photos.

———

Two hours later, my cell phone buzzed, just a number on the screen. And it wasn't an 800 number.

"Hello?" I said, punching in the speaker.

"Hi, Cate. It's Dorothy."

I was a stunned. Dorothy? Dorothy, Jesus. "Hi, Dorothy, is everything okay? How's your granddaughter?"

"She's doing better—that's why I'm calling. I'm at a pay phone. You have no idea how hard it is to find one these days. I'll be brief."

"Take your time."

"It's a good bet that your phone is tapped. My stopping at your house probably amped up the surveillance."

"A little paranoid, don't you think?" I said. "You are on my cell; it's a lot harder to bug."

"I've been this way a long time; it's hard to change. I'll be brief. Thank you for whatever you did to help find that donor. If it's one of your children, please don't tell me. The match was as good as it can get, and the transplant of the bone marrow and cells was done two weeks ago. It will take time to find out what the effect is, but the doctors are extremely hopeful. It will be at least Christmas before we know if it's beginning to work. So, whatever you did, thank you."

"You are welcome. It wasn't as difficult as you might think. I'm glad that we could help. And we do not know officially who the recipient was, so there's that as well."

"Thank you; *we* thank you," she said, then paused. "You said that the FBI had been there to interview you. You didn't completely understand why."

"I didn't then, but I do now. Agent Talant stopped by again, more questions. I told him that you visited."

"My God, Cate. I don't want you caught up in all this."

"Don't worry; I don't know where you are, what your last name is, anything. I could tell him almost nothing, other than that your granddaughter was ill. That's it. He's fishing; I can see it. But I'm also afraid for you."

"I'll be all right—don't worry about me," Dorothy said. "I brought this all on you and Joe. I'm going to stay away; you won't hear from me again."

I couldn't let her go. "Could Mom and Dad have been murdered by someone trying to find you? You knew things; you were there. You said in your diary that you identified the FBI agent who ran out of the house. His name was Michael Talant, wasn't it?"

Dorothy paused again. "Yes, that's the name."

"The FBI agent who interviewed us is his grandson; this is all too much of a coincidence."

A long pause. "I agree. Who is the agent?"

"Special Agent George Talant; he is out of the Washington office. His sister is Senator Jeanne Ellen Talant; she is running for president."

"Jeanne Talant, her? She is the granddaughter of the man who killed my friends?"

"Yes," I said. "I am beginning to believe the government was behind a lot of what happened. You said there was another man with Talant that afternoon?"

"Yes, his name was Zeke Allanson—at least that's the name he gave. We never confirmed it. Allanson was a student at the University of Michigan. He was one of the senior people in the Michigan SDS; he came down to assist us. He was worthless, and the more he hung around, the more I thought he was creepy, maybe even an informant."

"Describe him."

"Average height, white, full black beard, and a head of black curly hair—all too perfect, I thought. So did Abe Klausnick; he got into it with Allanson. He's also the one who provided the dynamite. He supposedly took off the week before the convention started and returned to Michigan. Then he appears that day at the house with Talant, and all hell blew up. After that, I assumed he was FBI, an undercover agent; so did my friend Debbie. To this day I believe they blew up the house and killed Abe and Barbara. The other two policemen were collateral damage."

"The FBI still blames you and your friend for the explosion."

"Yes, of course. Maybe to cover Talant and Allanson's work, I don't know. Dad told me it was in his notes. He was writing a story about the convention, the police riot, and the explosion. He was tying it together in the weeks after Mom died; he said it was his therapy. It was going to be a multi-part article in the *Daily News*."

"I found those notes and photos; they were in a box of his things. You continued to talk to Dad after you identified Talant? You helped him?"

"Yes, then he died in that accident. On the day of his funeral, when everyone was at the cemetery, I went into our house and took all the notes and documents I could find. Dad had hidden them; he told me where. There are also photos Debbie took when he met with Talant at the restaurant that day. I couldn't take them with me, so I put them in one of Mom's storage boxes; they were in a manilla envelope. They are with the ones she kept in the cabinet under all the family diaries."

"I am looking at them right now—everything is here," I said. "Miraculously, they survived the past fifty years. They have been on a shelf in my garage for most of them. It's almost exactly the way you described it."

"Almost?"

"Did Abe Klausnick have a beard?"

"Yes, and a full head of wild hair. Handsome guy. I think he and Dumas were into each other."

"It looks like the FBI set him up as the guy who bought the dynamite."

"It was Allanson."

"Not if they wanted to protect him," I said. "I wonder if he is still alive. Have you ever tried to find Zeke Allanson?"

"No," Dorothy said.

"Maybe it's time to see if the son of a bitch is still alive. Maybe he can help fill in the blanks. But there's one thing I can tell you: Michael Talant is still alive and is doing everything to hide the truth so he can to protect his family—be careful."

Chapter 26
If You Are Being Followed, You Really Aren't Paranoid

Dorothy: Now
Grand Haven, Michigan
Late October 2019

It was a long plane trip from Colorado to Michigan. A weather delay in Denver, and a plane change in Midway, made me four hours late to Gerald R. Ford Airport in Grand Rapids. Mitch stayed in Grand Haven on this trip. He and a couple of his buddies were scouting for the coming deer season, a tradition going back thirty years. The start of the season was a month away; he would pick me up when I returned. We wives all knew it was a way to spend a few days during football season in the cabin. It was jointly owned and buried deep in the forest east of Baldwin. I do look forward to the end of the hunting season; they usually return with enough venison for the year.

During the return trip from Colorado, I grew even more paranoid. I watched for the same faces following me. When I got off the plane in Chicago Midway, the first person I looked for was an FBI type. I swear I could smell them, the same in Grand Rapids. When Mitch picked me up, we took a different road home—stopping at one point so we could see if anyone followed us. I told him about the kids and my conversation with Cate. Mitch is getting into this; I'm not sure if he's humoring me or joining me in my paranoia. As they say, if you *are* being followed, you really aren't paranoid. We drove around our neighborhood; there were no unidentified cars or trucks. We took a few minutes and talked to a few of the neighbors; most have been here a long time. Mitch told them about some kids driving too fast as an excuse. No one saw anything out of the ordinary.

That evening, I sat at the dining room table and started searching for Zeke Allanson on the laptop computer. I guessed his name was Ezekiel—but to be honest, it could have been made up. Everything about the man could have been a fiction. If so, I'd know soon enough—I thought.

To my shock, a man with that name was right here in Michigan, not forty miles away. His name was in an article about a well-respected FBI agent retiring. The archived story was in the *Grand Rapids Press*. Being a subscriber, I logged in. The article was dated September 14, 1999. It was short and concise.

Ezekiel X. Allanson Retires
Former FBI Agent Hangs It Up

Ezekiel Allanson, Zeke to his associates, retired last evening at a party with his friends at the Elk Lodge in Grand Rapids. They celebrated Zeke's thirty-four years in the FBI. He spent those years as a special agent during the troubled times of the Vietnam War, assisting in multiple kidnapping and financial fraud cases throughout the Midwest, and eventually aided in the operations at the FBI's Detroit office. Originally from Grosse Pointe, Michigan, Zeke joined the FBI soon after he graduated from Oakland University in 1965.

Bingo, it had to be him. Directly below that first search listing was his Facebook profile. I was shocked. The man was my age and had a Facebook page. Even I didn't have a

Facebook page. All the kids do; no way to stop that. Me, I wouldn't even consider it. But there he was. It was thin, just two photos, one of him that I recognized. He had twelve friends—now that was pathetic—and two were veterinary hospitals. He listed himself as retired, his former job as an FBI agent, and that he lives in Cedar Springs—that, I couldn't believe—and was originally from Grosse Pointe, Michigan. The bio picture on the page was of a double-wide trailer—no face. The background header was a photo of a dozen cats.

"Mitch, do you know where there's a trailer park in Cedar Springs?"

"Yes, it's on the north side of town, off 18 Mile Road. A little trashy but does what it's supposed to. Why?"

"I found Zeke Allanson, or at least he lived in that trailer park three years ago. That's the date of his last post on Facebook. You want to take a ride tomorrow to find this guy?"

"Not tomorrow. Rotary lunch, second Tuesday—you know that."

"How about Wednesday?"

"It's a date. I would like to meet this guy—should I be packing?"

"Cute. He's a retired FBI agent. You wouldn't have a chance."

"Such confidence."

I couldn't find a specific address. just the picture he posted of his trailer. I printed it out. I also searched through the obituaries in the *Press* and a couple of other papers—nothing for an Ezekiel Allanson. If I had access to police data, I could probably find more: DMV, trailer registration. I sure wasn't going to ask them for help.

I would call Cate back after I confirmed that Allanson was still alive. After that, I wasn't sure what I'd do.

———

It was one of those last days of fall, still warm but quickly chills down at night. It took an hour to reach the trailer park in Cedar Springs. To say it was depressing was to glamorize the place. Single trailer homes, interspersed with more affluent double-wides, sat side by side in a somewhat orderly fashion. Each trailer had a shingle of concrete to its left side for the ubiquitous pickup truck or old clunker. Rust was the dominant color theme.

I pointed to the sign that read OFFICE; Mitch pulled into one of the two parking spots. A small, faded sign read, "For Future Residents of Great Oaks Terrace." A woman in shorts and a flowered muumuu top sat in a plastic lawn chair, a paperback book in her lap, a low table with a full ashtray to her right side. Before we made five steps from our truck, she yelled, "Can I help you folks?"

She knew we weren't here to check out the potential for accommodations; our Ford F-150 was worth more than the first ten trailers we passed on the way to the office.

I did the talking. Mitch hung back.

"Maybe you can, ma'am. This is going to sound strange and all. I'm looking for someone."

"That's not too strange for this place; you wouldn't be the first, lady. Most the time, it's the sheriff."

"You see, my parents died when I was young. I had one of those DNA things done, hoping to find out who I was and all. You understand?"

"Like they talk about on TV? Ancestry.com or something? Always thought it was a way to separate you from your money, a scam." She looked at our new pickup. "But I's can see that ain't your problem, honey. So?"

"Well, I had the test done, and they said I had a match to a relative, somebody named Ezekiel Allanson. I never heard of him till now. As I said, it's all strange. For seventy years, I thought I was alone in this world, no relatives or family, and then this test says that I have a cousin. And not fifty miles from my home—we've just come over from near Jackson. Damnedest thing, I'll tell you."

She studied the two of us, then lit a cigarette. "Look, honey, I don't know anything about all this DNA shit. Magic as far as I'm concerned. It's voodoo mumbo-jumbo. What do you want me to do?"

"Is Ezekiel Allanson still living here? I want to meet him. I've got seventy-five years of questions. You'd be a big help if you'd tell us that he does and in which trailer. Oh, and my name is Debbie. This is my husband, Dave."

She continued staring. I guessed that the glass next to the ashtray was not filled with iced tea. "I'm Julie. Been manager here for fifteen years. Always wondered about that DNA thing; there was a show on *Ellen* about it. I guess it wouldn't hurt—now if I could only remember which space he's in."

Mitch removed a fifty from his money clip. He handed it to Julie. "Maybe this will help jog your memory."

"Honey, you paid too much to jog this addled brain. Not that I'm complaining, thank you. Zeke stays to himself. I haven't seen him for a few days. I do a welfare check just to make sure he's alive. He's got emphysema and some heart issues; I got a touch myself. These stupid cancer sticks will do that. Ain't gonna stop; too late for me. Zeke's in slot 283. It's around the corner there, on Cherry Lane. Old double-wide, rusty awning to the right side over the door, a beat-up old yellow car in the apron on the left. I hope he's related. He could use some help."

"Thank you."

"Zeke should be in. Knock loud—his hearing is bad. Tell him that Julie said good morning." She crushed the cigarette.

I tapped on the screen door of the trailer; the inside door was open. The aroma of bacon and nicotine drifted out through the mesh. I tapped again.

"Give me a goddamn minute, would you, Julie? Damn, woman," a hoarse voice said from inside. A shadow appeared in the door. "Who the fuck are you?"

"A ghost from your past, Zeke Allanson."

The shadow didn't move. A meow broke the silence; a tawny-colored cat walked between the shadow's legs.

"Go back to your bed, J. Edgar," the shadow said.

"Zeke, it's been more than fifty years. The least you could do is let me in," I said.

"And who the hell are you?"

"Bobbie Davis, Zeke. The last time I saw you was when you were running out of the back door of a house in Chicago just before it exploded, killing four people."

The shadow started coughing, big deep coughs, hack on hack. The shadow turned away from the door, crossed the room unsteadily, then collapsed onto a pea-green couch. I pulled the screen door open; we followed Zeke into the living room. He put on a transparent plastic mask over his nose and mouth; a thin, clear tube ran to the oxygen canister next to the couch.

"You okay?" I asked.

He glared at the two of us, and in a muffled voice said, "No, I'm fucken dying. Why the hell are you here?" He took a succession of deep breaths, then pulled the mask away. He visibly relaxed. "Without my canisters, I'd be dead in a week. Sit. I knew someday you would show up, or that other bitch, Debbie something. Someday, I just knew it." He held the mask to his face. "Today must be my fucken birthday."

"Debbie Toomey, she died last year. She died alone because of you and Michael Talant not telling the truth about what happened."

"And you—they let you go? You get out of prison?"

I looked around the living room. I knew now why my nose and lungs were starting to close; I counted at least eight cats on climbers, couches, chairs, and beds. Where there's eight, there are more.

"They never found me, Zeke. I've been hiding since that day. They want me for murder; you know that. But I didn't do it; you know that, too. I want you to tell them—go to the FBI, get me out from under all this. For once, do something right with your miserable life."

"Me? You were the fucken revolutionaries hell bent on destroying the country. We were there to stop you. I remember every minute I was with you and that group of sunshine radicals. That guy your husband?" He pointed to Mitch, then coughed. "Have you told him what you were like back then? The drugs, the boyfriends, the stuff all twisted up in your head. Yes, I saw it all; it all went into my reports. You were one twisted up bitch."

"You're a bastard," I said. "Did you put in your reports that it was you who bought the dynamite? You who brought it to the house."

"No. Who the fuck cares anymore? Yeah, I bought it, Talant set it up. Gave me the place in Indiana and the extra money I needed. You fuckers didn't have enough."

"I want you to tell the FBI, tell them what happened."

"What I'll tell them is that you bought the dynamite— fuck, it was you making the bombs. I saw them on the table and what that Polack was doing. I'll tell them it was you— all you." He grinned through the oxygen mask.

"You son of a bitch," Mitch said.

Allanson chuckled and stroked the neck of an orange cat. "Yeah, we were there, me and Talant. Talant wanted to get the dynamite out of the house, I don't know why. The whole operation was shutting down now that the convention was over. He wanted the dynamite gone, said it was too dangerous—the son of bitch was growing a conscious. When we went down the stairs, that fucking Polack wanted to know why we were there. Then the kid pulled a gun, and Talant pulled his; it was a standoff. Then a girl came down behind me with a baseball bat; took a swing at me and missed. Then the Polack lunged at Talant, trying to knock him down. Talant smashed him across the head, hard, fucking hard, with his fist. The girl screamed. I grabbed her hand and pulled her down the stairs. She stumbled and I smashed her hard into the concrete floor. It was over in seconds. Talant picked up the bat and made sure they were dead. Me, I really don't know. Maybe they were, maybe not."

"Maybe? Maybe?" I yelled, reimagining what Allanson was telling us.

"Whatever, they deserved it. They were going to kill people—you were going to kill people. Talant then calmly walked over to the cans of gasoline and poured one all over a stack of boxes and junk. He looked at me and said, 'No evidence—it will look like a fucking accident.' He was smiling; the man was batshit crazy right then. He could be a mean bastard—that's why Washington liked him, I guess. He then took a couple of the fuses, calmly stuck them in the ends of some of the bundles of sticks, then walked over to the stairs, dropped a match on the gas, and we ran up the stairs. We busted out the back door smack into you and that other bitch. You should have been killed, caught in the explosion. In fact, for a long time I believed you were dead." He started coughing, then wheezed out, "None of you were to be left alive. Those were our orders. Leave no one."

"Who told you to leave no one alive?" Mitch asked.

"I assume the higher-ups, maybe Washington. Talant was the team leader; he told me what to do. He's the one who brought me down from Ann Arbor. You know, my nose was never right after that Polack punched me. When I saw that he was dead, I laughed—I fucken laughed. So, Bobbie Davis, or whatever you are calling yourself, fuck you. I hope they find you, throw you in prison—maybe you'll die there." He pushed his mask to his face and started sucking his oxygen again.

"We've got to get out of here," Mitch said. "This asshole won't do anything to help. And he's not worth shit."

"Help? Help what? Maybe I'll turn you in for the reward. Got to be sizable by now." One of the cats—a striped, gray, feral-looking thing—climbed over the orange cat and onto Allanson's lap. "That's a good boy, Elliot. They'll be leaving soon; I know you're hungry."

"I wouldn't know about the reward," I said. "It's been

fifty years—look at you now. Alone, sick, bitter, and cats. I was hoping you could help clear my name, but I see that God's vengeance has triumphed."

"Triumphed? God damn, woman, we all live in the world we create. This is my heaven, just a fucken paradise. Let me tell you something you don't know; I was there—and I got this when it happened." Allanson raised his arm and pulled up the sleeve of his sweatshirt; a scar wrapped his left arm a few inches above his wrist. "Your fucken dog did this to me. Damn near ripped off my arm. Still causes me problems, pain, stiffness."

"What the hell are you talking about?" Mitch said.

"Wouldn't you like to know?" He continued to grin. "It's been twenty years since they pushed me out of the FBI, said I was unreliable, had a drug problem—allowed me to retire, the fuckers. And they've treated me like shit since. I wanted disability. What could I do? Talant told me to keep my mouth shut. Wouldn't do any good if I did say something; it would be my word against his. Probably end up in a ditch or something. So, like a good soldier, I kept to myself, real quiet. It's okay, no big deal. I went where they sent me, no field work. The checks came—finally even finagled a disability. And, until that bitch Toomey turned herself in, I couldn't have cared less." A strange smile came over Allanson. With his left hand, he stroked both cats. It was a gaunt, toothy grin. "Hey, that day your mother died, I was there, in the house, looking for your old man's notes."

"What? You were there?" I said.

"Talant sent me in. He waited in the car. We wanted to know what your old man knew about the explosion, what *you*, Roberta Davis, knew. He was sure your old man knew where you were, he even hoped that you were in the house when it exploded. He was still pissed about the decoy trick at the restaurant. Even Washington was pissed at him for that. I went in through the unlocked back door and walked down the hallway. I heard the shower running; no one was supposed to be there—that's what Talant said. Then that fucken dog came out of nowhere. I ran down the hall. When I passed the bathroom, the door opened. A naked woman stood there, screaming. I pushed her away; she fell. Then that fucken dog had me by my arm. I dragged him down the hallway, trying to throw him off. I pulled open the first door I came to and tossed the fucker in. If I had a gun, I'd have shot the son of a bitch—hate dogs, worthless shitters." The cats purred in unison.

"That's why Tack was in the garage!" I said. "What do you mean my father's notes?"

"What?" Allanson said. "All this was your old man's fault. He wanted a meeting with Talant; he wanted to know about the explosion. Told us he had photos. Jesus Christ, reporters think they are fucken immortal. Can't be touched. That's why I was at your house, to find his damn notes and photos."

"You saw my father?"

"Yeah, sure, a week or so later."

A hideous grin slowly grew on Allanson's face. "Talant knew him and set up a meeting along a canal in Chicago somewhere. Talant drove. Real private; nighttime—near a bridge; there were lights above. Your old man picked the spot—he showed up drunk, yelling. He was crazy, over the edge. Started pushing Talant around. The two of them got into it. He was screaming something I couldn't understand. All I heard was the word *wife*. He said it three or four times. Then, he had a pistol in his hand and was waving it around; he swung it toward Talant. Talant whacked him on the side of the head with his own revolver; he collapsed to the ground. Talant hit him hard in the face and head a bunch of times. We dragged him to his car and dropped him in the front seat. I made sure the engine was running and aimed it at the bridge. Talant edged up in his car behind the car, tapped the bumpers, I dropped it in gear, then Talant pushed the car straight and hard toward the abutment. He got up enough speed and the car slammed head-on into the concrete wall. The stupid fuck."

I was stunned. This piece of shit had admitted to complicity in the deaths of my mother and father. If he hadn't been there, she wouldn't have fallen; she would not have died. He knocked her down. Dad knew or suspected. They crashed the car into the concrete wall. They killed him. Dad had a gun—I wish to the Lord above I had one now.

"We need to get out of here, Dorothy. This shit isn't worth it," Mitch said, then he sneezed. "We got what we came for."

"Dorothy? Fucken Dorothy? That your name now? You should have left this all alone. Talant's probably been dead for years; you're in the clear. I sure as hell don't give a fuck about you. You should have left this all alone. Done nothing —nothing."

"Michael Talant is still alive," I said. "And his grandson— also an FBI agent—is hunting for answers. I'm sure you are on his list. If I can find you, they will, too. He will rain holy hell on you. They are playing for bigger things now. They will find you."

"You think I'm going to tell this story to the FBI? No fucken way. I remember what's in that report. That's the story, the *real* story they'll hear. Hell, it's the story that Talant constructed."

"You are a dead man."

Allanson sat there, the grin gone, his hand on the cats. He squeezed. The gray cat howled and jumped off his lap. "Well, fuck me, then. You couldn't leave this alone. Talant, alive? Jesus, I knew his son, don't remember the name, the one that got killed. Mike wasn't the same after that. I heard he helped raise those grandkids. And now his grand-daughter is running for president—I know all about that. I keep up with the news. Old Mike is cleaning it all up; no detail too small, he used to say. Talant will probably kill me anyway. Why the hell are you here?"

"I came for your head. You were a slimy little, dope-smoking weasel back then, Zeke Allanson, and fifty years later, nothing has changed. But you aren't worth it. You will die here, and before they find you, the cats will eat your liver. That's my vengeance."

Allanson stared at us from his open door, and as we pulled away from the trailer, he gave us the finger.

"My God, what the hell was all that? I don't know what to say," Mitch said as we turned back onto Highway 131. He reached into his breast pocket and handed me the digital recorder. "If it comes to it, there's more than enough here to get an attorney to look at what happened back then—and no wonder the Talants are scared."

It took an hour of the filtered air in the F-150 to open our throats and lungs.

Chapter 27
One Thing Often Does Lead to Another

George Talant: Now
Annapolis, Maryland
Late October 2019

I watched the latest debate with great interest. Jeanne, as always, stayed back until the last fifteen minutes, then destroyed the others. All their promises, promises that they hadn't kept as politicians, she reminded them of every one of them. Two were current governors, three were congressmen—two women and a man. One other was a senator from California, and two were worn-out politicians making their final attempts at the presidency. She showed strong and bright through all their malarkey and false sincerity; she was good, damn good, and I was proud of my sister and her performance. I was also troubled about what she and Gramps were doing. They were putting me in a bad spot. The worst case was that I had to choose my oath or my family.

The next morning, on my desk was the report from Special Agent Doris Twiley out of the Grand Rapids office. I'd read a lot of reports over my years, but this was one of the strangest and, considering the result, most disturbing and personally dangerous.

We found Ezekiel X. Allanson through his SSI and FBI pension records. He was living in Cedar Springs, Michigan. He was seventy-seven. I said *was* because when Agent Twiley, following up at my request, knocked on the door of the double-wide trailer he lived in, she knew immediately she had a problem. The door was partially open, and the smell of decay pushed its way out the thin crack.

While she stood there, a woman approached her and said she hadn't seen Allanson for a few days. The report notes her name as Julie Loon, the trailer park manager. Twiley identified herself and then went into the house. She found Mr. Allanson dead on the couch; pending an autopsy, she guessed he'd been dead at least four days. There were no obvious signs of foul play, no wounds or trauma. The man was still wearing his oxygen mask and appeared to be trying to fix his oxygen lines. The tank was on the floor between his legs. When checked, the tank was empty. And the house was full of cats. Agent Twiley then called in the sheriff.

I am trained not believe in coincidences when it comes to crime, criminals, and attendant and collateral damage. One thing often does lead to another. Why Mr. Allanson was found dead in the middle of an ongoing investigation is not just suspicious—considering the troubling comments my sister told me. I was convinced that something else happened, that Mr. Allanson may have been murdered.

The report also includes comments made by Ms. Loon about a couple that visited Mr. Allanson four or five days earlier; she wasn't exactly sure when. She did note that there were CCTV cameras on the property. The man and woman were in their seventies; the woman did all the talking. They drove a fancy-schmancy pickup truck; she did not know the make. They said something about DNA and Allanson; she couldn't remember why. They spent about fifteen minutes with Allanson, then left. She couldn't remember their names.

Agent Twiley asked Ms. Loon if Mr. Allanson was alive after the two people left.

"Oh, yes," she replied. "I went over to see Zeke; brought him a piece of cake I'd bought down at the store. He was all agitated, but still alive and kicking. He acted nervous, more so than usual. Said the damnedest thing. 'If I die, make sure all the cats are cared for. Would you do that for me, Julie?'"

She said she would. The report notes that there was significant predation on the body by the cats. It would probably result in their euthanization.

My first thought, as I closed the file, was Roberta Susan Davis.

———

Dorothy: Now
Grand Haven, Michigan
Late October 2019

I am terrified. I haven't been this scared in a long time. I'm afraid for Mitch and my family. I have made what peace God will allow me, but they don't deserve any of this. There is no forgiveness for me for what I planned back then. During the four years Debbie and I hid at her aunt's house, we talked a lot about all the radical things we believed. We evolved and went from righteous to repentant. Those dead in the house were my fault. Sure, Allanson and Talant killed them, but it was my idea about the bombings. I started the wheel rolling, and six died because of me—yes, I blame myself for my parents' deaths. Listening to Allanson brag about those days, what happened, it drove a stake through my heart. Mitch understood.

Finding out that Allanson was dead put it all in perspective. Mitch said the man was probably murdered. His death was too much of a coincidence so soon after we were there. Michael Talant would do anything, even murder, to keep the past buried.

We found out a week after we'd spoken with Allanson. The doorbell rang; standing in the door was Deputy Sheriff Gary Ambrose. Mitch stood behind me.

"Hi, Gary, what's up?" Mitch said. Gary's father and Mitch had gone to school together; we've known the deputy sheriff since he was a baby.

"You got a few minutes to talk? Something's come up—this is official."

I took a deep breath.

"Coffee, Gary?" I said as I nodded my head. Gary followed Mitch and me down the hallway.

"No, thanks, I'm good."

"Let's go out on the deck. It's such a great day," Mitch said. "How's your dad?"

"Good. He can't wait for deer season. He keeps saying that this will be his last. Then again, he's said that the last three years. He's tough."

"He is that. Tell him the cabin's ready. I was up there last week. There were good signs everywhere."

"I will. Great day," Ambrose said as he looked out over Lake Michigan. "But down to business. Were you two up in Cedar Springs last week? Wednesday?"

Our story was good; Mitch and I talked a lot about it.

"Yes," Mitch said.

"Can I ask why?" Gary said.

"I wanted to find out more about my family," I said. "I'm an orphan. You may or not know that, Gary. Your dad knows. Well, I took one of those DNA tests to see if I had any relatives, and a name popped up, Ezekiel Allanson. I had no idea who the guy was. It showed up in the test, then I looked him up on Facebook."

"And he lived where?"

"In Cedar Springs. We drove up to find him," I said. "It was a nice day for a drive. I also found him through a Google search. It was weird. We talked to the trailer park manager, June or Julia or something. I didn't have his address or a space number."

"Her name is Julie, Julie Loon," Gary said.

"Right, Julie. She pointed out his trailer. We talked to this Ezekiel Allanson, a bizarre and spooky guy. Mitch and I agreed before we met him that if he seemed weird, not to say anything about who we were. Then there were the cats —good God, Gary; there had to be a dozen of them, all kinds. Mitch started to sneeze, and I started to have trouble breathing. Allanson got upset, told us to get out. We never said anything to him about why we were there. If I'm related, I want nothing to do with that guy. Why?"

"He's dead."

"What? . . . He was obviously sick. Used an oxygen mask —we could barely understand him. But dead?"

"Yes, it looks like it was natural, but the woman Julie made a fuss," Gary said. "The sheriff of Kent County called me. He said that the FBI was also involved, that the guy was a retired FBI agent. In fact, it was one of their agents that found him. I don't know why they were there, and they haven't offered either. Julie took down your license plate; you were the last people she said visited him. She talked to him after you left; he was upset. He wouldn't tell her why. He was found dead a week later."

"Good Lord," Mitch said. "That's sad. He didn't have anybody except those cats. Hope the SPCA or somebody could take care of them."

"The sheriff said that they might have to euthanize them all. It seems they messed with the body."

"Oh my God," I honestly said.

"My thoughts exactly," Gary said. "Anyway, I was following up for the Kent County sheriff. I'll pass on your comments; they jibe with what the sheriff told me. Sorry about all this; it's just one of the things we do. There are so many around here living desperate and lonely lives, so many public services that people don't use."

"You said the FBI. This guy Allanson was an agent?" I asked.

"Yes, the deputy said that he was an FBI agent, out of

the Detroit office. Retired years ago, lives on social security and his pension. Still a terrible way to die."

"And an FBI agent found him? Why were they checking on him?"

"I have no idea. Maybe they do that, follow up on their own. Don't know."

"Sad. He was a weird guy, I'll tell you that," Mitch added.

"I'll leave you two. Thanks for the information." He stopped and turned to me. "So, you never asked him if you were related?"

"Gary, if you saw this guy, would you want to know if he was your relative—or worse, who *learns* you are related to him?"

"I understand. I'll tell Dad hello."

We walked to the front door and watched Deputy Sheriff Ambrose climb into his unit. He waved as he backed out of the driveway.

"Did we do the right thing?" I asked Mitch.

"Dorothy, we had nothing to do with that man's death. But that guy Talant's fingers are all over this. If he was murdered, then it's a good bet that the killer is now looking for you. We need to be prepared."

I took Mitch's hand. "I love you."

Chapter 28
The Sins of the Grandfather

Joe: Now
La Jolla, California
November 2019

It was good to get back into the paint. For me, there's something primal and therapeutic about the aromas of linseed oil and turpentine. You can have your acrylics, and even watercolor painting; they just don't reach into the senses like oil paint. Best we keep it our secret, though. If the Feds find out about the off-gassing of turpentine, they will shut down the whole game. I love the smells, the textures, the patience required, the layering—love it all. My subject today is a simple still life, a ceramic pitcher in blue and white, three lemons, a half-full glass and a bottle of red wine, a handful of fresh olives on a branch, and a large chunk of sausage. The sausage is now three inches shorter than when I started. The bottle of wine has also suffered.

"Hi, Sis," I said, clicking on the phone's speaker. I was going to let it go to voice. I answered when I saw her name. "The fog still in? Clear and sunny here."

"Hi, Joe. It's Dorothy."

I was not expecting a Dorothy. "Dorothy? Are you in Carmel, on Cate's phone?"

"No, Joe, it's a conference call," Cate said.

"How do you do that? I need to learn."

"Don't get distracted, Joe. Dorothy called me; you need to hear this. Dorothy, play that again."

"Joe, my husband and I recorded this a week ago," Dorothy said. That name . . . I hear Bobbie, hard for me to think Dorothy. "Let me start it over. This is part of a conversation we had with that son of a bitch retired FBI agent."

"Is that Zeke Allanson, the one you mentioned in your diary?" I asked.

"Yes. Here it is, listen," Dorothy said.

She played the conversation.

"Oh my God," I said when it stopped. "Did he just admit to being in the house when Mom died? He pushed her?"

"Yes, Joe," Dorothy said. "And said he was also there when Dad died. They murdered him. It was Michael Talant."

"How did you find him? Where is he?" I asked.

For the next ten minutes Dorothy told us how she found Allanson and her visit with her husband. Then Cate started to talk about the Talants, all three of them. She speculated about why the interest in Roberta—after fifty years.

"They are running scared, afraid of what you might say, Dorothy," Cate said.

"These are heavy, heavy hitters," I said. "My cynicism tells me that they want all this gone. They do not want you, or this guy Allanson, popping up. I read Jeanne Ellen Talant's autobiography. That woman has a huge ego, and she has the power and people to back it up. If the sins of the grandfather come out, it will taint the children, in this case, the grandchildren. I knew there was a reason why that FBI guy knocked on your door."

"He knows that Roberta is alive," Cate said.

"How'd he find that out? . . . Cate, you didn't?"

"Yes, I told him. We talked about it, Joe, but that was all I said. Not her name, or anything other than she asked for help for her sick granddaughter."

"Dorothy, nothing has changed," I said. "Our Cate still

has the biggest and most naïve heart of any of the Davises or Kents."

"There's something else, and this is scary," Dorothy said. "Zeke Allanson was found dead in his trailer. The deputy sheriff stopped by and questioned us. The manager saw us; she took down our license plate. The FBI found the body. They were obviously looking for him—only the Talants knew about him. And I have a good idea why. The sheriff believed our story."

"Are you going into hiding again?" I said.

"Yes, at our house," Dorothy said. "You two have done so much, thank you. Someday . . ." There was a long pause. "Goodbye." The phone clicked.

"Well, damn," I said. "I'll fly up tomorrow evening. We need to talk."

"Call me when you get on the plane. I'll pick you up," Cate said. I was surprised there was no argument.

———

Cate was standing at the curb in front of the Monterey airport terminal next to her Range Rover. She didn't smile; just waved when she saw me. A man I recognized stood next to her; he was wearing, I kid you not, a cowboy hat.

"Joe, this is my friend Ben Taylor," Cate said. "He dropped in unexpectedly after we talked."

I extended my hand. "Ben, a pleasure. Good to see you again." I'm always polite to Cate's friends.

"I'm a fan of your work. I saw two of your paintings at the National Portrait Gallery. You do make a statement."

"Cate? This cowboy knows my work—that's what, three people now?" I said from the back seat.

"And so modest," Cate said, looking at Ben.

It was quiet until Cate reached Ocean Avenue in Carmel.

"This town hasn't changed in the last ten years," Ben said. "Maybe a few new or different shops, but mostly it's the same."

"And most of the residents, too. A few more Texans now. Some young tech money has moved in, but mostly the same, just older. We don't hanker to strangers much," Cate said.

"You almost have to have a passport and visa to enter," I added. "There's talk about requiring shots."

"Surprisingly, it's becoming that way in some towns in Colorado," Ben added. "It's getting territorial up there; prices for places going through the roof. Outsiders don't settle down there; they spend the summers, jack up home prices. A lot of the locals are getting fed up with it. I've lived there my whole life. I admit, I'm sad to see the changes."

"Yes, but . . ." I said.

"Yes, it's better than a lot of places," Ben added.

Luckily, when I was last here, we made a Costco run; the liquor cabinet was full. I found the bottle of my current favorite rye, WhistlePig. I cracked the seal and we retired to the library.

"Joe, Ben called after we talked yesterday. He was in San Francisco for a meeting with his agent. I invited him down; we had dinner at Venti's. I saw him a few weeks ago at Jules's party."

"Jules had a real cowboy at the party—good for him," I said. "He invited me, but I declined."

"You'd have enjoyed it. There were authors who wrote about zombies and clowns," she said.

"Ah yes, Jules Wallace throws great parties. You do what, Ben?"

"I'm a writer, like Cate."

"Oh God, not another one," I said.

"He was also Colorado's attorney general a few years ago."

"Last century," Ben added.

"And an overachiever. Cate likes those. Westerns?"

"No, not primarily, though I've taken a few awards for them. I like war thrillers; throw in a little tech, and there I am."

I snapped my fingers. *"The Sharp Break of the Sun."*

Ben smiled. "Yes, that's my current offering. It's selling well. You've read it?"

"No, but it was sitting on a table in a bookstore I frequent. Currently, I'm into political fiction."

"Don't start, Joe. Ben won't be interested."

Ben bit. "And which book is that?"

"Senator Jeanne Ellen Talant's *Once More into the Breach*."

For the next two hours, we told Ben everything about what had happened to our family over the last fifty years, the strange involvement and intersection with the Talant family, our speculations, and the truth as we saw it. It was three in the morning when our therapy session ended. We ran out of steam; the bottle of rye whiskey died a heroic death.

"Cate and Joe, you know the chances of anything coming out of this affecting your sister—indictments, or even a criminal investigation—are slim," Ben said. "Too many years, no witnesses. It's a period I know well, and today it's also a time that people want to forget. It was our war, Joe. We were there; we know what it was like. Your sister Bobbie fought at home; she's as much a casualty as we were. Only she's still fighting for her life and her family now. From what you've said, she's had a good life. All considered, it would be unfortunate and unnecessary to put her through all this again. I'm not sure that a federal prosecutor would even try. But now things have changed. The death of Allanson put a twist in all this."

"I'm going to bed," I said. My good leg had stiffened up. It had been a long day. "You two have a good night. I'll see you in the morning."

"It's already morning, Joe," Cate said.

"Yeah, but not a new day," I answered.

Chapter 29
The Whole World is Watching

Dorothy: Now
Grand Haven, Michigan

I wanted out. Out of the house, out of the city we lived in, out of the state. I wanted to see Susan so bad my eyes hurt from all my crying. This man, this FBI agent, this Michael Talant, someone sworn to protect us, had set the wheels in motion fifty years ago to force a corrupt political agenda on the American people. Back then I was doing everything I could to stop them, and in doing so became like them. My lies became my facts. Hate was easy; Talant's prejudices were wrapped in the flag; and they used the fear that was ginned up in the American people, from Wall Street to Santa Monica Boulevard, against them. Families were torn apart; young men and women died for the politicians in Washington. We sang "The Times They Are A-Changin'." The fabric of our staid republic was being torn asunder. Feminism, black power, hippies, and anti-war marches all added to the enmities between the generations. Slogans ruled: "Hell no, we won't go." "Power to the people." "Never trust the man, man." "Give peace a chance" morphed from "We shall overcome" to "Make love, not war" and "Don't trust anyone over thirty" and "The whole world is watching." "God is dead" became "Jesus Christ Super-star." "Question authority" became "I am not a crook." And it was all gift-wrapped in sex, drugs, and rock 'n' roll. Mitch had questions about my old life; I had answers he did not want to hear.

And now this man, Michael Talant, wants me dead—all to hide the past, and to protect the future, his family's future. What about mine?

"You hungry?" Mitch asked. I was nursing a drink. I needed it to calm my nerves.

"Not sure I can keep anything down," I answered.

"All the alarms are set, cameras are running, we will be fine," he said reassuringly. I saw his pistol on his hip. "Let me make you some soup, chicken noodle."

We *will* be fine—I honestly believe him. We haven't stayed together for all these years out of habit. Mitch saved my life, saved me from myself. I love the man, and I know he loves me. Our lives are for each other and our children. My greatest unhappiness is that I can't have the kids living next door to us. Their lives took them to other places. Their lives are full, and I have five grandchildren. In the winter of 1968, the odds would have been ten to one against any of this, maybe even higher.

"Did you want to put the truck in the garage?" I asked.

"It's good there in the driveway; I'm going out early. Jack wants to meet about next spring at the store. I can leave without waking you," Mitch said.

"You know I'll be awake. And Jack must learn you won't always be there for him. It's all his now."

"He's owned the store for three years. I think he just likes to kick ideas around, and it keeps me in the game—at least a little."

Some nights Lake Michigan can be a thunderous wonder, all churned up and crashing. Tonight, it was so quiet and smooth, I swear you could hear the foghorn from Muskegon, ten miles up the beach. It is nights like these that the stars light up the sky and you can follow the shore lights for fifty miles. And on some winter's nights, the aurora borealis dances across the surface like fairy magic. This evening it was stars and a half-moon.

About midnight, the first sign that something was wrong was Mitch whispering in my ear. "There's someone on the deck."

"Just a raccoon or a deer," I mumbled.

A human shadow, cast by the moon, crossed the window shade.

"That's not a deer," I said, now fully awake. Mitch was still in his clothes. "Why are you dressed?"

"Get dressed. No lights; I don't want a confrontation. We need to get out."

In the dim light, I saw he was still wearing the automatic. This was now fucking serious.

I pulled on pants and a shirt, then grabbed my charm bracelet from the dresser.

"You don't need that," Mitch said.

"It's my good luck charm."

"When we get to the truck, call the police, tell them there is an intruder." He passed me my cell phone. "We'll go out through the side door of the garage."

"Maybe there's more than one?"

Mitch removed the Glock from its holster. "Then, let's hope there's only one."

We crossed through the house, into the garage, and to the side door. Behind us, the crash of the glass of the rear sliding door to the family room shattered the silence—goddamn the son of a bitch. We ran along the side of the house. The motion lights clicked on, flooding the side yard, exposing us to God knows what. We reached the truck. Mitch opened my door; I climbed in. He ran to the driver's door and yanked it open. From behind I heard the snap of a pistol. Next to Mitch, his window crazed, and a hole appeared.

"Gun," I yelled.

Mitch swung up his pistol and fired down the length of

the house, then climbed in and jerked the door shut. In three seconds, we were squealing backward into the street.

Another hole appeared in the front windshield. The glass crazed; neither of us were hit. I punched in 9-1-1 as Mitch fishtailed down Acorn Road. More dings as bullets hit the truck's tailgate. I waited for an impact, pain, or worse.

Fifty feet down the road, we passed a parked gray Hyundai.

"You recognize that car?" I asked as the 9-1-1 operator answered my call.

"No, it must be his," Mitch answered. "Gray Hyundai Elantra."

"What is your emergency?" came a voice over the car's speakers.

"We are being shot at; I live at 119 Acorn Road at the lake. Someone tried to break into our house. We escaped in our truck. They are shooting at us."

"Do you know who?"

"No, we don't. I'm Dorothy Cooper. We are leaving the house in our truck, a black Ford pickup, Michigan license plate . . . Mitch?"

"CCF 0756."

"CCF 0756," I repeated.

"Are they following you?" the operator asked. "Can you drive somewhere safe?"

"I don't know. Mitch, someplace safe?"

"I can try to make Highway 31."

Suddenly our truck was slammed into its left rear corner. The truck twisted; Mitch corrected. "The son of a bitch just rammed us," he yelled.

"Who rammed you?" 9-1-1 asked.

Mitch jammed the pedal to the floor; the truck roared. The gray car was invisible; he was following close with no headlights.

"I'm going to 3rd Street then to Pine. I will use the on-ramp to get to the highway. I can outrun him."

"Mitch, he's accelerating. I can see him in the mirror," I screamed.

"I am sending police to your location. Please stay on the line."

"Make it fast," I said.

The engine roared so loud I had to yell. To the right, across a lagoon filled with cattails, the corporation yard for Grand Haven Gravel was lit up by the high-powered lights mounted on tall stanchions. A massive red ship unloading gravel was moored behind two of the cone-shaped piles of sand and gravel.

"Hold on," Mitch yelled.

He slammed on the brakes. The Hyundai, half the weight of the truck and not anticipating Mitch's move, was traveling too fast to stop. It slid on the pavement and slammed into the back of the Ford. The car's front end slid under the high tow-hitch of the pickup; our truck's tow-rig ripped away the Hyundai's front hood and bumper. Mitch slammed down the pedal again; I heard tearing metal.

Mitch accelerated. Out the window, only the roof of the car was visible. It had swung out to parallel us. The hood was folded back, almost blocking the driver's view. Then the car came alongside, then the *pop, pop* of a pistol. The windows in the back seat exploded. The truck thundered and roared. We pulled away.

Ahead, the red stop sign for the intersection flared in our headlights. We blew through the crossing. Mitch pulled the wheel hard right; the back end fishtailed through the turn. Beyond, straight ahead, the lights of the riverfront corporation yard lit up a half-dozen pyramid-shaped mountains of rock and gravel. Mitch pushed the truck hard. The sedan was still stuck on our tail; twenty feet didn't separate us. Then we left the asphalt of the county road and hit the gravel corporation yard—dust and stones flew up. The following car was completely engulfed.

"Tighten your seat belt. Put your hands across your face," Mitch yelled.

"What are you going to do?"

"Crash this truck into that asshole."

"Mitch!" I screamed.

Illuminated by the lights was the fifty-foot-high wall of a ship's red hull. Above, the unloading gravel spilled out of chutes onto the cone-shaped piles. The truck roared like a wild animal—faster and faster Mitch pushed it. The sedan, lost in our dust, had to be immediately behind us. I squinted into the gray cloud and saw nothing until a ghostly pair of headlights clicked on. The killer had to be following our taillights; there was no way he could see anything.

Mitch screamed, "Hold on!"

Mitch crashed into the first massive sand pile, driving upward. The airbags exploded. I slammed into my seat belt, knocking me almost senseless. The air blew from my lungs; the airbag exploded into my face. A split-second later, the sedan rammed into us. The smaller car drove under the high undercarriage of the truck's rear end, lifting us, like a massive wedge, off the ground. The road dust overwhelmed us; I began to cough uncontrollably. I reached for Mitch; he had already bailed out.

God, I hurt. I released my seat belt and fumbled for the door. The charms in my bracelet caught the door handle, pinning my wrist against the door. It was twisted—I couldn't open the door. The smell of gasoline now mixed with the dust. I slammed my fists hard trying to force it open. I was blind; my charms were caught on the handle. I tried to use my left hand to pull it away; it got tangled in the airbag. I screamed and coughed. Then flames lit up the truck cab's interior. I shrieked. Mitch yanked the door open; the charm bracelet broke as I tumbled out the door.

"I got you," Mitch yelled. "I got you."

The car's impact had lifted our truck more than two feet off the gravel road. Mitch picked me up and carried me away from the fire. I looked back at the crash. More fire came from inside the sedan's engine compartment. A dark shape was draped out the front window. I heard screaming, then the fire surged. Mitch lowered me to my feet. I couldn't look anymore at the tangled car and truck. Mitch stood next to me; his pistol was aimed at the car. It wasn't necessary. Illuminated by the overhead lights, all I saw was a body. It was sprawled half in and out of the front windshield, the driver's face buried in the burning engine compartment. Mitch calmly walked back to the truck, pulled open the back door, and removed a fire extinguisher. He aimed it first at the interior of the truck, then at the crushed front of the sedan. The flames were quickly shut down. Beyond, through the smoke and dust, I saw blue flashing lights and heard sirens heading toward us.

Chapter 30
I Want Retribution

Cate: Now
Carmel, California
Late November 2019

I clicked off the phone. My brother and Ben looked at me in stunned silence.

"Well, damn," Ben finally said. "Thank God they are all right."

"What the hell was the guy thinking?" Joe said. "He could just break in and kill them? He had to have killed Allanson, then was trying to eliminate Roberta. Michael Talant must be so afraid that someone will find out about his history that he must eliminate the only witnesses left. If he'd have done nothing, nothing would have happened— none of this."

Dorothy had called. It was one-thirty in the morning in Michigan, ten-thirty in California. She was distraught; I did what I could to calm her. She told us about the break-in, the chase, the crash, and the driver's exit through the front windshield, killing him. She stopped a few times to gather herself as she explained what had happened. There was no identification on the body, no wallet, nothing. The police were checking on the car the man was driving, maybe they will learn something.

"Are you and Mitch, okay?" I asked.

"Yes, I can't believe this happened. But we are good, a little bruised, but good."

My heart went out to Dorothy and Mitch. I heard my sister's resolve and resiliency; Mitch filled in additional information while Dorothy gathered herself. I was shaking when he finished. Someday I want to meet this guy.

"They will check the body's fingerprints to confirm its identity," Ben said. "Dorothy said they found a key card in the man's pocket; they will find out where was staying. My guess, he was a professional. The Glock pistol that was found, along with the additional magazine in his coat pocket and the small snub-nosed revolver and holster on his ankle, makes it obvious. But sloppy."

Earlier, the three of us had spent the day doing touristy things. We went to the aquarium in Monterey, drove Seventeen Mile Drive, walked along the beach, and had a wonderful dinner at the Pebble Beach Lodge, sort of a post-Thanksgiving dinner. We returned to the cottage and were sitting in the library; a fire was burning when my phone rang. Dorothy and Mitch went on, almost nonstop, for a half hour. She sounded so much like our mother; it was eerie. When they finished, I asked about Susan.

"She is doing better; they believe that the transplant has helped," Dorothy said. The change in the conversation also helped to get her mind off what had happened.

"That's wonderful," I said. We agreed to talk later in the week.

"As I said at lunch," Ben said, "I don't believe, at this time, there's a DA or federal prosecutor who would bring charges against your sister. She is the only remaining witness to what happened that day. And the one material witness, retired agent Michael Talant, is the only man who could testify to the crime—but connecting him to all this would be almost impossible. His testimony could place your sister there, but it would also make him complicit in some type of cover-up. He's already said he was somewhere else. To claim that he saw your sister at the house, he would have to change his story. And there's no one now to back him up since Allanson is dead."

"I don't give a damn about that," Joe said. "Those two, Talant and Allanson, blew up the house and killed four people, and Talant and the FBI were responsible for supplying the dynamite to Bobbie. What breaks my heart is what happened to our parents. Mother died because Allanson broke into the house, obviously under orders from Talant and maybe even Washington. And Allanson claims that Talant murdered Dad and covered up that crime as well."

"There's no way to prove any of this," I said. "We just have the taped conversation with a dead man, who may or may not have been murdered."

"And again," Ben said, "in today's climate, and even with the best in forensic science, there's no prosecutor who'd take the time. It will always be a tragedy, and unless there's a confession by Talant, which is unlikely, justice will never be served."

"Talant was behind this attack on Dorothy," I said. "Who else could it be? He has to be connected to the man who died trying to kill Dorothy."

"That will be hard to prove. Best to leave this with the Michigan authorities," Ben said. "They are right there. Your sister's family is prominent in the region; it will be pursued. Maybe they can even connect him to Allanson's death. But it will take time."

"I want retribution; I want to get even," Joe said. I could see he was working himself into a state. "Michael Talant destroyed our family. He is the face of the institutions that took us to war; he manipulated the evidence; he lied about what he saw and did. His actions led directly to the deaths of an FBI agent, a policeman, Bobbie's friends, and our parents. I demand justice."

"And what would that be?" I asked.

"Make them afraid. Expose them for what they are," Joe said. "So much so, they lose what they want most. For me, that's a good place to start."

———

Our family, the Kents, can be traced back through the New and Old Worlds over five hundred years. I've walked through the village in Surrey where our forefathers and - mothers married, raised children, and begat other Kents. I met relatives during book tours and signings. Our family in America is a tree well planted and nurtured; third, fourth, and fifth cousins populate America. It was in 1756, when two brothers, Gideon and Rupert Kent, sailed to the New World in the stout English ship *Solace*. There's a tale involving an unpaid loan as the reason they left England. I can attest that they were not shipped to the Americas as criminals, like some to Australia. The boys, twenty-three and twenty-one, respectively, settled in the village of Ipswich, Massachusetts. A hamlet that was already more than a hundred years old when the men opened a furniture shop that sold locally made goods and took orders for finer pieces imported from England. They married into established Massachusetts families. Gideon Kent was the first to start a journal; his was as much a political treatise as a diary. His brother soon followed suit, the women also kept diaries, and the tradition began. Their testimonies sit on my shelves. Twenty years later, during the winter of 1775, they sided with the revolutionaries and fought against the British. In a remarkable coincidence, Rupert was at the Battle for Bunker Hill when he lost his right leg; his ancestor Joe Davis would lose his in Vietnam. I've kept that little tidbit from Joe; he might or might not appreciate the link.

This compilation of our family's history is a serious responsibility. First, it is essential to those who will follow us, and secondly, it is out of respect to those who came before us. And to be honest, it is seriously cool to read the diaries of my ancestors whose DNA I and my family carry forward.

I persuaded Ben into staying over another night; his flight was early evening from San Jose to Denver. Joe was heading home the following evening. We spent the day talking about what had happened, possible options, even courses of action. We knew that the best thing would be to let it all settle down, do nothing. While I was making dinner, the phone rang.

The boys looked at me while I talked. My side of the conversation confused them.

"Yes, thank you. I'll see you at one. Do you have . . . of course you do." I clicked off. "Well, that was the California manager for the Elect Jeanne Ellen Talant for President campaign. Ms. Talant is the guest of honor at a lunch at the Pebble Beach Lodge at eleven tomorrow morning. If I were free at one, she wants to stop by and meet me. She has admired my books and would like to have a conversation—completely private, of course—about soliciting my support."

"Well, damn," Ben said. "That woman has balls. Does she think you don't know what's going on?"

"She knows exactly what's going on," I said. "She wants to know what I know—and how much a threat I am."

"There is no way you are meeting that woman alone. I'm sitting in," Joe said.

"I would not have it any other way," I agreed.

"I'll leave you two with her," Ben said. "I'll hang out in your library, just to make sure there are no fisticuffs." He smiled. I enjoyed this Colorado cowboy's company.

"We could use a nonaligned third party," I said.

"Use the terrace. I can listen through the library window," he answered.

She was fifteen minutes late. Three black Tahoe SUVs stopped in front of my cottage, completely blocking the number one tourist route through this part of the village.

Jeanne Ellen Talant exited from the rear seat of the middle vehicle. Two security men had exited the first Tahoe and stood next to the car; these were rent-a-cops. I guess we are a strange and dangerous electorate.

Talant turned and looked out to the cove. A band of fog had ominously settled along the horizon. Another woman exited the opposite side; I assumed it was her campaign manager. A broad-shouldered black man in a nice suit climbed the steps to the door. I met him at the landing.

"Ms. Wallace?" the man asked.

"Yes, I am. Please invite Senator Talant up."

"Good afternoon, Ms. Wallace, I am so pleased to meet you," Talant said when she reached the landing. "Thank you for taking the time." She extended her hand, and I took it.

"You are welcome," I said. "It's not every day that I meet the next president of the United States. Please come in."

"This is Darius—my guy, as we say. He's going to take a quick look inside. Do you mind?"

"Absolutely not. Please look around," I said. "And this is my brother Joe Davis; he is spending a few days with me. I also have a writer friend working in my library; he's harmless."

Joe walked out from behind me, his hand extended. "It's a pleasure, Senator Talant, a real pleasure."

Joe startled her. She quickly recovered and shook his hand. We all followed Darius down my hallway.

"May I suggest the terrace off the kitchen? The sun is out; it may be one of the last nice days of the year. I made tea, and I have coffee—maybe something stronger?"

"Thank you, but I'm fine. I've been drinking coffee since five this morning. The lunch at the lodge was delicious."

"Yes, I know the restaurant well. My late husband and I ate there often."

"My condolences. I saw your interview on *Hello America*."

"Thank you," I answered.

"Joe, I also have been told that you are one of our great

American artists, a national treasure. One of the curators at the Smithsonian told me."

"Well, I'm a treasure—wow. That title and two bucks will get you a cup of Starbucks coffee."

"He also mentioned that you were known for your humor."

Joe just grinned. We sat. I had a carafe of ice water on the table.

The banter was getting on my nerves. "Senator, the world knows that I carefully keep my political views to myself. I try hard to keep them out of my books; historical facts drive the backstories. I have not and will never endorse a particular candidate. So, why are you here?"

Talant's face took on a dark tone; her pale Irish complexion shifted to rose, highlighting her red hair. "You know damn well why I am here—all this is your sister and family's fault."

The storm quickly rolled in. "My family?" I said. "What are you talking about? Joe and I have never had anything to do with you or your family. And yet here you sit, implying something. What is it?"

"You know—both of you know."

"I have no idea. Joe, do you have any idea what she's talking about?"

"None, unless it's about Roberta, our missing sister," Joe said. "Let me think—yes, fifty-one years ago your grandfather, FBI Special Agent Michael Talant, pushed his way into my parents' home and demanded that we tell him where Roberta Davis was. That was way before your time. So yes, there was contact with the Talant family. It was the fall of 1968, September to be exact. This happened the week after the police riots at the Democratic convention in Chicago. I was still doing rehab for my missing leg, this right one; it was lost during the Tet Offensive. None of us knew anything. We had no idea what Agent Michael Talant was talking about. I was there. I told him that."

"You met my grandfather?" Talant said—there was surprise in her voice.

"Yes, I did—fifty-one years ago, almost to the day. And my sister and I talked with your brother, George, just a few months ago. He's been like a dog with a bone on this cold case."

"George interviewed me twice," I added.

"George? He was here?" Talant said, she tried to look surprised. "It must be for a legitimate FBI investigation."

"Please, Senator, you know he was here. He had questions about our missing sister. It has been a long time—Joe and I have believed Roberta was dead. Her absence, like the deaths of our parents, left a great void in our hearts. To lose all three in just a few weeks nearly destroyed Joe and me."

"All three?" The shock on her face was either real or well rehearsed.

"You didn't know?" I said. "Your grandfather didn't tell you? Please, Senator Talant, that's why you are here, isn't it? To clean up the mess your grandfather made and is still making. You are here to smooth over the rough spots—damage control I think it's called in your world. We have learned from an unimpeachable source what happened that day when four people died; we know who was directly responsible. We also have it on tape from another witness who was there that day. And thank God for that. We've just learned that that witness was found dead a few days ago. The local sheriff suspects foul play. Senator, I would be cautious about where you take this. It's a slippery slope."

"You? You are telling *me* what to do? Where is your sister? She is a criminal and a murderer. You are aiding and abetting a wanted person, a fugitive. I can, and I will, have you arrested and thrown in jail."

"Please, Senator," I said. "You can't wave your hand and demand that charges be brought against Joe and me—especially now. Don't you have one of those interminable candidate debates set up for next week in Denver? It would ring like a publicity stunt. How would all this look? You have no evidence, certainly not like what we have. And there's a good chance that the man involved in the death of that witness is also dead. He died in a car accident while trying to murder two people two days ago. So, you can be damn sure we won't tell you where she is—even if we knew. There may be somebody out there thinking about harming us. Setting us up. Damn, woman, what is your family trying to do?"

She put up both hands; it was not in surrender. "Look, I know your sister is alive. Where is she?"

"Of course you do," Joe said. "Your brother told you, but I'm also guessing your grandfather confirmed it. We have no idea where Roberta Davis is. You say she is alive; then you know where she is. What are you Talants trying to do to us? Tell us where she is, Senator. We miss our older sister. If you know she's alive, then where is she?"

"I don't know where she is."

"Then she's dead," I said.

"I've been told—"

"Again, by your grandfather, your brother?" I demanded. "They know? That means you know. And if you know, then the FBI told you. Where is our sister?"

Talant stood, her hands on the table. "I don't know."

"Then you lied," Joe said. "This charade is so wrong. You demand, threaten, cajole. You have nothing. Where is our sister, Roberta Davis?"

Talant stiffened, then carefully lifted her hands off the table. "Let's slow this down. I'm sorry. In time I can be helpful. In my position there are things I can do to . . . help your sister."

I stood and took two steps toward the woman; I was six inches taller. I pointed my finger. "My sister made some bad decisions, but she is not guilty of murder, or specifically any of the crimes she's been implicated in. We all carry sins— only God forgives sins. I suggest that you look to your own family for the killer—in the eyes of our society, murder is the most unforgivable crime. Your grandfather killed four people when he blew up that house that day and then killed our parents to cover it up. We have proof."

I hadn't punched her, but she staggered back.

"You are lying. My grandfather is an honorable man, a war hero. He raised George and me after the death of our father. I am who I am because of my grandfather Michael Talant."

"Then I would be careful," Joe said. "The sins of the grandfather and all."

"Is that a threat?"

"Senator Talant," I said. "I'm just a simple writer who has survived traumas that I would not wish on anyone, even you. All this could have remained untouched, left alone. But guilt and fear, your grandfather's guilt and your fear, have made people do things that you will later wish you'd left alone. You are now at that place. Drop all this, or it won't turn out well."

We glared at each other. There was a knock at the frame of the kitchen door. Darius stood there.

"Excuse me, ma'am," Darius said. "Ms. Johnson says that we need to move on; the plane is ready. We have the fundraiser in Pasadena at five."

"This is not over," Talant said, turning back to us.

"Senator Talant, this is a road you do not want to go down. I will do what is necessary to protect my family. Only you can stop this; we suggest that you do. Safe travels."

Talant marched past Darius; we heard her heels click down the hallway. Then the door slammed. In moments the lane out front was quiet, just the sound of the surf rolling in and out.

Ben joined us.

"You heard?"

"Yes." He pointed to the open window. "A quid pro quo? All to protect her campaign. Curious what people will do when threatened."

Chapter 31
I Will Make It Worth Your Time

Cate: Now
Carmel, California
November 2019

Two days later, after Ben had returned to Colorado and Joe to La Jolla, my day had become a catastrophe. Somehow the word got out to the media about Senator Talant's visit to Carmel. First, it was the local newspaper wondering if I'd broken my rule about endorsing candidates. I said no, it was just a friendly visit—a fan to a writer. Then the San Francisco and Los Angeles newspapers chimed in, speculating about a hundred of the wrong things. This morning a couple of bloggers called. I found that humorous —bloggers using a phone. I chastised them; my phone number is private. They laughed.

My phone rang again. "Hello," I said, now exasperated. "Marsha, what a delight . . . Yes, Senator Talant did stop by . . . Friendly? Yes, why do you ask? . . . My dear, we need to talk . . . A follow-up to the story of a few months back? . . . Love to. Call me tomorrow to schedule. In fact, Marsha, I'll have a scoop for you."

"Is this wise?" Joe asked when we talked on the phone. "A lot of weird shit could come down."

"And maybe it will also stop the cartload of it headed at us," I said.

Marsha and I talked the next morning. She was in Denver. The fifth or sixth debate of the presidential candidates was Tuesday night; I don't keep count. She was covering it.

"Can you do the interview tomorrow?" I asked. "It's a timing thing."

"I can't, it's Sunday. There's a push here because of the debate. How about late next week? Our viewers' response to our last talk was off the charts. I will call you at 9:00 a.m. That work?" she said.

"No, Marsha, it won't. In fact, how about a live interview, on air, tomorrow morning. We can meet at your affiliate here in Monterey, use their studio."

"I don't know. What's so important?"

"I'm publishing a new book. It's nonfiction. It's about the impact that partisan politics and the heavy hand of government had on the American people during the troubled decade of the 1960s."

"A nonfiction book? Why would that be this important right now?"

"I will leave that to the reader to decide. And it does tie in to one of the current candidates and the debate Tuesday night."

"The network gave me some leeway here. I'll make a few calls, see what we can work out. You've intrigued me."

"I will make it worth your time."

———

Hello America, the Sunday 8:00 a.m. live network New York show, required me to be in the local affiliate's Monterey, California, studio at 4:30 a.m. The show would be broadcast initially from New York at 5:00 a.m., West Coast time. It would be shown on tape delay here on the West Coast at 8:00 a.m. New York media still controls everything. Marsha

Templeton and Curt Jefferies were already waiting at the studio. From the looks on their faces, they hadn't slept.

I'd been to this local studio a few times for interviews and was on good terms with the station manager and the crew. While early for them, they were excited to offer their bit to the national broadcast. The large bag of fresh pastries I brought didn't hurt.

Marsha said that we had been placed in a five-minute window in the second hour of the show just after 9:00 a.m., New York time.

"So, what's the scoop?" she asked.

"You will see. What do you know about the 1968 Democratic convention in Chicago?"

"We studied that in political science. It turned into a battle between the police and the demonstrators. In time, some have come to believe that the government may have had a hand in increasing the agitation, maybe even stoked the fire. In the end, the Democrats failed, and Nixon triumphed and won the election."

"Let's start there. My new book is titled *White Rabbit*."

"Like the song from Jefferson Airplane?"

"You are too young to remember them," I said.

"Too young? I have the album *Surrealistic Pillow* on my phone."

I grinned. "Good, we are on the same page."

After the commercial break, we were signaled that we had thirty seconds. I sat with Marsha. A view of the morning sun reflecting off the Monterey boat harbor was projected behind us on the massive wall of the in-studio monitor.

"We have a busy week ahead of us, America. The Democratic and Republican debates are this week, the release of the new Tom Cruise movie, and how much damage the hurricane marching up the Eastern Seaboard will do," Anne Rutledge, the host for *Hello America*, said as we returned. "However, this morning, one of our most enjoyed authors is once again visiting us from California. Marsha Templeton is with Catherine Davis in Monterey, California. Good morning, Marsha, and it is good to see you again, Ms. Davis."

"Good morning, Anne. Yes, I am pleased to again talk with Catherine Davis. Ms. Davis is author of more than thirty-five novels that, in one form or another, have told the story of America from revolutionary days up until the years following World War II. Her novels are known for their depth, accuracy, and vitality, and especially strong female characters. A few have found their way to television, and her incredible novel *Two Souls Lost in the Woods*, about Michigan in the 1930s, was made into a critically acclaimed movie."

Marsha was reading the teleprompter. The text was almost exactly from our previous interview; I was okay with that.

"Ms. Davis, I believe you have a new novel coming out," Marsha said, ending her introduction.

I smiled and took a deep breath. "Thank you, Marsha, and most especially for the kind words—and the plug. The writing profession is difficult these days with all the other distractions we have in our daily lives. I'm just glad that people can take some time and enjoy my stories. And, yes, I have a new book coming this fall, just in time for Christmas."

"Well, my gift list just got easier," Marsha said, looking at the camera. "A title?"

I smiled again. I'm so good at this. "The novel is titled *White Rabbit*."

"From the Jefferson Airplane song?"

"Yes, and it also suggests Lewis Carroll's wonderful books, *Alice's Adventures in Wonderland* (also known as *Alice in Wonderland*) and *Through the Looking Glass*. Both the Jefferson Airplane song and the novel present nonsense characters and not-so-vague references to drugs, the regimentation of societies and politics, and especially that many things around us are not what they seem to be."

"Wow, a little deep for this early in the morning," Marsha said with a laugh. "So, the novel is nonfiction?"

"Yes and no. I will leave that to the reader to determine."

"Intriguing. The song was released in 1967 and was wildly popular; in fact, it's often called one of the most popular songs of those difficult years. So, the book is about 1968?"

"Yes, and about the present as well. It is about how events fifty years ago still resonate through families and societies. I was fifteen. My brother had lost his leg in a fire-fight near Khe Sanh during the Tet Offensive that February. We lost our greatest political and social hopes for the future that year, Robert Kennedy and Martin Luther King Jr.; both were assassinated—and controversy still exists about those killings. There were political demonstrations and riots at the nominating conventions in Miami and Chicago, and the government was doing its best to spy on every American. It was the seminal year in the battle for the future of America. It was the youthful Baby Boomers, my age cohort, against those that saved the world from Hitler, Mussolini, and Tojo. Both felt entitled to the future; both fought to make their vision for America real. In the end, there were no winners, just survivors."

"*White Rabbit*, is this an autobiography?"

"In some ways, yes, Marsha. I changed some names to protect a few innocent people, but I have not changed all of them. My brother Joe and I are two of these survivors. That year we lost three people who were special to us."

"Three? Who were they?"

"My sister, Roberta, disappeared that fall. She was one of those who were protesting the war and what America was doing around the world. She was implicated in the deaths of four people in an explosion of a house in Chicago a few days after the convention concluded. She has been blamed for their deaths; at the time some called it murder. And soon after Roberta disappeared, both our parents died under mysterious circumstances. Both deaths could be interpreted as accidents. We have found, through new sources, that they probably died from the direct actions of governmental agencies."

"Murdered?" Marsha said. I could tell she was getting into this. I looked at the clock; I had only a couple of minutes left. I wasn't going to tell the story; just light the fuse.

"Yes, we believe so. We have also learned that the FBI may have been involved. As you may or may not know, during that dangerous time, the FBI director, J. Edgar Hoover, had formed a unit within the FBI to surveil Americans; it was called COINTELPRO. This surveillance unit was nationwide and would eventually involve investigating thousands of Americans."

"I didn't know."

"Most Americans don't. My own investigations and this book are about a group of rogue agents in the FBI who were directly involved in investigating my family. These investigations led to the disappearance of my sister and our parents' death."

"And these agents are still alive, even fifty years later?"

"We are not entirely sure, Marsha. They would all be well over seventy years old, some much, much older. No one in this group has been arrested and charged for these crimes. My sister was implicated; we believe that she was a scapegoat for the real murderers. A friend of my sister was arrested a few years ago and charged with the crime; she died soon after from cancer. And some of these officials have lived out their lives, had families, and watched with pride as members of their families reached the pinnacles of political success here in America—all on the ghosts of those who died fifty-one years ago."

"Do you have names?"

"Yes. We will work with the proper authorities and turn over what we know. However, Marsha, they continue to pursue my family even today with threats and intimidations. Their actions have led to the recent deaths of two people and attacks on others."

"Today? Deaths and attacks, today? My God, fifty years later?"

"Yes."

"I wish we had more time," Marsha said.

"Don't we all."

"Ms. Davis, as always, you surprise us. Look for Ms. Catherine Davis's new novel, *White Rabbit*, this fall, and I assure you, you will not be disappointed. Back to New York."

Chapter 32
Pandora's Box

George Talant: Now
Bay View Active Adult Community
Annapolis, Maryland

I was waiting in my grandfather's room when he returned from lunch. He did not expect me, I didn't call ahead. He was in a wheelchair, one of the team members (as they were called) was pushing him; both the wheelchair and the attendant were new.

"Did you call, Buddy? I don't remember," Gramps said. He turned to the young man; he was black and maybe eighteen. "Dion, if you can get me near the couch, I'll slide out, that work?"

"Yes, Mr. Talant."

I watched as they maneuvered to the couch and in one motion Gramps slipped out and over. He smiled, I guess it was a small victory.

"Dion, this is my grandson, George Talant. He is an FBI agent, like I was back in the day." He pointed to the largest plaque on the wall behind him. "George, Dion DuBois. He's been a big help this past week."

I shook Dion's hand, it was strong. "You look familiar, did you play high school football?"

"Yes, sir, running back, Annapolis High School. I'm taking a year off to heal my Achilles, got messed up the last game of the year. Then maybe I can get into Maryland; they are holding a scholarship for me. But it will take a year to heal."

"Good for you. I wish you luck."

"Thank you, Mr. Talant. I'll leave you now. Do you need anything, Mr. Talant?" Dion was looking at Mike.

"No, I'm good. Thanks. I'm going to take a nap later; you can get me for dinner about five. That work for you?"

"Yes, sir. Five sharp." He turned to me. "Nice to meet you, sir."

"And you too, Dion, and good luck," I said.

"Thank you."

"Would you close the door on your way out?" I said and waited.

Gramps turned to me and glared. "What the hell are you doing here, Buddy?"

"I'm here because I was pulled from the field and I'm on a type of probation, pending a disciplinary hearing and clarification of a lot of shit. My deputy director has me on a short chain, my career is on a tightrope, and you put me there." I was so pissed at him.

"What do they know? And I haven't clue what you're talking about?"

"The deputy director came into my office and dropped a stack of papers on my desk that show a paper trail. It appears that there was an incident in Michigan where a Dalton Ward tried to kill a couple, a couple that had visited a man by the name of Allanson, who had been murdered a few days earlier. Ward was killed in the altercation, the couple survived. He was tracked to a hotel room in a Hampton Inn; in the room's safe were his wallet and driver's license, two cell phones, and a Glock semi-automatic."

"And this has what to do with me?"

"The last phone numbers, incoming and outgoing, in fact

the only phone numbers on one of the cell phones were to a phone bought at a Target store in Bethesda."

"And this means what?"

I love this man, he is everything to me, yet this fucking game he was playing was running out of road. "The cell number was to a phone I *bought* for you. The cell phone has my name all over it, I bought it with a credit card."

"That was stupid. You are a police officer; you know you should never buy a pre-paid phone with a credit card—cash, Buddy, cash."

I was stunned. "What the hell was Dalton Ward doing in Michigan? And why was he calling you?"

"He was doing a bit of work for me, cleaning up a few things. What did he tell you? I know the man, he's as tight as a Chesapeake clam." Gramps tried to form a smile; it didn't work.

"Didn't you hear me? Ward is dead, his prints were matched to the ones on file. He had rented a car at the Detroit airport. He flew in from Dulles. The room was rented to a Tom Teller, a fake name. The manager recognized Dalton from his driver's license photo—the mug shot taken in the Grand Haven morgue no one could have identified."

"Ward is dead, amazing. I thought he was impossible to kill. Do you know how many times he'd been wounded on the job? He finally took disability, he even wanted to refuse that, just so he could stay with the Bureau. Tough guy."

"He was nuts," I said. "That's why the Bureau allowed him disability; they didn't want the embarrassment of his extra-curricular activities made public. How many times did you bring him home to dinner? Mom didn't want us around him, yet you still brought him over."

"There's a thing called loyalty, Buddy. Something you should think about. I was loyal to Dalton, and he was loyal to me."

"Ward was directly connected—by the Michigan State police—to the death of Ezekiel Allanson. Allanson was found dead in his trailer. He is the same Allanson who is mentioned in the Roberta Davis files, your files; he was your partner. Why is he dead?"

"I have no idea."

Gramps sat there looking at me, I was stunned. "What the hell is going on?"

"Who were the people who were allegedly attacked by Mr. Ward?"

"They were a prominent couple in Grand Haven, Michigan, the Coopers, Mitch and Dorothy. They have no idea why Ward tried to shoot them and then run them off the road."

"I'd dig deeper, if I were you."

"What do you know?"

"I have no idea what you are talking about."

"Where's the phone?"

"What phone?"

"The phone I gave you, the one that Ward called."

"I lost it. And that's probably a good thing for you."

————

George Talant: Now
Senate Offices
Washington, DC

Yesterday, I was thinking—as I was sitting in my office imagining what my life would be without a job—about the Roberta Davis case, as I now call it, when it took a bizarre turn when an unsolicited package of documents arrived. There was no cover letter, just photocopies of reporter's notes, a tape of a conversation, and a packet of photos. I have a very good idea where they came from. All I wanted was to close this case that had troubled my grandfather. I had not wanted to crack open Pandora's box, but there it is.

This was a week after my confrontation with Gramps and Jeanne. I returned and had been waiting for Jeanne in her office for almost a half hour, when the door from the hallway burst open and my sister hurried in. In her wake were her chief of staff, her campaign manager, and two others I did not recognize. Following them was the majority leader of the Senate and two others. No one was smiling.

"Hi, George, sorry I'm late," Jeanne said. "I need a few minutes, then we can talk. That okay?"

"Who is this?" the majority leader asked.

"My brother. He is an FBI special agent." She let the introduction hang in the air; she did not introduce me.

"Now the FBI? What the fuck?" He turned and walked into my sister's office. The rest, including my sister, followed; the door slammed.

I looked at Beth Ellington, Jeanne's assistant.

"It has been like this all morning, senators and campaign people coming and going. And I don't know why—they will not tell me anything."

"Sometimes it's better not to know. Keeps you clear of the storm debris," I said.

For ten minutes the yelling was palpable, yet indistinguishable through the thick door. Then it opened, a tad more civilized this time, and all the people, led by the majority leader, filed out. Jeanne Ellen stood in her office door watching them leave. She mumbled something about not letting the door hit them in the ass as they left.

"That didn't look like fun," I said.

She cocked her head, inviting me in. I followed.

"The newest health bill—haggling is going on; seems worse than it is. Hasn't a chance in hell, has so much pork in it you could open a barbeque joint. How's Gramps?"

"The stroke was bad. If the staff hadn't found him, he'd have died on the floor of his studio. Luckily, they sent someone to his room to take him to breakfast. They believe it happened just before that."

"He's tough," Jeanne said. "He'll pull through."

"I talked to the doctor; he is not sure that he will survive. It was massive."

Jeanne walked to her C Street window. "You should have

left this alone, George. None of this needed to be investigated, none of it. I'd hate to think this had—you had—something to do with his stroke."

I was stunned. "You're blaming me for Gramps's stroke? You can say that after what I discovered the two of you have been doing these past couple of months?"

"I told you to stay the fuck away from this," Jeanne said, turning from the window.

"Why the hell was Dalton Ward involved? That man was dangerous, borderline psychotic."

"He was Gramps's man—you know that. He would do anything for him."

She was right about that. The Talants have known Dalton Ward since we were kids; he worked with Dad. He was there in Idaho when he died. Ward was a rookie agent at the time of the shooting, and until taking disability in 2003, I believed him to be a solid FBI agent. Yesterday, after I'd gone through his personnel file, I realized why our mother told us to stay clear—the man was a wreck.

"Did Gramps hire Ward, or was it you?"

"Just stay out of this. You will destroy a great man and ruin your career."

"Did you hire Ward?"

She raised her right hand and extended her index finger and pointed it. "This is your mess, George. Ward was cleaning it up. Ward just got out of control; patience wasn't one of his virtues."

"The man was certifiably psychotic, paranoid, and a dozen other levels of crazy."

"He was a tool, that's all."

"You and Grandfather are up to your necks in this . . ."

"No, this is your mess. You own it, then you broke it. We were trying to fix it."

"Like hell. Gramps was responsible for the deaths of six people; I have the proof. Then he covered it up, purged the files, and sanitized the whole thing."

"And if you hadn't investigated, none of this would be

happening. You are destroying an honorable man who served our country. He took care of our family—he took you under his wing, made you who you are."

"And he destroyed another family in the process. Dammit, Jeanne, can't you see this?"

"Just leave it alone. Gramps said to put it all on him if it came to this. He told me, 'Jeanne, I'll take the fall. What is important is that you keep your hands clean. You have important work to do. Dump it on me. Besides, I'll probably be gone anyway.'"

"You are lying, he never said that. What have you done?" I demanded.

"Done? I've done nothing. It was all our grandfather. He contacted Ward. It was Ward who took out that fool Allanson."

"How do you know about Allanson?"

"He was the killer. He did it all—that's what Gramps said. He told me. He set off the bomb, he murdered the Davises, he's the one that did all of it," Jeanne said with a smile.

"Then who was the couple that Ward tried to run off the road?"

"I don't know, maybe somebody who got in his way, call it road rage. Hey, I've got a great idea. Maybe you should keep this investigation going, talk to the Michigan State Police, explain away the cell phones, tell them about Chicago, give them the dope on Allanson. Drag that bitch Catherine Davis in; get her legions of fans involved. After her little Sunday show a few weeks ago, it seems she knows nothing about managing the press and how to get them on her side."

"Catherine Davis told me that you were involved, that everything I knew was a lie."

"And what are you going to do about it?"

———

Washington is fond of saying (in fact, survives on it) that news stories have a life; they are born, age, then die. The big stories have big lives, bigger headlines, then faster deaths. The story of a house explosion that killed four people a few days after the riots at the Democratic convention in 1968 that may have resulted in the deaths of two people fifty years later had the life span of a gnat. To say that someone cared isn't an exaggeration; it's a lie—no one cared. There is a wide difference, though, between caring and justice. I am in the justice business. So was my father, and at one time so was my grandfather.

With the approval of the director, I held a news conference that announced the closing of a fifty-year-old cold case. Four reporters showed up. These days it's fashionable to impugn the reputation of the Bureau when it was under J. Edgar Hoover. I kept my remarks civil and to the point. New evidence had come to light that confirms that a rogue FBI agent had acquired explosives and was directly involved in the deaths of four people. He was under orders from senior FBI agents and worked directly for them.

"Do you know who those senior officials were?" the reporter from the *Washington Post* asked.

"We believe that the authority came from the highest position in the Bureau," I said.

"J. Edgar Hoover ordered this?"

"We have not found definitive information, only that these agents would not have acted without such authority."

"There's a reference to this incident in Senator Talant's autobiography. Are you saying that the story was incorrect, that your sister fabricated the story?" Earlier, I'd pointed out the bio to the reporter.

"I am not. I am saying that new information has come to light, competent information, that revises and updates what we knew. My sister will answer that question herself."

Gramps passed away quietly. Jeanne and I were there at his side. Our brother, James, cried when I told him that Gramps had died, one of the first tears I have ever seen my damaged brother shed. What was Gramps's legacy? I look at my family, since I'm now the titular head, and wonder. All families have dark shadows in their past.

Jeanne Ellen announced a week before Christmas that she was withdrawing from the campaign. She used the patented explanation that she wanted to spend more time with her family, concentrate on ongoing legislation, and mourn the loss of our heroic grandfather. I also learned from her office assistant that the three largest contributors to the Talant campaign withdrew their support after my press conference. Jeanne Ellen is politically young; she came away clean. She is a solid reelection candidate, and the presidential cycle does come around every four years. Maybe by then she will be talking to me.

Growing up, and except for my years in the Navy, I have spent every Christmas with my grandfather. Large Irish family gatherings they were; Grandmother, Dad and Mom, Jeanne and James, even a few cousins and Bureau friends. Then, as the years passed, we lost Dad, then James to the home. My kids were added, and some years we'd have a few strays, as Gramps called them, join our celebration. For the last twenty years, since Grams's death, the group dwindled again—but never, until this year, did they not include Michael Allen Talant. He was the head of around seventy-five years of Christmases.

This year his seat is vacant at the table and there is a great hole in my heart. Mike was my hero, my mentor, my Olympian God. He was always there, our North Star, the lodestone of our family—and for many others as well. To learn and then have to accept that he was a killer, no matter his reason, broke me. Gramps was a leader of men. Hundreds of agents owed their careers—and even a few, their lives—to Mike Talant. He was a man who followed orders and gave orders; in fact, order itself coalesced around him. I find it unbearable to believe he did what he is accused of doing—yet the evidence is almost impossible to ignore.

My grandfather had been at war his whole life. First with

his father, then with the Nazis, then a succession of perceived enemies of America: Hollywood communists, Bolsheviks, anti-war radicals, China, Russia, and toward the end of his career, the beginnings of the extreme right, the one that killed his son. He had been a soldier in two wars, the first in Europe and the other at home. He served his country well and honorably. However, did his actions in Chicago come from hatred or a true sense of duty? The ethical arguments are eternal, as was his duty to protect America. And this duty continued even to his grand-daughter and what he believed is her important role for the future.

I can't buy it, ethics and free will notwithstanding. Michael Talant was a good man who did bad things. He was a religious man, a righteous man, who rationalized his actions. This is what broke my heart: his support of the convenient universal lie that the ends justified the means.

Michael A. Talant will be buried next to his brothers and sisters in Arlington Cemetery. He will be honored for his service, not because of his actions, but because we need to believe in men and women like Michael Talant who protect and serve us. Our national narrative, our diary, is found in those white stones.

The sins of the father do come to haunt the sons and daughters. Someday, I hope that I can come to terms with what he did and can then seek some forgiveness from the Davis family.

Chapter 33
The White Rabbit

Cate: Now
Near Red Cliff, Colorado
Late December 2019

I did spend two weeks in London with Alice and Derek Pengrove. We did see *Guys and Dolls*, and I did have a great time. And the guy from Colorado sent me an email wishing me a Happy Thanksgiving along with an invitation. I accepted his offer; we spent a quiet postcard Colorado post-Christmas together.

The day after Christmas, my sister called. It is a wonder and a blessing to have a sister, again. She had news about the man who tried to kill them. She also added that a lot of this information had been sent to the FBI a month earlier by the Michigan State Police. I said nothing about my package that I sent to Special Agent Talant.

"The sheriff of Kent County, where Allanson's body was found," Dorothy began, "has been pursuing a few leads. He was leaning toward a malfunction of Allanson's oxygen machine, or that he couldn't replace the cylinder quick enough. When his body was found, the canister in the apparatus was empty. There was also some bruising around the face where the mask would fit. The county coroner says that

that might have been caused by holding the mask tight to the face, and if the air were cut off, he could have suffocated. There was some hemorrhaging in the eyes, but if the apparatus had malfunctioned, it might have also caused the hemorrhaging."

"So, there are suspicions about his death?"

"Yes. Julie Loon, the trailer park manager, has a few of those CCTV cameras set up around the park. She was concerned about residents and trash issues, who was staying where, even some pilfering by the residents. It also caught the comings and goings of the residents and guests; she gave a digital copy of videos the week before and after Allanson's death to the sheriff."

"Did she seem like the type to be that sophisticated?" I asked.

"No, she says she has a nephew that ran the equipment; he's also out on bail for being a peeping Tom. Some of the cameras were aimed at certain units—but that's another story. The Kent sheriff told Mitch's friend, the sheriff of our county, that the cameras showed us coming and going the day we told him we were there, confirming our story. It also showed the manager visiting Allanson a few hours after we left, confirming that he was alive after. It also shows other residents entering and leaving the property. One car, a brand-new gray Hyundai Elantra, also entered and left. It came in about ten minutes before we arrived and left about ten minutes after we left. Our truck is fairly distinctive, or at least it was."

"Did the manager know the car?"

"No. In fact, she didn't remember it. She'd only come out about five minutes before we arrived, and after we left, she went back inside. It was all on the cameras."

"And the car?" I said curiously.

"The sheriff didn't pay it any mind until the next day after the attack on us. Grand Haven police put an all-points out for information about the gray Hyundai involved in our crash. They gave out the license number; it was an Indiana plate. It was rented at the Detroit airport. The Kent sheriff picked up the Hyundai on a traffic camera on the main highway a mile from the trailer park; he matched it to the car on the trailer park videos. The video was from early the next morning, the day after we were there. That put the guy in the area about the time Allanson died. The Hyundai was later confirmed to be rented to a Dalton Ward, from Virginia."

"So, he killed Allanson?" I asked.

"Probably. There's more. Our deputies are pretty good here in Michigan. They found four cell phones in Ward's hotel room safe. They were the kinds bought at grocery stores and big-box outlets. With the help of the Michigan State Crime Laboratory, they traced the numbers that had been called. One of the numbers went to a phone that had been purchased in a Target store in Bethesda, Maryland. A credit card was used to buy that phone. The card belongs to a George Talant."

I nearly dropped the phone. Ben looked at me with a very strange look. "What?" he mouthed.

"Dalton Ward, the presumed killer of Zeke Allanson and the man who attacked Dorothy and her husband, called a phone bought by FBI Special Agent George Talant."

Ben's eyes got large and twinkled. I am beginning to like this man, a lot.

"Yes," Dorothy continued, "they are pursuing the connections through the Michigan State Police and the Grand Rapids office of the FBI. One agent knew George Talant; she'd sent the report of Allanson's death to him in Washington. Of course, they didn't know who George Talant was until a court order checking his credit card information alerted them. Then FBI agents from the Grand Rapids office stopped by the sheriff's office here in Grand Haven. I'm not sure how long my secret is going to last. If they go after Talant, he may try and barter me. He will make them look. He may even have them go after you and Joe; he knows you know about me."

"I don't believe that George Talant had anything to do with all this. It has to fall on his grandfather," I said. "It might even include his sister."

"Maybe George bought his grandfather the phone," Ben said. "I bought my mother her phones before she passed on. It's possible."

"Who's that, Cate?" Dorothy said.

"Just a friend, a trusted friend."

"How trusted?"

"Very trusted, okay?"

"Oh, my sister is being testy and defensive—must be the boyfriend."

———

It snowed during the night. I rolled out of my warm bed and draped the heavy Indian robe over my shoulders, and, using my nose, followed the intoxicating scent of bacon and coffee down the stairs to the kitchen. Ben was sitting at the massive central island, pounding away at his laptop. Beyond the windows, the mountains, virginal and white, climbed upward to the bright blue morning sky. The rising sun cast sharp shadows halfway up the mountain's flanks.

"It's so quiet, I could hear the clicking of your keyboard," I said.

"It's my favorite time. It's magical. I often leave for Mexico about now, before the snow makes the roads impassable. The cups are hanging under the cabinets." He pointed.

"Thank you for letting me impose," I said.

"You are not imposing. I did make the offer," Ben answered.

"I'm sure that you didn't think I would take you up on your offer when the rivers were frozen."

"*Au contraire*, I hoped you would. What do you want for breakfast?"

"A real cowboy breakfast," I said.

"Done and done. Start with the coffee. That's no girly-girl Kona stuff there. It will put hair on your chest."

"Thanks for the image."

Two hours later, I sat buttoned up in a thick, colorful blanket coat, earmuffs, cowboy hat, warm gloves, all atop a gorgeous black stallion. Ben rode a palomino. Mine was called Blackie. I was hoping for something more dangerous, like Desperado or Midnight.

"A friend's little girl named him; they share the same birthday," Ben said. "This boy here is Finn, Gaelic for 'fair'. He's about as mellow as you can get." He slapped the horse on the flank of his neck. "Tough, strong, takes the cold, and even though mellow, he can be stubborn."

"That reminds me of John," I said out loud.

Ben smiled.

We rode into the mountains. The six inches of snow softened the landscape; the scrub pine branches wore snowy caps. The thin branches of the aspen groves were pattern studies of white on white. Animal tracks on the road were dense and numerous. We weren't the first out this morning.

"My indigenous herd of elk," Ben said, looking at the imprints. "They come down out of the high mountains about now; there's more food down here. They tend to stay in the hollows until the sun gets high. Stinky fellows—play havoc with my fences—but make you feel real-life Colorado."

A rabbit bolted across the road. "I didn't know there were white rabbits here," I said, watching the hare bound through the snow, then stop and look at us.

"That's a snowshoe rabbit. They are gray in the summer; turn white in winter."

The rabbit, its long legs gliding across the surface, disappeared down into the elk hollow.

"*Una señal de Dios,*" Ben said.

"A sign from God? A white rabbit?"

"Do you mind?"

Ben held up a cigar. There was nothing I could refuse him.

The smoke from the cigar held like a cloud in the still air. If he pulled out a harmonica, it would be the perfect soundtrack.

"Susan is doing well," I said. "Each day brings them closer to believing in a miracle. Louise asks me if I know anything more about the transplant. I hate to lie to her."

"A blessed fib. Someday you can tell her, maybe even introduce her to Susan. I think she'd like that."

"Dorothy and Mitch take it day by day. Dorothy wants this all behind her but is afraid for her children and grand-children. If there are innocents, it is our children. Each day brings a little more separation. There's much I want to know, and I know that I will never know it all."

"We know what we know," Ben said with a laugh.

"Please . . ." I stood up in the stirrups and looked around, truly God's quiet country. "Maybe we should write a book together, like *Game of Thrones: The Rockies*. We could cook up something special and grandiose with flying horses, a white buffalo, Indian shamans, and evil government agents."

"Little lady, I'm the solitary cowboy type—independent, dark, forbidding, quick to temper, fast with the gun, and I like children and dogs. They call me pilgrim."

"Well, pilgrim, I'm surprised that you don't have a dog," I said.

"I did, a long history of them. Loved them all. Had to put down the last one a summer ago. His heart just gave out, and now I'm too old for a dog. I don't want them to outlive me. Wouldn't be fair."

We rode high up to the ridgeline, and between the peaks, looked fifty miles across the rough Colorado mountains. Below, two dozen elk pushed their way down the slope. Yearlings gamboled along next to their mothers. From far off, a short bark and then a howl echoed through the canyons.

"My wolfpack. There's six, I've been told," Ben said. "I've only seen a single male. He was studying me; I'm guessing he wanted to know if I was a friend or foe."

"We are interlopers in this world. We barely fit in."

"So true, but on a morning like this, I'm reminded of a set of lines from Carroll's *Alice* story. You mentioned the book in your interview. I went back to it: 'I wonder if the snow *loves* the trees and fields, that it kisses them so gently? And then it covers them up snug, you know, with a white quilt; and perhaps it says, "Go to sleep, darlings, till the summer comes again."'"

"Yes, 'curiouser and curiouser,' I believe," I answered, thinking about my next day's entry into my journal. "Dear Grace, I saw a white rabbit this morning."

A look at: The Chronicles of Sharon O'Mara
The Complete Series

Meet Sharon O'Mara—a tough rebel with a caring soul.

In *Land Swap for Death*, Sharon has just returned from Iraq and the Army's military police. Assigned to settle a life insurance claim, she struggles with the insane thought that the man's death was no accident—but rather, a brutal murder.

Book two, *Containers for Death*, trails a wet and raucous ride from Mexico's Baja beaches to San Francisco's darkest alleys when what starts as a luxurious vacation getaway for Sharon turns terribly wrong after she finds a shipping container filled with knockoff luxury handbags and death.

Toulouse for Death follows a Toulouse Lautrec painting being stolen by Nazis, a dying friend's wish, and an old evil that returns to the twenty first century... Will Sharon and her friends survive a night of unmitigated terror?

In *12th Man for Death*, Sharon is hired for a simple job—find out who killed the great America's Cup skipper and technical genius, Catherine Voss.

A man is found dead on second base in the San Francisco Giants' ballpark in book five, *Diamonds for Death*. How he got there, no one knows. But one thing is certain—Sharon must go to Cuba to find out.

During *Limerick for Death*, Sharon heads to Ireland to help her friend with his newfound inheritance—an old and dilapidated baronial estate that overlooks the Celtic Sea and holds untold secrets. But the insatiable greed of an evil developer, smugglers with secret tunnel, and local Cork County history stand in her way.

Get ready to enjoy the award-winning Sharon O'Mara mystery series. The Chronicles of Sharon O'Mara: The Complete Series includes Land Swap for Death, Containers for Death, Toulouse for Death, 12th Man for Death, Diamonds for Death, and Limerick for Death.

AVAILABLE JULY 2022

About the Author

Gregory C. Randall was born in Michigan and raised near Chicago. As a youth, he spent his summers on his grandparent's cherry farm in Michigan. He now lives in the Bay Area of California. He is an author of more than twenty thrillers, mysteries, and family centered novels.

Made in the USA
Monee, IL
10 July 2022

99433211R00198